LOS ANGELES GOTHIC

Elizabeth Jeeves

ISBN: 979-8-218-73862-4

Author's Note:

This novel contains scenes of graphic violence, harsh language, drug use, and sexual content, as well as exploring themes of sexual assault and bigotry. Reader's discretion is advised.

Dedicated to the angel who saved me.
Connor, I owe everything to you.

M's Journal
September 20th, 1996

Visions... always those damn visions. This time, was a dream about the end of the world. This city, sitting atop hills of gold-plated rot, had crumbled. But destruction and mayhem reigned. Were so many corpses. So much death. Pray that this does not come to fruition in my lifetime... or my niece's.

I've seen horrors throughout my life. Things unspeakable. Always comes down to the acts of men. The heinous nature of all sentient beings would always outweigh the desire to do good. In '86, finally managed to find a way to suppress my visions. Didn't have to look at horrors anymore. Just comes along now and again in the form of migraines and dreams. I settled in... eventually. Built myself a nest. Kept my niece and I safe... and disappeared into legend. Not like that's the only thing we lost that year...

L.A. always had the habit of bleeding its own brand of "wonder and magic" into the rest of the city: delusions of grandeur overtaking the masses like a plague. Gripping minds and replacing logic and trust in nature with broken promises from movie execs and music producers until every individual is stripped of their dignity and becomes a slave to a lustrous idea. Nothing more than that. An idea... Los Angeles is a strange and sensuous place.

All chaos out there. On days like today, feels like making sense of it is a fool's errand. Guess when you're in my profession, should be grateful for the unfaithful husbands with their prolific call girls, and the occasional missing persons. Without, be out of a job.

Even still, cheating spouses and sex workers are not to blame. Just playing out a scene written a thousand years ago. It's the 1 in 100 case. The one that breaks your perception of reality. The one that makes you question if any of it is worth it.

Legends in L.A. are plentiful. Even have a few myself. Never a shortage of "Once upon a time..." It's the "Happily ever after" that I can't find.

-M.

Act 1: Tall Tales from the San Fernando Valley

1

A teenage Elf, Joana Larsson, was found murdered in Beverly Hills. She was stabbed forty-seven times and was dumped in an alley by a high-end clothing boutique. The store owner found her as they went to open for the morning, seeing pools of blood before coming across the corpse, dressed in a torn bikini and nothing else. Police arrived at the scene in record time and declared Larsson dead at 8:37 a.m. on September 20th. She was only nineteen.

Morgana Scriven placed the bloody newspaper down on her dining room table. A ring of ichor from her morning meal had stained the corner of the paper just above the article. She ran her thumb over the sticky stain and grimaced. This was the last news story that Morgana read, an article published by her very own Cryptid Chronicle. Morgana may be just an intern, but it was stories like this that drove her to be a full-fledged reporter.

In a tightly packed, three-bedroom apartment, not particularly well kept or even in a good neighborhood, Morgana meticulously pinned up her long blonde hair. Being a Vampire, she needed to do so without the aid of a mirror, relying heavily on touch and muscle memory. Had her apartment been newer and fitted with mirrors not made with silver, she'd be better off. Even still, she managed to do all her makeup in a compact, using grays and beiges to complement her naturally albino skin. Not all Vampires were albino, just this one; it was a trait that was more common in Trueborn than in the Turned.

Though, as a trade-off, Morgana, or Morgan in less professional settings, was born without any fun powers or ability to be attuned to magic. In fact, she saw magic as a form of science… and don't get her started on religion. She could, however, stand in daylight— a privilege she was very privy to.

Morgan was taught young the dangers of being a Turned. Her parents' deaths by sunlight were enough to awaken the fear of her existence. Upon seeing those burnt, mangled corpses, Morgan vowed never to turn a single living creature, under any circumstances. She went so far as to never feed off a living being. She merely drank blood from pre-sealed packs, like morbid Capri-Suns. She may have overreacted in some eyes, but to her, it's kept her sane for almost a decade. Despite the tenth anniversary of that tragic day fast approaching, Morgan was confident that this year, 1996, was going to be her year.

Morgan fitted herself into a contouring pair of smart jeans, a black halter top, and slid her pale feet into a pair of fire-red stilettos. Fully dressed, she felt smart and sexy.

"You're awfully dolled up for work," said the tawny Wood-Elf standing outside of the master bathroom. Merely a half bath, no shower. That had to be shared between Morgana, her best friend Raphael, their roommate Seth, and her rather cantankerous boyfriend, Dr. Balam Sequoia.

"I am," Morgan said plainly, patting her head lightly to make sure she was straight. To her chagrin, she was not and went back to work. "It's my first day on the floor. I wanna make a good impression."

"In jeans?" Balam scoffed.

"What's up your ass?" She replied, leaning on the sink and turning to face him, her delicate features illuminated by the fluorescent lights, softly flicking. Diamond-pink eyes met his, there was a lingering pause that felt heavier than an overweight Giant.

"You know *exactly* what's up my ass," he said with folded arms. "Meet you in the car."

As he exited their room and then their apartment, Morgan thought of what it could be that had him so upset. All she could think of was that he disapproved of this internship. But that was highly unjustified. She waited two years to get this position and fought dozens of other Journalism Majors for the exact same slot, only to win the vote by a narrow margin. Now that she was in, working the floor, nothing was going to stop her from being the next big thing at the Cryptid Chronicle.

It was like a dream, the only paper in Los Angeles that catered to the needs and problems of the Non-Human. One would think that two hundred years after the integration of mythic beings and Preternatural humanoids would lead to a better life for most of them. But that wasn't the American way; colonization left Orcs and Wood-Elves disparaged. Domhainn, Medusae, Taknolings, and many others all fled their home of Ile de Lenora from the persecution of the High-Elf Legion and found no harbor that they could truly call home. The only ones who had any weight in the city of glitz and glamor were the High-Elves and the Vampires, but when each composed one of the most populous gangs in the county, they had at least some sort of upper hand. As an intern reporter, Morgan would have an up-close-and-personal look at it all.

She smiled, wondering what her first story would be. Would it be gang violence, thugs in possession of magical weapons? Or maybe something in the entertainment division, reporting on stars and their exploits? Or perhaps something mundane, like the controversial tax cuts for Little Lenoran businesses. Ultimately, Morgan desperately wanted to be attached to the follow-up on the Larsson story. Such a gruesome murder can only have a spiraling mystery attached to it. She doubted an intern like her would be given such responsibility so soon; that was a duty reserved for more senior reporters, but she could dream.

Despite an assuredly awkward car ride to come, she was ready for her day. Morgan felt bulletproof, that nothing could destabilize her. Even in this dark and dangerous city, she was going to thrive.

Red. The color of the doors. Endless white on all sides. The hall was void of sound, with no real structure to bounce audio waves. The high ceiling above seemed to flicker and fade as if it were slowly evaporating. Beyond the strobing veil, tendrils of old, calcified flesh, leathery like an alligator's skin, knit together in a sky of nightmares. Eyes adorned its every surface like the suction cups on the

tentacle of an octopus. The icy blue glare stared with malicious pupils, like that of a goat. An unearthly shriek could be heard echoing from the endless path ahead— a sound that no mortal ears were meant to hear. The doors began to knock from the other side, followed by another baleful howl.

Sudden and sharp pounding on Raphael's door jarred him awake. Sticky eyes and throbbing head, he was yet again shocked at how easily he was given free liquor. It was the only thing that helped the insomnia, but he probably should slow down. He was only Human after all. The rapping came again, faster this time. He groaned, rubbing his face, squashing sepia brown skin, and looking down at his digital alarm clock: 7:48 a.m.

"Fuck… I'm coming!" he whined, slumping out of his bed. He grabbed a dirty *Filter* t-shirt off his desk and pulled it over his head, otherwise only wearing boxers. He shambled to the door, trudging through a floor cluttered with dirty clothing and scattered take-out containers.

"Raphie, are you still asleep? You need to get to class soon," the woman knocking spoke. He instantly recognized the scolding voice on the other end as his best friend and roommate, Morgan.

He reached the door and swung it open, leaning on the handle and poking his head out. Long, black, curly hair hung beside his face, as unkempt as his scruffy chin. "My alarm doesn't go off for another ten minutes, so I don't see why you're trippin'," he said, his voice groggy.

"Why is your alarm set to go off right before you have to leave?" Morgan asked, raising a blonde eyebrow. She had been best friends with Raphael since they were children. Always an independent and responsible student, she was also the first Preternatural person to befriend him. Kids of significantly different races didn't hang out back then, but there were no Vampires at the school. She climbed the social ranks and he stayed the nerdy kid, but they remained fast friends. Morgan watched over him, and he did the same for her. No matter what.

"If I'm being honest, I just fell asleep…like a few hours

ago… so I'm dropping this class… see ya," he said, going to close the door, but Morgan stuck her red pump between the door and the frame, wedging it open.

"What's going on with you?" She said with a tinge of worry in her voice, "Are you feeling okay?"

"I was just dumped? On top of that, it's insomnia, when it's not fucking nightmares… this isn't news to you," he said unamused.

"I'm sorry. I just… You don't look well."

"That's 'cause I'm really fucking not," he said with a scoff. "Be glad you can't get sick."

"I'm immune to disease. That doesn't mean I can't get hung over… Don't you think cleaning up in here might let you relax? I know I'd like to avoid unwanted tenants if you catch my drift. I'm sure Balam feels the same."

"What, mice? Roaches? Isn't Balam a Wood-Elf? I thought they loved nature," Raphie joked, met with a look of disgust from his friend and schoolmate.

"I'm not even gonna dignify that with a response," she retorted. "If you can promise to at least get to the laundry then I won't tell him about the racist ass remark."

"Dude, it was just a joke, don't be like that," Raphie said, opening the door more, the look of smugness transferring to Morgan. "If it makes you feel better, I already planned to clean up a bit."

"Awesome. I'm gonna stop by M's after work. I was hoping you'd meet me there?" Morgan said.

"Honestly… I'm not feeling too social. Hug her for me, I'm sure she'd rather see her niece than, ya know, your stoner thrall."

"Thrall?!" Morgan said, offended. "Is that how you think of me? Like a slave driver?"

"No, no, no, more like a Lich who thinks she's everyone's mom," Raphie said with a smug smirk.

"Oh, you're a dick," She shook her head and gestured to her body. "I'm the hottest Lich there ever was if that was the case."

"Yeah, you're gonna be all the talk of the water cooler when you get in there today," he said, deflecting and changing the subject.

"Damn straight. But it's going to be because of my superior intellect and master sleuthing skills!" She said with an inflated confidence.

Raphie laughed.

"Yeah, sure. Go for it, Blondie. Be the Phyllis Barks you always thought you'd be or whatever." Raphie nodded sharply.

"Wow, you and Balam going to the assholes convention today or what?" She said with an incredulous laugh. "Look, I have no idea when Balam or Seth are coming home, but probably before me. So straighten up, and then you can enjoy your day."

"Gee, Mom," Raphie said, squatting down and trying not to lose it. "Thanks for the permission."

"Don't forget to brush your teeth, drink water, and go fuck yourself," she joked, flipping Raphie the bird.

"I love you, too, Blondie," Raphie replied, waving goodbye, the gesture devolving into a lewd stroking motion. They both laughed until Morgan was out of the apartment. Raphie was grateful for Morgan, despite her preppy, perfectionist attitude, she could still be lighthearted and real with him.

As the door closed behind her, the alarm in Raphie's bedroom went off, blaring out rock music, "Brain Stew", a very ironic choice at that. Raphie was exhausted and turned to collapse, face first, into his bed.

He groaned, rolling over as the song reached its climax. He rubbed his face and begrudgingly began his day.

2

Morgana watched out the window of the passenger side as Balam drove them down Ventura Boulevard. She unabashedly observed the streets with her roseate eyes, the other undead wore their refractium masks and gloves to hide their skin from the sun, turning their faces into featureless, opalescent mannequins. A group of Valkyries flew a few stories above street level, holes designed in their jackets to allow their angelic wings to be free. A Giant, eight feet tall, strode down the street, making eye contact with her as they hit a red light. Morgan gave the goliath humanoid a modest smile, her fangs appearing out from just behind her red-painted lips, a stark contrast to her pale, white skin; he returned one in kind.

"Are you even listening to me?" Balam said, aggressively gripping the steering wheel.

"What's there to listen to?" She asked, not looking him in the eye.

"You're going to be gone out here all the time, and you won't even do me the decency of looking at me?" He whined.

"I told you about this. This internship is all I've ever wanted, and now I have a real chance to prove myself on the floor," she said with a scoff. "I thought you'd be proud of me."

"I never said I wasn't proud," he interjected and shook his head, the tips of his bone-white antlers grazing the roof. "I'm just pissed you signed up for such an extensive program in Studio fucking City."

"My only other option was to work for PNN in WeHo," she said with a sigh. "Why are you so against this?"

"You're a Vampire, Batty Girl… people still wanna stake you. And didn't you hear about the girl they found yesterday?" Balam said, though there was more behind his tone than just worry. "And who the fuck is going to keep the apartment clean? Certainly not Raphie or Seth."

"Hey, that's not fair. Raphie does pick up after himself. More than I can say for you," she said with an eye roll. The car began moving again.

"Whatever… I'm gonna miss your fucking cooking, too… and that's not even talking about *my* needs," Balam groaned.

"When I signed up for the program you said it would be okay if we fucked less," Morgan said, her pitch hiking further in defense.

"You're remembering wrong," Balam retorted. Morgan didn't respond. "We haven't been intimate, much as it is, and I was worried this would happen."

Meticulously, she checked her hair in the visor mirror shortly before they reached her destination. *Shit, I need to replace those gods damned silver mirrors at home,* she thought, slightly envious of Non-Vampires at that moment.

"You trying to look pretty for your coworkers? Any of them you're interested in fucking instead?" Balam said, turning his head to see her primp herself.

"Oh my gods, you're, like, really on one today, aren't you?… I like to feel cute. I thought you would like my look, too. Shouldn't have even bothered," she said, crossing her arms as they approached the squat but still sizable building. "The least you could have done is wait for me to get home tonight before you berate me."

"Look… I didn't mean to start shit…" he said, sighing. "I just worry."

Balam pulled his silver EV1 up to the curb before what Morgan saw as her inevitable future: The Cryptid Chronicle. It was one of the few papers in the nation that catered to Non-Humans, including Preternatural peoples and their issues, a transformative place. It even boasted an Orc as the chief editor: Colt Harding, a serious, award-winning journalist also known for being a serious, award-winning jackass to anyone beneath him.

Morgan said nothing more, merely unbuckled herself. She glanced to the side and saw the group of men, all of various races, loitering just before the Chronicle steps. A Human among them watched her intently as she exited.

"Please don't stay mad at me," he said, taking her free hand softly. "I just want what's best for both of us."

"Okay," Morgan said, reluctant to forgive him. "I-I gotta go, babe."

"Can I at least get a kiss before you go?" he practically whimpered.

"Sure." She sighed heavily as she leaned in to peck her ruby-red lips on his.

"Have a better day," He said, watching her exit the vehicle, keenly eyeing her rump in tight-fitting jeans.

"You too… see you tonight?" She replied.

"Yeah, I'll be home late, though."

"Then see you tonight," she said, closing the door and making her way towards the Chronicle.

As soon as she was out of the car and Balam was peeling off, the Human man whistled at her.

"Hey, mama, you white as hell. Where you from?" He said with a chuckle from his peers. Morgan kept walking.

"We got some real good dope, keeps your dick nice and hard, hit me up after work," he continued, causing his posse to begin laughing. She pressed on, even still, trying to ignore him and eliciting a scoff from the man. "Eh, fuck you anyway."

Morgan took a deep breath as she climbed the steps to the brightly colored, modern art building. A uniquely shaped structure, it desired to be "hip" but looked manufactured by Fisher-Price. Thankfully the clashing colors of purple, green, and yellow were merely just the ugly shell to the beautiful interior, something much more simplistic, perhaps due to lack of budget.

"Yo, biter," the man behind her said. Morgan froze, hearing the slur. She turned on her heel to face him, only to see a woman in a pantsuit and refractium set; her face a bald, faceless, opalescent, glimmering rainbow in the light. "Don't they keep you locked up in Transylvaniatown until Halloween?"

"I said I don't want trouble, again," the Vampire said, marching up the steps.

"You should stay outta the daylight, honey," one of the other men threatened. "Might get burned if something happened to that stupid mask."

She stormed past Morgan, up the steps. She couldn't see her eyes but was certain that the poor woman had looked at her. Morgan's heart bled. Being sexually harassed was one thing, but coming under threats of a hate crime was something else entirely.

"Are you okay?" Morgan tried to say, but she was already in the building. Morgan glanced back at the posse of creeps. With yet another voluntary sigh, she opened the door herself.

3

"You're six minutes late, Scriven." A booming voice sounded seconds after Morgan entered the open, air-conditioned main floor. Crossing from the adjacent wall closest to her was Colt Harding, her editor, supervisor, and, for now, the only one capable of stopping her from actually generating college credits.

Looking down at her wrist, there was a slim, gold watch that matched her earrings: a Christmas/moving-in gift from Balam. According to the hands, she was on time. She was about to protest, then remembered it was a few minutes slow when she first acquired it. Not being a watch gal, she only now found the opportunity to wear it, despite its beauty, thus never adjusting the time: ten minutes behind.

"Oh, gods. I'm so sorry—" She began.

"Don't start with excuses, Scriven, the news has no time for it," he said, plain and cold. He wasn't even looking at her, too busy reading what looked like an early print-off of a new issue. He turned to another employee and gave them some distinct instructions before pushing his wireframe glasses back up his large nose and turning back to glare at Morgan. "Ah, and you're in jeans, how dreadfully unprofessional."

"I-I've worn jeans before," she stammered, unprepared to already be grilled.

"Right. But you're now on the floor," he said, approaching her and gesturing to the dozens of busily typing and scrambling journalists. Harding was not a bad-looking man, despite a receding hairline that he fixed by shaving his head; his face was chiseled and always bore a 5 o'clock shadow. Like most Orcs, he had two tusk-like teeth that protruded from his bottom jaw. His skin was a rich emerald and rough to the touch, though Morgan could only assume the texture. His orange eyes weren't frightening per se, but the constant expression of disapproval coming from someone two heads taller and three times her size was intimidating… and yet.

"That means you're in the pen with the big dogs now," he continued, giving extra condescending and animated facial expressions to match the words. "And the big dogs don't fuck around. So, unless you want to get eaten alive, I'd suggest wearing something more work-appropriate. Like a skirt, or a dress… or something."

He pushed past her, not so much as acknowledging her shock, mouth agape. She turned to look at him but he was already moved on to his next underling. His path seemed to be leading him around a circuit of the building.

"I mean… I-I can change if you think it's that great of an issue," she said, trying to hide the sass in her tone.

"Not necessary," he said, not looking at her but instead turning his attention to the male intern who just stepped up to him.

"Hey Jackson, you catch the game last night?" He said, his demeanor changing almost immediately.

"Yes, sir, Mr. Harding," Jackson replied. "Real nail-biter."

"Yeah tell me about it, I was almost out a hundred bucks. If you could please take these prints to Dalkom that would be great," Colt said, Jackson nodded and headed on his way. Colt turned back to Morgan to ensure she was following. She was not. This seemed to irritate him further. "You coming, Buffy?"

She caught up, again trying to hide her visible irritation at the highly offensive reference. She, like most Vampires, hated that movie and questioned how it even got made. Once he heard the tapping of her heels behind him, he continued. "There we go, don't be shy. You're going to be working with one of my junior reporters this morning. Whatever she needs, you're there to help make it happen. That may mean getting coffee, but that may also mean checking in on sources, making phone calls, and doing all the legwork that she doesn't want to do. That's your job."

"Rad, who am I working with?" Morgan said, smiling for the first time since she walked in.

"Is that you, girlie?!" a familiar voice called from above. Leaning over the landing guard rail of the second floor, was Morgan's long-time friend and former upperclassman, Eliza Wagner. The woman cleaned up well, in a masculine dress shirt and slacks that accentuated her muscular body. From underneath her shoulder-length, black hair, two horns the color of red brick sprouted from her crown. Other than her heterochromia, these were the only two features that showed she was a Taknoling and not simply Human.

"Eliza?!" Morgan bounced with brief excitement.

"Oh Jesus Christ, you two know each other already?" Colt said, shaking his head.

He sighed, watching Eliza as she descended the stairs.

"Yup. We used to date in high school." Morgan grinned.

"Damn skippy. Met working the school paper together." Eliza admitted, wrapping her arm around her still-friendly ex. "How have you been, girlie?"

"Doing well! Already got the internship, obviously. But look at you! Reporter already!" Morgan swooned, gleeful to see evidence of her friend's success.

"Well, it's no cakewalk, but you were never afraid of a little hard work, were ya?" Eliza mused, sparing a glance at Colt as they separated the hug. His face was simultaneously boggled and annoyed.

"Perfect, I just teamed up the lesbians with chemistry," he scoffed. "This isn't going to be a problem, is it, Wagner?"

"No, sir," Eliza replied with confidence. "I'm ready to keep my time with her strictly professional."

"However," Eliza muttered to Morgan. "I'm going to this guy Dave's house tonight in Hollywood. Big place. Lots of booze and honeys. You should come."

"Well, that clock starts now, ladies," Colt said, looking at his digital watch and pressing a button to observe one of its many faces. "I don't want either of you here past your time. I'm not paying for any unnecessary overtime today."

"Don't worry, boss," Eliza said with a salute. "I don't plan on being here any later than I have to."

Once he was out of earshot, Morgan felt comfortable enough to speak. "Like, what's his beef?"

"You'd need a front-page special issue to break down that answer," Eliza said plainly. "Take it with a grain of salt and you'll get used to it. After all, you're 'the intern.' Let me show you my cubicle."

Work for the beginning of the day was simple, Eliza's desk was a disaster and so Morgan spent a full two hours just organizing and filing away old documents wherever in the Chronicle they belonged. Eliza was hard at work typing up her latest draft for the new issue. The story was about a group of young Vampires having an orgy in Echo Park last night. They were caught mid-act, apparently having been trying to do some illegal blood ritual that had no real basis in actual magic. Regardless, they were all arrested for attempted use of magic and indecent exposure. It was enough to garner the attention of the Department of Supernatural Affairs, which doesn't bode well for the Vampires.

Once she reached the end of her task, she noticed a corner of a photo. It stuck out of one of many disorganized folders that had been covered by other papers, stacked in the corner of Eliza's minimal desk. What was clearly shown was black curly hair and velvet skin, the color of a doe's coat.

The name scribbled next to the photo was Chrissy Donavon. Chrissy was smoking a cigarette outside of a nightclub with two other women, a Domhainn girl with jet-black hair, facing away from the camera, and a Catfolk woman with silver hair and black ears with white tips. They were all dressed provocatively, likely to prostitute themselves.

"Who is this?" Morgan said with conviction.

"Oh, her?" Eliza turned from her computer to Morgan "Missing persons case, we got the info for it this last week but every news outlet and their mother has already covered this story. Harding told me not to waste my time with it."

Morgan grabbed the folder it came from and opened it to see the notes on the story. It declared Chrissy was barely 17 and dropped out of high school. She was last spotted screaming for help, mostly naked, in Hollywood on the corner of La Cienega and Waring. The longer Morgan observed the more she realized the parallels present; this story was alarmingly similar to Joana Larsson's.

"Why?" Morgan's tone hardened.

"'Cause he's the Chief Editor? Come on, you're not that new."

Morgan didn't reply. She instead left the cubicle and

marched her way to the staircase and up to Harding's office. She saw him climb the stairs at the other end, knowing full well he'd have to pass her to leave; she had him cornered.

"Where the hell are you going?" Eliza asked leaning back in her chair and poking her head out of the cubicle.

"I have a question. It'll only take a second." Morgan ascended the stairs, her red pumps creating a rapid-fire sound against the metal steps. As she crested the top she saw Colt's door close, a smokey glass labeled 'Chief Editor' stood in her way. As soon as the door clicked she gave a brief but poignant series of knocks on the metal.

"Oh sweet merciful God, WHAT?!" he lamented from the other side.

"Mr. Harding. It's Morgana… Morgana Scriven," she said. "I just had a question. It's silly, really…"

There was silence for a long moment. "Well, ya gonna fuckin' come in?"

"You need to invite me, sir."

"Oh, whatever. Yes. Enter."

"Of course," Morgan quickly opened and closed the door, admiring the large office, decorated in a sharp, classical style. The room itself was old-fashioned; frames and running boards were ornately carved of wood and lacquered to be smooth and warm in color. It even went as far as to have a minibar. Colt sat on a couch that faced his desk, double the size of any two other desks in the building put together. He stretched his arms across the black leather, his head thrown back as well, with eyes closed. "I'm sorry to bother you, I was just wondering about a story."

"Spit it out, Transylvanian Barbie, we're burning through my first ten of the day," he said, still keeping his eyes closed.

"It's about the Donavon story?"

"What? What Donavon story?"

"The one about the Human girl who went missing in Hollywood? I'm curious as to why you put a kibosh on that. It just seems important," Morgan pushed.

Colt opened his eyes and blinked hard.

"I think I remember that one. Look… I'm gonna be

transparent," Colt warned, something that made her wonder what he thought he had been this whole time. "As important as the Chronicle is to us and our readers, we are still a sister news source to the Preternatural News Network, so we don't have as much control, funding, or, again, being blunt, readers as half of the other papers. On top of that, Chronicle readers are usually Non-Humans. They don't wanna read a story about another missing Human girl when that's gonna be on every other paper in the county."

"But.Hollywood is our backyard. Isn't that the kind, neighborly thing to do? Raise awareness?" Morgan said, standing her ground. "Besides, we're the Cryptid Chronicle. We're the heroes of the unsung!"

"Did you just try to pep talk me?" Colt said, lifting his head fully then leaning forward, "I'm gonna love bursting your bubble; last year, more than 35,000 people went missing in LA County alone, most of them beneath the age of eighteen…"

Morgan's gusto melted away, like putting a blow torch to a popsicle, quickly becoming overtaken by grim reality. "But that doesn't mean we shouldn't care."

Colt scoffed and rested his elbows on his knees.

"Look, Scriven, you want this goddamn story so bad, fine. I'll make you a deal: if you can actually manage to find something that's new and not just a reiteration of the same old thing, then you can publish the Donavon story with your name on it. You have until Halloween to get me something worth publishing."

Morgan's eyes became alight with excitement. Her own story! On her first day on the floor, nonetheless. Such a thing was unheard of. "Thank you, Mr. Harding! I—"

"I'm not done… You think you know the news better than me, then prove it. If I don't have a publishable story by the 31st of October, then you're done. Out of the internship program."

"What!?" She cried, her blood turning to ice. "Y-you can't —"

"Yes. Yes, I abso-fucking-lutely can. You got a month to convince me you've got something worth selling." He ordered.

"It took me two years to get chosen for the p-program!"

She stammered, "I-if I get fired, there's no way I'll get back in! N-no papers or networks will take me!!"

"And if you don't have anything worth selling, then you're not worth taking," Colt hounded. "Now drag your preppy, overconfident ass out of my office and get it to work. I'd like to rest. Thank you."

"Alright," Morgan said with a stealthy yet smug look. "You're on."

4

After a few minutes of groveling about his exhaustion, Raphie pulled himself out of bed. Their Westlake apartment, while small, had enough of a living space for Raphie and his three roommates to live comfortably. Their beaten-up wooden floors were protected in places by worn rugs. An old tan couch fit for three sat up against their sliding glass door, leading out onto their tight-fit balcony. Adjacent was the ornately maintained green suede of Seth's armchair. Though the man was hardly home, it, and the blanket along its back, were off-limits. A modest TV sat on a wooden stand across from the couch, a PlayStation and VCR in its cubbies.

There was enough space for a round table and a few chairs off to the left, though most of the hanging out took place at what the roommates called "the Bar", a half wall meant to divide the living room and kitchen. They had nailed a board of lacquered wood to the top, against the landlord's wishes, and placed two stools on the living room side.

Raphie made his way into the kitchen and started with what he needed the most, a cup of tea. Once he made sure the coffee maker was clear of grounds, he started the machine, sure there was at least enough water in it for tea. Rather than start making loud, gurgling noises, it instead dripped a few drops of brown, viscous fluid into the pot.

"What the…?" Raphie said, leaning down to inspect it closely.

As he grabbed for the empty pot, the device began to buck and growl. Spider legs sprouted from its mechanical cracks, the coffee maker becoming misshapen and dancing across the countertop.

"God fucking damnit! I don't need this right now!" Raphie shouted, quick to grab their broom from beside the refrigerator and swat at the creature. It began to change shape as it moved, keeping the texture and color of the device as it took on an almost hermit-crablike appearance.

"Get the hell out!" He called, swatting at the animal with the broom as it scuttled across the floor. Like a hockey player, he tried to swat the pest toward the back door. But like a bad hockey player, he scored on his own goal.

"Damnit, no! Not in my room!"

By the time he reached the door, the creature had taken the form of one of the many objects he owned.

"Fucking mimics!" he spat, pushing objects around with the broom head. "You better not eat any of my stuff, you little creep."

It would be a slow and arduous process to find the mimic. Raphie was sure to shut the door and seal the opening with t-shirts, leaving his window wide open, screen removed. The first items he checked were his surfboard and guitar, both more difficult to replace than anything else.

After scouring his room and carefully nudging each object, the space looked much cleaner. He wished it were under different circumstances. While on his hands and knees scanning under his bed, he noticed a Chinese food container twitch.

"Got you, motherfucker," He said, spraying hairspray to stiffen its transformation. The box tried to shift shape, legs sprouting from its corners as the flaps opened to reveal its sharp teeth and thick, wriggling tongue. Thankfully, due to its diet of inorganic objects, mimic bites were rare, but Raphie wasn't taking any chances with a cornered animal. Once the creature was stiff and immobile, Raphie swept it into the dustpan and tossed it out his bedroom window.

"There… now you're someone else's problem," he said, feeling a tinge of guilt that one of his neighbors would have to deal with the same struggle, but this was more humane than an exterminator.

Slumping at his desk chair with a sense of relief, Raphie ran his hands over his face, stretching the scruffy skin. *Back to work,* he thought.

*****

One would think that the rather attractive apartment complex would take a little better care of its community centers, but the laundromat built into it was utterly subpar. Raphael chalked it up to the number of residents who were also students, many of them male, and didn't seem to care. Raphie wasn't particularly cleanly himself, but he at least respected the need to have working washing machines.

At the time Raphael passed the facility, he saw that it was down to just two of the five machines. A small line of residents snaked through the door to the laundromat and into the inner courtyard, which was surprisingly floral.

Fantastic, he sarcastically thought. *Fuck this.*

With his basket held under the crook of his arm, mostly full of black clothing, flannels, and band shirts, Raphie returned to their second-story apartment and retrieved his skateboard. As he left the apartment, suite 161, he was met with the always startling visage of their Cryptid neighbor. The seven-and-a-half-foot-tall, skeletal creature waved at him with long, bony fingers.

"Greetings, Human Neighbor," He said in his low, groaning monotone. His jaw never moved, his face appearing like a fleshless skull with antlers sprouting from the top of the brow, just black pits where the eyes should be. "I hope that you are finding this day cheerful."

"Afternoon, Tom," he replied, giving a half-hearted smile "It's going. How about you?"

"A most acceptable day it is," the Cryptid said. "The wind is carrying whispering voices."

"Good to know," Raphie said with a nod, making his way

down the steps "You take care, say hi to the wife for me."

"An achievable request. Enjoy your daily consciousness, Human Neighbor."

After a moment or two balancing, Raphie headed down the block to the coin laundry on his board. If he was lucky enough, he could be there before the rush. A task, so far, he's done nothing but fail at. The warm day was softened by a cool breeze brought in from the coast. This temporarily eliminated the smog, turning the top of every hill into a scenic view. This was a lovely detour to Raphael, his wide mouth curling upward into a smile. The sun felt warm on his sepia skin, with highlights of bronze, like Grecian armor, giving him a much-needed dose of Vitamin D and waking him up. These sights, combined with the wind in his long, spiraling hair and the grunge music that blared in the headphones of his Walkman, gave him a blissful sensation of calm. He preferred music over the sounds of the city, especially over the strange sensation when the sound of airplanes suddenly cut out. Naturally, he was never looking to see what happened to the planes; the sound just ceased.

Relaxation was a state he often had difficulty finding without liquor or pot, having overbooked his school schedule at the start of the semester. He handled the previous year so well that he had felt that increasing the workload would have zero consequences; he greatly underestimated the amount of dedication three-hundred-level classes required. What drove Raphie to the point of finally dropping classes was the lack of time he got to spend with his boyfriend, Oliver. He was perfect for him, or at least he *was*.

Things changed two days ago when Oliver came over to spend some time with Raphie. They argued, heated. Oliver grilled Raphie about his lack of dedication to him, solely because of his workload. Raphie pleaded and managed to convince Oliver to stay. Things worked out, they made up and made love. Oliver had always been hesitant to date trans folk before Raphie. But once they made that first connection it was decided.

Things took a turn for the worse when it was all said and done. Raphie and Oliver laid on the bed, in the afterglow. Something changed in Oliver, sudden and cruel. He stood up, got dressed, and told Raphie he was leaving him for good. Raphie, torn by his words, asked him if the sex was truly that bad. The words Oliver said next, Raphie will never forget: "No… that's the only thing that was ever good." Tears formed in Raphie's eyes as he thought about this feeling of abandonment. He swallowed them down, determined to "be a man about it."

After several minutes of skating along the uneven streets, he arrived at his local laundromat. It seemed empty; a few people sat scattered among the wooden benches, waiting for their clothing to finish. Along the back wall, machines were open.

Fuckin' sweet. He gave a half-hearted smile, making his way to the back. It took him only a few minutes to get it loaded and running. He plopped back into an empty bench and pulled out a small but thick paperback on Advanced Philosophy from the bottom of the basket and a highlighter pen from the front pocket of his black jeans. If he had to be waiting about, he might as well study.

A few minutes into reading, a figure encroached on his light. He peered from behind his book to see an Elf woman he would come to describe as "enchanting", though "bewitching" was a more appropriate word. She was petite, though far from frail. She wore a tank top that was cut low on the sides, showing a lacy black bra beneath. Her legs were draped in a skirt with two layers of black cloth. The innermost was a form-fitting satin, the other flowing and gossamer, like smoke from a campfire. All of her ruddy, exposed skin — arms, legs, back, neck — was covered in ornate and beautiful tattoos. Her hair was dyed a bright, sea-foam green and styled into a pixie cut that exposed her pointed ears.

From behind large, round sunglasses, her eyes would dart to the side, catching a glimpse of Raphie desperately attempting to look casual. She clearly saw through his flimsy guise to his obvious infatuation. Her eyes gleamed a green that matched her hair and had the striking power of a tsunami. Her black lips grimaced. Was she amused? Irritated? It was beyond Raphie's understanding; he'd never been good at reading faces. By the time he had decided to glance up at her, she had turned away and was back to pulling out her dry laundry.

He pulled back his headphones and tried to think of a reason to speak to her. Historically, Raphie had been lucky in that all of his partners had always approached him first. More than a few had claimed to be pulled in by his steely, perpetually pissed, look that had made him appear brooding and mysterious. It could be that his eyebrows have always grown thick and angular, making him look as if he'd been pushed to the limits of his patience. He had never once outwardly tried to look this way, and in fact, he tried to be as laid back as he could be. It was easier managing anxiety with a stoner, grunge attitude.

Scenarios like this one were often tricky for him, thusly, trying to look relaxed and "chill" did not come as an easy task. Instead of being either relaxed or chill, he formed a wearisome, awkward grin.

Thankfully for Raphie's dignity, she had already turned and made her way to leave the stuffy building. His eyes shot down to where she stood and saw a small bundle of black lace. He dropped his book and CD player into his basket, stood, and swooped up the article of clothing in one motion. With a few long strides, Raphael caught up to the mystery woman, her modest load of clothing stuffed into a dark green duffel bag.

"Miss! Excuse me, miss!" he barked from still within the building, but had approached by the time she turned to see him. She stood next to a beat-up Ford Bronco with the roof chopped off. It was an off-white color that had chipped in multiple places as if it had been used to go off-road. There he was, frozen in his tracks about six feet apart from her, paralyzed by her gaze that rivaled the waters of the Pacific Ocean. His skin crawled as if she had immersed him in those very same waters.

"Um… I think you dropped this."

He held his hand out to give her the item. Once his arm had fully extended, the bundle unfurled and revealed itself to be a risqué pair of panties, see-through in almost all places. He became flushed and did the first thing his mind felt natural: switch his grip to just his forefinger and thumb. Naturally.

"Thanks…" the Elf woman said reluctantly, her voice was soft but deeper than the average girl's. Not that anything about her was average. She took them from him with a look of visible confusion. "You know they're clean right?"

"Yeah. I know," he responded faster than he should have. "But it's, ya know… personal."

"Riiight," she said arching a dark, manicured eyebrow. "I mean it's cool, not everyone is into strangers' panties." Her tone was humorous, desperately trying to make the situation less uncomfortable.

"No, it's okay, I'm bisexual," he replied.

Holy shit, stop talking, he thought.

"Nice," she smirked, her soft, lightly freckled face beaming in his direction. "Me too."

Holy shit. Holy shit. Holy shit.

Raphael began to sweat, a single drop trailing down his brow.

"Nice. Me too," he parroted.

She laughed. Her smile made him feel like his whole body was being torched. His stomach knotted; she was the most beautiful Elf he'd ever seen.

"Well, I've got to fold my panties," she joked, her voice mellow and sweet, like hot tea and honey, opening her door and climbing into her large vehicle. After a few attempts, the vehicle started. "Thanks again. See ya round, maybe."

"Of course. And see ya round," Raphie echoed, stepping back and watching her slowly pull out and drive off. Once she was out of sight, a realization came to Raphie:

Damnit! I didn't even ask for her name!

5

In the southeast corner of West Hollywood, sat a drab little apartment building painted the color of dried mustard. Morgan entered and briefly scanned the lobby. A set of stairs flanked the left of the narrow corridor, and on the right was a desk where a blonde Dwarven girl in pigtails sat, head resting on her fist and reading *People* magazine. Domhainn starlet Kacey Blackwish was on the cover, something about her new husband being a Human. It appalled Morgan that some people still treated inter-species marriage like a big ordeal.

"Back to see your grandma?" The girl said without looking up from her magazine, the rock-like flesh of her cheek scrunched just as any other's would.

"My aunt," Morgan corrected with a furrowed brow.

"Whatever," the stony woman replied.

Morgan rolled her eyes and pressed on down the hall, up the set of stairs, passing four apartments, to stand before the frosted door. Its inscription became clearer as she approached: Lunar Light Investigations. Beneath it hung a dust-caked sign that said "Sorry, We're Closed". Morgan wondered if she had ever moved the sign… and how she could find business. According to her Auntie M, "the case finds her."

Upon the final steps down the silent corridor, Morgan reached into her small beige shoulder bag, pulled out her keys, and found a single, weathered, brass one among the others. She unlocked the door, opening and entering in stride. The rather large, shadowy, one-bedroom apartment opened to a narrow hall before expanding into a chaotic mess. The room looked less like someone's home and more akin to an abandoned office from the 70s with its stacks of paper, notebooks, files, and boxes marked "Evidence".

Turning the corner to the click of a gun becoming cocked caused Morgan's skin to freeze. She looked up to see two cored barrels of a sawed-off shotgun. Morgan dropped low out of instinct, almost to her knees.

"Holy shit! Auntie M!" she yelped in defense.

"Goddammit, kid," the gruff-voiced woman spoke, lowering

her weapon with her dark, strong hand. "One of these days you're gonna get your head blown off coming in here without knocking."

"Why did you give me a key then?" Morgan chuckled uncomfortably and rose to meet the gaze of her seven-foot-tall aunt.

"Emergencies," the woman spoke, the bottom of her humanoid face almost disappearing into the massive wool collar of her aviator's jacket. Her legs were kept hidden by baggy cargo pants, but they could not hide the almost bird-like feet. Her face was mostly taken up by her eyes, two almond-shaped, wine-red orbs like headlamps with black pupils. From her head, two long, feather-like antennae protruded, the same color as the soft grey fur that seemed to cover many parts of her body.

"I'll be sure to knock next time," Morgan said with an eye roll.

"Now that you're not cannon fodder," the large moth-like woman spoke, holding her arms out. "Where's my hug?"

Morgan stepped forward with arms outstretched and gave her Aunt M a wide hug. Aunt M did the same with one long arm. Morgan's arms couldn't wrap fully around her waist, but grazed against the unique, scaly texture of her wings. Each of them was tucked gently under her coat, with enough exposed behind her to dangle down like elaborate coattails.

"It's good to see you, Auntie M," Morgan said. "I'm sorry I didn't come last week. Class has me by the balls already."

"Expected as such," Aunt M said, ending their hug with a soft pat on Morgan's back. "An adult now, have to accept you're too busy for your auntie… speaking of which, how's the internship?"

"It's going. Already had my shift today," Morgan said to her massive aunt. The woman turned around and placed her gun next to a telescopic camera on her currently 'active' desk.

With her back turned, Morgan had a chance to look at Aunt M's highly disorganized home and place of business. Any and all open space, including parts of the kitchen, was dedicated fully to her profession. Scattered across the area were a few dozen lamps, all of different styles, shapes, and sizes. Each had old, low-wattage bulbs; some would flicker or fade out, and others glowed bright only occasionally, holding that brightness for a time before going as dim as the rest. Each cord was haphazardly duct-taped to the floors and walls, connecting to jury-rigged power strips. All around them, moths of different varieties flittered about, landing on the brighter bulbs.

Despite all the lamps, the only source of natural light in the apartment was from a single window in the wall furthest from where Morgan stood. The window itself was shuttered and looked to be that way for some time, judging by the dust. Past a tower of stuffed folders and lamps, on the wall beside the window, was a placard: "Maxine Mothman: Private Investigator." Beneath this plaque, a badge was framed with a black & white photograph of her old team labeled: "M. Mothman, FBI." Beside it, in a matching frame, the badge of her father: "N. Scriven, FBI."

"This place is a fire hazard, Auntie M," Morgan said.

"Believe me, kid," Maxine retorted. "Causing fire is least of my worries. Besides, I'd feel it coming."

"If you insist?" Morgan said suspiciously, stepping over some hefty stacks of paper to stand next to her aunt, bumping a desk corner as she did. "I never really understood how your sixth sense worked."

"Me neither," Maxine said with a smile, her mouth and nose humanoid, if not sharply defined. "Just does, end up where I need to be every time—"

"Without fail," Morgan completed.

"Take it, I've said that frequently?" Maxine skewed her face, somewhat disappointed, but couldn't help but chuckle beneath her breath. "Get as old as me, turn into a broken record."

"Not at all, Auntie M," Morgan said with a smile, crossing to sit in a chair beside the desk where Maxine stood. "You're always full of surprises."

There on the wall before her was a corkboard with several scribbled notes and pictures, a few of which were linked together by thumbtacks and string. As Maxine organized the scattered papers on her desk into their respective folders,

Morgan took several moments to observe the clues to the unknown case. At the center, gathering the most connected strings, was a picture of a Domhainn girl. She was young, though age is hard to tell with Elves, but judging from the picture, she was in a prom dress of sorts. Her hair was raven black, straight, and pinned behind her long, pointed ears. Her skin was smooth and grey like stones in a Zen garden, her eyes a bright gold and happy.

"Who's she?" Morgan said and pointed to the photo.

"Her? She's a case I'm working on; missing persons. Had some solid leads but they went cold, info wells ran dry." Maxine looked at the picture with her cold, dark eyes, reflecting the light of the many lamps that filled the room. She lifted a mug of black coffee and sipped it, still observing the girl's photo.

"What's her name?" Morgan asked with genuine concern.

"Franques, Tori Franques. Was hired by her parents; poor girl's only eighteen and went missing shortly after high school graduation," Maxine said.

"That's awful… what do you know?" Morgan asked, placing a hand over her heart.

"Not much. Got involved in nightlife, mother said, no idea where. Word is with a Vampire, but got gut feeling it's something else." Maxine looked perturbed as she spoke, reaching into her jacket pocket and pulling out a cigarette and lighter.

"I'll put my ear to the ground, maybe I'll find something," Morgan gave a displeased frown. She shuffled her feet and looked at the floor. Taking a deep breath and gathering the guts she needed, "Hey… I have a somewhat related question to ask you."

"Shoot," the mothwoman replied.

"I'm working on a story… my own story…"

"Fantastic, congrats," She said in that hopelessly positive way only a parental figure could. "Knew they'd see your talent."

"It's uh… about a missing girl, actually…" she said with undercurrents of reluctance. "Her name is Chrissy Donavon. I was hoping you might know where to start."

"Missing persons, huh… seems to be a lot of those lately," Maxine shifted her weight, a look of concern washing over her dark, alien features. "Where was she last seen?"

"La Cienega and Waring," Morgan replied, thinking back to her notes. "She was half-naked and acting strangely. Some bystander tried to help her, but someone else called her to a nearby building? The police apparently combed the area and found it was all up for lease. Nothing inside."

"Hmmm," she said, looking off into space and lighting her cigarette. "Talked to the parents?"

"Her mother was interviewed by the cops and my friend at the Chronicle… but nothing came of the story."

"Not what I asked," She said, taking a draw, letting the smoke wisps escape from her lips. "Did *you* talk to the mom?"

"Not yet."

"Start there," Maxine began. "Talk to her, and when you can, use the archives at the Chronicle. Remember, you work at a paper."

"Right… I'm just a little overwhelmed, is all," Morgan said with a weak grin.

"Not sure I like you chasing crime stories," Maxine grunted. "Need any help?"

"You've already helped a lot." She stood with a little bounce.

"Sure… just… tell me if trouble starts brewing," Maxine said, drawing on her smoke.

"Of course… Those things will kill you, ya know?" Morgan said disapprovingly. "Plus, you're going to set this room on fire, like I said."

"Use an ashtray," Maxine defended. From the outside looking in, it would seem the niece was the more responsible family member. "Watch it, missy. All have our vices. Better than drinking myself into a stupor like little friend, you paid the way for. Where is Raphie, by the way? Not coming with?"

"He's at home," Morgan said.

"Why's that?" Maxine said smugly.

"He is too hungover and is dropping his class," Morgan said, realizing what she was tricked into admitting.

"Right," Maxine said, as if Morgan had just spouted gibberish. "Just don't want you expending your savings. Know your folks left a substantial sum, and trust you're smart. But they also wanted me to watch after you."

"Thank you, Auntie M, I appreciate you caring. But you taught me to take care of myself." Morgan stood on her toes and hugged her aunt again. "I promise I'll be okay."

"Trust you will," Maxine replied, squeezing her adopted niece. "Your old man always said you'd make it far. Can't see him being wrong now."

"Thank you… I really miss them, but I know they always wanted what's best for me… So I keep moving," Morgan lamented, but kept her composure as always.

"Rode the bus alone?" Maxine said, crossing her arms.

"Yeah… so?" Morgan laughed.

"Just want you safe."

"Auntie M… I'm not a little girl… and I'm a Vampire, it's more likely that people will avoid me than try to give me problems."

"Suppose."

"Hey, I gotta get goin," Morgan said. "Please, don't stress about me."

Maxine sighed, turning to the corkboard once her niece had said her goodbyes and left. Her big, watery eyes focused on the photo of the missing girl.

"Be careful, princess."

The sounds of guitar cords could be heard echoing from the small room that belonged to Raphael. As he strummed, his fingers slipped, and a note fell flat.

"Damnit," he said, repositioning his fingers and trying the riff again. He tried a few more times and ended up getting more flat notes. "God damnit!"

He tuned his guitar a bit and tried again. It was then that he heard the front door open, his ajar. Balam's voice could be heard over the music; rather than stop playing, Raphie was nosy and turned the volume on his amp down, making it easier to hear.

"Yeah, no," Balam said, before giggling. Raphie raised a brow. "I can't have that anymore… but I do like it…."

It was clear to Raphie that Balam was on his cell phone, being a doctor, he was the only person in the household to own one. Everyone else got by with pagers and payphones. Raphie didn't think cell phones were all that impressive and didn't see them being anything more than a gimmicky device. Even still, Raphie listened with intent.

"Oh yeah?" Balam said, a certain flirtatious tone in his voice. The smile on his face was transparent through his tone alone. "Maybe when I see you again, you can show me… I can do that for you…God damn… don't tease me like that… Okay… Yeah, I'm home now, so I gotta go… I'll see you soon."

Rather than wait, Raphie turned off his amp, set down his guitar, and exited the room.

"Oh! Raphie!" Balam practically jumped and quickly put away his phone. "I thought you had class today."

"Yeah, I dropped it," he said, looking at Balam past his nose. "Who, uh… who were you talking to?"

"Oh, just one of the other doctors from the clinic," Balam said with a smile, making his way to the fridge for a bottle of water.

"You… sounded awfully close to them. Must be a really good coworker," Raphie highlighted.

"Um… yeah… we're good friends," Balam said nervously.

"Right… " Raphie replied, leaning on the Bar and grabbing an apple out of a basket. "Just uh… don't get too close now."

"Raphie…" Balam said with a sigh, "If I wanted your opinion, I'd give it to you… Thanks for the tip, but everything is fine. Okay? I have another shift at 6, so if you don't mind…"

With that, Balam marched off to his room and slammed the door. Raphie chuckled in disbelief.

"Fuck." Raphie said under his breath.

6

It was roughly 7:30 p.m. when someone finally unlocked the front door to Apartment 161. Raphael didn't move off of the couch, he didn't care if the entrant was a burglar or a serial killer, or the fucking messiah. The door swung open, letting the Bruce Springsteen music he was playing on full blast out into the undeserving world.

"Raph?" Morgan said, walking in and placing her bags and keys on the entry table. She flicked the light switch, lighting the once clean apartment living room transformed into a room littered with beer cans and a half-eaten *DiGiorno* pizza. He held his arm over his eyes, half draped over the couch, hissing like a cat.

"I wish you could appreciate the irony of what you just did," Morgan spoke honestly. "Damn… Springsteen, you must really be deprcssed."

"I got dumped, dude. How many times do I have to fucking say it? " He paused, changing his tone. "Sorry… Grab me another beer out of the fridge, and you can turn it off." Raphael sighed.

"Alrighty then. Deal," she said, concerned. She crossed over to their kitchenette, spotting the space on the counter.

"Where's the coffee machine?"

"Mimic," Raphie groaned, waving a dismissive hand at her. "I got rid of it already."

"Lovely…" Morgan said with a sigh. "Gonna have to replace that now."

Morgan went into the fridge and pulled out two locally brewed beers called *Aeldar Ale* from a six-pack that was already three short. "You didn't drink all this today, did you?"

"Does it matter?" He slurred, mostly too apathetic to speak properly.

"Since you're not undead like me, and thus can die of alcohol poisoning," she said, turning around and kicking the fridge door shut with her heel. "Yes. These things are like 9%. But since I already agreed, at least come sit with me at the Bar. You probably should stretch if you've been there as long as I assume you have."

"Okay," he said begrudgingly. "Fine."

As Raphie approached she turned the overly loud and melodramatic music off, then popped the caps off both drinks. Once he had pulled up one of two stools on the opposite side, he sat down and grabbed a beer, almost immediately putting his head on the Bar top.

"You sure you're okay?" She said, holding up her hand. "You were much better this morning."

"Yeah…" he said, thinking about what transpired with Balam a few hours prior. "You uh… might wanna sit down first."

"Why?" Morgan pushed, standing up straight. "What happened?"

"…Balam was acting really strange today."

"How so?"

"He was on the phone with someone and he was…" Raphie skewed his face. "Off…"

"How off?" Morgan inquired, her eyes stern and her defenses ready.

"I don't know, just off. He was like… flirting or some shit."

"What did he say?" Morgan continued. "Raph, if you're saying what I think you're saying, you better have some good proof."

"I can't remember what he said specifically, just that it felt off," Raphie insisted. "I'm just reporting what I heard, that's all."

"You know what?" Morgan intruded. "Just keep it to yourself. I don't want to hear it."

"But, Blondie—"

"I'm sure you misheard, okay? Balam would never hurt me like that. And just because you're hurting yourself, I don't think it's cool to project relationship problems on others."

"I'm not projecting. Look, forget I said anything. You're probably right. I just misheard, is all."

A pregnant pause followed.

"So… how was your day?" Raphie asked timidly.

"Interesting. I had Harding breathing down my neck the moment I entered the office," she scoffed. "Can you believe jeans aren't work appropriate for a *NEWSPAPER*? In LA?"

"That is kinda stupid." Raphie pulled a face, then his memory sparked, and he smirked. "Hey, isn't he that hot older Orc who runs the paper? Maybe I'll rebound on him."

"Eww. That's not even funny," Morgan rolled her eyes. "He's like fifty, is balding, and—"

"'Has a chiseled jaw, and, like, a sexy scruffy thing goin on, and arms like a linebacker,'" Raphie quoted, doing his best impersonation of Morgan, gushing. He looked smugly at her and took a drink. "I remember what you said when you started. Verbatim… you don't forget a description like that. Besides not like you're gonna fuck him."

"You're right. He's my boss. That would be inappropriate," Morgan gave a disgusted look and drank her beer as if to cleanse the taste. "And all attraction was dissolved as soon as I realized how much of an asshole he was."

"Maybe he's just wound too tight… needs some release," Raphie jested, making a lewd gesture with his hand and his mouth, bulging his cheek with his tongue.

"I get it! Oh, my gods, you're awful!" Morgan laughed in disbelief and shook her head. "Honestly… I'm glad to see you joking. I didn't think you would when I walked in."

"Yeah," he said, slumping down, being brought back to sobering reality.

"Okay," Morgan said, "I wasn't considering going, but I'll give you a choice: I heard that they still have some copies of *Resident Evil* at the mall, and if we hurry, we might just be able to make it before it closes and get a copy."

Raphie raised an eyebrow, decently interested. "That's tempting. What's the other option?"

"Well, remember Eliza? My ex? She's my new supervisor, and she invited me to a party in North Hollywood tonight. Big house, lotta cute single guys and girls."

"Is there free booze?" Raphie asked plainly.

"Yup."

"I'll buy the taxi!" Raphie said, jumping off his stool and grabbing the phone off the adjacent wall.

"Atta boy," Morgan smiled.

*****

Dave's party was as wild as Eliza said it would be: live music, lots of booze, tons of cute people. What more could a bisexual college student ask for? For Morgan, it was a change of pace. She usually preferred clubs. Raphael, being no stranger to such environments, instantaneously got them both drinks in red cups. The red ale was strong, Dwarven—robust, earthy, and nutty. Even Morgan seemed to perk up a bit when drinking it, but it did nothing for Raphael. As of late, his alcohol tolerance seemed to be through the roof. When he did drink enough, he often skipped being drunk and went straight to the hangover.

He was standing among a group of fellow students and alumni from Avalon University, but mentally was hardly present. Morgan seemed to know them. She did all the talking; Morgan always did. Raphie was in no way feeling social. Oliver used him and then left him, so cold it almost felt transactional. Raphie couldn't believe him. It didn't make any sense. He felt deep down that Morgan was right; maybe if Oliver was willing to do this, it was a sign he was never meant for him.

He looked up from his foamy drink and saw her past two of his classmates: the Elven, aquamarine goddess. She was wearing a short, form-fitting, black dress with a draping hem and bell sleeves. Atop her head was a wide-brimmed, black hat hiding her pointed ears. She seemed to step from a dark dream, not a nightmare, but rather a Gothic fantasy. A tall tale in Doc Martens. She held a red cup in both hands, standing off to the side, looking around as if waiting for someone. Her eyes met his. He felt cold, even in the crowded and hazy living area. She smiled at him. The world froze.

"You okay, Raph?" Morgan asked worriedly. "You look

like you saw a ghost."

Eliza had overheard Morgan speak as she approached the circle. She slapped her hand hard on Raphie's shoulder, jarring him. Eliza gestured forward with her drink hand, "Nope, worse. He's been hexed."

Raphie scoffed in irritation, looking at Eliza, who seemed to completely ignore his expression. Eliza was just as tall as Raphie, but she was twice as strong. At first, he thought it was just because she was a Taknoling, but he could feel her muscles even through her oversized sweater. By the time he looked forward again, he had lost sight of his mysterious vixen.

"What do you mean?" Morgan furrowed her brow in confusion

"W-who was that?" Raphael looked pale, like death had passed by him and given him a second chance. "You come here often, right, Eliza? Who was that girl? The one with the teal hair."

"You don't wanna tango with that one, buddy," Eliza said, taking a swig of her beer.

"Why not?" Morgan said, "My boy needs a rebound."

"Yeah, why not?" Raphie said, wiggling out of her grip and looking for the mystery woman. "She was nice to me at the laundromat."

"Oh shit, you've spoken to her?" Eliza scoffed, finishing her beer and tossing it into a trash can. "You're screwed buddy, that gal is bad news. She's a witch. I'm not talking the tarot cards, gemstones, and happy thoughts kind. I mean she's the real deal: the kind you hear about in the Pre-War legends. Belongs to a pretty serious local coven, too."

"That seems narrow-minded of you, Eliza," Morgan spoke up. "Especially from a Taknoling."

"Well it might be easier for you to trust magic being a Vampire, but I've seen the likes of every person get chewed up and spit out by that firecracker and her fucked up friends, that's all I'm saying. And it only takes getting burned by them once," Eliza protested, turning to Morgan to finish her debate.

"What's her name?" Raphie asked.

"Demy. Demy Moon," Eliza answered. "Look, magic is

hella illegal and dangerous, and our comrade isn't necessarily the best at self-control. Am I right, bud— fuck he's gone."

Morgan chuckled, seeing Raphie head into the crowd in search of the legendary, sublime Ms. Moon. "You couldn't stop him if you pinned him down."

Eliza shook her head. "His funeral."

Raphie wandered around the elephantine, three-story Victorian. Every room, even those cleared of any furniture, was packed. He searched the entire ground floor and into the backyard, then the front yard. From there, the second and third stories. He needed to find her.

He unintentionally brushed shoulders with strangers who would not make way or simply didn't pay attention to him. Raphie was sure he got some dirty looks, but couldn't care less. He searched the top floor, peering into the open rooms and even daring to peek into one of the closed ones. The party-goers on the other side didn't seem too pleased as their moans and cries of pleasure turned to shouts of anger and the throwing of pillows. Still no dice.

You've gotta be out there somewhere. It's not even that late. He thought, stepping down a short, narrow staircase and looking over the banister of the second story. His whole sweep couldn't have taken more than ten minutes, but it felt like an eternity.

The large crowd seemed to have gotten larger since he disappeared upstairs. His eyes scanned the now jam-packed ground floor, hoping, praying for that splash of turquoise that made him feel weak. Instead, he saw pale skin and blonde hair; he smiled, but a heavy sigh followed.

"Raphie!" Morgan funneled her hands over her mouth to shout over the loud music and drunken crowd. She saw him look in her direction, but as soon as she called, he turned and went back upstairs. She tried to push past the same groups of people as Raphie, but they were now less responsive.

Back upstairs, Raphie had found an open bedroom painted a soft yellow, most likely a guest bedroom. Though judging by the sheer number of rooms ready to sleep, crashing here was a regular occurrence. A window on the far end of the yellow room led out onto the roof and was left wide open. Taking advantage, Raphie climbed out.

The initial incline was steep, but he felt as if he could just get a bird's eye view of the front and backyard he would see her. After going up a few feet, he realized how difficult climbing such a slanted roof would be. He squatted down and sat beside the window, looking out from the Hollywood manor and into the glow of LA. The nighttime lights were his favorite part of the city; on a breezy day like today, the smog was lifted, and you could see for miles. Each bundle of lights was its own little world, culture, and community. For a moment, the sight relaxed Raphie… for a moment.

Letting off a sigh of disappointment, Raphie began to accept that this mysterious Demy Moon was nowhere to be seen. Their meetings to be dismissed as coincidences. Bending his knees, he folded his arms on them and rested his chin. *Is that it? Was that the last time I saw her?* He thought, alone again.

"Hey," a woman's soft voice spoke. He lifted his head to Morgan, hanging half out the window. "How are ya doin', big guy?"

"Fine," he said muffled and somber.

"You don't seem fine," she said, sitting on the windowsill and turning to dangle her legs out. "And how often do you say 'fine' and actually mean it?"

Raphie remained silent.

"Look, I know this Demy girl seems right in your ballpark…" Morgan began, her tone low and nurturing. "But maybe that's not such a good thing. Maybe you need something out of your ordinary."

"That's just it, Morgan," He spoke again "There's something about her that is completely different than anyone I've ever met. I just have to talk to her one more time."

"I've heard she's pretty unique," Morgan said, rubbing the back of her neck nervously. Raphie's head whipped around.

"What else did Eliza say?" he asked pointedly.

"I don't know, to be honest, she was drunk and kinda rambling about some weird conspiracy theory type shit," she said, now tracing her finger around the rim of her cup. "Eliza has always been hard to read when it comes to other women.

That's why we didn't work out. I just think she's looking out for us. She's your friend, too, ya know?"

"Yeah… I guess," Raphie said.

"Look, all I'm saying is— is that her?" As if summoned by their conversation, three goth figures walked from the house to meet another group that had just pulled up in a blacked-out pickup truck. Among the three was the woman of Raphie's dreams, her wide-brimmed hat blocked her face, but he recognized the tattoos on her legs and the accents of blue-green that shone like Malachite at the bottom of a river bed.

"Yes! Blondie, that's her!" he said, trying to stand but knowing Morgan blocked the only way in the house.

"Alright," she sighed, "let's go get the girl."

7

Six friends, dressed in mostly black, gathered in and around the bed of a large, black Dodge Ram. Each of them, despite their gloomy wardrobe, had accents of color in various places across their bodies, ranging from accessory choices to hair colors. Demy Moon was among the three outside the truck, with two women as darkly dressed as she. The pale one was in a pin-up style outfit that fit her wide-hipped figure well; she had big black hair and even bigger makeup. The other was a woman in shorts, ripped tights, and a *Black Sabbath* shirt cut into a crop, exposing her brassy skin. Her hair was navy blue and cut into a chin-length bob. Morgan was too far away to see the others as she approached.

The one with navy hair noticed them approaching and nudged Demy with her elbow. She had a mean look about her, her eyebrows hidden by her bangs, but somehow still came across as arched in irritation. Raphie slowed his stride, stopping a few feet from where they stood in the currently open road. Morgan kept her distance, standing in the driveway and observing. Demy and Raphie seemed to immediately connect; the others, however, seemed to shift and observe them as they approached. The pinup girl carried a cane, stained ebony, and the other brandished a wooden baseball bat. Neither gave Morgan the sense that they were just accessories; they were weapons.

It was then that Morgan could make out the other two, who were sitting in the bed of the truck. They were both Orcs, instantly identifiable by their green flesh. One was a woman, dressed in a more bohemian style, with braided brown hair. The other was a man who stood as he approached. He was wearing a tight red t-shirt that seemed to be stretched over his yoked arms and chest like a second skin. The man stepped down from the truck and steadied himself with hands clad in black riding gloves with what looked like spiked knuckles. The woman remained in the truck.

"Can we help you?" the cerulean-haired woman spoke, lifting her bat to point at Raphie. The rockabilly woman tightened her grip on her cane, and the Orcish man cracked his knuckles.

"I, uh, actually wanted to talk to Ms. Moon…" Raphie nearly tripped over his words but found himself in time. He looked Demy directly in the eye. "If you wouldn't mind for just a moment…"

Demy chewed on her cheek in deep thought but did not reply.

"Is this guy a problem, Demy?" the Orc echoed. Though he did not speak loudly, it carried through the hills.

"Naw, I've met him before. I'll be done in a second, guys," she said stepping forward to meet Raphie. Once she was closer to him, she spoke again. "Hey. Small world."

"Yeah, and here I thought LA was a big city." Raphie smiled. Demy kept looking past him at Morgan watching them talk.

"Oh, she's my friend and roommate, Morgan," he turned and gestured to the Vampire. "She's just really protective of me, is all. Usually, she's a great wingwoman."

Raphael gave a somewhat forced chuckle through the awkwardness. He scratched his head, appearing particularly stumped. He seemed to be losing her a bit. *Just say it*. Morgan thought.

"Do you wanna go with me?" he said without fear of being rejected. "Out… go out… with me? Sometime. It doesn't have to be now… but… I saw you again and I knew if I didn't say anything I'd regret it forever."

Demy smirked, "How'd you know my last name?"

"I asked a friend. Eliza, she's inside still I think…" he said plainly "I'm Raphael by the way, everyone calls me Raphie though."

"Demytria." She replied, "But Demy is easier for most."

She looked back at her friends. The blue-haired one held her arms open as if to ask, "What are you doing?"

The Elf turned back to Raphie, smiling. "How attached are you to this party?" she asked.

"Not particularly," he said with a grin of swelling confidence.

"Are you down with magic?"

"I mean… As long as we're not killing anybody."

"We're not," Demy said. "Wanna come with us?"

It was then that Morgan took a few long strides and grabbed Raphie's arms. "Hi! I'm Morgan, Raphie's best friend since grade school. Can I borrow him for a moment?"

"Sure?" Demy said with a look of confusion, turning back to return the shrug.

"What are you doing?" Raphie gave a hushed but panicked cry. "She asked me to come with her!"

"Do you know the first thing about these guys?" She argued, sparing a glance at Demy, who raised an eyebrow in response.

"Do you?" Raphie challenged Morgan. "You're not salty because she's an Elf, right?"

"Motherfucker, I'm banging an Elf."

"You're gonna use the 'brown friend' excuse on me? Really?" Raphie said and skewed the corner of his lips.

"I meant if they're talking *real magic,* that shit's super illegal," She said folding her arms like a disappointed mother. "Just promise me you'll be careful."

"Eliza has you paranoid," Raphie shook his head. "Look," he reached into his pocket and pulled out a small black pager

"My beeper's on, page me if you think I've been gone too long or whatever. If I don't call back within an hour of your page then you can call the search party. Okay?"

"Fiiiine!" Morgan was not pleased but she'd comply if only because he was dumped days prior. "Just come home sometime tomorrow morning so I don't have to call the cops… Or Aunt M."

"Oh lord," Raphie looked a bit frightened. "Yeah, don't call her, I'd very much like for her to not fly in playing superhero."

"Well, come home safe and I won't call her." Her mouth shifted to one side, as did her stance. "Go. Go paint the town black or whatever."

"I'll be okay, Blondie," he said, turning to jog back to Demy. "Promise."

After a few more seconds of talking like flirty school kids, they all piled into the truck, the sixth individual poked his head out from the driver's side window, a decrepit-looking Ghoul. His skin was pale and thin, his veins visible across his dead flesh. A tinge of green seemed to pervade his face, especially around his lips, which harbored a row of carnivorous teeth. Morgan raised her brow in contemplation. It was rare to see a Ghoul on this end of town.

"You guys ready? We're on a schedule." He spoke loud enough for Morgan to hear the gurgling in his throat.

"Sorry, Gruel," she heard Demy say as they hopped into the vehicle. The rest was muted by the sounds of the party in the background. Morgan waved to them as they drove off, her fake smile turning to a frown once the truck was out of sight.

"You better not break that promise, Raphael Shapira," she said to herself.

"He won't," Eliza said, now sounding less drunk and approaching Morgan. "Raphie may easily swoon, but he's not stupid. He'll know when to get out of things when he's in too deep. You're the one who has that problem."

"Excuse me?" Morgan whipped her head around.

"I'm just kiddin'," she chuckled, sarcasm dripping from every syllable. "You're the toughest chick I know, Morgan. Tough enough to deal with Harding's ass. And the *boyfriend*."

Eliza shuddered at the last word, like it left a bad taste in her mouth. Morgan giggled and shook her head.

"Hey, Balam is a solid guy," Morgan said defensively. "He's a fucking doctor, vegetarian Wood-Elf for the gods' sakes. He couldn't be trouble if he tried."

"I suppose you're right," Eliza scrunched her lips, defeated. "He sounds 'G' rated, but I think that's good for a one-woman army like you."

"Thank you," Morgan looked to her feet, unable to hide a blush thanks to her albino complexion. "You're too nice."

"I mean, I couldn't do it for you. I didn't have the mettle, not at the time. But Balam, he's a good guy. It makes me happy you got someone who takes care of you while letting you be you, and that's something you deserve."

"You're right," Morgan said, thinking of her boyfriend. Her smile faltered. "He's pretty great."

"Hey, I know you're worried, but don't be. Raphie is fine." Eliza commented, misunderstanding Morgan's shift in demeanor.

"Right," she agreed, only half paying attention to what was said.

"Okay, I'm almost sober, let's go hang out for a minute then I'll take you home. But we're going to Shelly's first, I'm starving."

"I'm down, I don't hate their coffee," Morgan followed Eliza back into the house. Turning back at the front door to look at the moonlit sky, she thought for a moment about Raphie's relationship troubles, and how they almost seemed less than her own.

8

The bed of the black pickup was in rough condition, though a pair of blankets had been laid down so the passengers riding in it had a bit more comfort. Raphie kept his back to the driver's side corner. In the bed with him sat the Orcs and the girl with navy blue hair, keeping their heads low in case of police. Now and then, Raphie would glance back into the cab and lock eyes with Demy until he would look away sheepishly. The navy-haired Human had not stopped mad dogging him since they left, and seemed the one most perturbed by this interaction with Demy. Raphie, trying to be the peacekeeper, turned to her and spoke.

"Hey," he opened with a half smile. "I don't think we got the chance to get introduced before we took off. I'm Raphie."

He held his hand out for her to shake, instead, she just twirled her baseball bat in her hands. He let his hand fall in disappointment after realizing she wouldn't reciprocate. His eyes drifted to the male Orc.

"Ed," the Orc spoke instead, his voice coarse and deep, and gestured lazily to each person. "My sister, 'Ruthless' Rhonda, and this ray of sunshine is Amy. You've already met our sweet Demy, the dark thing sitting beside her is Trina, and the creepy fella behind the wheel goes by Gruel. Never heard his real name."

"It's a pleasure to meet you all," Raphie said with a genuine smile. "So, where are we headed? After party?"

"Yeah," Amy scoffed. "It's a party, alright. A real private party… You should feel lucky you got invited… you're gonna keep it on the down low, right?"

"Of course?" Raphie said, feeling his heart race with sudden worry.

Rhonda stared at Amy and shook her head.

"Why do they call you 'Ruthless?'" he asked daringly, though she didn't seem to notice he was talking to her as she still leered at Amy.

"She's deaf," Ed said, tapping on Rhonda's shoulder and signing to her. She signed back, glancing at Raphie occasionally.

"She says, 'You ask a lot of questions.'" Ed translated, as she continued to sign before stopping and smiling at Raphie. "But since you asked, it was because someone kept pestering her about whether she could read lips. He mouthed something rotten, and she ripped his ear off."

"Word," Raphie choked, kind of chuckling. The others stayed quiet. "Wait, really?"

Before anyone could respond, the truck hit a bump that jostled the passengers. Raphie peeked out over the side of the vehicle to see they were deeper in the city and out of the hills, pulling up to an abandoned shop. From the looks of the signage, it used to sell music, now it was a withered husk of a building, the economic stresses of the past decade having taken its toll on the structure. Raphie raised a brow, but had certainly partied in sketchier locales.

"So what are we…" he said, turning back to see the other occupants bailing out of the vehicle the moment the truck was parked. "Doing… here?"

Not to be left behind, Raphie vaulted over the side of the bed. This was the first time he'd meet eyes with Gruel the Ghoul. He was short, slightly portly, with speckled green skin with splotches of dead flesh held in a permanent state of decay. His head was topped with a black mop, stopping just above his sunken and shadowy eyes. Those eyes, bloodshot and yellowed, stared into Raphie with an unseen intent.

"Well, hello there," Gruel rumbled, his voice naturally guttural and strained. "You must be the new guy."

"New guy?" Raphie said.

"Demy told me about you in the cab… said you were… cool." Gruel looked Raphie up and down, a wicked smile of sharp teeth on his face. Raphie felt like he was being sized up, despite the cheery tone coming from the Ghoul. "You're gonna have fun with us tonight, don't worry."

He patted Raphie on the arm, a bit harder than he should have, nearly knocking him off balance. Raphie chuckled it off and rubbed his arm discreetly, following Gruel around the truck to meet with the others. Gathered in a small circle, Demytria Moon stood with her friends, her freckled cheeks raised high with a charming smile as they laughed and gabbed. Raphie tried to fight his blushing face, grateful for a darker complexion.

"Where the fuck is Adrian? They were supposed to meet us here, and we're technically late," Amy huffed, marching over to Gruel, the others' attention on their conversation.

"Dunno, probably got held up with the Brothers Estrada again. You know how they are." Gruel said, picking his tooth with a sharp nail. "We can just chill for a moment."

"Chill? This place is a hot zone! We should be in and out like greased lightning, not waiting in a group."

"I said chill, Amy," Gruel said with a low growl.

"Please keep your voice down, Amy," Ed had said. "You said it yourself, it's dangerous."

Raphie strode up next to Demy, the only one he knew out of this group, and the one he wanted to get to know the most. She had stepped away, looking at the locked cage of the shop windows, contemplating.

"Hey. How goes it?" He said, eying the graffiti that had been plastered across nearly every surface of the building. Some of it was even good. Raphie was quick to judge the lazier works.

"It goes."

"So… what's up with the abandoned music shop?" He dared to ask.

"It's not what the shop is, it's that it's abandoned," Demy said with that same charming smile. "We only need a place to be uninterrupted, and no one place is safe to practice twice."

"Practice. You mean magic?" Raphie felt suddenly quite clammy, realizing what he might have agreed to.

"Exactly," she nodded. "Though our organization prefers to call these acts rituals since it's partially spiritual."

"So you guys are like a covenant or something?"

"Coven, yes. We call ourselves the Corvus Enclave, and we're actively recruiting… if you're interested."

"I've never done magic before," Raphie gulped, "But I'm down to give anything a try once, I suppose. What is it you guys do? No one seems to want to tell me." Raphie inquired.

"You'll see soon enough. I promise. Don't stress either, you're not getting sacrificed or anything… tonight…"

"Oh, good," Raphie laughed nervously.

"I'm kidding, Raphie, I'm Pagan. We don't do living sacrifices," Demy gave a soft giggle at Raphie's bashful demeanor. "Or undead ones either."

"Speak for yourself," Amy had come up idly swinging her wooden bat. She leaned up against the wall, suggestively looking Demy up and down, "I'd sacrifice your friend for a McDouble."

"You're such an ass, Amy," Demy said shaking her head, then turning to Raphie "Don't listen to her."

"You know I'm only fucking with him, he's too jumpy not to," Amy scoffed, lifting Demy's chin to face her with a gloved hand. "Besides, it would upset you, and I wouldn't dream of hurting my precious Moonstone."

Demy smiled, an expression that radiated a flirtatious aura almost as magical as her fantastical abilities. Amy leaned in and kissed her on her soft, black lips, pressing her body closer the longer they kissed. Demy reached up and cupped her partner's face, softly tracing her fingers over her high cheekbones and sharp jaw. Amy opened her right eye and gave Raphie a prize-winning look of victory. The two broke their kiss, leaving Raphie somewhat stunned in silence.

"Oh, I didn't know you two were an item," Raphie said as he played off the heartache.

"Raphie," Demy began, seeing the disturbance across his mug, "Amy *is* my girlfriend… but I know you weren't just trying to be friends with me. Have you ever heard of polyamory?"

"Um… Probably? Maybe you could explain. For the sake of the group?" Raphie joked, getting another giggle out of Demy — and an eye twitch from Amy.

"We're in an open relationship," Demy said, Amy wrapping her arm around her. "Amy and I have been together just about a year, but we still see other people. Sometimes alone, sometimes together. Neither is mutually exclusive."

"I hope that doesn't bother you, Raphie," Amy said with a tone of genuine concern, but a pompous look that could only belong to a romantic rival.

"Not at all!" Raphael said, rubbing the back of his neck, "I don't mind sharing affection."

"That's the spirit. What's a little healthy competition amongst friends anyway?" Amy said, reaching out and giving what was supposed to look like a gentle jab, but was actually a rough punch.

"Yeah… right." Raphie rubbed his arm.

"Wow, Amy called you a friend," Trina cackled "That must mean she fancies you or at least doesn't want to kill ya, yet."

Amy's arrogance melted from her face. "Wait… let's not get too hasty."

"Aw, I know you're gettin' soft," Trina chastised, to which Amy removed her arm from Demy only to flip her off.

"I'll turn your caked-up ass into a rabbit," she barked.

"Voices *down,"* Gruel demanded, a guttural growl creeping through his words.

"Hey… if we're going full disclosure," Raphael took advantage of the discord and spoke directly to Demy again. "I'm transgender. Been on T for years. Something told me you wouldn't mind, but you deserve to know."

"You're right," Demy grinned, intoxicating him with her visage of happiness. "I don't mind in the slightest."

The two looked at each other and beamed, their eyes locked in a moment of mutual understanding. A symbiosis that could only be described as a queer hive-mind; telepathy of sexual and gender identity unique to each interaction. No magic. No gimmick. Just unity.

"It's show time," Ed called, begetting silence, as a black panel van pulled up from the opposite end of thc shop. From inside came two more women. Each unique in their own style, but clad in similar black or dark colors with small accents of brighter colors. The first of the women was of Asian descent, young, soft-skinned, and with braided brown hair that trailed to her hips. Not once did she raise her head from the notebook she was vigorously writing in.

The other, Hispanic, appeared to be a bit older and with a completely shaved head and dark eye makeup. In fact, Raphie questioned the first impression of their gender. They wore a heavy black jacket and had what looked like the bottoms of military fatigues.

"Why are there only two of you?" Gruel asked immediately.

"The Brothers Estrada are out, guess they had to skip town," the person with the buzz cut spoke. "Something to do with crossing a local dealer."

"And what about Scottie?" Gruel said, shrugging and exasperated.

"He called out last week, couldn't get the night off," they

said.

"Any word on the out-of-towners?" Gruel turned to Trina, who shook her head. "We can't do this missing 30%… we need at least 80 to pull this off."

"Looks like it's your lucky day, Raphie," Demy said soft and breviloquent. "We have an extra member today! It was meant to work out!"

"What, hon? The scrub?" Amy whined, gesturing lazily to Raphie. "He's said it himself, he's never touched magic in his life. What makes you think he's capable of doing something this big?"

"I hate to be the bearer of bad news, but Amy has a point," Ed added, Rhonda signed to the group simultaneously.

"I'm with Rhonda," the shaved-headed person said, noticing the sign language. "Let's give him a shot. Worst case scenario, we fail and come back next month, right?

"No. We don't! If we fail, we fail… that's it." Gruel said with contained rage, boiling away to reluctance, "We don't get a mulligan on this… but ultimately, I trust Demy's ability. If she could teach most of you morons what you know she can teach the kid."

"Thanks?" Raphie said, positive he was just inadvertently called a moron. However, it dawned on him at that moment what Gruel had said. *Demy* taught most of them what they knew. The concept blew him away, meaning Demy was beyond just an amateur mage… she was a truly powerful witch.

"You got a name?" the androgynous person spoke up again. "I'm Adrian, Miss Socialite here is my apprentice, Ferrah."

"Pardon me if you don't care about being torn down to a molecular level," Ferrah retorted. "Otherwise, I need to focus on getting these seals exactly right."

"Torn to…" Raphie choked. "What??"

"Don't stress," Demy intervened, "We're professionals. They asked you your name?"

"Oh, right. I'm Raphie. Don't mind me, I'm just along for the ride," He said, nervously shifting on his heels.

"You got the knife?" Ed asked.

"You mean the Blade of Entering?" Adrian said, pulling out a rather stylized and impractical-looking dagger. "Never leave home without it."

Adrian stepped forward and slashed wide at the chained-up door. A purple, flaming gash formed in the space they'd struck, slowly opening and oozing violet plasma onto the floor, only to fizzle out immediately. The gash opened wider, allowing for a person to squeeze through easily. One by one, the group piled into the abandoned shop.

Gruel and Raphie were the last to enter, Gruel standing with his arm outstretched in a gesture of humility. "After you, amigo." He said, to which Raphie sneered a bit.

"Yeah, sure," Raphie mumbled, climbing through the surprisingly cool-to-the-touch flames. Once Gruel was in, the hole began to slowly seal itself back up, appearing as if it were never there to begin with. Within was nothing to write home about: dusty, abandoned shelves, counter space, a few empty racks where clothes used to be, and a couple of dirty band posters. Though Raphie pegged one poster of *Siouxsie Sioux and the Banshees* as being in decent condition. He mused on taking it before he left, if nothing else, as a gift for Morgan, as that was definitely her type of music.

"Okay… let's get started." Gruel began, clapping his grubby hands together. "Ferrah, have the new guy distribute the seals with you. Ed, Rhonda, start drawing the binding circle. The rest of us, grab your tools and cleanse the area."

Before he could question any of it, Ferrah approached him and handed him a stack of parchments, each with the same, circular, eldritch symbol— akin to a pentacle with more points and breaks in the ring. Raphie recognized some of the runes from his History class. They were some kind of seal, ancient and eastern, one of the many to be outlawed under the sweeping global bans that came after the War.

"Place each one of these on the center of the walls and the corners. I'll get our ceiling," Ferrah said, cold and impatient. "Don't fuck it up, or it's more than just my ass that will be on the line."

"Geez…" Raphie scoffed, "Are you sure you even want me doing it?"

Ferrah rolled her eyes, took the papers back, and marched

on. Raphie turned to Demy, who shrugged.

"What are ya gonna do? That's just Ferrah," She said with a small chuckle. She looked him in the eye, and her face changed. "You doin' okay?"

"Y-yeah," he stuttered a bit, he wasn't aware his discomfort was so clear, normally he just kept his "resting bitch face" and used that as the ultimate mask. Somehow, this mystical witch could see through that. To distract himself, he marched over to the Siouxsie Sioux poster, stood on his tiptoes, and began to peel it off the wall.

"Yeah, I'm fine… I just have never actually seen a mage before. I thought they were all gone," Raphie replied finally, taking the poster off bit by bit, careful not to rip it.

"Technically, we were. After the Great War, all magic got outlawed by the Branson Act except basic cantrips, nothing with any real power. Most mages and witches no longer had legitimate ways to study magic. So people like Trina, Amy, and the others use whatever wooden object they can find and enchant as a wand." Demy gestured loosely to herself. "And find a teacher wherever they can."

"You taught them magic? C—… could you teach me?" Raphie said, blown away by the concept. Pulling the poster down completely, he needed to give an extra hard tug. As it ripped free, he fell backward onto a counter, his hands pushing through the glass display and shattering it. He yelped in pain as his palm and wrist were cut, thankfully not very deeply.

Demy gasped and helped him up. "Holy shit, Raphie, are you okay?"

"Yeah… I'm fine…" he grunted, blood dripping from his hand. Demy quickly reached into her bag and pulled a small container of salve as well as a bandage roll.

"Nice one. You an acrobat or something?" Amy chastised as she walked past, not caring to stop and help her girlfriend.

"You are not fine, you're gushing blood," Demy said with a sneer toward her partner. "And ignore her."

As she fitted him with the bandage and salve, his hand instantly felt better, cooler, and fought off that biting sting.

"Thanks," he smiled. "I am admittedly kinda a klutz.

Dexterity is not my strong suit."

"Maybe," Demy giggled, standing up.

"You said the others use wands… but what do you use?"

Demy said nothing and merely smirked, just taking the poster and rolling it up nice and neat for him. Raphie admired her in her little black dress, the flowing bell sleeves and hem making her look like something of a shadowy apparition; every inch of exposed skin was covered in an ornate elemental tattoo. Raphie was in all senses of the word, hexed by this beautiful Elf. She *could* be sacrificing him and he might not protest.

"What the fuck is this?!" Gruel had shouted after a minute.

"It's the blood you asked for," Trina replied, timid and soft.

"IT'S FROM A BLOOD PACK!" He gurgled, "This is antibiotic-filled, processed, animal blood garbage. I said we needed humanoid blood. You thought I wouldn't notice? Did you think *they* wouldn't notice?"

Demy and Raphie marched back over to the center of the group, where the commotion was arising.

"You never said humanoid, man," Ed said apprehensively.

"Ed… can it," Gruel replied. "I know what I said to her. Trina just fucked up."

"What seems to be the problem?" Demy stepped up, "Why are we trying to get the cops called on us?"

"Trina here," Gruel said, gripping Trina's arm and shaking her violently. "Forgot the key ingredient."

It was then that Raphie saw the full extent of the magical ring the Orc siblings had crafted in the center of the room. Like the seal, an eight-pointed pentacle, candles along the perimeter, a ring of salt forming an outer circle, and at its center was an archaic and unidentifiable symbol, now permanently etched into the concrete floors. Raphie gulped, beginning to doubt his desire to be sacrificed.

"Gruel, cool it," Demy said, stepping forward and separating the two.

"Yeah, it's fine." Adrian said, picking in their ear, "We'll come back next month."

"NO!" Gruel hissed. "This has to be done tonight!"

"Why is this so important we do this now?" Ed mentioned.

"You know exactly why, but thanks to *someone*, we're in mixed company. So I don't think I'm going to fucking discuss, you-know-what, thank you very much." Gruel grumbled, turning and looking a Raphie. It was odd, but he seemed to sniff the air.

"We could just use your blood, Trina, since it's your fault," Amy joked.

"Shut the fuck up, Amy. That's not funny." Trina fought.

"Besides, we don't wanna use just anybody's blood. Only the right kind will do, and that's why Gruel's panties are in a twist," Adrian answered, rather pragmatically.

Gruel approached Raphie now that Demy was holding hands with her Rockabilly friend. Without hesitation, Gruel grabbed Raphie's wrist forcibly and lifted his wound to his nose. "You.... You're perfect."

Gruel gave Raphie no time to protest, pulling him with force toward the center of the circle where he tore off the bandages and squeezed Raphie's freshly bleeding palm. The red ichor dripped down into the carving on the floor as Raphie yelped in pain.

"Gruel! What the fuck are you doing!?" Demy cried. "Stop it!"

Gruel released Raphie, who swung at him wildly. Gruel dodged and cackled. "Sit down, rookie," he said, withdrawing a branch of yew with a leather wrap handle. With a flick of his wrist and a muttering of an incantation, Raphie was frozen. His body was wrapped in a field of force that prevented him from even speaking. He could feel the energy pulsing over his body, rushing across his frame like liquid fire, but never burning the flesh. He could only move his eyes to Demy, who looked horrified at what she was witnessing.

"Imprison. A simple but quite effective spell. You're helping us exponentially, kid. Now you can just sit back and watch." The others seemed no less perturbed, except for Amy, who merely grinned, fighting the urges to cackle and failing to hide it.

"Stop this now. We're leaving," Demy said, waving her hand, her palm glowing as teal as her hair. In a flash of light, Raphie was capable of moving again.

"What the fuck, dude?" Raphie barked.

"You're just going to leave before we've completed the ritual? This is integral for the next phase, and you know that."

"And you can do it without me," Demy said, grabbing Raphie by the non-wounded hand. "If you can't on your own, then maybe you shouldn't at all… Call me when it's time for the next coven meeting. I'm getting him out of here. Come on, Raphie."

"Really, Moonstone?" Amy protested. "You ditching out on us before we do anything fun?"

"I think I've had enough fun," Raphie challenged, glaring at Amy, who seemed all too content with all of this.

Adrian stepped forward and slashed their knife across the door to reopen the portal and let them out.

"Thanks, Adrian, see you around," Demy said with a meek smile to the shaved-headed person. The two climbed out and the portal closed.

"Fuck… what the fuck… what the fuck are they doing with my blood? What is happening, Demy?" Raphie pressed, looking her in the eye with fear.

"Nothing that will bring you any more harm, I assure you…" Demy took him by the hand and guided him across the street, marching forward with purpose. "It's a binding ritual. They want to access… other planes… but we don't even know if it will work—"

A loud, thundering boom rendered them both deaf temporarily. Glass shattered and nearly struck them as the force exploded outward from the abandoned record shop. Raphie and Demy covered their faces, Demy holding her hand out as if to stop anything that came their way. It seemed to work as they came out completely unscathed. As they peeked again, they saw the other members of the coven barreling out of the building as the, originally thought to be defunct, alarm rang loudly.

"GO! GO! Everybody scatter!" Gruel shouted, and they did, hopping into their getaway vehicles.

"Come on!" Demy took Raphie back to the other side of the street, climbing into Adrian's van with Trina and Ferrah.

Immediately, Adrian started the vehicle and went into escape mode, driving like a maniac to get out of dodge, just in time to hear sirens in the distance.

"Adrian…" Demy asked. "Did it work?"

"Not quite…" Adrian replied.

Raphie looked to the other two women, a look of shock along their faces. Whatever they had seen had shaken them to their cores. Raphie felt his wounded hand and wondered what he got himself into.

9

Entering the Cryptid Chronicle the next morning was a bit different from how it normally was. A sudden heatwave made the walk over unbearable; as Morgan pushed open the door, she was met with a wall of warm air. She grimaced and scrunched her nose. She wore a simple black pencil skirt and coral blouse with a collar left open due to the heat. She skipped the stockings as well, all for the better.

Broken A/C was hardly all that was amiss. Rather than be met with the bustling activity she had before, she was met with a rather quiet and empty floor. Upon closer inspection, 90% of the staff was gathering around a hanging television, volume set to max. Morgan raised a brow and headed in, once she got closer she saw and could hear that it was the news. PNN to be specific, the parent company of the Cryptid Chronicle.

"…Paramedics arrived at the scene and found that the man in question was in stable condition. But that didn't stop him from sharing his story," the news anchor stated.

"She came out of nowhere, man," the interviewee said. "She landed, and that was it, my car was done. Yo, she owes me a new car, man. That [censored] ain't right."

Morgan couldn't see the screen too well from here, her eyes not as sharp as other Vampires, and opted to, begrudgingly, pull her pink-framed glasses from her purse and place them on the bridge of her nose. She hated having to wear them ever since she was a kid. If she didn't hate having her eyeballs touched, she'd try contacts; between that and tight spaces, she possessed genuine phobias.

Once her glasses were on, she could finally see what they were staring at. Her heart sank. It was none other than her Aunt, Maxine Mothman. An image was taken of her blocking a speeding car from crushing a bystander. Using her 10ft wingspan as a shield, the car buckled around her wing like it was made of tinfoil. Morgan clasped a hand over her mouth.

"Maxine Mothman fled shortly after the impact, flying away from the scene. Authorities are debating whether this is a criminal act, but as the man is alive and well, Police Chief Lawrence Jacobson may let this one slide as he has in the past," the News anchor declared. "The other potential victim fled from the scene as well and is described as an Elf with colorful hair. If any viewers have details on the location of Maxine Mothman or the mystery woman, call our studio hotline and report what you know."

"Holy shit," one of the Chronicle staff had said.

"Mothman is back!" Another had cheered.

"Motherfucker…" Morgan muttered to herself. She tried to lay low, turning away only to collide chest-first with Eliza.

"Morning, Girlie." She said with a grin. "Crazy news, right? Straight up superhero shit."

"Yep…" Morgan stayed stiff, looking away from the screen.

"Wait… don't you know Mothman somehow?" She asked, begetting looks from some of her coworkers.

"Yep. And my dad was Elvis." Morgan said with a forced laugh, several people turning back to the screen. Morgan stood on her toes and whispered through gritted teeth, "Ixnay the othmay."

"What? Why?" Eliza squinted. Morgan didn't need to explain herself. She had a high-profile relative, which was enough reason for her to lay low and pretend that they didn't know each other. Especially when M pulls stunts like this. People finding out that they were related would potentially pollute her career path. She wanted to do this herself, no LA nepotism involved. Morgan would feel guilty going about it this way if she didn't know M was incredibly paranoid and secretive herself. She didn't even have her address publicly listed, and that was before the PI era.

"ALRIGHT!" A booming voice echoed across the floor. Colt Harding barreled down the stairs and pushed into the crowd to disperse it. "I am NOT paying you all to stand around and watch OTHER people make the fucking news. Get your asses in gear and report on some shit, god damnit!"

The group scattered like startled rabbits, each quickly moving to their station and acting like they were working. Eliza and Morgan were no different, making their way to their nearby cubicle and pretending to have already been working.

"Jesus Christ… the lot of you. Unbelievable," Colt said with a cocky, tusked smirk, putting his hands in his pockets. Due to the heat, he had unbuttoned his shirt, revealing a simple white tank top that clung to his chest. Morgan couldn't help but notice, and he noticed her. "Did you get new glasses, Scriven?"

"Not new, no," she said, adjusting them out of embarrassment . "Just been needing to wear them more, working here."

"Looks good on you. You got a cute librarian thing going on," he said plainly, turning her face pink. "That was wildly inappropriate to say, wasn't it? This fuckin' weather has my brain cooked, and we can't seem to get half of the A/C units to work on top of that."

"No worries." Morgan gave a little wave as a gesture for him not to stress about the comment. She didn't entirely hate it. "It's hot out."

"Right. Wagner, check your inbox. I sent you a couple of stories, and I need you both to bust them out pronto. With the Mothman story, we'll need to postpone a page's worth of shorts. I need those adjusted for their new print date ahead of tomorrow." Colt began to step backward and head to his next charge. "Change of pace, ladies, and if you need to stay later, go right ahead. I know I am."

As he turned away, Morgan maintained her gaze, her head following Colt as he strutted away. She'd never seen so much of his body before, especially so close. He was definitely a health nut or gym rat. The dampness that caused his undershirt to so revealingly cling to his emerald skin outlined muscles that made him further look the part. Morgan bit the very edge of her lip, feeling her whole body become flushed. She'd blame it on the heatwave, but there was more than just heat fueling her flush.

"Oh my god… You think he's hot," Eliza said in a whispered yell. "You wanna fuck him don't you?"

"What are you talking about?" Morgan whipped her head around, pursing her lips and scrunching her brow.

"You totally do… You were just undressing our boss with your eyes," Eliza cackled in disbelief. "I saw you bite your fucking lip."

"My lip itched, I didn't want my lipstick to smear," Morgan lied.

"Do you even wear lipstick? I thought your lips were just always that perfect," Eliza grinned mockingly. "I've always loved your lips."

"Thank you," Morgan replied with a modest smile.

"Oh my god, you want to fuck Harding," Eliza said, refusing to let the subject go. "You didn't hold it together when *he* called you cute. I could see the pink on your face."

Morgan blushed on cue, her stark white complexion making any bit of bashfulness obvious. She held her head down in shame, knowing that there was a deep-down desire for Mr. Harding. She found him attractive since day one. She'd also been with Balam going on two years, which only aided to complicate things. Why did she have so much random desire these days? Was it really because they hadn't been intimate like they once were? Morgan's thoughts began to stumble from speculation into complete stress from there.

"You awake over there?" Eliza said, waving to Morgan, snapping her out of her inner thoughts.

"Yeah… just thinking."

"Well, save your filthy fantasies for private and take these issues down to the archive, will you?" Eliza said, handing her the stack.

"Sure…" At the mention of the archive, Morgan's thoughts were thrust back into her battle plan for finding what happened to Chrissy Donavon. "Hey, do you mind if I look something up while I'm down there? I won't take long, I promise."

"Whatever, just file those away first."

"Of course," Morgan said with a closed-lip smile, making her way through the floor cubicles toward the back of the building.

She did her best to politely smile at the various people she saw. There were Orcs, Giants, Valkyries, Taknolings, Vampires, and every variety of Elf, but it was rare to see a Human passing through the halls. Once she reached the tightly packed room of 8-foot tall filing cabinets, Morgan immediately got to work on filing away the issues. From there, she began her search into the most recent archival papers from both the Chronicle and any of their competitors.

Searching through months of Chronicle backlogs took much longer than Morgan expected, but she needed to keep searching for any additional information on Chrissy, beyond what the original story file told. To her surprise, none of the other papers mentioned her by name. The closest she could find was the declaration from the LAPD that they established a special victims task force to look for the collection of girls missing; that told Morgan they were considering this as a sex crime.

Naturally, Joana Larsson was something she stumbled across. She was declared missing two weeks before she was found dead and was last seen working at the Elf-run night club called The Keep in Little Lenora. The owners demanded a warrant to investigate, but the judge hasn't given one yet. Now that her body had been found, it was only a matter of time. It was a thread to follow.

What she did find, or rather struggled to find, was any information on Chrissy Donavon that she didn't already know. And what little she did find was pitiful at that. It was as if they were covering the absolute minimum of the story, if at all.

"What the fuck?" She grumbled.

"I agree. What the fuck are you doing down here?" Harding said, his booming voice causing Morgan to leap in place.

"I'm sorry, Mr. Harding, I just lost track of time, I think."

She said, shuffling her papers.

"Well, the floor needs its lackeys… so quit playing with yourself and get back up there. The guys want coffee," he said, irritation growing.

"Question," she asked, ignoring his crass comment.

"Shoot," Harding said as a verbal eye roll.

"You said the Donavon story was oversaturated, but I can't find anything about her," Morgan said. "Why'd you kill it?"

"Goddamn, you're such a blonde. I already told you why, Scriven," Harding said, rubbing his brow. "She's Human, we're a Non-Human geared paper. We can't kick out Non-Human stories for one about a Human that nobody knows anything about, and if she's not just one Human, she's part of the missing girls already getting printspace elsewhere. We focus on our own. Direct orders from up top."

"Isn't that a little problematic? Just because she's Human doesn't mean she isn't someone's daughter." Morgan said, shifting her weight onto one hip, as a vague memory stirred.

"Hey, I told you if you could find more info, I'd give you the story and let you stay in the program. But, I need your ass upfront. Search for answers on your own time, Nancy Drew."

"You got it," Morgan said, knowing that the Orc was partially right.

Morgan arrived in Inglewood just after noon. She walked down the pavement watching kids play in the street; a few Human men sitting on a porch watched her as she walked by. One of them catcalled her, and she did her best to ignore them. She felt the burning of their eyes on her, even still, as she walked, she clutched her pepper spray. Superhuman strength was all good and well, but being assaulted by multiple full-grown men would still be more than a challenge for Morgan. So instead, she just walked with purpose.

While Chrissy was the one missing, it was the neighbor's

house that had a broken-in door and several shattered windows covered in damaged police tape. Morgan steadied her breath and pressed on. She knocked at Chrissy's relatively pristine door and waited a few moments. This gave her time to observe the property. The grass had died, as had the flowers in the planters. A collection of toys was sprawled out on the patio; chalk, jacks, and a beat-up, old tricycle were among the things she spotted. Receiving no response, she reached to the side and rang the doorbell. After another few painstaking seconds, the door unlocked.

To Morgan's surprise, a young girl with soft coppery skin and big curly hair answered. In her hands, she held a furry white bunny with a twitching nose. "Oh, hello," Morgan said, leaning down to speak closer. "Are your parents home?"

"Mommy!" The little girl shouted, turning into the house. Even yelling, she had a sweet voice. "There's a tall lady at the door."

Morgan couldn't help but chuckle to herself. "That's a really cute bunny."

"Her name is Glue 'cause she's white and sticks with me," she replied quickly. Though when the older, pear-shaped woman entered the entryway, she scuttled away, ducking her head into her pet.

"Shea, what the hell did I tell you about answering the door? Go put Glue away and set the table," the woman said, gently admonishing the girl named Shea. "Can I help you?"

"Hi, are you…" She shuffled through her notes, blanking on the woman's name. "Ursula Donavon?"

"Who's asking?" The woman said, looking Morgan up and down, paying special attention to her teeth.

"My name is Morgana Scriven. I'm a… reporter for the Cryptid Chronicle. I just wanted to ask you a few questions about your daughter, Chrissy," she said, maintaining an even professional tone.

The woman's face drooped, her eyes falling to the floor, becoming distant. When she looked up again, she gave a frustrated sigh through her nose. "I don't know what I can tell you that I haven't already told everyone else…"

“I’m following her story. I want to find answers. You and your family deserve them,” she said, with fire in her voice.

“Fine… then ask them, but make it quick, I got pasta boiling,” Ursula said, shaking her head, agitation clear in her tone.

“I won’t take much of your time, ma’am,” Morgan replied, pulling out a pen from behind her ear and placing the tip against her notepad. “Your daughter was last spotted in Hollywood. I’ve looked at the report, and she was coaxed back into the building where she came. Do you have any clue what your daughter was doing there?”

“I don’t know a god damned thing about it. She did whatever she wanted. Nothing I said or begged meant shit to her,” she said already flustered and impatient. Morgan raised a brow and began taking notes.

“Did she ever mention who she was with?”

“No. I said I don’t know,” she scoffed. “She told me once that she was gonna catch her break working for some Vamp woman in Transylvaniatown. I have no idea her name, so don’t ask. Owned someplace called the Bourbon something or other.”

“The Bourbon Belfry?” Morgan asked. She’d been there once before; it was more of a strip club than a nightclub. What stood out the most was its location: Transylvaniatown, a place not generally safe for young Human girls. “And you don’t know anyone else she worked with, possibly?”

“I said I don’t know,” Ursula huffed.

“Fair enough,” Morgan said with a pause, introspecting for a moment. “Do you think she was romantically involved with this Vampire?”

“With a woman? She was wild, not disgusting.”

“Right,” Morgan said, taken aback. “I understand the concept may be unnerving to you, but it's a real possibility. I’m very intrigued by who she was with before her disappearance. I’m just looking for answers, same as you.”

“I don’t need answers. She ran away from home. Threw up a big stink. She never came back. She wants to be gone.”

“Ma’am… don’t you want to find her?” Morgan said,

growing confused at the incredulous woman's words. "She could be in mortal danger."

"If she's in any danger, she put herself there."

"Another girl around her age was brutally murdered this week, Mrs. Donavon, and I don't think she put herself in danger either."

"That's *Miss* Donavon… and I'll be damned if I am going to be lectured on my doorstep by some prissy biter."

It was then Ursula slammed the door in Morgan's face. She was lost, utterly baffled at how a mother could be so careless about the disappearance of her daughter, completely ignoring the attitude toward her kind. She wanted to knock again but there was nothing that this woman would give her any more than she already had. As she turned to walk down the driveway, she stopped and looked back. There was only one place she *would* find the answers.

10

Infinite light washed over all things Raphie could see. He was alone, no longer holding Demy's hand tightly. There was nothingness, only white, but it was no longer blinding. He couldn't decipher walls, windows, or doors; however, somehow, he stood on a floor, incapable of seeing where it began or ended.

He took a few steps and felt the world tumble. Despite the lack of dimension, he could tell space rotated like a carnival funhouse. For a fleeting moment, Raphie could see the frames of blood-red doors along what he now perceived to be an infinite corridor. He stepped again, seeing more of the endless hall as he moved. His vision was drawn to the nonexistent ceiling and the terrible sky. There was an archway into a dark void, filled with stars uncountable. The longer Raphie looked, the more he realized they were, in fact, a trillion eyes, staring back at him. In a sudden and terrible cacophony, clouds of grey ash erupted from the furthest reaches of the void like an infernal assault on the all-seeing oblivion.

Raphie's alarm rang into his mind, digital klaxons firing like massive cannons inches from his head. His body jolted, waking him up in a flailing of limbs. He was sweating, his body instantly chilled by the feeling of air on his face. He was still fully dressed from the night before. He shook his head and rubbed his face, aghast at what he did remember… he glanced down at his hand, freshly bandaged again. He ran his other fingers over it and sighed.

Raphie's hand slammed down his alarm so hard it bounced even as it paused. Once he was in silence, he sat up and looked about to ensure he was, in fact, in his room and his room only. He blinked and tried to focus on his *Iron Maiden* poster of Eddie as "The Trooper". Eventually, the red and brown blur became what it was meant to be. Even still, Raphie's head pounded so roughly that the world seemed to shift with each wave of throbbing pain. He'd never been so badly hungover, including the time he downed an entire bottle of sour apple schnapps by himself. He shifted, and the world seemed to shift as the bed didn't move, and he wondered if this was a hangover after all.

As he turned to the tendrils and eyes depicted in his drawings, pinned along his opposite wall, he felt the vomit coming, standing and bolting to the bathroom. As he blew past the entry hall, Morgan was striding in. She stopped just short of a collision, allowing him to cross the living room, past the kitchen, and into the main bathroom.

"Raph, you just getting up?" Morgan asked, putting her bags down and approaching the bathroom door, "Are you okay?"

"I'm good," He replied from the other side of the door after a moment, over the sound of the running sink.

"When did you eventually come in?" She asked, pressing herself against the door worriedly. "You were out cold when I checked on you this morning."

He didn't reply right away, splashing water against his face and then quickly brushing his teeth rather than immediately responding.

"I'm not sure," he finally said, staring in the mirror, his eyes had bags beneath them, and his skin washed out. "I think 4, 5 am? Not long before you were awake, I'm sure."

"Gods," Morgan said in awe. "What happened?"

"We had drinks, hung out with some of her goth friends," he said before exiting the bathroom, and before he had to look Morgan in the eye.

"You look exhausted. Where did you go?"

"Just some abandoned place near Downtown. You know how alt kids are. Why?" He said, trying to stay as close to the truth as he could.

"The story Eliza and I worked on today… Someone was fucking with some major magic near there… The DSA is getting called in," Morgan said, already, her doubts were clear in her voice.

"That's…¿que?" Raphie replied, blinking rapidly to look bewildered.

"Oh my gods, what happened to your hand?" She said, noticing the bandages, "Raphie, what did you do?"

"I just hurt myself on some broken glass. Honestly. It was a stupid accident…" he said as blankly as he could, his body beginning to sweat again.

"You're a terrible fucking liar," Morgan pushed, crossing her arms and tapping her foot.

"What?!" Raphie said, doing his best to maintain the flabbergasted act. "No! I didn't do anything, I swear to God. We just hung out."

Morgan narrowed her eyes. "You better not have."

"I didn't," He insisted, though it felt wrong lying. It was not something he did often, and Morgan had always caught him. But he barely understood what had happened, let alone his part in it.

"Is your hand okay?" She said, taking it and looking at the rather meticulous bandage job.

"I'm fine," He smiled, seeing the bossy demeanor slip into actual care. "Demy is apparently an excellent healer. It doesn't even hurt at all... How have you been?"

Morgan hesitated to answer. "You know that scoop I got about the missing girl? Harding said the story was oversaturated, but I can't find anything about her in any papers. I mean, there may be ones we don't have in our archive, but… that's weird, right?" Morgan rattled off this information to a half-coherent Raphie, though he did his best to absorb it.

"Huh," Raphie said. "That's interesting."

"It gets weirder. I spoke to the mother, I'm not sure if it was me being a Vampire or the fact that she's a shit mom, but she was very off-putting. I did get a lead from her, though," Morgan said, taking off her shoes and beginning to unbutton her top. Raphie gasped and turned to face the bathroom as her hot pink bra beneath began to show. "Oh, come on, we've known each other since we were kids."

"Even still…" Raphie said, keeping his back turned. "Please continue."

"A nightclub in Transylvaniatown. The Bourbon Belfry. Kinda sleazy when I went. I heard a rumor it was run by the T-Town Tyrants, so I never went back. But that makes sense as to where the photo I found at the Chronicle came from." Morgan, now in just panties and a bra, moved into the bathroom and ran the shower. Without care, she bent over in front of Raphie, unwittingly presenting her backside, revealing her only tattoo, a Blue Morpho butterfly on her hip. Raphie made a swift stride to the couch, giving Morgan complete privacy. "I'm not trying to give in to stereotypes, but a teen Human girl at a T-Town club? They'll, pun intended, eat her alive. So why was she there, on the other end of town from where she was last seen?"

"Bar crawl maybe?" Raphie contributed.

"She's underage… and even with a good fake ID, there's no bar crawl that leads from T-Town to WeHo. There just isn't." Morgan pressed on. Raphie saw her bra tossed aside in the mirror of the bathroom. "So, I'm going there. Tonight."

"What!?" Raphie shot up, just as she slammed the door shut. He approached and cracked it so she could hear him over the sound of the shower. "Blondie! You can't be serious. You're just an intern, not a super-powered P.I. like your aunt… You could get yourself in some serious trouble… let me go with you at least."

"Raph, you're an angel," Morgan said briefly poking her

soaked head from out behind the shower curtain "But, yeah, no."

"No? Excuse the fuck out of me?" Raphie barked, his voice lousy with offense.

"First off, you're a Human. Man or not, being seen with a Human at night in T-Town could get us *both* jumped. I can draw less suspicion and most likely be safer on my own. Secondly, I don't need a man to hold my hand. Harding doesn't believe I'm capable of finding the story I *know* is there, and I don't need help."

Raphie gave a heavy sigh, knowing that Morgan had sunk her fangs into the meat of a story. He'd known her long enough to understand she wasn't going to let go until she drew blood. All he could do was try to curb her more reckless tendencies. "Fine. I know you won't listen to me regardless. All I can say is follow your heart and trust your gut. Don't put yourself in a bad position, and get the fuck out if things seem shady… but you'll do whatever you feel is necessary."

11

In the entirety of LA, there was no place quite like Transylvaniatown. Founded in the 40s, with construction funded by the Vampire Nation themselves, it was a historic and unique part of the city. Brick buildings with darkened windows, layered in refractium, lined wide streets. Blood-based restaurants, the latest in gothic fashion, and of course, the most riveting nightlife to be had in this or any life.

Outside the Bourbon Belfry, a two-story building adorned with neon, Morgan waited for her turn to enter. She kept to herself, trying not to look suspicious or nervous. But when surrounded by so many Vampires, you never know what kind of encounters you'll have.

Morgan entered the cool-lit nightclub. Red and blue light colored the spaces left by fishnet stockings, ending where her go-go boots began. The sensuous exposure of flesh halted again just before her hip, covered by the strapless, black, vinyl dress her body was poured into. Over the dress, she wore a bolero jacket with holographic fibers sewn throughout it. Her hair was parted drastically to the side, showing off her dark eye makeup done in a punk style. A small clutch hung off her shoulder, within it were only four items: her wallet, her pager, pepper spray, and a disposable camera.

She noticed select groups of people would turn to look and undress her with their eyes. She smirked, strutting in with the confidence of a club veteran. She scanned the room for a moment and noticed that almost everyone here was watching the single dancer on stage, a half-naked Ghoul with ultra-short hair. The main stage was on the ground floor, so she found the metal spiral staircase and climbed it post-haste.

Immediately her ears were flooded with the industrial music and sounds of roaring club-goers. Dancers of all genders performed from cages hung high above the floor, connected to a rafter where people congregated. The night was still young enough to let her traverse the dance floor relatively easily, but the slowness left her feeling trapped.

Despite having no requirement for oxygen, she quickly found herself short of breath, raggedly trying to find her way off the dance floor. Around her, she saw the debaucherous amenities the Bourbon Belfry offered. On the dance floor, Vampires sank their teeth into each other, letting the blood trickle down their pallid flesh. Turning away from the carnal display, she saw another man snorting fine white powder off small square mirrors. She almost collided with a tray of wineglasses filled with blood, carried by a horned server in a skimpy outfit, her Taknoling tail fed through a manufactured hole in her shorts. The server's crimson eyes practically glowed as she flashed her fangs with a venomous grin, before moving on. It wasn't long, and Morgan saw that more eyes were aimed towards her, searching for their next fix of pleasure.

Overwhelmed and lost, pushing through the crowd just to get to the other end, the bodies of the dance floor surged around her; Morgan felt the very real urge to breathe. At last, she found a wall with a direct staircase up to the catwalk. She gripped the simple metal railing as she climbed, the whiteness of her knuckles went unseen on her skin. The clamping sensation around her chest loosened as the crowd lessened, and she felt as though she no longer needed to breathe, but her heart still fluttered with panic.

"C-come on, Scriven," she whispered to herself, trembling, "Get it t-together."

She found herself leaning against the railing of a large metal catwalk over the wide-open warehouse-turned-dance floor. Easily a hundred more people had filled the floor since she arrived, many of them in different styles of goth or alternative, and almost all of them Vampires or some form of undead. Even the DJ was withered away, appearing as an urbanite stripped to his skeleton; a banner with the words "DJ SkeleGore" was strung up on the front of his turntable. Scanning the room, she now looked for some sort of back route; after a minute, Morgan noticed a door labeled "Staff Only" in the adjacent corner.

"Bingo." Morgan noticed most people along the catwalk were too busy trying to get to where they wanted or making out to pay attention to her. She was amazed she could turn heads and become unremarkable all with one disguise. A waitress burst out from the other side of the door, hustling to get downstairs as Morgan speed-walked up, preventing the door from shutting with the very tip of her boot.

Careful not to draw unwanted attention, she slipped inside. The transition from muted to fluorescent light was harsh on Morgan's eyes, adjusting to the drastic change. She looked back and forth down the hallway, seeing that her best option would be to follow the long path to the right. She'd not seen a soul yet, but someone would come eventually. She prepared a line about looking for the ladies' room, tapping into her inner "dumb blonde" and hating it.

The only real facility on the top floor was a large dressing room: coed, and thankfully for Morgan, empty. The room was shadowy with dim lighting, the walls lined with wine-colored velvet. At the far end were three fully lit vanity mirrors, each workspace cluttered with makeup supplies. Scanning the surfaces gained Morgan no further insight into her story. About to walk away, she saw a Polaroid photo pinned to the corner of the furthest mirror. Curious, Morgan leaned in to inspect the photo, seeing that it was taken in what appeared to be this room. There, among two other humanoids, was Chrissy Donavon.

"Gotcha," Morgan whispered, quickly withdrawing her camera and snapping a photo."Intern, my ass."

She looked closer, immediately recognizing the silver bob hair and white-tipped cat ears from the original photo on Eliza's desk. The other figure was a man Morgan didn't recognize. Footsteps could be heard on the gantry. She made herself scarce, narrowly avoiding a group of entertainers entering the dressing room for their break.

Morgan found herself down on the ground floor again, this time in the belly of the Belfry. She almost crossed paths with security once or twice but managed to hold back, hiding in a corner or behind a support beam until the coast was clear. It wasn't long until she ended up at a door marked "Management Office," the sounds of distressed conversation coming from within.

She closed her eyes and concentrated, filtering the dull roar of the club. With a minor effort, she hyper-focused her directional hearing and honed in on the voices, one masculine and one feminine, though neither particularly professional.

"I'm still fucking beside myself," the feminine one spoke, drunk by the sound of her slurred words, made even less intelligible by her Transylvanian accent. "Who the fuck does she think she is walking in here throwing accusations? That bitch."

"Yeah," the male said plainly. He sounded American. "I dunno, Yessenia. You don't think it was a little close? She knew about the girl and the Lounge."

Morgan raised a brow and reached into her bag for her camera. She looked around for some sort of visual access to the office. Above the door sat a shutter vent that connected to nothing save the other side. It was cracked just enough for the camera lens to see through.

"She got lucky," Yessenia scolded. "Talked to some little shit on the grapevine who doesn't know fuck all about what they're even saying. That being said… we need to clamp down on the streets. Sending that psychopath here… rots my stomach. Send some of the boys South and put the squeeze on the loudmouths. It's Friday night, someone is where they shouldn't be right now."

"Banger territory?" the man debated.

"Morale in LA is weak. Things are shifting, and we've got the chance to increase our grip on the South and West," Yessenia said with a charge. "And once we have the region in our fist we can push toward Little Lenora, and snuff out those Elf fucks."

"Don't you think the boss man will be displeased if we start a war after all his hard work?"

"You keep that pretty head of yours focused on who to flay, Strix," Yessenia chastised. "And I'll worry about that creep. He wants the Elf Mafia and us to get along. He tries to get us to hold hands and sing songs and shit like he's forgotten what they did to the homeland. Never again."

Not knowing how much longer she could eavesdrop, Morgan took her chance, standing on her tiptoes, extending her arm as far as she could, and pushing the camera up against the slats. She couldn't see how clear a shot she had, but trusted it would have to do for now. The camera shuttered.

CLICK.

"Did you hear that?" Strix said.

"Yeah, I did," Yessenia said and pointed to the door with her chin. Strix obeyed.

She turned to the other end of the hall, the only way out of the corridor, and saw that there was a security guard, an undead Orc. He was busy chatting up a performer, yet to notice Morgan, but blocked her way out. *Shit. Fuck. Oh, fuck oh fuck.* She thought, knowing that the "lost girl" routine probably won't work on the gang bosses. The door swung open.

12

"Can I help you?" the tall Vampire named Strix spoke. His flesh was a grayish taupe, like petrified driftwood. He was dressed in a black shirt and bulky black pants. His head was shaved bald, and a black goatee covered his chin and upper lip.

Morgan could see Yessenia in the back, sitting cross-legged on her desk, subtly swaying her feet, dressed up with high-heeled combat boots that laced up to her knee. She was wearing pleather leggings with a white crop top and suspenders. Her hip-length white hair was parted far to one side and styled with product to look windswept. On a face that contorted into a wicked and constant evil grin were two black eyes with blood-red irises, like a raptor's eyes. The crime boss leaned forward to see who was causing the noise.

"I was told to speak to Yessenia," Morgan said, putting on a vapid air. "I'm here to audition as a dancer."

"One second," he said, closing the door. They spoke in a hushed tone, so much so that Morgan could no longer hear.

"There's a girl here who says she's got a dancer audition with you?" Strix questioned. "You got an interview tonight?"

"No," Yess sighed. "But the boys have been busting their asses recruiting, so it wouldn't surprise me… what she look like?"

"Pretty hot. Maybe you should give her an 'audition,'" he said with a wink.

"Maybe we should… I could use some steam released," Yess winked back. "Bring her in."

After a few seconds, Morgan was sitting across from Yessenia, who now leaned against her desk, looking the pale girl up and down with her blood-red eyes. Behind her, the imposing, fit man shut and locked the door. "Alright, first things first, you got a name, pet?" The silver-haired Vampiress asked.

"My name?" Morgan giggled as she thought frantically. She gave a confident smile and looked Yessenia in the eye. "Chastity, Chastity Vaughn."

"Chastity," Yess stuck out her bottom lip and nodded in approval. "Not bad. An appropriately ironic name. We don't do last names. Drop that. Why do you want to work as a performer at the Bourbon Belfry?"

"Well, I've lived in LA almost my entire life. I couldn't resist searching for more… the next rush. It was only a matter of time.

I knew it would be me in one of those cages or on that pole," Morgan said, further selling the character of 'Chastity.'

"Another thing," Yessenia leaned in, narrowing her eyes, looking Morgan dead in hers. "Have we met somewhere?"

Morgan kept her grin even through the panic, wondering how she could have been recognized. She dressed nothing like this in her day-to-day. The idea that this devious crime boss spotted her at work or among those on the street was asinine. "Um... I've been here before?"

Yessenia looked her over once more before giving a shrug, accepting what Morgan had said. A quiet victory.

"Well, Chastity, I'm going to be honest with you. We pride ourselves on offering our guests the best possible T-Town experience. We thusly cater to a wide variety of clientèle." Yessenia kept her red lips formed into a devilish smile throughout. "So I'm sure, being a local, you know that means each one of our entertainers offers above and beyond."

"I think I get it," Morgan said, still trying to feign full confidence. "I'm cool getting personal if that's what you're saying... as long as the money's good."

Yessenia's smile widened, revealing her long, wicked fangs. Her soft, ivory skin was flawless, or at least her foundation was. Her lips were painted a deep red, like wine, and looked just as delectable.

"I like your style. What do you say we test your mettle and get this audition started in earnest?" Yessenia said, nodding to Strix, who turned to the nearby boombox. He grabbed a tape and threw it in. The beat of "Sweet Dreams" began to play, as the Vampires now scrutinized her. Yessenia sat back in her plush office chair. "I want you to start with your best lap dance."

"Of c-course," Morgan said, hiding her trepidation with another fake giggle. As long as she got through this, whether she was good or not, she would get out of this place without harm. She stood and crossed over to Yessenia, her hips swaying to the beat as she walked, trailing her fingers across the dark wood of the desk. Yessenia bit her lip and leaned back into the red leather seat. Morgan, not having choreography, did her best to look sexy; caressing her body, she moved her hips with the song's tempo. She placed a boot between Yessenia's legs, grabbed her hand, and forced it onto her fishnet-clad thighs.

Channeling her cheerleader experience from high school, she deftly mounted the chair, straddling Yessenia. Her movements varied from swift and erotic to slow and sensual, but all synchronized with the music. Yessenia let her hands wander Morgan's waist, smiling like a shark. She pulled close, Morgan's back pressed firmly against her chest. With one hand, she moved some of Morgan's hair aside and pulled down her gossamer jacket, exposing her shoulder.

"Hold still, cutie," she growled, letting her red lips dance across Morgan's flesh ever so gingerly. Morgan shuddered, knowing fully what she planned to do, but too paralyzed to stop it. As expected, Yessenia's fangs sank into her flesh, causing a pained whimper. Yessenia kept digging, drawing out Morgan's thick, cold blood and drinking straight from her wounds. Both Yessenia's hands clamped tightly around her arm and waist, keeping Morgan in place. Her eyes fluttered, trying to fight through the pain, but making cries that could only be described as pleasure.

As Yess drank from her shoulder, Morgan felt something boil inside her, burning her skin. Her eyes rolled back, aroused beyond anything previously imagined. Never bitten by a Vampire until this very moment, she was enjoying every second as each pull of the mouth seemed to pull directly at her core. She moaned louder, Strix stirring where he stood, adjusting his pants a bit at the sight. Morgan's eyes drifted to him and flashed a hungry look. After what felt like an eternity of pleasure, Yessenia released Morgan. Once her fangs were extracted, only a few droplets of blood leaked from the four puncture wounds as the holes began to clot.

"Alright, good enough, toots. Go sit back down," Yessenia said, dismissing her with a gesture. "Another request." She stood and approached, now hovering over Morgan and eying her with devious intent. Morgan shifted slightly when Yessenia reached into her breast pocket and pulled out a fold of hundred-dollar bills. "I'll pay you $200 to put on a more hands-on, intimate show. In this office."

Morgan could see the money clip and knew this woman was serious. A crawling, icy sensation ran up her spine. She had the opportunity to get close to the gang that undoubtedly had been involved with Chrissy Donavon's disappearance. To do so, she betrayed her boyfriend, not that he ever got her this hot. It bothered Morgan… how naturally she whispered, "Yes." Something was awakening within her, a smolder turning into a blazing inferno.

"...follow your heart and trust your gut." Raphie had said. *"... do whatever you feel is necessary."* She knew Balam would never approve in a million years. Raphie would have her back at the end of the day, which made her feel safe… and that was all she needed.

"Alright," Morgan answered with a nod. "I'll do it."

"Awesome, Strix, grab the camera," Yessenia said, briefly clapping. He turned and unlocked a closet door. "You don't mind if we keep a record of this? Do you?"

"Am I signing a contract first?" Morgan challenged.

"Ooh look at you, Chastity knows her shit," Yessenia crooned as Strix set a Super 8mm camera on a tripod that shuddered under its bulk. "No, sweetheart, we hire so many people. We don't keep a paper trail. For now, consider this a hands-in audition, and I like to keep… a personal record of auditions."

Morgan thought it over; the consequences of this getting out could be dire… no one would want to hire the bimbo reporter. Yet, as she eyed Yessenia up and down, her tight leggings and curvy body caused Morgan's stomach to knot with excitement. It had been so long since she'd been with a woman. *What could one night hurt?* She thought.

"You in or out, sweetheart?" Yessenia barked.

Rather than respond, Morgan simply leaned back, lifting her vinyl dress and spreading her legs. She rested one leg on the couch's arm, revealing her black thong caged by the ultra-fine fishnet. With her sharp, pink nails, Morgan cut the crotch of her stockings. Yessenia grinned and hit record.

"That's what's up." The elder Vampiress grinned, checking the viewfinder. Morgan looked up and bit her bottom lip, her ring and middle finger touching the very edges of her petals. She let out a sweet and breathy moan, already feeling her body become hot at the idea of being filmed, let alone by someone so attractive. "You don't seem to be a stranger to this, Miss Vaughn."

"I-I never said I w-was," she moaned.

"I guess so," Yessenia opened her eyes and looked up past the camera, directly into 'Chastity's', shimmering like pink crystals. The two held gaze for a moment, though Morgan never stopped her performance. Yessenia bit her lip in admiration when Morgan reached her limit. Bucking her hips upward, she threw her head back and screamed, a result that had become increasingly rare for her. Her body spasmed and twitched, her legs and arms shaking as she collapsed onto the couch.

"You got the job. When can you start?" Yessenia said

"I-I'm free T-Tuesday and Wednesday nights," Morgan stammered. She slowly sat up, giving a satisfied sigh. "And Saturdays."

"We'll ramp things up a bit," Yessenia grinned, razor-sharp fangs on display. "Double your money, and you let me play with you next."

"Okay…" Morgan replied almost reflexively. She knew the only way to get to the heart of this mystery was to follow the path as it was carved. "Sure."

"Alright, I love your moxie, sweetheart." Yessenia smiled, taking the camera off the tripod and handing it to Strix and retreating behind her desk, only to retrieve a small wooden box. Yess gave a fanged grin upon opening it, pulling out a blood-red, 8" plastic vibrator.

Morgan felt her heart flutter, more like a living heartbeat, but her blood burned nonetheless. She had forgotten that Strix was still in the room. As the camera changed hands, she opened her eyes, looking up at him with irradiating lust. He gave her an equally fanged smile. He was attractive himself: sharp features, full lips, shaved head, preternaturally strong arms. His presence only further aided this process.

A moan escaped her mouth with a flutter. The sudden vibration caused her hips to jolt, though Yessenia's rough hands kept her in place. She looked up at Strix as he resumed filming. Her hand instinctively reached out, pulling on his shirt and untucking it from his pants. She could now clearly see his hulking mass, poorly hidden by his slacks. Yessenia used the vibrator's tip to prod gently at Morgan's womanhood, her long, pointed tongue flickering at her button. Morgan gave another yell of pleasure, gripping the shirt tighter and placing the other on Yessenia's head.

"Ah-ah," Yessenia gave a playful scold, lifting Morgan's arm off her head with ease and pinning her down by the wrist against the couch. " 'Hands on' is meant for me." Yessenia removed the toy and replaced it with her tongue.

Morgan gave Strix another desperate look.

"Holy shit," Strix said in awe, catching the moment of climax on film. Morgan's eyes rolled back in her head, her mouth agape, screaming at the top of her lungs and arching her back. This pushed her hips into Yessenia's mouth, forcing her to drink directly from her chalice.

"Holy shit is right," Yessenia mused, returning her mouth to Morgan shortly thereafter. Still holding her wrist, Yess wrapped her arms under Morgan's thighs and lifted her by the hips.

Just as she crested the peak of orgasm, Morgan was dropped back onto the couch, left a throbbing mess. Yessenia returned to the box, undoing her top and suspenders simultaneously. "Triple your money again… get on your knees."

Morgan was still in a haze not thinking, she looked up to Strix and met his ruby eyes. There was no hesitation anymore. She'd not felt this good in ages, and with Strix standing over her, she knew it wasn't just her and Yessenia who were about to have fun. "Alright," she grinned looking over to the quickly stripping Yessenia, her body flawless and fit. "Let's rock."

13

The taxi pulled up to Morgan's apartment at around 1:30 am. Exiting, she noticed the tears in her stockings, a reminder of the acts she committed. She gave a farewell wave to the driver, then put in her code to enter the perimeter gate.

She felt exposed facing the long walk down the open, outdoor entryway of the complex to quiet Apartment 161. Yessenia had left marks on her upper arms and inner thighs. As bitey as the elder Vampiress became, Morgan gave as good as she got. Thanks to Vampiric advanced healing, the marks were already beginning to fade.

Her fears were realized. Tom was standing outside in the open, a basket of laundry beneath his massive arm.

"Good evening, Vampire Neighbor," the skeletal Cryptid said, his voice deep but politely low. "You are home late."

"Hey, Tom," She said as she walked past him. "I went to a party."

"Another party? Your schedule does not usually permit such instances of merrymaking."

"Y-yeah, it's unusual," she said, reaching her front door and fiddling for her keys.

"Do not play too hard, Vampire Neighbor. The walking dead can feel the grim sensation of fatigue, as well."

"I'll be okay. Don't worry," she said, waiting to open the door, hopeful that the conversation would end and Balam wouldn't hear it.

"Sleep well. Do not let your dreams envelop you overmuch," he said ducking to enter his own apartment. Morgan paused, shook her head, and dismissed Tom for being Tom.

Her living room was still unkempt, though that's what she came to expect living with three men. Seth and Raphie's doors were shut, no sign of either of them. Her bedroom door, however, was slightly ajar, a dim light shining through. She wished it were dark. Morgan was capable of navigating the dark thanks to her undead senses, but the light posed a sense of dread; Balam may be sitting awake, still waiting for her.

She pushed the door open; the hinges creaked. Her body cringed at the sound. Looking upon the bed, Morgan saw that Balam was asleep, slumped, half-sitting, Tom Clancy novel fallen out of his listless hand. She smiled at her sweet, unknowing boyfriend; he bought her excuse of another party, being a college student provided an easy slew of excuses. He'd tried to stay awake for her, again, but he was always working and always drained.

Morgan crossed to him, grateful to be walking on carpet and not tile or wood. She picked up his book and placed it on the nightstand. When she reached to turn out the light, she saw his light-maroon face and white antlers illuminated in the soft glow. She sat gingerly beside him. His expression looked relaxed, serene, almost innocent. She needed to make it right somehow. Telling the truth would be too explosive. But she couldn't do nothing, her heart wouldn't allow it.

She kissed his forehead, caressing his chest through his shirt. Her lips began to wander his skin as he stirred beneath her. She suckled his neck, an impulsive desire to sink her teeth in rattled her thoughts. Thankfully, she found some will and fought the urge. He groaned again, this time lifting his head. His hand touched her head out of instinct, running his fingers through her teased, golden hair. "Oh fuck… Morg? When did you… fuck… when did you get home?"

"Just now. Sorry to wake you," she cooed.

"Don't be, batty girl," he smiled, running his knuckles along her cheek. Her hand wandered between his legs, over the single sheet and comforter. He was without pants, only boxers, and a solid white T-shirt. Her hand found his member rather quickly, massaging him. He groaned, sighing in pleasure. She pulled the blankets off him and continued to tease him through his boxers. After a moment, she slithered down his form and served him with her lips; he grinned at her, fully awake.

When she'd rise again to kiss him, he took her into his arms and kissed back. The moment their lips touched, she straddled him. A few seconds into their deep embrace, she was perfectly positioned. They moaned in synch, clutching one another with growing ferocity.

While caressing her, he reached up to the zipper on her vinyl dress. With one swift movement, he managed to disrobe her entirely, save her boots and legwear; his hand massaged her hips, fingers tracing over the blue butterfly.

Morgan arched her back and rolled her hips, lost in the sensation of their binding. She gripped his sun-bleached hair and bit her lip, her hips lifting and dropping. Softly at first, but soon she was rising and crashing violently onto Balam, giving loud and ecstatic moans each time their pelvises met. She came down hard and froze, her legs spasming in ecstasy. He took one of her breasts into his mouth and teased at her erect nipple with his tongue and teeth. As her shuddering started to slow, he switched his mouth to the other, feeling her womanhood's eagerness for him to join her in climax.

She gasped, finally losing steam. Balam seized the opportunity, rising and putting her onto her back, still gripping her fishnet-clad thighs. Her hair spread outward like liquid gold. Her eyes, like cherry blossoms, gazed up at him with burning lust that could sear steel. He whipped off his top and cast it aside, his red flesh smooth, like terra-cotta. He gripped both of her wrists and pinned them down with all his strength. With his new dominating stance, he powered on, a steam engine finally free of its train.

"Th-th-thank you, doctor," she purred, knowing how badly that aroused him.

Her eyes rolled back into her head. Her face at first appeared anguished, then evolved into howls of ecstasy. Balam held her head still and maintained his grip on now both of her wrists with his other hand. She looked into his loving eyes, even at his most aggressive, his face was benevolent to her. He gave a wicked smile but did not hesitate, making it clear his craving for her at this moment had overwhelmed him.

Knowing what she knew, what she had just experienced mere hours ago, Morgan's body could have caught fire to the very bed. The secret acted as a catalyst for a chain of the greatest orgasms Balam had ever given her. There was a flame alight in her belly, his seed failed to extinguish, only causing the flame to surge. The blaze erupted, and with it came a rush of admission.

"I love you!" she screamed. "I love you so much!"

In this moment, she seemed apathetic to the lies she had woven, more concerned with the texture and taste of one another's flesh and the rush such secrets provided.

M's Journal

October 7th, 1996

Got a case. Parents came to me. Daughter moved out after graduation. Got caught up in Hollywood. Became a ghost. Been chasing leads for weeks. Not many friends. Folks deathly afraid. No one cares to look too long for a Domhainn girl. So I have to, again, I guess. Not reluctant to look. But reluctant to live in a society that can't seem to give a shit. Back to the easy life as soon as possible: that's the motto.

Would have given up ages ago if it weren't for Morgan. She kept me focused on being present. That kid is so damn strong. Can't imagine being so young, losing both your parents. Never had a family, Noah and Odessa were the closest thing I had. They're gone and somehow the state was so kind enough to bless me, a queer Mothwoman, guardianship of an 11-year-old girl.

Maybe that's why I'm trying so hard to look for this girl, Tori Franques. She's 18... only a few years younger than my Morgan. Don't know what I'd do if anything happened to her... Yes, I do. I'd go to prison. Chained with rune-inscribed cold iron and thrown in a 10x10.

Do I regret how I've handled situations in the past? Hell yes. Every fucking day. Move forward trying to take my mistakes and learn from them the best I fucking can. Kinda heinous. How easily I could fall back into those old patterns. Won't forget the words the FBI director told Noah and I when we confronted him back in '71... after the Ozarks. "You're not cryptozoologists, you're monster exterminators." Genuinely think he forgot that I was a Cryptid and not just another preternatural like Noah. Then again, back then, we were all just "Supernatural Aberrations." Not that Director Samson was a friend of the people. If that's the type who's still in charge, gods help us.

Best lead is still my old Transylvanian chum, Yessenia. That bitch has only gotten nastier with age. Like milk. She claimed not to know the girl. But I can smell her bullshit. Not like I'll be able to get back in the Bourbon Belfry without a Sanguimancy-powered needle in my eye socket. Doesn't mean stopping there. Just need to view things from new angle. Gonna start looking into Elf Mafia. Lotta power players already... not pleased.

-M

Act 2: Astarte

1

It was 6 am. Morgan's alarm clock sprang to life with pop music. Her eyes shot open, her body lay still beneath the cotton covers, with extra layers on her side only. Balam stirred, she hurriedly shut off the alarm, knowing that if it woke him, she'd never hear the end of it. She rose, stretching her arms, back, and calves. Grabbing a robe, she headed to the shower, unclaimed this early in the morning.

At 6:15, she felt the hot water pour over her cool body. She craned her neck and let the water soak her scalp and run down her face. She let out a sigh of release, the conditioner rinsing out of her hair, leaving her ultra-fine mane silky smooth. As she brushed her fingers through the spilling sunshine that was her hair, her other hand found her womanhood.

It was 6:50. With one hand, Morgan brushed, using a special paste designed for undead teeth. In her other hand, she finished brushing her freshly blow-dried golden locks. After rinsing her mouth, she looked into the empty mirror. Though only her bubble-gum pink robe filled the reflection, she somehow could find the exact spot where her eyes should be. She stared into emptiness until she could imagine her face and her eyes in the antiquated silver mirror, and disparaged herself.

7:20 had come, and she was fully made up, returning to her room to dress. She put on a grey crop top, not feeling a bra today. Balam stirred again, in reaction to the sliver of light shining into the room through their drapes. Morgan didn't see him awaken, as he rolled over and watched her dress. He smiled, the light illuminating her body perfectly. "Good morning, batty girl."

"Oh! You're awake. Good morning," She said, returning the smile. "I was trying not to wake you."

"It's fine, you didn't," He said, propping himself upon his hand. Morgan was now working every weeknight, but somehow, they had managed to find time to have sex virtually every night, a welcome change of pace.

"I'm glad," Morgan laughed, raising a brow at his staring. She slid a pair of washed-out, blue jeans, with tears in the knees, over her plush bottom.

"You're just so beautiful," he said with fluttering eyes. "Like god damn, I've never seen someone as stunning as you."

"Thank you," she said with a bashful glance at her feet.

"And I have you all to myself," he said as he continued to admire her with confidence. Her smile faltered for a fraction of a second upon hearing that comment. "You wouldn't have time to take those jeans back off, would you?"

"I wish," she said, striding over to the bed. She leaned over him, a hand beside either of his shoulders. Her lips kissed his, maroon in color and soft to the touch, and locked with him for several moments. His hands wandered up to her waist and under her top, grazing her breasts with his fingertips; she kissed him deeper in response. Just at the moment she almost changed her mind, she leaned back and stood up. "I'm afraid I'm on a tight schedule again."

"That's okay." Balam laid his head down, obviously disappointed. "I understand you're busy, been a tough year, but I think it will all be worth it."

Morgan remembered her endgame, Chrissy Donavon, her reason for all of this. "You're right." Morgan's lips curled into a half smile as she picked up her white Converse sneakers. "It will be."

By the time it was 8 a.m., Morgan was sitting in class waiting for the rest of her classmates to situate themselves. She spaced out as the professor began; Broadcast Journalism Appreciation was the last thing she wanted to "appreciate." All that Morgan could focus on was her new job. It took hold of her like a virus, infecting every fiber of her physical and mental being. She'd never felt so alive as she did when she was on stage, or when she was giving a private "show." It was always different, though it had yet to match the quality of what her "boss" Yessenia provided during her interview.

It still baffled Morgan how easy it had been to become a member of staff, but she relished the opportunity. What didn't baffle her was this story. She knew she had found the right channel; she just needed to get the tuning exact, and she'd have her answers. She opened a file on her laptop that was labeled "BB", within which she had typed out all her notes. She observed what she had found out in the nearly two weeks she'd worked there: work schedules, staff names, clientèle, all of it. She had the name of the Catfolk, Tabby, but Morgan had yet to share a shift that gave her the chance to speak with her. She would, she'd make sure of it.

"Ms. Scriven!" The professor called. Prof. Cromwell was a shrill hag of an old woman in the most literal sense. She was undead of some kind, Morgan never bothered to find out if she was a Ghoul, Vampire, or Lich. "You haven't once looked up from your computer, so perhaps you've been taking diligent notes? Perhaps you could also tell the class why and when Walter Cronkite became an important figure?"

"Um…" Some of the class started to giggle like the immature brats they were. Morgan felt the pressure, having not realized how much time had passed. Had she known how absorbed she would get in her notes, she wouldn't have opened the documents in class. Looking up at the projector slide with virtually no information on what was asked, she could see the look of disdain on Cromwell's weathered face.

"Well…" Morgan began to draw from her memory, refusing to be caught off guard by the sideways comments. She endured, "He launched TV's first 30-minute broadcast in 1963, if you mean like originally. But he reported on the JFK Assassination, the Flatwood Bomber, the moon landing, Vietnam, the civil rights movement, the Supernatural Equality March… so, like, any of those?"

The class began to laugh. "Thank you very much, Ms. Scriven, that will do."

Around 4:30 pm. Morgan burst through the door of Apartment 161, took off her bags, and set them down. The door barely closed behind her before she reached her bedroom. Balam was still at work and would be for several hours, exactly what Morgan needed. With just a bit of extra time, Morgan collided with the bed, face first and fully dressed — shoes and all.

At about 5:30 pm, she awoke, rising with a groan and stretching her sore limbs and neck. In their closet, hidden behind thick winter coats, was a plastic bin. Within her prom dress. She lifted the frilly pink dress out of the bin to reveal a black backpack stuffed to the brim. She fetched the bag, returned the dress, and then the bin. The contents of the backpack had everything she needed to transform herself into Chastity Vaughn. She would do her make-up on the metro, as she had the past four nights she had performed. This left little chance that she could be mistaken, or recognized rather, as Morgana Scriven.

At 7 sharp, she was inside the Bourbon Belfry, teasing her hair and switching into the punked-out look she had adopted for the character. She considered shaving her head and using wigs, but she knew Balam would have a shit fit if she got anything shorter than shoulder length. For now, she'd just have to deal with styling her thin, delicate hair.

"It's 8 o'clock, ghouls and boys." One of the floor managers said, poking his head into the third-floor dressing room. Morgan knew his name, Mordecai, one of Yessenia's top cronies. "Opening time, that means you, new girl, you're up."

He gestured to Morgan, she flashed a cocky grin back and sauntered in his direction.

It was shortly after 8:10 that her boots hit the stage; enough people had filled the bar area that she could finally start her set. Morgan had always loved to dance, a cheerleader in high school, as well as a Swing Club member. But it was nothing compared to this. The rush she felt when her top came off and she danced for the lustful undead patrons was harder, in her mind, than any drug that could be produced. As long as she was wrapped around the pole, she felt powerful. She danced for a few songs only, but by the time she'd finished, her audience had tripled.

"Give a round of applause. You know you wanna buy what Chastity was selling you!" the DJ announced. The crowd roared. She knew hardly any of them could afford the rates, but so many people hungry for her alone made her burn. "Look for her on the floor this evening, and maybe you'll be lucky enough to win her favor." The announcer continued to spin Chastity even after she had left the sight of the crowd.

At 10:45, she was assigned a cage, the applause from below as she entered felt riveting, even if they did that anytime anyone entered the cage. This was one of the moments out of the night she had the best view of the building. While the world observed her body, she observed the other dancers, the patrons, the security— scrutinizing every minute detail. A pattern was soon to arise.

She noticed one of the dancers attracted more attention than her: the Catfolk. While the only major difference between Tabby and the Vampires was cat ears and a tail, her talent stood her apart from the others. She was topless, her tan, athletic body exposed, obviously not undead; while Morgan initially considered this to be the main attractor, even she couldn't deny the allure of her dancing. The way her body moved was hypnotic, with intoxicating eroticism. She was positive Tabby was the woman in the photograph with Chrissy. She had to be. In time, Morgan knew she would lead to the next clue.

By 11:45, the Bourbon Belfry was brimming with patrons. Morgan was enjoying the few moments of reprieve between dancing her heart out or sleuthing. She drank from a blood pack provided for the staff in a dark corner of the top-floor dressing room. This room was twice the size of the one below, complete with the luxury of not doubling as a storage room. She waited here often on her breaks, hoping to overhear something useful.

For the first time since she'd arrived, the most sought-after girl in the building was on break at the same time as her. The bronze-fleshed Catfolk adjusted her silver bob wig in one of the mirrors, tucking away a few of her natural black hairs poking out. Her tail and ears seemed to possess perfect, snowy white stripes. Morgan sucked down her meal and tossed it aside, striding over to take up the empty seat beside her.

Morgan pretended to fix her hair and check on her uncharacteristically punk look; still on point. She finally looked over at the Catfolk woman, who was still too focused on touch-ups to truly notice her.

"Hi, I don't think we've had a chance to meet; I've seen you work and you're amazing," Morgan began, gushing like a drunk valley girl in a bar bathroom. "I'm Chastity."

"Tabby," She replied, closing her bronzer and turning to face Morgan. "You're the new girl, right? I've seen your set. You're a natural."

"Thanks!" Morgan blushed, genuinely complemented by the beautiful, athletic woman. "I have to be honest, like, despite all that I do out there, I'm kinda shy— haven't made many friends here yet."

"On and off the stage are two very different worlds, baby," Tabby began, a certain sagacity to the way she spoke. "How'd you find the gig?"

"My friend Chrissy, Chrissy Donavon. Not sure if you'd know her," Morgan spun. "She worked here for a while."

"Chrissy?" Tabby said, her ears perked up in excitement. "You knew Chrissy?"

"Yeah, we went to high school together," Morgan continued to lie, her ditsy character helping sell it. "You haven't talked to her lately, have you?"

"I was gonna ask you the same thing." Tabby's words hung like a grave omen. "I haven't seen her in a while. Though it makes sense why you're such a good dancer, being friends with Chrissy."

"She do well?"

"Do well? The girl was the house special for a solid month," Tabby began. "She started with one set, then time in the cage, then two sets… not unlike you. But in the VIP rooms, is where she excelled. Suddenly, she's a 'Top Performer.' High-profile clients would come here specifically for her. Guess she must have finally blown the right bachelor, cause she left shortly after one of her most profitable nights. Tried to pry an answer out of Yess. She just told me to 'Stay sexy and shut my slut mouth.'"

"Jeez, I'm sorry she said that," Morgan said, her true empathy breaking through her disguise momentarily.

"I've gotten used to it. Take lip from your boss, not your customers. That's why I learned kickboxing at the same time as pole dancing. Body certainly didn't suffer from it, that's for sure," Tabby gave a cocky smirk, but her eyes seemed to be cold. Jaded even.

"You do have a rockin' bod. Like, for real," Morgan said,

once again tapping into genuine opinion. "And you haven't heard a word since?"

"Not a peep," Tabby said solemnly. "My bet, some trust fund baby up in a penthouse offered her enough money and blow to make Tony Montana blush. 'Cause the last thing I heard that girl spill, she was invited to a Hollywood party."

Morgan felt the hairs on the back of her neck stand on end. She was getting closer; there was a missing stepping stone to the next piece hidden within this establishment. She just needed to know where.

"Speaking of which," Tabby said, reaching into her makeup bag and removing what looked like a small compact with a Van Gogh image in tiny sequins on its top. Pressing the button, she opened the container and revealed a mound of white powder. With her pinky nail, she dipped in and collected an amount underneath. "You want some?"

If Morgan's nerves weren't already on fire, they were ablaze then. She stammered, incapable of forming words.

"It'll help. Take the edge off, give you energy… everything *feels* better, which in our line of work is a godsend," Tabby said, setting it down in front of her. Morgan looked at it, torn between her desire to remain a professional and the need to impress. She watched the Catfolk close one of her nostrils and snort the rest through her other. She shuddered, her tail swaying, her ears twitching. "Mmmf. Much better."

Morgan reached in the same way Tabby did with her nail and collected a small amount. She stared at it for a long while, her undead heart pounding like a slow-beating drum. She could feel Tabby watching, her eyes boring into the side of her head. *Fine.* She did as Tabby did, closing one nostril and snorting it up with the other. It felt like a punch directly to the back of her eyes. She squinted and rubbed her nose with the back of her hand, fighting the urge to sneeze. As she shook her head and sighed, she felt like a layer of stress had just been lifted, like peeling back the comforter on a hot night.

"Fuck…" Morgan said, blinking rapidly and feeling a sudden rush of energy. "Shit."

"First time?" Tabby said, her tail now perfectly stiff as she leaned on the countertop.

"Yup," she said with a sniffle and a chuckle. "Not bad."

Morgan and Tabby's attentions were drawn to the door as Mordecai burst through to call the next girl.

"Chastity," He said, pointing to Morgan. "You, uh, got a client, again."

"What, really?" Morgan said, becoming more flushed and still sniffling. "Again?"

"Right on schedule, baby," Tabby said with a gloomy smile. "You're headed to the big leagues."

Midnight. She was alone with a man in one of the private chambers, dimly lit with black candles. His hair was wavy and styled loosely; he was clean-cut, suave, and well-dressed. Like so many others like him, he had a pair of piercing red eyes that seemed to glow in the dark room. She locked eyes with him, and he flashed her a half-smile, his fangs much larger than her own, a symbol of his potential age. Her body trembled in anticipation, cast aflame by the nose candy she chose to partake in. His burgundy shirt was half unbuttoned, revealing his hairless, muscular chest. Morgan had chosen her song for the private room at the start of the evening, the staff had already placed the tape in the stereo. She sauntered over to the massive velvet couch he sat upon, pressing play as she passed.

He eyed her up and down with hunger, his venomous smile framed by a sharp jaw. She strode over to him with rhythmic strides, her hips rolling in tune with the music. As she stood before him, the stranger leaned against the back of the red sofa, unmoving but poised to strike should he so desire. She was soon pressed against him, grinding on him with both knees on the seat.

"You can touch," she whispered, biting on his ear. "Just no marks on my neck or arms."

"I can work with that." The stranger obliged, caressing her thighs, waist, and back, his fingers toying with her bra strap.

"Go ahead," she said with a heavy, false breath. Within a second, he unhooked and removed the black lace, tossing it aside with little care. His lips pressed against her exposed nipple, and he did something she never expected: he bit down. She cried out in pain and pleasure as he drank blood from her wounded breast. After all, she never told him that was off limits, and she was glad. He would bite her a few more places, her inner thigh and her shoulders, to name a few.

"Perhaps I should give you what you're here for," she teased. The stranger began to unbuckle his belt, Morgan teasing him through his pants, feeling the effect she had. He presented himself for her and, with ardor, her lips enveloped him.

2:38 am. The door to Apartment 161 creaked back open. "Fuck" Morgan whispered to the door, snaking her way through the barely open crack. After pulling her bulky bag through, she shut it, thankfully without an additional creak. No one was awake, yet again, only her. She, barefoot, tiptoed her way into her bedroom. She had learned to time it perfectly. Carefully, she hid her backpack in the plastic tote, beneath the prom dress, and stored it away until tomorrow. Morgan was relieved that her boyfriend was such a heavy sleeper. Stripping down to her panties, she tossed on a worn t-shirt before climbing into bed with her cuckold of a boyfriend.

As she lay with him, Balam rolled to his side and wrapped his arm around her. Her body lost all its heat, and back came the guilt. She stared up at the ceiling, praying for the same sandman with whom Balam was so close to spirit her away from the turmoil of dual life. Eventually, Morgan found a brief moment of mental peace, or possibly exhaustion, and her eyes fluttered to sleep.

It was 6 am. Morgan's alarm clock sprang to life with pop music.

2

Morgan watched Raphie emerge from his bedroom, yawning and scratching the back of his head. He squinted, struggling to adjust to a sunlit room. As he crossed to the Bar, he saw Morgan sitting at their tiny dining room table in her fuzzy, pink robe, hunched over a cup of coffee from their new, non-sentient machine. Her mug was full but no longer steaming.

"Morgan?" he asked, rubbing his eyes. Seeing his friend, he grabbed an orange from the basket on the Bar and moved to sit beside her. "I don't think I've ever seen you just sitting on a weekday morning... You came home late again last night."

"I'm sorry," She said reflexively, "I didn't mean to wake anyone."

"No need, I don't sleep...Everything okay, Blondie?"

"I'm okay," Morgan said with a forced smile. "Balam was out before me this morning, and class doesn't start until noon, so... I did some assignments, and now..."

"You were alone with your thoughts?" Raphie grimaced, but his tone was endearing. "Wanna talk about it?"

Morgan was silent. She wasn't a liar, at least not before the last couple of weeks. She held her mug shakily, nearly spilling. Raphie reached out to take it, but still, she stared blankly forward, trembling.

"Morgan... please talk to me. You've barely said a word since you went to that club," Raphie said, sick with worry. "You know you can tell me anything."

"Do you think it's worth doing something evil if it means doing something truly good?" Morgan lifted her head, her eyes swollen with tears. "Do you think you can still be a good person even if you're doing something awful?"

"What happened? Dude, you gotta tell me. I'm gonna help you," he leaned in closer and wrapped his arm around her shoulder in an effort to console her. "Please, tell me it doesn't have to do with that club."

Morgan laid her head on his shoulder, letting out an honest and ugly sob.

"Oh Blondie, it's okay," Raphie scooted his chair directly beside her and fully embraced her. Morgan cried in his arms for a few minutes, Raphie didn't know what to say that would get her to open up. He simply kissed the top of her tangled blonde head and told her it would be alright. It was all Morgan could ask for.

"I'm cheating on him, Raph," Morgan finally spoke, catching her shallow breath.

"Okay," he said with a temperate reply. "With who?"

"It's c-complicated."

"Ah… How complicated?"

"Um…" Morgan sat up, sniffling and staring onward, struggling to say what had transpired outright, fighting her natural stammer. "I-I got inside. I got in at the B-Bourbon Belfry, and I picked up the first piece of the trail of C-Chrissy Donavon. She, at least for some amount of time, worked there. Th-the whole fucking place is run by a gang, Raph. The T-Town Tyrants. They have to have something to do with her disappearance."

"Okay," Raphie interrupted, a bit hesitant in his asking, "But how did you get your in?"

"I… I did things…" Morgan began, and Raphie took her hand.

"Morgan, fuck. I'm so sorry."

"You don't understand… I debased m-myself… I let this b-boss woman fuck me while I sucked her henchman off… And I reveled in every fucking second of it," Morgan wept, finally feeling like she could divulge all the gruesome details. "So much so, I went back the next night… I danced for the early crowd, and they loved me. So I'm now a regular entertainer at o-one of the sleaziest, criminally run clubs in LA, and I've been sleeping with strangers every night I've been there… and I c-c-can't fucking get enough, Raph. I keep hoping someone will buy me for the night. Like, I don't know what the hell is wrong with me!"

"I… am not quite sure what to say." Raphie took a few deep breaths and continued to hold Morgan's hand tightly. "I don't think anything is wrong with you… But there… *might* be something wrong with your relationship. Do you think Balam knows?"

"No." Morgan shook her head. "We've been having sex regularly too… It's never been better."

"Fuck, Blondie," Raphie sighed hanging his head "This is bad."

"You're damn right it is!" Morgan gave a sarcastic giggle, a sign the stalwart Vampiress was losing her control. She was aware Raphie knew her too well not to see it. "I don't know how to fix this… I'm so close to finding the next piece and helping this poor girl."

"I'm gonna say something, and I want you to take it with a grain of salt…" Raphie began.

"Are you sure you wanna say it?" Morgan growled.

"You don't scare me, " Raphie laughed. "I know deep down you're as goddamn beautiful as you are on the outside. Listen, I know you want to help this girl. You want to see all of this made right. But it might be that, without knowing, you found a way of finally giving yourself what you want."

Morgan snapped her head to him. As her tears had faded, she was still visibly upset, more frustrated than sad at this point.

"You took to this story the moment you saw a pattern no one else did, and you were fucking right —which means I'm sorry— But when you moved in with Balam you just about hemorrhaged your bank account bringing me here with you guys… this brings me to my hypothesis: maybe you only said 'yes' to moving in with Balam because you didn't want him to be hurt if you said 'no'. Maybe you feel you're in too deep, to be honest about how you feel… that you weren't ready."

Raphie paused and watched Morgan stare off into the distance in a moment of dissociation. Not out of shock, but rather panic that another voiced her thoughts. Nevertheless, Raphie continued, "I also think you should let your Aunt know what you've found and back out now."

"And what, tell her that I cheated on my boyfriend of almost two years with multiple strangers, some of whom are gang members?" Morgan rolled her eyes at the prospect and pulled her hands away. "Yeah, that's gonna go over *real* well. Not to mention, if I back out now, then I may never get that story. I'll be out of the internship program for good and will have sabotaged my relationship for nothing."

"I'm not saying it's optimal, but if you don't bring in an actual professional, then you're going to end up in a situation you don't like so much… and she'll find out eventually anyway," Raphie raised his voice, finally taking his stance.

"What happened to always having my back?" Morgan retorted.

"I do have your back!" Raphie pushed. "I'm watching it so you don't get hurt. I love you, dude. You're my best fucking friend. I don't want to lose you."

Morgan froze, she felt her face become flushed, she seldom heard Raphie be so affectionate to anyone, herself included. She smiled softly, taking Raphie's hand back. "I'm sorry. I know I shouldn't ever doubt you… You're the one person other than my Aunt that's stayed with me through my antics… and now Balam… I can't tell him… He'll never understand… he's going to ask me to leave. Fuck, Raph, I'm so stupid."

"You're not stupid," Raphie furrowed his brow "You're a fucking genius and your GPA proves it. You just made a fucked choice that forced you to make more fucked choices. So if you're right and you're as close as you say you are, then you need to make one more fucked choice: If you're certain of a lead you might have found, you need to follow it, whatever that yields. I trust you didn't use a real name?"

"Of course not," Morgan smirked.

"What did you pick?" Raphie smirked back.

"Chastity Vaughn," She said saucily.

"Ooh, props." Raphie nodded and gave a wink. He hesitated before asking the next question. "Are they paying you at least?"

"Yeah, under the table. Which explains how Chrissy got the job…" A smile broke Morgan's straight face, incapable of hiding her pride. She stood up and ran into her bedroom, returning shortly thereafter with the backpack. She opened it, and Raphie saw the collection of skimpy clothes folded tightly together as well as a pair of thigh high boots. She pushed the clothing aside and pulled out a small black pouch attached to a garter. She reached in and pulled out a roll of cash, mostly 20s. She handed him the money. "This was just from last night… two clients and a few hours of dancing."

"Holy fuck…" Raphie looked floored; he'd not seen that much money in one wad in real life. "Um… okay, after this next shift you go D.B. Cooper on their asses. Take anything not nailed down."

"I don't even feel right owning it, let alone spending it,"

Morgan said, looking down at her bare feet, ashamed. "It feels like blood money."

"Well… maybe you need to freeze your assets." Raphie handed her the money back "Get yourself a vehicle. Not like Balam is particularly concerned with finances right now, so he won't question it. It would help you make a quick getaway if you need to, at least."

"I'm not going to need to run away… they don't think I'm anything but some girl seduced by the attention." She paused and thought deeply about how true that was.

Raphie went to speak but was interrupted by a knock at their front door. "Oh, sweet. Demytria's here."

"Shit, I didn't know she was coming. Don't let her in just yet," Morgan panicked, threw the money in her wallet, zipped up the bag, and retreated to the bedroom. Raphie raised an eyebrow at his friend's frantic behavior. "Kay!" she shouted from the main bedroom.

As he approached the door, the knocking repeated. "Coming!" he answered. When he opened the door, Demy stood on the other side in a worn brown coat, a deep burgundy dress, torn tights, and her go-to, chunky boots. Hanging by a hemp string was an animal scale pendant that was bound in wire. Her cute pointed ears were adorned with silver and black hoops and studs. The corner of her red velvet lips was curled upward the moment he came into sight, her eyes hidden behind her round, black sunglasses. "Good morning! I'm sorry, I didn't know I was running behind."

"Don't worry," Demy said. "I'm early. Usually am. Just a knack I have, I guess."

"That's better than being flaky," Raphie grinned. "You're welcome to come in. Did you have any trouble finding the place?"

"Not really, once I realized the 100s were on the *second* floor. Why are they like that?"

"Oh well, the ground floor apartments used to be businesses back in the '60s… before the murders," Raphie replied, with a tinge of foreboding.

"Spooky…"

"Um, let me change and I'll be right out!" Raphie ran to his bedroom.

Taking off her sunglasses as she entered, Demy looked around the modestly decorated apartment, absorbing the nuances of Raphie's living situation. She started to approach the glass sliding door across from her; it led out to a quaint patio with a few chairs. The view was worth a look, a practically framed portrait of the hills. She smiled and stepped closer, but the sound of another door opening caught her attention.

Out stepped Morgan, with straight, blonde hair, jeans, and a *Bob Dylan* t-shirt that had the sleeves cut off. Morgan didn't feel as well-manicured as when they had first met. Demy, on the other hand, was strikingly pretty, and Morgan witnessed this for the first time.

"Hi, I don't know if you remember me—" Morgan began stepping forward, nervously extending her hand.

"I remember you, you're Raphie's best friend." Demy took her hand, shaking it gently; there was an almost stillness in the air when they touched. Demy took her hand back and kept her face as straight as she could. "He told me a little bit about you, last time we hung out. You work for a newspaper?"

"Yeah, I'm an intern at the Cryptid Chronicle," Morgan answered honestly, but shyness came across.

"Nice," Demy spoke. "You guys are one of the few good guys out there in the media."

"Thank you, I feel the same."

"If you ever need a hand like… investigating… I'd be totally down to help if I can. I know a lot of people in this city and can always put my ear to the ground for you," Demy said with a positive smile.

Morgan raised a brow; something set off her senses, but she wasn't sure what. She remembered dismissing Eliza's warning at the party, but in hindsight, she seemed seriously disturbed by whatever Demy Moon was about. Though now, staring at the Elf in the morning light, she understood fully how enchanting Demy was. How could Morgan blame Raphie for being naive when she felt just as intoxicated? "So you and Raph are dating now?"

"You could say that." Demy smiled. She seemed warm and kind. Eliza was just being a bitch. Or maybe she's an ex. Either way, she didn't feel threatened around the curvy tattooed woman— quite the opposite.

"Okay," Raphie exited his room dressed in distressed jeans, a black tee, and a plaid jacket wrapped about his waist that matched Demy's dress in color. "Ready, sorry to keep you waiting."

"Don't be, I said I was early," Demy reassured, acknowledging Raphie only to turn back to Morgan, her blue eyes lined with a wickedly sharp wing, smoking out around the edges of her lid. Something about her eyes, Morgan had a soft spot for the part of the body anyway… but hers were otherworldly.

"It was nice talking to you, Morgan."

"Yeah, I look forward to seeing you again," Morgan said, giving an almost flirtatious smile.

Raphie grabbed his keys and bag and escorted Demy out of the apartment, saying "Goodbye" to Morgan; his face bore a look of worry even still. Despite all his protests, Morgan refused to accept she was in any danger.

What she couldn't wrap her head around was her heightened sexual appetite. She felt guilt in her gut, wishing she could still pretend Balam was enough. She walked out onto the patio, looking out into the city. Her mind began to wander, as did her hands. She sat down in one of the chairs and lay back. She opened the fly of her jeans and indulged her shameful thoughts.

3

Raphie and Demy walked for over a mile, though the time flew by thanks to endless conversation. They talked about music tastes and found they had a great amount of overlap. They talked about where they were from; Raphie was born and raised in LA, whereas Demy immigrated from Romania when she was a child. The daughter of a High-Elf woman and a Human, she was only a Half-Elf, which explained the relatively smaller points of her ears. She mentioned something about being an orphan but said nothing more.

Both Raphie and Demy possessed immense love for the City of Angels, currently overtaken by October and all that it means. Autumn was in full swing, leaves crunching everywhere they walked. Occasionally, they would come across the orange, black, and deep crimson of the decorations outside people's homes and businesses— faces of skeletons, pumpkins, and ghosts jumping out in the dark. Thankfully, with the few people who decorated, you didn't see many Vampire or werewolf decorations this deep in the city; generally, now found to be in poor taste.

While they were both talking about how they loved the Getty, their hands brushed. Rather than act coy or pretend it was unintentional, Raphie reached for her hand. She accepted and they walked, linked, through the city streets. This was the first moment the entire walk that either had become silent. Occasionally Demy would say where to turn and Raphie would follow without question.

"You know," Raphie spoke up for the first time in almost fifteen minutes. "I'm not saying we're lost, but you know your way around, right?"

"Yeah, I mean, I'm an Elf, so I don't get turned around easily," Demy said casually. "But I'm pretty familiar with the streets of certain neighborhoods."

"Oh, I do not doubt either of those things, no ma'am," Raphie said, "But what I've come to learn is that: there's no such thing as lost, just not knowing the *true* destination."

Demy stopped in her tracks beneath the shade of a magnolia tree. He pivoted around to gaze into her bright blue eyes, albeit shielded, holding both her hands now.

"You know, Raphie, I like that mentality. I like a lot about you. I'm just glad we met, period…"

"Me too," Raphie said, fingers tracing over her knuckles. "I can't stop thinking about you if I'm being real."

"My thoughts have been extra crowded because of you,

too," Demy said, biting her bottom lip. Raphie melted. The two stood there on a residential street for some time. Raphie wanted to kiss her and she him, though some invisible barrier kept them apart. Demy turned with him still taking his hand, "Come on, we're almost there."

"Where are we going?" Raphie questioned with muffled anxiety. "We're not doing any crazy, magical rituals, are we?"

"It's going to be nothing like the other night. Honestly, I still don't know what got over Gruel. I'm deeply sorry," Demy said with a sigh.

"It's okay. He seems a little unhinged… and that's not any fault of yours," Raphie said. "I'm just a bit on edge still if I'm gonna be perfectly honest."

"I won't ask anything like that of you anytime soon," Demy replied. "Please, I know it's a lot to ask, but I need you to keep what you know quiet."

"I promise," Raphie said with a nervous laugh. "Now, where are we going?"

Demy turned back and beamed, "It's a surprise, trust."

"I can do surprises," Raphie said, keeping up with the determined, aquamarine woman. "Life has been bursting with surprises since I met you… Not about to ask it to stop."

"How much do you know about magic?" Demy asked, leading him behind a series of houses backed up against the wall of the 101 Freeway.

"Well… not a lot," he admitted. "My mom was super religious growing up. Hell, my dad converted for her. But Jewish, not Pagan. So there wasn't any magic in our house… school obviously hasn't helped much, either."

"Ah, say no more." She said with a little wave. She found an entrance, a tear in the fence, and a break in the concrete retaining wall. She slouched down low and slid down the length of the steep, dirt hill, lightly floating at the very end as she landed. "Come on!"

"Um… okay. I guess we're doing this," he thought out loud, climbing over the break and sliding down as she did. Without magic Levitation, he didn't stick the landing. He stumbled, arms flailing, and nearly lost his balance and fell into traffic.

Recovering at last, he stood triumphantly. "Nailed it!"

"Yep," Demy said, unable to hold in her laughter. Raphie felt a rush of euphoria hearing the sincerity of it; knowing he was the cause made his heart skip a beat. "Come on, almost there."

"Sure," Raphie whined, but followed up behind her with eagerness.

After a few minutes of following along the edge of the freeway, they came across a bridge; a camp had been established beneath. Several disheveled individuals sprinkled the makeshift encampment. Raphie was no stranger to the homeless; he even knew a few. They approached a ramshackle tent made out of a broken E-Z Up, aluminum siding, and a parachute.

"Yo, Puck, I'm here for my commission."

"Ah shit, Demy, is that you?" A man said from the tent, the sound of his voice suggested he was choking. A hard cough later, and out spilled a cloud of skunky smoke. Like a stage magician, the man named Puck arose. He was older, blowzy with big, wild, ginger hair. He wore a pair of star-shaped, Elton John sunglasses, an army jacket, a torn-up pair of pants, and a *Care Bears* t-shirt. He carried a hockey stick, adorned with Christmas lights that somehow flickered without any visible power source. "I said it'd take a week."

"You did, last week," she said, sternly.

"Damnit, is it Wednesday again?" the scruffy man said disappointedly. "It's always hump day somewhere, right?"

"That doesn't make any sense." Demy shook her head.

"My bad, it's always 4:20 somewhere. You know what I mean, bub?" He said to Raphie with a slight cough and a filthy grin.

"Right," Raphie chuckled.

"Ah… do you know about liminal spaces?" Puck said, his head perking up.

"Uhhh…" Raphie looked to Demy to save him from the conversation.

"Do you have it ready or not, Puck? I already paid you," she said, running her hand through her short, teal hair.

"Certainly!" Puck said, "Well, almost done. I didn't get to

put any final coats on her. So she might get dirty and be difficult to clean, but she'll do. She'll do."

He hobbled to the backside of his tent, where a workbench had been set up with a decent display of tools as well as bins and buckets full of odd trinkets; animal bones, feathers, stones, pieces of metal, jewelry, and the like.

On top of his workbench was a foot-and-a-half-long piece of driftwood that had been sanded down and finished with a cherry stain, making the light-colored wood a bright crimson. He held it up, brandishing it like a sword.

"You the lucky man?" Puck said to Raphie.

"I guess?" he answered, tilting his head to face Demy, who gave a reassuring nod. "Yes. I. Am… the lucky man."

Puck handed the piece of wood to Raphie, who could now clearly see a Hebrew inscription wrapped around its circumference.

"Love is Mana?" Raphie read aloud. "How'd you know I was Jewish?"

Demy arched her brow. "I didn't."

Raphie smiled brightly, examining the piece of finely decorated driftwood. "Thank you," he looked up to Puck "Thank *you*."

"No prob, Bob," Puck said, "Now you do know what you have, right?"

"Naw," Raphie said, still beaming.

"Jesus, Demy, you're gonna train this one, *too*?" He clasped his hand over his head. "Just don't do it anywhere near here, I don't want the cops to come… and a fire to start…"

Puck retreated to his tent.

"Thank you, Puck," She called over her shoulder.

"Knock before you exit, my siblings!" he flashed a peace sign out the tent opening. The two chuckled under their breaths and made their way out of the camp.

"Train…" Raphie said, stunned, "Does that mean?"

"Yeah," Demy confirmed before he could say it. "I'm going to teach you how to use magic. You have it within you already, felt it that night at the music shop. I feel it now that you have this." She gestured down to the item he still held gingerly.

"That means," Raphie couldn't keep his eyes off the stick. "This is my wand."

"Bingo," Demy said with a cocksure smile, pleased with his gift.

"Thank you… thank you so much… when do we start?" Raphie said like a child with a new toy.

"Soon." She said, looking at him with loving eyes. "Just promise me we'll keep it on the down-low for now. Not everyone was necessarily gung-ho or even on board with my decision to do this. Particularly Gruel and Amy… but I wanted to give you the opportunity."

"That's… wow… I understand that means a lot, Demytria. I hope you know you didn't have to do this. I'm grateful and genuinely excited, but not at the expense of your friends and partner."

"Don't worry," she smiled. "I wouldn't do this if I didn't have faith in you. Hell, faith is all I run on these days. Not much hard evidence, ya know?"

"Yeah, true dat," Raphie said with a sigh, remembering his best friend's plight.

Demy led them both up a section of hill, flat enough for them to scale. With a little balance control, the two made their way off the freeway and back onto the streets. They walked a block to a cozy park, barely over a mile from Avalon U, and tucked in an open lot between two multi-story structures. They loitered there for a moment, the morning sun coming down, though in the distance, grey rainclouds rolled in. They decided to seek shelter beneath one of the park's trees. Demy opted to stand, while Raphie sat up against the thick bark, admiring his wand.

"You like it?" She blushed, leaning on the tree.

"Yes," he said, still gleeful. "I genuinely love it."

"Good," Demy said with a look of reverence. "I'm gonna be real with you, Raphie…"

Raphie rose to meet her eye to eye, his heart racing as she spoke, anxious of what she might say. "I'm listening."

"I think you're hot shit…" Demy said. "You're cute, funny, and exceptionally kind. I mean, see how you look after your friend. She needs it right now."

"How did you know?" Raphie said, confused. "Did she say something to you?"

"Eyes are the window to the soul." Speaking from the heart, Demy obviously believed her words. "You can learn a hell of a lot with a few seconds of eye contact."

"Oh yeah?" Raphie said, the corners of his lips curling up arrogantly, "What are mine saying?"

"You tell me." Demy took off her sunglasses and looked Raphael dead in the eyes. The flawless, crystalline turquoise of her irises was the most hauntingly beautiful thing he'd seen in this strange world. Her freckled, round cheeks crested the edge of her eyes, the bottom lids forced upward by her radiant smile. He leaned closer, Demy eying his lips.

He didn't move more than a few inches before she cleared the rest of the distance, her wine-red lips kissing his. Demy shifted; Raphie reached up and cupped her soft face, his hand moving back to graze the back of her neck, the longer their kiss lasted. Demy backed away first, her cheeks flushed and heart racing. Raphie was the same, astonished by her worldly, as well as spiritual, beauty.

A car horn from the curb nearby broke their fairy tale world. Adrian from the ritual was behind the wheel of their blacked-out van and laying on the horn.

"Get a room!" they shouted crassly.

"Please stop," Demy said plainly, without fight. "I don't want to draw any unnecessary attention to your rape van."

Adrian's mouth fell agape. "Rude."

"Do you need a ride?" Demy asked, turning back to gaze at Raphie one last time.

"Naw, you go with your friends. I'm good."

"I'll see you soon, Raphie." Demy smiled and strutted her way over to the van, the side door sliding open. Trina held it for Demy to enter, giving Raphie a wave before slamming it shut again. The van peeled off, taking with it the woman who had his heart.

4

Raphie ended up in World History 320 nearly fifteen minutes late. The professor, a Dwarf man in his mid-forties by the name of Eliott VanderGraf, had his back turned to the class as he lectured, attention on the wall before him, where the projector cast its images. Among the raked class seats, the albino Vampiress who was Raphie's best friend waved vigorously to grab his attention. He kept his head down, ignoring some upset grumbles, and moved as quietly as he could to sit next to his friend, in the one class they still shared this year.

"You're late," Morgan whispered to him as he sat down, noticing the red wand poking partially out of his bag "What's with the stick?"

"Yeah, I know… and it's a long story," he whispered back, stuffing the wand away. "What are we talkin' about today?"

"So from this point," VanderGraf went on, "the world was forced to acknowledge the existence of Non-Humans. Until then, it was all just stories or isolated pockets in select locales. Legends and hearsay. Much like how many Cryptids are still handled today. When the Mighty Elementals cleared from the Straits of Ile De Lenora, so many races that were considered legends reached the shores of North America and Europe. This mass exodus was called 'The Emergence.' Also, thank you for finally joining us, Raphael." Prof. VanderGraf spoke, turning around and giving Raphie a sharp stare. "I'm assuming since you're late, you had plenty of time to complete the reading. Mind if you tell me what the Mighty Elementals were and when they vanished?"

"Uh…" Raphie glanced at Morgan, who was hunched down beneath her laptop screen, mouthing the answer to him; the light of the screen reflected in her pink-framed glasses "They were massive living storms that prevented long-distance boat travel, which barred most Non-Human societies from the world. They cleared once in the BC era, which is where most fairy tale origins come from, again in 1700 with the Domhainn Mass Exodus, and vanished for good in 1799."

"Excellent," he clicked his pen and crossed his arms. "Now,

can you answer it without Morgana's help?"

Morgan lifted her head, face loaded with guilt, and softly said, "Sorry."

Raphie's chipper demeanor began to crumble as he realized he was on his own with his pants down. "No, I can't, Prof. VanderGraf."

"I thought so," VanderGraf said with a disapproving frown. "I need to talk to you in private after class for a moment."

"Of course."

After the lengthy lecture came to a close, the class packed up and urgently exited with a chattering ruckus. Raphael took his time, waiting for all those in his row to clear out before he finally stood. Despite being called out during class, Raphie neglected to take any real notes. Instead, his notebook now featured two highly detailed portraits of Demy that Raphie had sketched by hand. Morgan watched him place the finishing touches as she packed up her laptop along with her textbook. She had remained beside Raphie the whole while, her expressions like shifting sands, wavering between a bittersweet smile and a wistful look.

At the end of the aisle, Morgan gripped Raphie's jacket sleeve and gave a soft tug against the flannel fabric. "Hey, I'll wait for you as long as I can, but I have to be back home soon." She spoke in a low voice as the sounds of idle chit-chat and footsteps began to diminish.

"Yeah, I know, your jobs are demanding. You do what you got to do, Blondie," Raphie gave a half-smile, distress and social anxiety clear in his eyes.

"You'll be fine," Morgan pecked Raphie's cheek. "Good luck."

As she turned to exit, he felt the spot on his cheek. She wasn't wearing lipstick, so he didn't feel any worry that she left a mark, but he felt its lingering presence nonetheless. He was lucky to have her as a friend… so her kiss must carry that luck with it.

Raphie hiked down the stairs and made his way to Prof. VanderGraf, his skin appeared like smooth limestone, complete with ribbons of darker streaks in his rock-like flesh. He was handsome, with dark swept-back hair, and streaks of gray decorating his head and goatee. He sat behind a metal desk, reading the previous class's assignments and swiftly marking each with a red pen.

"You wanted to speak to me, Prof. VanderGraf?" Raphie practically whimpered, hanging his head as if the ceiling had shrunk.

"Yes, I did," he said, placing his pen down, taking off his glasses, and peering into Raphie's dark eyes with his own. "You've been late six times already this term. You also neglected to turn in last week's timeline assignment which is going to hurt your overall grade. What's up?"

"Just not applying myself, I guess," Raphie waffled, knowing what these conversations entailed and trying to expedite the process.

"That's bullshit," VanderGraf scoffed "You were in my class last year and you murdered the curve. So why is it this year you seem to have less and less focus as the days go on?"

"I don't know," Raphie said, his brows drooping.

"Not an acceptable answer," he said, standing and crossing to his podium, stepping up on the stool to be eye level with Raphie. "What's your major again?"

"Undecided." The word left Raphael's mouth like a razor blade, wounding his tongue and causing him to forcefully purse his lips together. He yearned to conjure a quick excuse but had none. "But I'm working with my councilors."

"Still? In the first semester of your Junior year…" VanderGraf sighed. "May I see your notes from today?"

"What? Why?" Raphie whipped his head up.

"I'm not going to scold you if you didn't take notes, I just want to prove something," VanderGraf's tone was calm but had an underlying tension like an inactive volcano beneath his rocky flesh. With some hesitation, Raphie handed his notebook over. The professor looked through the notebook to find the two lifelike drawings Raphie had done that day. Any other pages from the current week would have been cluttered with unusual doodles, disturbing eyeball creatures, and psychedelic asymmetrical spirals, except for a few of Morgan. VanderGraf turned back to the page to see his most recent drawing: Demy at a 45° angle, looking off into the distance. A mere snapshot of reality that Raphael had given permanence to.

"You're an amazing artist, Raphie," VanderGraf arched his brow and pouted his bottom lip, impressed with the sketches.

"Thank you," Raphie said, blushing slightly. "Those are honestly just doodles—"

"What's her name?"

"Demytria," Raphie said her name, and it seemed to heal the invisible wounds his previous words had left.

"She's very beautiful," VanderGraf began, behind his words, he held a 'but' like a blade, poised to strike. "But I'm going to say something you're going to hate."

"Sure," Raphie said, fighting the urge to roll his eyes fully into his head.

"You're a brilliant mind. You have a near-photographic memory, incredible talent, and you're going to squander it on a girl. Look, Raphie, you're young, I get it. And I know this girl might feel like 'the one', but you're missing 'the one' opportunity you have to set your life on a path to success. If she respects you, she'll stick around through your schooling. But she shouldn't be impeding your education."

"She's not," Raphie fought honestly. He knew Demy had been distracting him, yes, but he was already checking out before Oliver left him. "I've honestly just been burned out. I'm not sure what I want to do, I love my art, but like… what am I gonna do with that?"

"You could switch to an Art Major, it's not too late since you've probably got more than enough GE by now," the professor suggested.

"I've thought about that, but I don't think *I* could make a living as a comic artist. Is it what I want? Yes. But I don't know," Raphie sighed, for the first time he was being honest with someone about how schooling made him feel.

"Have you considered being a storyboard artist? You live in LA, you could make a lot of money doing that."

"That's where my councilors are pointing me," Raphie said. "I don't know… It all just feels pointless."

“Don’t tell me you’re considering dropping out.”

Raphie shrugged.

“No,” VanderGraf retorted bluntly, his tone shifting and his face growing cold. “Listen and listen well, Raphael: You’re just a Human among the hundreds of Non-Humans, the real people Avalon U was built for. You may be Hispanic and transgender, but at the end of the day, you’re a dime a dozen for this school. So if you want to throw away your opportunity to graduate among the brightest minds from the most diverse school in the country, then go right ahead. Because they will *NOT* hesitate to throw you to the wayside and call the next number. Do I make myself clear?”

Raphie stood frozen, unsure of how to take the professor’s rant. Uncertain whether he was supposed to answer, he opted to nod.

“Good… now I don’t know what you gained from this, but I hope it’s the right thing. Have a good day, Raphael.” VanderGraf gave a gracious bow of his head and returned to his desk.

Raphie climbed the stairs of the raked building and out into the world. He frowned; Morgan was nowhere to be seen along the enclosed corridor. He made his way to the main courtyard, thoughts of the future now weighing on his mind and putting his skull under pressure.

One look at his wand, and suddenly, he felt the uncertainty relent.

5

Never had Morgan intended to perform lewd acts for strangers when taking this job. She knew it was wrong: Chastity didn’t. The longer she played the role, the harder it became to think like herself. The concept frightened her, much in the same way being used by strong and dangerous Vampires did; the same fear that sparked the fire. And the cycle continued.

She wasn’t supposed to enjoy this so much or at all, and

yet. She was in her early twenties, a Trueborn Vampire. Her lust felt insatiable, and to Morgan, it seemed natural to let it manifest as a character. A character that had so seamlessly blended in with the underworld around her that she was labeled a "Top Performer".

Over several shifts, it was easier for Morgan to lose sight of why Chastity was created in the first place: to tell the story of a missing girl, to help find her, and to put all those responsible behind bars. With the data she'd collected here, the lawless depravity, she'd be able to have this building put out of commission. But where would that leave her investigation? Where would that leave Chrissy Donavon? No, Morgan would have to wait until she had every domino aligned before she could watch them fall.

One particular day, she was working the stage, looking for changes in the pattern, when she saw a man in an all-black suit, still with refractium gloves and mask, enter carrying a metal box. His movements were stiff and jerky, like he had worn-out joints. He was immediately met by Mordecai, who ushered him back to the office. After a few seconds, he left with his metal box. She took mental note of this stranger, especially since he was still wearing his fract underground.

Achieving the rank of Top Performer got her not one, but three sets on the ground floor stage as well as a dedicated cage above the DJ. According to Yessenia, if any other dancers were in there and she wanted to work "Too fucking bad". It made Morgan gleeful to know she was desired by nearly the entire underground Vampire community; it only further fueled the wicked urges she felt.

Tonight had been a usual shift for Chastity. After some time in the main cage, Morgan wandered the halls of the Belfry, observing the behavior of other staff members. Many dancers scowled at her sidelong. She knew she stirred things up in a bad way. It was now she regretted not being more low-profile. At least she used a fake name, unlike Chrissy. But Chrissy was still a kid at the end of the day. That fact caused a shiver to run up Morgan's spine.

On her route, she found the main office. Its door was left ajar. She pushed the door open more and saw it was empty.

Thinking quickly, she entered alone and shut it firmly behind her. The first thing Morgan tried was the closet that held her incriminating tape with Yess and Strix. She needed to get that back someday… or destroy it. The metal cabinet that contained the videos was locked up tight, and while Morgan was certain she could pop the lock with brute force, it would be too suspicious.

Next, she moved to the desk, the computer was simple, and slightly antiquated, with a solid blue background and dusty vents. Morgan noticed a black floppy disk half out of the tower. Curiously, she pushed it in. As soon as it loaded, a window with the words "Enter Password" appeared. Morgan, puzzled, tried to figure out what Yessenia would use as a password. So she tested a few.

TYRANTS REIGN

DENIED

HOMELAND

DENIED

Morgan looked for clues and saw a Dodger's baseball on the desk, raising a brow.

GODODGERS

Even still, DENIED.

"Shit." Morgan stood, crossing her arms in frustration. The sound of Yessenia's voice was swiftly followed by the door handle turning. Morgan moved to the couch, plopping down and acting relaxed.

"Yes, sir… if you'd want to come tonight you can have a sample," Yess said as she entered, talking into a flip phone, antenna extended. "Excellent, we'll be seeing you soon…"

She closed the phone and glared at Morgan, casually lounging in her office.

"The fuck are you doing in here?"

"Taking a break," Morgan said, "And the door was open."

"That's what the backrooms are for," Yessenia said, her vile grin unwavering. "Unless that's not all you're here for."

"You're right… I was feeling kinda lonely." Morgan sauntered up to her boss, playing with her short tie, prepared to roll with the punches again.

"Fuck it, I got time," Yessenia said, slamming and locking the door behind her.

*****

Back at the hallowed grounds of Apartment 161, Raphael sat alone in his poorly lit bedroom, the rain pattering against the window, *Alice In Chains* playing low on his boombox. He worked, hunched over an old artist's workbench, diligently going back and forth between pages of a textbook and his notes and documentation. The book itself was a snore to navigate. Raphie had a difficult time focusing. Especially given the task at hand, as a Jewish-Latino-American, he couldn't care less about the history of power struggles in Ile de Lenora *after* The Emergence.

He turned a page in his notebook, back to the drawing he was working on of Demy from that first night at the party, leaning against the wall, one foot up, watching out for her friends. She was smiling, as she often did. He always took the time to define her features with shading and felt it a crime to improperly portray her.

He looked up at the drawings visible above his desk, designs that he'd based on metal album covers and spiraling, eyeball nightmares that were his dream-inspired creations. He pushed them aside to reveal a drawing of Morgan. Picture-perfect. From her high cheeks to her wide smile to the relaxed way she sits. It was all there. He smiled and pulled out his recently finished work of Demy and pinned it beside Morgan. He let his doodles fall back into place to cover both girls, a secret he may not be particularly ashamed of having, but a secret still.

A knocking came from the front door. Raphie raised a brow, turned down his music, and stood from his desk, welcoming an excuse to escape the monotony of his homework. He spared a glance through the patio door. The gloomy sky had opened up, pouring down rain upon the thirsty California earth.

He pondered who he knew that would have traveled through this. Los Angelean roads aren't particularly well known for being their best during the rain. In particular, the rain that wasn't expected.

Raphie didn't bother to look through the peephole. They couldn't be worse than the homework, so he simply opened the door.

"Demytria?" He exclaimed, shocked to see the girl he'd become so infatuated with, drenched from head to toe. "You're soaking wet. You're gonna get sick! Come in and let's get you warm," Raphie belabored, knowing she wasn't wearing much to begin with under her weathered, albeit bulky, coat.

She didn't say a word but rather stood there, mouth hanging open and swaying aimlessly. Raphie's face contorted, and he went to speak again, stepping forward from behind the door, but before he could, Demy gripped the back of his head and neck and pulled him into a deep, passionate kiss. He held her hips and pulled her into the apartment, shutting the door behind them, their bodies pressed softly against one another. Raphie's worries melted the longer her lonely lips melded with his. He wanted to ask why she was here again, soaking wet and pale as an undead.

After losing time in a loving embrace, they finally broke off one another. "Okay… I'm really happy you're here. Like… fuck, dude," Raphie laughed, running his hand through his fluffed hair, showing off his cut jawline on accident. "But… what happened? Are you okay?"

"I don't know…" Demy said honestly, at last, turning her gaze to the floor in embarrassment, "Amy and I aren't a thing anymore, I guess? And maybe the whole Corvus Enclave? A lot is happening very fast, and I don't know how to deal with it and… I just want you to hold me… that's what I do know."

Raphie took Demy's hands; she was freezing, but her tremors were not shivers. She had a look in her eyes, the same he had in his when his blood was used in some sort of eldritch ritual, the effects of which he was still blind to. She was in shock, and she wasn't ready to speak about it.

"I can do that," he answered, curling her hand up into his. "You don't have to say shit… I won't ask. Just please: Come sit with me."

"Okay." She was on the verge of tears; she had not been so kindly treated by someone who knew so little of her. They'd hung out a handful of times… and yet he treated her with the same patience and kindness he did on the first day they met.

He led her into the living room, holding her hand the whole time. He grabbed a blanket draped on the side of the untouched lounge chair. "Seth can fucking sue me." He wrapped her in the wool Afghan, the fluffy cloth clinging to her wet body and giving immediate relief. For the first time since she arrived, she took a deep breath and stopped shaking.

"I'd like to get out of these clothes if that's possible," Demy said, her words floating like bubbles.

"Oh, right. Absolutely," Raphie said "Look, I'm sure Morgan wouldn't care if I lent you some of her clothes. Just like a t-shirt and sweats to get you dry. And you can change in the bathroom, right there."

"Actually," Demy glanced up, with wanting eyes. "I'd like to just go to your room… If that's okay."

"M-my room?" He stared through his cracked door, to the pit of despair that was his room, "Yeah, I mean, It's not picked up."

"I don't mind a messy room, Raphie…" Her voice was stressed and tired.

"Anything you need," he said, face stern, breath balanced. Wrapping his arm around Demy, he walked her to his room, opened the door, and guided her on a safe path to the bed. By the time he'd closed his bedroom door, making faces of celebratory disbelief, she had shed her boots, blanket, and jacket. She peeled the red velvet dress off her body and tossed it aside with her other articles.

Raphie approached the bed. He didn't seem so meek or bashful, radiating sex and confidence. She blushed at his presence, her body growing hotter the closer he was. Her eyes indulged in his visage, and he saw it: how tantalized she was. He bit his lip subtly, looking down at her voluptuous curves, clung to by scanty black underwear. All of her limbs, much of her neck, sides, and back were completely covered in tattoos.

Many took the form of mythic animals or symbols representing her faith. He placed his knee beside her on the bed's edge, just brushing against her stocking-clad thigh.

Her hands began to unfasten his belt.

Raphie gasped, his breath flimsy as if his heart faltered. Demy's hand reached into his pants and stroked him through his tightly fitted boxers. He had removed his packer once he was home alone, not that it would have impeded her anyway. She caressed his folds as he tried to undress. His wobbly movements were made more ungainly by her fingertips teasing his engorged phallus. After a moment, he noticed her hand was no longer petting him, both her hands now wandering up his hips. Even still, he felt his manhood massaged.

"H-how are you doing that??" He said, in no way protesting as frustrated little moans escaped his lips.

"Spirit Hand," she said smugly, "It's a form of telekinesis. Just a cantrip but very versatile."

"Feels more powerful than that," he groaned.

Demy chuckled and felt up under his shirt. Her eyes widened. A muscular abdomen was apparently not what she expected. Pleased, she pulled his shirt off. He was hesitant at first, but aided her after a second or two.

Abdomen, pelvis, pecs, all of it perfectly toned like Grecian armor. "Fuck," Demy choked again.

"Is it okay?" Raphie said, confidence dissolving as he spoke, hands partially covering two crescent scars under his pecs.

Demy had yet to notice them. When she did tilt her head up to see his concerned face, she still hardly noticed.

"Yes," biting her bottom lip, she leaned up to kiss him. His glower softened the longer she held him. "Make love to me."

"I think I can make that happen," Raphie smiled and let his hand slowly work back to the hem of her purposefully torn tights and tugged at them as he lowered himself to kiss her again.

She broke off their kiss only for a second to whisper, "Rip them."

He did so without hesitation, making her gasp again. His

zeal begot pleasant yips from her. Within a few seconds, he shredded through her tights and gently toyed with the strap of her panties.

Their lips grazed one another, giving each other clement kisses. Raphie traced her full thighs with his strong fingers. She arched her back and let out a soft whimper as just a small testament to her desire. He smirked.

Somehow, Raphie just knew when and where to touch his partners; all had been transformed into a squirming, mindless state by the end. He wove the strap of her panties into his fingers, her hands gripped his, but didn't stop him from sliding them down. They both blushed, though Raphie could not resist peeking. He leaned back as he pulled her elegant garment down her inked legs. Each limb was a tapestry, with a unique story, one Raphie was dying to learn.

She bit her knuckle, her breath labored as soon as she was exposed. He gave gentle pecks against her, his whiskers tickling her skin. The witch bit her finger harder as he peered up at her, locking gazes with her crystalline, impossibly turquoise eyes.

"Do you want more?" Raphie asked, both teasing and assuring, she enjoyed the moment as he predicted. "We move at your pace."

She nodded vigorously, "Please."

He failed to hide his smile at the desperation in her voice. Raphie lowered himself to her petals and gripped both sides of her hips. The moment he touched her, doused with excitement, she bucked again. He used as much of his strength as he could to keep her rump on the bed. Though when coupled with her sensual, ragged breath, he found her animated state invigorating. She gripped Raphie's head, her fist full of his long curls. She didn't attempt to control him in the slightest; rather, it seemed she just needed to grab hold of something as she cupped her breast with the other hand.

"You taste so sweet," Raphie gasped, planting abrupt and genial kisses on her soft belly, his hand taking the place of his lips. "Like an actual peach."

"Really?" Her face turned pink, her cheeks aglow like the setting sun.

"God yes," He said, tending to her with his hand. His fingers moved nimbly, mapping out every point of absolute pleasure just like his fingertips were at the frets of his guitar. "I can't believe no one's ever told you before."

He admired her naked body, taking time to observe each limb and the tapestries they presented. Her legs, both, were covered in waves of various shades of blue and grey, a sea serpent wrapped across her right leg. Upon closer inspection, Raphie noticed the grey on her left leg represented clouds, with various sea birds along their length, as well as lightning bolts that extended up to her side and reappeared on her right arm.

Flowers composed the sleeve of her left arm, eventually breaking to show mighty purple mountains, peaked with snow. Her right arm was the most intriguing, a plethora of roaring flames with a green wyvern locked in combat with a phoenix. So lost in her body art, he had almost missed Demy's climax.

Demy rambled curses, her eyes rolling back, her smokey painted lids fluttering. "Don't stop." She managed to say.

"Wouldn't dream of it, doll," Raphie replied, his hands bringing her to the brink of ecstasy.

Demy's magenta face was painted with an expression of satisfaction. She had shown up at his home unannounced and drenched from the rain. He took her in. He said nothing. He knew she needed the touch of someone warm and kind. She needed his touch. A person she could proudly call her boyfriend. Once he had pleased her fully, he spoke again.

"Demytria," Raphie said, his voice low and rumbling "You've become such light in my life. You make waking up in the morning worthwhile again."

"You're too kind," Demy said with a melancholy tone, tracing the lines of his midriff. "I don't know about being a light, though. I seem to feel pretty dim these days."

Raphael's hands moved to cup her cheek and caress it with his thumb. "Then let me return some of the light to you."

He leaned in, and she jumped up to meet him. They kissed passionately as the rain poured harder, ushered in by the cool night. Demy couldn't keep her hands to herself. They wanted one another more than either thought possible. They belonged together tonight. This was a fact in their minds.

"Please stay with me. It's already late and raining cats and dogs," Raphael said, breaking the kiss, a weak excuse to keep her in his arms.

"Will you promise me you'll do the same?" She said plainly, glancing out the window to the darkness enveloping the city.

"I'm not going anywhere, doll," Raphie smiled, stroking Demy's round, freckled cheek. "I promise."

6

In between her second and third sets, Morgan took up a spot in the dressing rooms on the second story. Her only real companion was Tabby, the buxom Catfolk veteran. She took more than one opportunity to bend her ear and get details on virtually any of the entertainers or staff. Some of the stories were so despicable that her stomach was put in knots. Thankfully, according to Tabby, the Belfry had become a "safer" place since Yessenia began running the show years ago. However, Tabby said she would prefer a different scent of candle in the VIP rooms.

Unfortunately, Tabby had a client. An unusual instance, as Morgan did not see her in the VIP rooms often. Perhaps it was that her rates were far higher than her own, causing Morgan to wonder if she should haggle for better pay. As she touched up her lipstick, she heard a bouncer talking with the Taknoling server at the opposite end of the room. She pretended not to listen and focused.

"You hear?" The man said, "The Moth has been seen scoping around T-Town."

Morgan knew too well who that was, and her skin froze.

"Yeah," the server said, unimpressed. "But Yess sent her running, unless she wants to fight all the Tyrants at once, she'd be better off looking elsewhere."

"What was she after anyway?"

"Don't know… Yess wouldn't say."

"Well… if it has anything to do with her derring-do bullshit then I don't want anything to do with it. I'm not paid enough to fight that monster."

Morgan felt a pang of anger hearing them talk so horridly about her aunt. Demonizing her, even if it was the gangster who was more terrified of Maxine. In all honesty, they should be afraid. Hell, Morgan was afraid of being found out by Aunt M. "*She'll find out eventually,*" Raphie had said. Morgan hoped he was wrong.

Startling her out of her eavesdropping and subsequent thoughts, Tabby plopped down hard in the seat beside her, entering from nowhere with feline grace.

"What's good, baby!?" Tabby snickered, clearly high.

"Not much, you?" Morgan answered honestly.

"You might wanna hear this," She said, leaning over and grinning, tail swishing behind her. "I just fucked the head of the Special Victims Task Force."

"You… what?"

"I fucked a top dog in the police force, a Detective Penelope Lan," Tabby said with a giggle "There's nothing more valuable than a pet piggy."

"Damn, good to know the cops are dirty too."

"It's less who it is and what I got from her in pillow talk," Tabby said, looking over her shoulder. "The task force…. They're aware of Chrissy… they think she's missing too."

"Fuck," Morgan played off, pretending to be ignorant "What else did she say?"

"That this place was off limits… Lan's not going to come back and is striking the Belfry from the records… part of some deal with Yessenia," Tabby went on. "I was a bargaining piece… which doesn't feel great, but at least the cops won't come around here anytime soon."

"Yeah, I suppose so." Morgan nodded, thinking about how deep the corruption ran in this city. "I just hope they actually try and find her still."

"So I've been meaning to ask," Morgan said, changing the subject but still inquiring, "You've been here years… why haven't you gotten the 'Top Performer' moniker? You're one of the best dancers I've ever seen."

"Well, I did… once," Tabby replied, endlessly adjusting her white bob wig. "But I backed out before long."

"Why?" Morgan turned to Tabby, her brow scrunched. "If I may ask."

"You may." Tabby took a deep breath and began, "Look, I don't wanna discourage you from your new spot because Top Performer is nothing to sneeze at. But I've seen what it takes to get that position, and what else it takes to maintain the status. I'm a lesbian; only ladies are allowed downstairs… and most men in here can't afford to change my mind. And I'm not gonna wait for a bouncer if a guy is too touchy for the price he paid." She flexed her arms and showed off her biceps. "That's why I carry guns."

Morgan giggled and nodded. "I respect you for having boundaries. Honestly, you're a hell of a strong woman. Even without your guns."

"I appreciate that," Tabby grinned, like Morgan, her canines were also fanged and sharp. "I respect the hell out of you not having any. You call me strong, but you must have so much understanding of self-worth that, I'm not gonna front, I'm a bit jealous."

"Shut. *Up.*" Morgan said, brushing her hair behind her ear.

"Hell naw! You're amazing out there! You're an inspiration to all of us."

"Thanks!" Morgan beamed.

"You're welcome, baby… just promise me you'll watch yourself… Top Performer unlocks a shit ton of doors. Just don't go through them all. 'Kay?"

"I think I understand," Morgan said, her face austere. She looked up at the collection of Polaroids and saw Chrissy's sweet, round face. Morgan was so close she could taste it.

"Let's take one. I wanna get a memory of you," Tabby said, pulling out a Polaroid camera. She leaned into Morgan and turned the camera backward. "Say: 'Skank!'"

"Skaaank."

The camera flashed and spat out the white photograph. Tabby immediately took it and shook it. The image soon became visible; they appeared as if they were in the middle of a genuine laugh. Tabby taped the still-developing photo on the mirror.

"That's a keeper," she said.

"Hey," Morgan asked, suddenly becoming coy. "Is there any way I could get more of… that stuff?"

"Stuff?" Tabby blinked confusedly. "Oh, the coke? Yeah sure, I can hook you up with some."

Morgan's grin became wide. Before either could say something else, Yessenia herself propped open the door and leaned against it.

"Chastity," she said coldly, her dark grin missing from her pallid face. "A word."

"Good luck, baby. I'm sure you're fine…" Tabby said with a smile, before turning to her boss. "Yess."

"Tabby," Yessenia gave a nod and a smirk to her veteran entertainer. Morgan walked up to her boss and followed the Vampire woman to the very same catwalk she had stood up on that first night. The lights flickered, splashing them both with strobes of white before shifting into a sequence of bright colors, then back again. Yessenia, holding a Real Bloody Mary, leaned over the banister toward the backside of the building, away from the main stage. The lights washed over her grim stature like a foreboding omen.

"Is everything okay, boss?" Morgan fought to be heard over the roaring music; even still, she sounded nervous.

Yess pointed out into the crowd, along the back wall, the curtained-off VIP tables were visible. Within, a man sat at the center of the space. His skin was a deep umber and wasn't washed out like a Vampire, so maybe a Human, as they sometimes dared to enter.

"You see that rich dude sandwiched in between the dancers?" Yessenia pointed out into the crowd

"Yes."

"He's a high roller. I put in a good word," Yessenia reached into her coat pocket and pulled out a small letter, sealed with wax, bearing a symbol of intertwined snakes. On the other side, the name 'Chastity Vaughn' was penned artistically. "He liked what he saw."

Yessenia turned back and smirked at Morgan, who, in turn, looked to her feet. Yessenia rolled her eyes and returned to watching the floor. She swirled her copper-tasting drink and took a sip while Morgan opened the letter and scanned it.

"This is an invitation," Morgan stated.

"No shit, Sherlock."

"But to what?"

"I don't know… that's for your eyes only," Yessenia said, turning around and taking another drink. "If you're smart, you'll hide that. Some of the others might get jealous even if you have Tabby in your corner."

Morgan looked down at the letter, folding it up tightly and putting it in the tip purse on her thigh. As she did, she peeled a chunk of the wax off and observed the now broken symbol. She cursed herself for not waiting to identify it better.

"So… ya gonna go?" Yess raised her brow in inquiry.

*****

"So… are you gonna go?" Raphael said, keeping pace beside Morgan as they walked down the streets of Studio City.

"I don't know yet," Morgan held a crate of four cups of coffee, watching the steam escape into the cool autumn air. Raphie had offered to come down and meet her for coffee since they'd hardly spoken since her 'second job' began. He didn't want their time together to end and offered to walk her to work. Regardless, he was already awake, the usual insomnia.

Raphie flashed her concerned looks as she spoke about her exploits. She was proud of how much she'd learned; it was plain to see. Raphael would never lecture her… though he would be honest if he felt she was being particularly foolish. *You need to tell someone,* he thought. *Someone who can help before you get too deep.*

She was dressed slick, as she always did for her internship. Black on black skirt, top, and suit jacket. Her legs made a deep chocolate brown by her opaque stockings, held up by a garter that could occasionally be seen through the small slit in her skirt when she walked; Raphie paid notice. Her solid white, square purse hung by a narrow strap on her shoulder.

Raphie was the opposite, dressed down in another bulky, flannel jacket with a hood over his *Fleetwood Mac* tee. He held his piping hot tea by its protective sleeve, sipping it as he walked. He kept his eye on his black Converse and tried to stay slightly ahead of or beside her, to avoid glancing at her body again.

"I should show you the letter, Raph," Morgan continued. "It's hella bureaucratic. You'd think it was, like, an invitation to the White House, not some rando's penthouse in Beverly Hills. It's all, 'We cordially invite you…' blah-die-fuckin'-blah. It says to dress professionally but also to 'consider my choice of undergarments.'"

"Heh, like what you're wearing but with a racy bra?" Raphie chuckled.

"Basically? I don't wanna like, show up in a cocktail dress either, … these people are the real deal. Thcy may be the ones responsible for Chrissy's disappearance." Morgan looked onward, determined. Raphie skewed his mouth and shook his head slightly.

"Does that mean you're actually going?" Raphie asked, the weight of worry in his words.

"I feel like I should. I've had to boink way too many dudes for it not to be worth it." Morgan laughed nervously, looking onward, avoiding eye contact with Raphie. He was genuinely afraid for her, and he made that clear. She may be a Vampire, but she's still just one woman, not that that ever stopped her before. "I'm really glad I can talk to you about this stuff, Raph. I can't quite put into words how heavily this has been weighing down on me, and you just being there has lifted so much of it, you don't even know."

"I'm glad I can be there for you," he said with a wavering smile. "I just wish you'd let me help."

"I know you're worried about me," she stated. "About my relationship with Balam and how that will affect us. About me and what could happen to me—"

"Yeah," Raphie interrupted with a skeptical laugh, "You go out almost every night and put yourself out there, that's one thing. But, dude, you're following the same path as a *missing* girl. You do know that, right? You know you could be fucking murdered or worse, right?"

"Yes, I fucking know," Morgan sighed, annoyed.

They turned the corner and into the sunlight. Morgan shielded her eyes with her hand, even Trueborn were sensitive to direct sunlight. The polygonal Cryptid Chronicle building came into view. Swirling, metal sculptures divided its front steps like a floating school of eels. He only had a few minutes more with his best friend, and right now, he was her only foundation.

"You know I can't go to Balam with this…" She sighed. "Any of it. Not only would he fail to understand the purpose of all this, but I can't trust he won't try to go to the police. That could jeopardize everything I worked toward. Plus, he'd think I'm some filthy hooker looking to cheat and I just can't handle the judgment."

"Are you sure that's how he'll react?" He said, skewing his face.

"It's not like he hasn't accused me of cheating before," she said, shaking her head.

"Well, haven't you?" He asked.

She remained silent.

"Haven't you?"

"Before this? No… but I thought about it," Morgan said honestly. "Not infrequently…"

"Blondie…" Raphie wanted to say more but he was speechless. He desperately wanted to make her feel secure, but he could also see clearly she was headed down a dark path.

"What?" She asked.

"Nothing… It's honestly nothing."

Morgan stopped just short of the Chronicle property, behind the smooth, concrete wall just before the steps. She turned, rested on the heel of her Mary Janes, and shifted her weight to her other foot.

"Thank you for keeping my secret," She looked up at him. Her pink diamond-like eyes glimmered in the light. "I know this can't be easy for you. I honestly don't know what I'm doing, but I'm doing it well… I'm hot on Chrissy's trail. I can feel it in my undead bones."

"You're welcome…" He squeaked, stunned by her beauty, as he always was. He cleared his throat and spoke again. "You deserve someone who cares, but I'm not going to control your life. And you're right… It's been rough. For the love of God, just please promise you'll page me if anything goes sour… fuck, I don't care how but I *will* be there."

"I promise," Morgan said, flashing him her fangs happily. "You're the best friend a girl could ask for. Other than M, you're my only family."

He wrapped his arms around her and took a deep breath as she did the same, resting her head on his shoulder. The facade broke as she started to whimper. It only took a matter of seconds for her to begin breathing deeply, counting backward from ten. "Deep breaths, Blondie… you got this."

"You're right," She said, lifting her head and squaring her shoulders. "I got this. Have a good day, Raph… be safe."

"Later," he replied. Morgan left his arms and climbed the steps to her place of work. He watched her and grimaced.

Be safe yourself, Blondie.

Fiddling with her purse and the coffees for her superiors, Morgan took a moment to scale the stairs, giving Raphie time to walk away and escape from earshot. But Morgan's ears were preternaturally gifted. She wouldn't be able to miss the sounds of conflict coming from across the street. She turned slowly to see the source of the commotion. Her heart sank, seeing that same Vampire from before, dressed professionally in a pantsuit, puff tie, and set of refractium. Morgan had found out her name, but still hadn't spoken: Victoria. Surrounding her were the very same thugs that harassed her and Morgan before.

Morgan took no time to wait and put the coffees at the base

of the eel-like statues. Marching across the street without care for traffic, Morgan could hear the words being said.

"I told you this area wasn't safe, biter." The grubby, scruffy man who seemed to be the ring leader spoke, his tone grim.

"I work here!" she argued. "You can't stop me from going to my job, prick."

"Oh, I'm a prick?" he cackled, approaching her closer. "Me and the boys oughta show you a prick."

"HEY!" Morgan shouted, striding up the sidewalk. "What the fuck are you doing to her?"

"We're just talking," one of the other men said, also Human.

"Yeah, little mama, nothing that concerns you. This is between us and the fangs," the ring leader said, brushing his fingers on Victoria's refractium-covered face. She shuddered and reeled back.

Morgan wasted no more time and bared her fangs. With a guttural hiss, she revealed her more animalistic side, her eyes darkening and her razor-sharp canines and incisors on full display.

"You think you can fuck with two Vampires?" She growled, "You wanna go today, little boy?"

The man reeled back as did his friends. Quickly, Victoria moved to stand beside Morgan, taking a boxer's stance.

"Come on, man, let's go…." one of the others said, a Dwarf who looked rather timid. "People are watching…"

"Fine… but this ain't over…" the ringleader said, turning away to take his posse with him. "Come on, let's bounce."

Once they were clear, Morgan stopped baring her fangs and took a deep breath, her eyes returning more to their soft pink color. She turned to Victoria and reached out a hand. "Are you okay?"

"Yeah… I'll be fine," she replied, futzing with her collar and tie. There was a certain terror still present in her voice.

"I'm so sorry… I know how guys like that can be," Morgan sympathized.

"Do you, Morgan?" Victoria replied, her tone shifting, looking Morgan in the eye behind her faceless mask, a distorted reflection of herself present in the refractium. "Do you really?

Because you've never had to wear this a day in your life."

She tugged at her gloves and snapped them against her wrist. Morgan was stunned, realizing that this Vampiress knew who she was as well; the accusations she was flinging were a shock to Morgan's senses.

"I-I-I just—"

"You don't wear a neon sign that says you're a Vampire… you can pretend to be Human all day long…"

With that, the woman stomped off, headed to the Chronicle. Morgan was left stunned, paralyzed. She had never been so blatantly told her privileges like that. Was she aware of them, yes, but to be told she's never known prejudice was asinine. Even still… she had a point, and that hurt Morgan's cold heart. She returned to the steps, grabbed the coffees, and with a sigh, continued about her day as best she could.

Balancing her bags and the drinks like a waitress, Morgan struggled as she entered the Chronicle. She needed to have her draft of the latest assignment ready to submit "the moment she walked in". It was a new project, something she was tasked with when she was here two days prior. It was a short one, a few paragraphs, and a photo of a local Cryptid from South Central named Teacher of the Year. Being cloudy-headed of late, she'd forgotten to have it stapled. Also still mixed in were her personal notes: various scribblings about the Donavon case not yet ready to present to Harding.

Caught up in the adrenaline of what had just transpired, Morgan didn't see her boss dashing by. The two collided with force, and Morgan's face pushed hard into his chest. The coffees were smacked from her hand by his and poured down the side of his blue dress shirt. Papers, both his and hers, scattered about the steps of the entryway. A few unfortunate ones landed in the puddle of spilled drink.

"Motherfucker…" He said in a scolding tone as his torso was drenched in piping hot beverage. "Thanks for the morning coffee."

"I'm so sorry, Mr. Harding. Oh my gods, I'm sorry." She immediately dove down, squatting and trying to reach about her feet to pick up the mess. In hysterics, Morgan tried her best to gather the documents before the paper soaked up the liquid.

“*90210*, how do you manage to fuck up going and getting coffee?” he blustered, letting his sleeve drip. “It’s not that fucking hard. I’ve seen teenage, disabled, high school dropouts working at McDonald’s with more skill and coordination. You’d best get your shit together, or else thank you’re lucky stars you got a pretty face 'cause right now that’s all you’ve got going for you.”

“I’m so sorry, Mr. Harding,” she repeated, her voice breaking and her saffron eyes weltering with tears. Her composure completely faltered upon noticing some of his documents were ruined. “I-I wasn’t paying attention. I’m so sorry.”

He inhaled heavily and sighed. He rubbed his forehead just above his brow as he watched her tears fall.

“Jesus Christ, don’t… stop that.” His tone changed, still gravelly and low, like he was forcing every word out. “It was… an accident… just watch where you’re fucking going coming in hot like that.”

“W-what?” She said, gazing up at him.

“Take those ruined drafts down to the print and get me fresh copies,” he said with a sigh. “I’m gonna go to the Lacoste across the street real quick.”

“Thank you, Mr. Harding,” she sheepishly avoided eye contact with the Orc so he couldn't see her few tears. “I’ve had a hard week so far… thank you.”

“Yeah, whatever… don’t mention it.” He gave an awkward smile, untucked his shirt, a few inches of green skin appearing for a moment, and headed out the door.

She took a deep breath and felt a weight had been lifted off her chest. Either Harding was feeling generous or the gods were actually smiling upon her; not that she believed in the gods. No matter, she was grateful to have just a moment of reprieve.

“Damn, you dodged a bullet,” Eliza said from the other side of the railing, just a few feet below. “I’m not looking up your skirt, I promise.”

Morgan rolled her eyes. She was certain Eliza was being honest, but she still kept her knees together. “Hey, Eliza… how ya been?”

"How've *you* been?" Eliza redirected, "You still following that Cristine Dogerman story?"

"I'm holding it together," Morgan grimaced. "And yes, I'm still looking for *Chrissy Donavon*; no one else is searching. Hell, even the LAPD task force got bribed to avoid her place of work. It's a shit show… someone needs to find her."

"And you're that someone? I get you're worried, but you sound like you're getting into some dangerous waters, girlie," Eliza said, scrunching her forehead. "Look, I heard you gotta go downstairs, so just hand me the draft and I'll finalize it for you."

"You'd do that?" Morgan said, mistrusting the kindness shown.

"Yeah, girlie, we're in this together."

"Thanks, Eliza," Morgan said, handing her a stack of loosely assembled papers, ignorant to the investigation notes among them. "You have no idea how much this helps."

7

Driving past luxury shops, silver hydrants, and beach-bronzed beauties, Morgan felt extremely out of place. She wasn't poor but felt like a pauper every time she came to Beverly Hills. Everything was lavish, big, bright, and extra. One building, in particular, the Babylon Tower, gave off more than a sense of superiority; the building seemed to breathe with an unearthly life. From its balconies to the steps out front, all were sculpted with excruciating detail, forming swirling patterns that gave the illusion of a liquid state.

Rather than gargoyles, avian reptiles framed the trim of the building. Morgan was sure this was merely her imagination, having never seen one move, but she was certain their positions had shifted when she wasn't looking. She watched them as she pulled up to the curbside valet. An Elvish boy was there, dressed as a forties bellhop. Luckily for him, the weather had cooled lately.

The taxi parked in front of the dark, Art Deco building.

Morgan looked up from her seat, the structure stretching almost out of sight. Every foot of the building seemed to have an ornate carving or sculpture. The valet stood with his hands folded, a placid smile painted on his ruddy face. He opened the door for Morgan as she scrounged for her wallet in her unstructured purse. Before she could, the driver was handed a small fold of bills.

"Keep the change," the valet instructed, placing his hand out for Morgan to exit. Leading with her long, stocking-clad legs, Morgan stepped onto the curb and rose, standing a few inches taller than the boy. "Head on up, miss. Ms. Abaddon should be there to greet you."

She nodded, pulled her overcoat tight, and ascended the stairs. Beneath, she wore a similar outfit to that morning, though she opted to change a few pieces to be more appealing: a tighter jacket, a set of gossamer black lingerie, and her taller, ankle-strap heels. She let her hair down, having curled it. She took twice as long on her makeup, springing for a more upscale sculpted look rather than the outlandish punk getup she normally donned as Chastity. Tonight, Chastity was more than just a stripper with a naughty streak. She was a high-class escort in Beverly Hills. Beyond that, she was the key to unlocking the next major portion of the mystery of Chrissy Donavon.

After scaling the steps imprinted with spirals, she gripped the solid gold handle and pulled open one of the enormous glass doors. Once passed the massive, dark-tinted doors, Morgan became awestruck by the amazing marble architecture. The lobby was as monumental as its entrance, an antique chandelier hanging from the ceiling like a crystal waterfall. The walls were a dark green marble, the floors off-white. Pillars that spanned the full three-story height of the lobby flanked the entryway, leading to the stairs covered with wine-red carpet. Morgan walked between them, dwarfed by their size. She looked at the bases of the plaster beams, each unique and oddly disturbing, featuring anguished faces, sharp teeth, and murderous eyes in most of the designs.

She was alone in the massive lobby. No security. No janitors. No cameras. No *sound*. If she didn't know better,

Morgan would assume the building was empty.

"Sure is lax security for the Ritz," Morgan thought aloud, strolling her way closer to the ornate stairs. She had not made it far into the entrance before the second pair of high heels on granite echoed throughout the empty building.

"Salut," a woman's voice said, approaching her flank. Morgan whipped her head around to see no one, only to be ambushed from the other side. "You must be Ms. Vaughn. We've been expecting you."

Morgan pivoted on her heel, facing a Domhainn woman with skin like distant storm clouds, her body poured into a black, high-low dress that left one of her legs exposed; her torso was decorated with sequins and beading. She was, in a word, gorgeous, with eyes like golden rings, her hair long, white, and carefully groomed. Morgan felt stunned, unable to speak. Perhaps it was the way this woman approached but something about her felt unnatural.

"Y-yes, I am. I'm M— Miss Chastity. Chastity Vaughn. It's a pleasure t-to meet you. I'm really excited to be here—" Morgan began gushing, a habit common to her character of Chastity. Already, she was silenced.

"Save it for Master," the Domhainn spoke, looking Morgan up and down, "Play your cards right and he might be your master, too. My name is Theodora Abaddon. That's Mistress Abaddon, or Madam to you."

Something about the way Abaddon carried herself made her uneasy. She felt a similar way when Yessenia first hired her, like they were carnivorous predators eyeing prey.

"Of course," Morgan gave an obedient nod.

"Come. The party is beginning upstairs. Most of the guests have already arrived." Theodora made her way to the elevator, beckoning Morgan to follow with a ringed finger.

After a silent ride in the elevator, Morgan and Theodora were brought to the penthouse floor. In the elegant lines of sixteen buttons, Morgan stared down— one seemed to be missing, something Morgan didn't expect in Beverly Hills. The doors split open, and immediately the smell of wine and spices filled the chamber. Swimming in the warm air of the floor,

Morgan felt entranced by the aroma. Music, jazz, low and mellow, echoed through the corridors.

"Stay close," Theodora barked, "You can easily get lost on these floors."

"Yes, Madam," Morgan took an opportunity to make a confused and apathetic face when Theodora wasn't looking. Morgan had to play along. For now.

The sound of music became louder as the aromas became stronger. Morgan smiled, hearing the pleasant sounds of party conversation layered with giggling women. Just shy of approaching, a set of gaudy doors propped open, and the two took a hard right into a quaint, minimalistic room with three lush chairs and a small table equidistant to them all. The walls were bare, with no windows or art, merely another door in the opposite corner. Morgan mused at the possibilities of what was behind it.

"Wait here and have a seat. Leave your coat and your bag in here," Theodora said, still holding the doorknob in her hand. "Do you like wine?"

She'd never drunk wine and was honestly just desperate to stop being so damn shaky. She gave an awkward smile. "Yes?"

"Red or white?"

"What?"

"Rosé it is." Theodora rolled her eyes and slammed the door.

Once she was alone, she truly felt the stress. But she wasn't willing to fuck tonight up under any circumstances. She reached into her bag and pulled out a gold, disk-like pill container with a green dragon painted on the top. She opened it, collected an amount of the powder with her nail, and placed it under her nose. With a strong draw, it was inhaled, and an almost orgasmic wave rolled over her. She let out a heavy sigh and closed the container, focused and ready with a smug smile.

Morgan sat, swaying her head to the muffled sound of music. She did not care for the cramped room she was dumped in. She walked over to the second door and gave it a rattle, but to no avail. With a mumbled curse, she began pacing. Without a window, Morgan felt like she was being slowly choked.

Plopping back down in a different chair, she proceeded to drum her own tune on her lap.

Amongst her rhythmic tapping, she missed the door behind her crack open. When she did her next anxious scan of the space, she froze, staring into the darkness on the other side of the door. She felt the insatiable urge to go investigate, but the knob on the door to the hall turned. Morgan faced it, expecting to see Theodora enter, but instead saw a goliath of a Human, shirtless in stark white pants and a kimono. She recognized him as the man she had seen at the Belfry. He was otherworldly, his body like sardonyx and just as chiseled. And yet, she felt most drawn to his eyes, like blue moons, sparkling in the softly lit room.

In one hand he balanced two glasses of wine in his fingers, one red and one pink. As he entered, Theodora came into view from behind him, she now possessed a clipboard and fountain pen. Morgan raised a brow as Theodora crossed opposite the tall, dark, and handsome stranger.

"Hello, you must be Ms. Vaughn," He said with a warm, friendly smile, perfect teeth behind full lips. "My assistant Ms. Abaddon told me you did not have a wine preference. I brought both of my favorite red and rosé, feel free to try either." He placed both down on the table before her.

"Th-thank you," She said apprehensively, reaching for the red regardless of her gut instinct.

"I am dreadfully sorry, where are my manners?" the stranger said. "My name is Dorian Ziusudra. Though I am not particularly fond of people using it."

"So what should I call you instead?" Morgan leaned in.

"Time will tell, my dear," he turned to Theodora and nodded. She stepped forward and handed the clipboard to Morgan, a thick stack of legal-looking papers bound together was attached. "I want to be formal with you, the best I can. Though forgive me if I falter momentarily here and there. I knew you were beautiful, but I was not imagining you would be so breathtaking up close."

"Oh my gods, thank you so much," Morgan gave him a grin, looking away as her cheeks flushed.

“Gods have nothing to do with it, Ms. Vaughn. Through the Lounge, people are the masters of their own destinies. Firstly, may I call you Chastity?” He said, widening his beguiling smile. Morgan couldn’t place his accent, but it was intoxicating and charming all the same.

“Yes, sir,” She said, catching on quickly.

“Splendid,” he glanced up at Theodora, who was tapping her wrist, imitating a watch. “Alright, let us get to it then. My parties are… exceptional to say the least. However, I do not achieve them by cutting corners. No. I want *everyone* to have the best possible experience by making sure everything involved is 100% consensual ahead of time. I have had Ms. Abaddon draft for me what you could expect to experience.”

Morgan looked at the well-written documents, each defining sexual acts in clinical and graphic detail. “Could I quickly read some of this? Promise, I’m a fast reader.”

“Naturally, Chastity,” He said with a nod, Theodora shaking her head and tapping her wrist more vigorously. “Your comfort is just as much my concern as my guests’. I mean, for all intents and purposes, you are also a guest. If you need anything, let any one of our staff know and we will take care of you. It is worth noting that security is always wearing brass masks, so you will be able to find them.”

Scanning for any signs of shady dealings, Morgan’s eyes darted from page to page. She quickly absorbed all she could. It was filthy, but it seemed perfectly legit. A simple contract stating if she finds tonight suitable for her tastes, she’ll be locked into five more parties; otherwise, there is no obligation to continue. With these parties came access to ‘Lounge Facilities’ and ‘rights by proxy’, similar to a rank within the club known as the Middle Echelon. Even a safe word system was built in, one that resembled a traffic light. Morgan was handed the pen. Close to the end, she noticed a section of blank lines.

“What’s this for?” She asked.

“That is for you,” Ziusudra replied. “Write down anything you are not comfortable with, and we will respect your boundary. Likewise, on one of the later pages, you can add something you would like to experience if you did not see it in the document.”

“Thank you… okay…” Morgan said, feeling suddenly overwhelmed. She was not kinky, at least not to the extent of what she was seeing. Bondage, whips, electricity, sex auction… it all was new to her, frightening her in the way that a rollercoaster would— encased in excitement. She got to work writing things she’d heard of that she knew she wouldn’t like, fisting of any kind the first. The second was no vomit or similar nastiness. She did make a note later that she was fine being bitten and biting undead. She now noticed the dotted line labeled “Signature.”

“Alright, Chastity,” Ziusudra said, his voice like a thunderstorm. “All we need to get started is your printed name and John Hancock. Chastity is your legal name, correct?”

“Yeah, of course,” Morgan lied reflexively.

“I love it,” he grinned again at her sassy response. “So if everything seems in order… would you kindly sign? Then we can begin to take care of you in earnest. Including a handsome financial compensation, if your performance is as my dear friend, Yessenia, described.”

Morgan clutched the antique-looking pen, finely polished but lovingly used. Her hand was frozen. This was leagues away from just dancing at the club and giving a backroom blow job. This was advanced S&M that she was willing to try, but had never experienced before. She had hoped to try it with Balam… *Balam*. His name still held her back, like a thread bearing a mountain climber. Sex with him had become less involved. Even as hard as she tried, he just seemed… checked out. But still, she hesitated. She could tell by the stillness of the room that Ziusudra and Theodora were boring eyes into her. She had to make a choice.

The tip of the pen glided across the document, signing in elegant cursive “Chastity Vaughn.” Beside it, she penned a fake birth date, and then the current date: October 13th, 1996. With a pearly smile, Ziusudra reached down and took the clipboard from her. Morgan immediately began drinking her wine, finishing half the glass in one go. Theodora seemed to find this mildly amusing.

“Excellent,” He said, handing the clipboard to his assistant and turning to speak to her. “I do not see why we cannot have her begin now, right, Ms. Abaddon?"

"Oui," the Domhainn replied.

"Are you ready, Chastity?" he held out his large, strong hand, hers dainty against his palms.

She looked up at him, admiring his physique. So eager was she to learn what was planned for her that her body had already begun to burn from the anticipation. "Born ready."

8

Just across from where Morgan was waiting was a room full of some of the most powerful individuals in all of LA. They congregated around the open space, scattered among a full wooden bar and multiple seating areas composed of pristine antique furniture. Women and men clothed only in collars, bow ties, and form-fitting undergarments paraded around serving each of the formally dressed patrons. Along the walls, Ziusudra's security watched unmoving, men in solid black suits and brass masks like human faces over refractium hoods, encasing their entire heads. No two masks were alike, some with sculpted-on beards and braided hair, others with scars and pits. Some with mouths, some without. Each possessed empty, shadowy eyes; the most unnerving detail by far.

Immediately, Morgan felt under-dressed, feeling more stripper-ish than she was intending. Though she asked Mr. Ziusudra if she should change, he informed her that the people she'd be entertaining were high-profile leaders: CEOs, TV executives, music producers. They would, quote, "prefer a girl that is dressed like the ones that work under them." What that statement implied made her queasy.

She found it both exciting and intriguing that so many women were guests. She had anticipated a sort of gentleman's club, but this group seemed to be highly inclusive; a good mix of Elves, Taknolings, and Orcs among the varieties she saw. It made her feel safer that so many Non-Humans were here. What removed that ease was that many of them hid their faces.

Their visages were half covered by elaborately designed masks of velvet or opaque silk. Morgan tried not to stare too long at anyone, though she eventually started gathering a few stray looks.

Morgan was taken off to the side near the bar, several of the patrons eying her as she walked by. Her blood began to rush, and the raw thrill started to envelop her. A smirk curled across her deep red lips, her fangs peeking out like the garter behind her skirt. She loved this, there was no denying it.

After taking up residence in a booth in the far corner, she took a chance to observe the room itself. Much like the rest of the building, it was carved and painted meticulously. Crystal lamp sconces hung from the walls, looking like transparent willows. Pillars and molding ran every edge, corner, and door frame the room had to offer. The ceiling was vaulted and painted a dark green, much like the exterior of the building. At the center, the highest point, a single chain, moderately thick, dangled down to the floor level. Her eyes followed it to see what appeared to be a set of manacles hanging from the end. Beneath was a rotunda stage, large enough to perform. Morgan had become familiar with these.

Strangely, to Morgan, the opposite end of the room was raised and possessed a railing, like a regal balcony. Ziusudra had been making his way to that end of the room, mingling with all his guests as he did. Once he took his position, he took a fork and clanked it against his wine glass. The attention of the room was immediately on him. Even Morgan, who was already facing that direction, was not as attentive. Yet another peculiar factor of this group.

"Sha hatti darisam, my good friends," he spoke up.

"Sha hatti darisam," the group echoed. Morgan seemed to be the only one who didn't. There was nothing like this in the agreement.

"To my old friends," Ziusudra began, his charismatic presence demanding attention, "Welcome back. To those who have only reached the Upper Echelon this evening. To you I say, welcome to the most exclusive decadence you will ever find. Now your tenure at the Lounge shall expand. Through us you will find power, you will find strength, and you will find eternal happiness… Let us join one another in a silent prayer to begin our evening."

This wasn't in the agreement either. Everyone hung their heads and closed their eyes, save the stoic guards. She awkwardly did the same, not praying but merely waiting. After a few seconds of the crushing silence, she opened her eyes, only to see two of the masked guards staring directly at her. She shut her eyes and waited for Ziusudra to speak again.

"Excellent. Without further ado, let us begin," Ziusudra said, an amenable smile on his face. "Tonight we have a very special addition to our company."

He outstretched his hand and gestured to Morgan across the way, all turning to her as he continued to speak. As everyone stared, Theodora strode gracefully toward Morgan. "It is my utmost pleasure to introduce you to Miss Chastity Vaughn. Let us toast in her honor, shall we? After all, she is our center stage act."

By the time he had raised his glass, Theodora was beside her. All raised their glasses in unison, calling her false name and drinking to it.

"It's time," the Domhainn said, taking Morgan by the hand rather firmly. Morgan slid out of the bench and promptly followed along, being brought to the stage at the room's center. She could see the eyes of those beside the stage undressing her. She smiled at a few of them; they remained expressionless.

In the space just beneath Ziusudra, was a collection of black chests, sealed tightly. Between the chains, the crowd, and the boxes she knew they were going to most likely take full advantage of what she signed off on. For a split second, she doubted her thoroughness in reading the forms.

"It appears before we have even begun, we have a bid for her to undress," Ziusudra grinned, taking a money clip from a gentleman near him. "Well, to get things moving, allow me to explain how this all works. If you want to see something happen or you want to bid on an act, approach either me or the lovely Ms. Abaddon. If there is an act in place, you have to outspend the previous bid by $100. Pricing is available at the bar. Charles here has already paid to see Ms. Vaughn undressed down to her delicates. Chastity, please satisfy my friend."

The Orcish man leaned over the banister and watched with thirsty eyes. She glanced up at the older gentleman, her roseate eyes locking with his. She smiled and gripped the lapels just above her button, tugging them down slightly. She bent over, granting people on the floor level a better view of her tightly pressed-together cleavage. A few stirred, growing just as excited as she was.

After a few seconds, she undid the first button and began to saunter across the room. Her hips swayed as she climbed the steps to the center stage. Her fingers sensually traced her body, right hand finding the zipper of her mini-skirt. The small round garment fell to her feet and she walked out of it with grace, not so much as breaking stride. She unbuttoned her blazer the rest of the way, tossing it up onto the "balcony". The Orc named Charles caught it.

Morgan didn't waste as much time with her top, pulling it open with force. Every button popped off and bounced onto the floor below the stage, revealing her lacy bra, as well as giving a better view of her matching panties and garter belt. She had barely gotten done revealing herself when Ziusudra called again.

"Alright! Looks like we have $300 to see Ms. Vaughn in chains," he said with a chuckle

But I just got started. She thought, used to much more showmanship on a stage. The moment her ruined blouse left her hands, two male servants had marched up, gripping her wrists. Her eyes widened, looking down at Theodora for guidance, only to see it was Theodora instructing them. She was roughly shackled, her arms hanging close together above her head. She watched them lock her in before lowering her eyes back to the crowd. Theodora, among them, licked her lips and laughed to herself. A Taknoling woman with a black bob haircut, a red dress, and a matching mask, approached Theodora and handed her a small fold of bills.

"Another $250 for the spreader," she said counting the money and putting it in her bra. She waved her fingers and one of the men moved to the leftmost case. Opening it revealed the expansive contents, with multiple layers of smaller toys and equipment. Within, they retrieved a matte black, steel bar with a manacle on each end.

Morgan shuddered, looking up to see Ziusudra watching her with admiration. He raised his wine glass to her, the yellowish, clear liquid swirling. His eyes taunted her, in this position, he could perform any perverted act he could imagine. Most of it she had just signed up for. But something told her that he got off on merely being a puppet master.

As her ankles became clamped and spread apart past her shoulders, she gave a desperate whimper, drowned out almost immediately by the laughter of the onlookers. She felt humiliated, her body half-naked and chained up before several dozen of the most powerful people in all of LA.

"100 for the blindfold," Theodora said from behind her, making her rounds.

Morgan gasped; she feared the possibility of having another panic attack by having her eyesight robbed from her. She watched in fear as the Elven man who helped shackle her wrapped a black blindfold around her eyes, the soft velvet pressed gingerly to her lids, and tied snugly about her head.

The sounds of glasses clinking in celebration and the secretive giggling became all she could hear. Still, she was desperate to focus on the next purchase. She blushed so brightly her cheeks burned, her reflexive breath sporadic and labored already. She tried to regain control of her lungs, but between the mocking voices and blindfold, she couldn't catch her breath if she tried.

"500 for a lashing," Ziusudra's tone was like a kid on Christmas. Morgan whimpered again.

"Ooh are we scared, bitch? I think you like this, don't you? You're just shaking with arousal already, you pitiful little tart," Theodora had whispered in her ear. Somehow, she never heard her approach. "Don't you dare come until they've paid you to. Do you understand me?"

"Y-yes," Morgan stammered out.

Sudden and sharp was a firm strike across Morgan's cheek; she yelped and sputtered.

"Yes, what!?" Theodora barked.

"Y-yes, m-madam…"

“Good,” Theodora struck and gripped Morgan's buttock tightly as her servants fetched a short lash with a leather-bound handle. “You and I are going to become very well acquainted, slut.”

As soon as the flogger was in Theodora’s hands, she had struck Morgan across her back. Barely before she’d let out a cry of pain, another crack snapped against her skin. It felt like the spots struck were set aflame by the contact, leaving streaks of burnt flesh. She felt tears pooling in her eyes and dampening the blindfold; the pain was searing, mind-numbing. After a few hits against her back, the chains became relaxed ever so slightly. Her mistress bent her over with a gray hand between her shoulder blades, palm pressing against her raw skin. Morgan panted at the lingering expectation of another inevitable strike. Just as her heart began to calm, it came, this time on her rump. Her yelp was even louder than before.

“Fffffuuuck!” she groaned. Theodora struck her again. And again. And again. Her white skin became pink, the blue butterfly on her hip looking as though it was flying through a sunset. Her body trembled. Her mind melted. Her head fell limp as she was repeatedly hit; her mouth agape, drooling like she’d become brain-dead.

“600 to strip her naked,” Ziusudra announced.

After a few seconds of pause, she felt the cold steel of the flat of a blade against her skin. She jolted at first, the icy metal shocking against her burning hot flesh.

“Hold still, little tart,” Theodora whispered again, assured no one else could hear the abuse. “Wouldn’t want to cut your pretty skin, would we? Not until someone pays for it.”

“Yes, Mistress. No, Mistress,” Morgan sputtered. Something about her accent made Theodora’s voice all the more arousing.

With an abrupt and sudden movement, her blade cut through her bra straps and released her breasts for all to see. The knife’s tip ran across her back, barely grazing the very fringes of her flesh, leaving small, almost invisible slashes. Morgan froze; her wrists held aloft were the only thing she allowed to shake. The blade cut through her panties just as harshly and tossed them aside. She expected the same of her garter and stockings, but it seemed those were acceptable.

Morgan turned her head, knowing fully she couldn't see what Theodora was doing. But even still, she felt the urge. She was so harsh, so wicked. Morgan's body could be pushed to its limit if this violent treatment continued. With permission or not.

"700 for nipple clamps," Ziusudra called out.

"Make that 800 for a clit clamp," Theodora added, her light footsteps moving around Morgan, the skin of her leg brushing against her bare flesh. She passed by Morgan's face, her exposed thigh grazing her cheek, and smelling of lilacs. "Fuck it, let's link them all together, yes? We have a chain harness in there somewhere."

Morgan was lifted back up and stretched back to a standing position. Without any further delay, the areas paid for were carefully stimulated before being pinched by small metal clamps with rubber tips. The three were linked together by a slim silver chain that was so taught, any movement on Morgan's part would tug at the clamps.

Softer than anyone should have been able to hear, Morgan cried, "Please gods.... Oh, gods... I can't..."

"Hush, harlot... or I'll break out the branding iron and give you something to really pray for." Theodora licked Morgan's flushed face, her long, forked tongue teasing her pale cheek.

"Please..." Morgan begged, her knees beginning to wobble. "I'm gonna..."

"You wanna come, little tart?" Theodora mocked with a devilish smile. "Une petite mort?"

Morgan nodded rapidly.

"Do you hear that, Master?" She said speaking to Ziusudra. "She wants to finish already."

He burst into a laughing fit, soon joined by those around him, and then the entire room. Morgan shook where she stood, body burning hotter the longer the clamps were on her. She couldn't move, even the slightest twitch could cause her to orgasm prematurely and without prompting.

"Anyone want to take her up on that offer?" Ziusudra jested, scanning the room. "Let this poor girl off so early?"

"I'll do it," a male voice said. Morgan recognized it. She'd heard that voice speak before. She tilted her head, and for the first time all night, she attempted the impossible: concentration. "$1200."

"Ah, Professor VanderGraf, please, you do not have to indulge her," Ziusudra answered. "She doesn't quite know how this all works."

VanderGraf? Morgan's thoughts raced. *My history professor? Oh fuck, what the fuck. Does he recognize me? This is bad, this is bad. I thought that this was for top dogs! Not college professors! Fuck, fuck!!*

"I'm not doing this to indulge her." VanderGraf said, "I mean… I'm not paying for her benefit."

"Oh?" Ziusudra humored the professor, most likely curious about what he wanted himself. "Pray tell."

"I want to fuck her."

VanderGraf was positioned on a rather sturdy crate behind Morgan, who whimpered, trying desperately to keep her voice down. He'd surely recognize her voice, too. It was now she wished someone had paid to put a ball gag in her mouth. The chains were lowered again so she could be properly bent over. It was then he muttered something so low only she could hear it, his voice rolling with sleaze. In this moment, something unearthly and foreign took over her… she smiled. A masochistic smile, one that signaled how much she was enjoying all of this… how much she loved what she experienced. She was grateful to have found herself in this position. In some dark, twisted way, she was grateful Chrissy Donavon had gone missing.

"Say please," he groaned.

"…Please…"

9

From the hot water of the spa bath, Morgan pulled herself up on a bench built into the spa wall and swept her long blonde locks back. With a sigh of relief, she closed her eyes, feeling clean and reinvigorated. After her encounter with VanderGraf, she needed it. Despite the debauched nature of the act, she never sensed that he knew who she was. At least she hoped he didn't. That would be something she'd have to unpack in the morning.

She had been left alone in the massive bathhouse. His servants were kind and caring, even Ms. Abaddon returned to help wash Morgan's hair and assure she was alright. They left shortly after, giving her time to relax by herself, though they didn't give her a clue as to what she was supposed to do once she was alone.

Curiously, she scanned the area; the tub itself took up half the room, the other half held a sauna and showers. It, like much of the rest of the place, was carved of fine stones to look like bizarre creatures and patterns. The water spilled from the wide, cap-toothed mouth of a stone sculpture of a stout bear creature. The ceiling itself seemed to have moths in mind when designing the patterns.

Along the far wall, she noticed an ornate clock, showing it was almost 2 am. Beneath it was a large, white robe that looked delightfully warm and fluffy. She swam her way across the dark pool, careful not to look down into the eerie abyss. She couldn't help but feel the sensation of being watched, the main reason she didn't go out into open water.

Once she had dried off, put on the robe, and looked to see where they put her clothes. The room swam. After VanderGraf, she served more people in one go tonight than ever before. She was exhausted and wanted help. Having someone offer to pamper her after she'd done them a service had been nice for a change. Regardless, she needed to find some clothes.

Never one to wait, Morgan opened the main door out into the corridors of the penthouse floor. Was all of this floor Ziusudra's? Was this all his building? It was never made clear to her. She stepped out, unknowingly and barefoot, into the eccentric estate. At this moment, she felt the truth of some of Raphie's worries.

Raphie. Even thinking his name warmed her cold heart. She was worrying him to death, and he more than had his hands full with school and a new girlfriend. She owed him for keeping the burden of her massive secret. She owed him for a lot of things.

Morgan found herself walking the stretch of a corridor for some time before finally deciding to turn a corner. To her, the floor seemed much smaller from the outside; architecture and dimensions were never her strong suit. Pressing down the corridor, she ended up back at the den where everything had happened. The doors were closed yet again. Attempting the knobs to find they were locked tight, she remembered the room across the hall where she left her bag. It was unlocked, and she entered.

Inside the room was pitch black; a simple flick of a light switch revealed that her purse was no longer present. The door in the corner was still ajar. Despite her belongings being missing, she was keen to know the contents. She approached with haste and went inside. Morgan searched in the dark, her Vampire eyes not needing to find a light. It was what looked like a storage area for the parties. Boxes of costumes littered the area and seemed to be the primary contents of the numerous, stuffed containers. She spared a glance at some of the less dusty boxes. One, in particular, sat alone, with a dustless top.

She opened the crate and looked inside. Her face contorted, confused, and disturbed by the contents. It looked like jewelry and trinkets, individual and personal. Some even had initials or names on them.

These were stolen. Morgan thought, her heart beginning to beat as she realized she was closing in on the trail, snapping back to her whole purpose for being here. She saw a few names: Rich, Andrea, Joana. She held the braided cloth with Joana printed on it, recalled the name of the deceased girl, and put it in her robe pocket. She continued to look, proving her intuition right; she found a charm bracelet with the initials CD.

"Chrissy Donavon," Morgan said aloud. She clutched the artifact for a moment, then slipped the silver chain over her wrist in an effort not to lose it.

"Ereh efas ton er'uoy." A woman's voice, distorted and distressed, startled Morgan to her feet. She turned around to see a servant girl, possibly no more than nineteen. She was blonde, with big, teased hair. She held an empty platter and a dirty rag despite being scantily dressed. She was not dressed like the others this evening; she was in a skimpy black leotard and pink leg warmers. She was barefoot, her feet filthy, and her body language and face spoke volumes of her misery. Morgan couldn't understand what she said, but she sensed the desperation in her tone.

"I'm sorry? I don't understand," Morgan approached the girl, who backed up nervously into the main hall.

"Nac llits uoy elihw, evael esaelp," The girl said, panicked, yelling, and bursting into a sprint down the hall. "Kcuts er'uoy fi pleh t'nac uoy!"

"Wait! I don't understand!" Morgan cried, chasing after her, bumping her shoulder on the doorframe as she followed, "I'm not gonna… hurt… you…" She was gone. There was no trace of her. Morgan stood and tried to parse what was said; she'd never heard such a strange tongue before.

A mass of darkness appeared far off down the hall. Morgan whipped her head around, thinking it was going to be the girl. She was perturbed when she saw a dog, black and brown like a Rottweiler. Unlike a standard dog, however, it possessed two long bull horns. It gave a silly howl and proceeded down the cross corridor. With a smile and a raised brow, Morgan felt compelled to follow.

Once she had reached the hall, it had somehow made it to the other end. It seemed impossibly far, though perhaps Morgan was just tired… or the optometrist was right about her needing glasses 24/7. She wasn't about to give in just yet, as the dog gave another strange howl.

She giggled at the absurdness of it all. "Stay! Good boy, stay!"

The dog walked on.

"No! Don't make me run! My feet hurt!" Morgan complained, breaking into a lazy jog to catch up with the beast. She reached the end of the three-way intersection of halls at last and the dog was nowhere to be seen. "Whaaat the fuuuck?"

When Morgan turned back to go down the hall she came, she was met with a solid wall. "Impossible," she said aloud, looking back and forth to see if she perchance took a wrong step and turned herself around. But no such hall existed. She was now staring down a single long corridor with no real clear end on either side. Morgan felt her heart race. She felt closed in on top of being lost and isolated.

She did the only thing she knew how to do, closed her eyes, took a deep breath, and breathed in and out to the count of ten —just as Auntie M taught her. After, she felt relieved a bit, though the penthouse still confused her. She was not sure if she'd seen anything penthouse-like other than the bath and the den where the party was held. She gave a nervous chuckle and turned around to head the other way.

Something was standing there.

Some unearthly thing hunched over with stubby legs that appeared to bend in places other than joints. It was top-heavy with long arms and fingers, like a chimpanzee with scaly flesh. Its body was wrapped in a blue t-shirt and a pair of khaki shorts that made it look approximately humanoid. "Approximately" was too kind; "bastardized" would be more appropriate. Morgan's cold skin crawled when she saw its head or lack thereof. It was as if someone had stretched a humanoid face over a dinner plate and placed it in the neck hole of the shirt. And the eyes. Glossed over, fake, like black oil.

Morgan and the thing were frozen, less than a hundred feet apart. It didn't seem to breathe, much like herself. But it didn't seem undead either. She could smell that it was… unnatural. Just when Morgan felt most at unease, it raised its palm, the size of her entire skull, and waved. Morgan was petrified, on the verge of urinating herself. She did what her heart felt was right: be kind to it. She waved back. What it did next was yet another bastardization of a humanoid trait: a smile without teeth. A black hole into an endless void shaped like what it *thought* happiness was.

The thing began sprinting.

10

Faster than she'd ever gone before, Morgan ran for her life, away from the creature that effortlessly kept pace. She didn't spare a glance back; she knew how close it was by the rapid pitter-patter of its misshapen feet. Using all her Preternatural strength and speed, she tried to gain some distance between them.

It can't keep up with a Vampire... it just can't... She thought, still too in shock to conjure a scream. At last, another intersecting corridor came into sight. Digging her bare feet into the carpet, feeling it tear under the friction, Morgan turned the corner hard and kept her speed as she entered the next hall.

She spared a glance back at last. Her eyes widened, and she finally managed to scream; it was behind her. Still. Closing the gap as if she had never tried to escape in the first place. It galloped, occasionally using its massive arms as legs, boosting its broken, alien movements.

"HELP!" she bellowed, her voice crackling like an antique radio. No answer. Nothing but what she now realized were breathy grunts from the creature behind her. No. Not breath. Laughter. It was enjoying this. "PLEASE, SOMEONE!"

She turned right into another corridor. She wagered that as long as she hugged the right wall, she couldn't get lost again. She couldn't attempt a door; if it was locked, she was dead. Even still, she needed to find a way out. *The building's not that big... it has to end soon... the elevator has to be here somewhere.* Silently, she prayed for the nightmare to end. Her muscles burned, and her throat was already hoarse from the earlier events. She couldn't help but curse herself, hating how stupid she was for going at this alone. How stupid she was for not listening to Raphael... how much she needed him in that moment, even if she wasn't sure what he'd even do.

Another turn and she had found a hall that ended in a set of double doors. Carved in the center of each was a rather unsettling face and a net of snakes behind it. A dead-end, and Morgan's only hope. Using all of her Vampiric gifts, Morgan dug in again and burst into a lightning-fast sprint, for the first time gaining some distance. The thing still galloped gleefully after her. Patting its massive hands roughly into the floor, it cackled louder and louder like the bark of hyenas, gnashing teeth at her heels.

Morgan gripped the door handle, locked. Even all her strength couldn't so much as budge the doors. It got closer. She pounded hard on the door with her fists, screaming at the top of her aching lungs.

"SOMEONE OPEN UP PLEASE! PLEASE HELP ME! GODS, SOMEONE PLEASE HELP!!!" she sobbed, scratching at the wood until the white finish peeled off in chunks. She sank to the floor and covered her eyes, waiting for the painful, agonizing end.

The pattering and cackling stopped, but she could sense a presence. The aroma of a woodland morning filled her senses, pleasantly replacing the sensory overload the creature caused. She still feared what it would do to her. Silence.

"I am here, my dear," a soothing voice said.

She uncurled from her fetal position slowly, her eyes puffy and red from the terrified sobbing. She sniffled and looked up to see Dorian Ziusudra standing above her. She was no longer in a dead-end corridor but in the center of a three-way intersection. The solid, white, French doors were without uncanny faces, twisted snakes, or scratch marks; the thing was nowhere to be seen.

"Please, let us get you off the floor, my dear. It is unbecoming of a lady of your caliber," he said, outstretched his hand. She felt safe enough to take it. He pulled her into his arms, softly holding her against him. For a brief moment, she imagined he was someone else and held him tightly. "Now tell me, what has you so disturbed?"

"I-I was b-b-being chased… th-this awful creature…" She looked down all the corridors, still panicking that it might ambush them both. "I-i-it was so fast and, oh gods…"

"Shhh," he held her head close to his chest. "It will be alright, Morgana."

She felt her skin freeze. His hands of comfort suddenly felt as if tools of torment, shackles no different than those she wore earlier. She thought of all the things that went wrong to lead up to this moment, what step she had failed at.

"How… how di— how did you—" she stammered, unsure whether to try and double down or confess.

"Know your name?" Ziusudra smiled down at the girl, too afraid to look back at him. "Knowledge is my business, Miss Scriven. I did not get as wealthy and as well-connected as I am without knowing who I have in my circle. I am very disappointed that you were not honest when I asked before."

"Wh-what am I supposed to say?" She started to lean away, but he didn't hold her back, making her feel somewhat at ease. As if he truly didn't mean her harm.

"I need you to tell me the truth… who are you? Why are you here?" He said sternly. "I want you to look me in the eyes when you say it."

Morgan trembled, glancing up at his six-pack and pecks that she still held close; her hands still held to his dark flesh.

"I'm Morgana Scriven," she choked. Her eyes finally matched his, nonplussed at how they seemed to glow. She smiled at his ethereal beauty. Something overtook her, perhaps it was the personality of 'Chastity' or her Vampiric nature. She felt a compulsion to confess and blushed at the reality of her truth. Eyes welled with tears, she spoke "I'm a slut… and I want to be used like a toy… by you, Master."

"Good girl," he grimaced.

He cupped her face and ran his fingers through her mostly dry hair. She rolled her face in his hand, kissing the base of his palm. She closed her eyes and allowed him to feel her body. She was ashamed and proud of her admission all at once. She didn't want to be monogamous; she didn't want what she once had. This new life, Chastity's life, is the life she wanted. For the first time, as an adult, her body felt free of moral and social shackles. She had the opportunity for freedom.

"Perfection. I will inform Yessenia that you will no longer be working at the Bourbon Belfry," his hands undid the tie on her robe and let the woolly garment fall to her feet. "You belong to the Lounge now."

"Of course, Master," She said as he caressed her face and placed his thumb into her mouth, which she dutifully sucked. She was telling the truth; she did enjoy being used, she did enjoy letting strangers take her. But she was still going to bring this house of cards down. She just had to do it from the inside, at the top.

Her body had finally calmed down from the adrenaline spike just in time to be heated back up by her new master's passionate touch. He removed his thumb from her mouth, tracing the digit along her lips before he leaned down to kiss her. As he did, his hands traced up and down her naked, pale body; she could grow used to this treatment.

With no effort at all, Ziusudra lifted Morgan into his arms, holding her like a bride. She, gazing into his bright white eyes the whole time, was mesmerized by their sparkling allure. From seemingly nowhere, two of the black-suited security guards, donning their brass, human masks, flanked either side of Ziusudra, stepping in front of him to open the double doors. Her eyes darted around, confused to see she was now in the bathhouse… this time far from alone. A congregation of eerie figures in faceless red cloaks waited in an organized pattern. The lights had been dimmed, and several elaborate candlesticks were distributed among the cloaked ones. They watched, unmoving; Morgan could feel nothing but dread staring back at them.

Impossible, she thought. *This room was on the other end of the building... it didn't have double doors... what's happening? Who are these people?! What are they going to do to me??*

As Ziusudra approached the edge of the concrete, she began to panic as she realized that beneath her was the massive, darkly infinite pool. She turned back to him, clutching him tightly to avoid looking down into the crushing darkness. "Wh-what's going on?" she choked.

"I know you're a journalist, Morgana," he gave a loving grin, a juxtaposition to her sense of danger. As he spoke, the figures began to chant in a language Morgan couldn't even begin to recognize. "It is a shame, you were such an amazing woman… You will find yourself in good company, I assure you."

"No," her heart sank, knowing what he meant. She tried to grip his kimono in a desperate attempt to stay on dry land. He must have seen the terror in her eyes as he tossed her with his full might into the utmost center of the pool before she could grasp him. "NO!"

"Sha hatti darisam." Those were the last words she heard him say before the hot water surrounded her again. Immediately, anxiety and survival instinct took full control, kicking and paddling in a sorrowful attempt to claw at the surface. The darkness began to swell around her, and she couldn't reach the surface no matter how hard she swam. Something had her.

She spared a glance down to see a humanoid hand gripping her ankle. She screamed nothingness, allowing water to fill her empty lungs. The girl from the abyss rose to grab her more, a look of hatred and despair on the cut and stretched skin that was once a humanoid face. Her mouth had been cut from ear to ear, the flesh of her cheeks pinned back to her head by bolts of metal. Eyelids were removed, rendering the specter's face into an endlessly frightening stare. The abomination got hold of Morgan's wrist, pulling off the silver charm bracelet, but giving her time to escape. Morgan kicked her away, slamming her foot into the woman's not-face. But by the time she had broken loose of her grip, a dozen more people, all with horrific piercings, extreme surgical modifications, and teeth filed to a point, rose from the depths to pull her down.

Morgan struggled. She fought, clawed, scratched, and pummeled. No use. All of her limbs were pinned, the rest of those hands touching her across her naked body. She gave a meaningless sob as the many mutilated monstrosities pulled her down into the abyss.

M's Journal

October 14th, 1996

Saved an Elf girl. 'Cause of a prophecy. Came fractured and painful like always. Almost got crushed by some bozo going 60+ through a red light. Managed to dig my boots into the ground and the fucker buckled around me. He survived. Barely. Just like that time in Quantico.

My wing got chipped. "Scales like plated armor." That's what I was told all those years ago, Francisca and those other Fed scientists. Claimed that my wings are stronger than solid titanium. Something about absorbing kinetic energy.

Don't know why I had to save her. Prophecy was obscure. More so than usual. She doesn't seem like anybody now. Don't know, maybe it was just a minor one, and got lucky. Always get lucky, right? Can't not be there at the right place or the right time unless I hole up in this decrepit old apartment and ride it out. I'm glad for leaving the house this time. She was young. Didn't deserve to be the next *Red Pavement*. Was kind, too.

Offered me help, thought I was tweaking. Don't blame her. Tend to trip over burnt-out tweakers in this town. It eats people alive and spits them out.

Tori Franques still missing. Have to try The Keep in Little Lenora. That was the last place Joana Larsson worked before she died. Has to be a connection...

-M

Act 3: Kings of Their Own Castle

1

At first, there was oblivion. An infinite void of crushing darkness beneath the endless depths so unknowable and massive that Morgana had forgotten entirely that she had been cast into Dorian Ziusudra's bath. The infinite black became a stirring of sensations and soon she had fully emerged from the abyss.

Time-shifted. Morgan found herself on top of something, staring up at a crimson sky, black sun at the edge of view. The very thing she lay upon was a tangled mass of lustful bodies intertwined in an otherworldly carnality. Never before had she felt such a horrifying blend of fear, pain, and pleasure: suffering and lust combined in rapturous harmony. Blades were drawn across her flesh, and metal wires fed through her skin. She was molested physically, the monsters taking her without remorse or respite, each taking their turns on her and each other with vile intentions. Like the woman she'd seen in the pool, her mouth was cut from ear to ear, giving her an eternal smile, spilling blood from the fresh wounds.

All of her senses were overloaded, her very mind infringed upon by nightmarish imagery even as she reached a fugue state of bliss. She screamed out a cry of desperation as visions of death and torture became all-encompassing. Glancing down the mountainous orgy, she saw the fate bestowed upon other souls and wept. She witnessed the endless charnel chambers, stretching downward for foreseeable miles, where a million souls were torn apart for the amusement of their mutilated captors.

Above her was an opening to the bleak crimson sky and empty black sun. A figure rose, eclipsing the bloodied heavens, wearing a gown made from the flesh of the unwilling; the very anatomies stitched together like a morbid cloak wrapped around their body. Fear, lust, passion, anger, and disgust all flashed into Morgan's mind at once, watching in terror as the shadow of the titanic being blotted out the black sun within the dead sky.

The figure extended their four arms, towering over Morgan's living throne. It looked into Morgan's eyes with its countless own, flashing a trillion impossible colors so fast that they at first appeared to glow white. Above this figure, the first sign of clouds gathered. Black and gray, swirling like a smokestack, an eye began to form. The storm swirled into a cyclone, and with it came a godlike wind that pulled many of the demons into its maw.

Within the eye of destruction, like a halo above the four-armed deity, lightning and hurricane winds ripped apart the massive chamber. In a torrent of engulfing storm, the clouds entered Morgan's body through her mouth, nose, and eyes, robbing her of all of her senses. The last thing Morgan heard as her body began to tumble miles below was a whisper, so low it should have been impossible for her to hear, and yet it was clear.

"Not today."

Then she awoke.

With a yelp of panic, Morgan shot up, immediately realizing she was no longer in the dream world. She touched her naked body, feeling that nothing had cut her flesh. No mutilated monsters were torturing her, no horned dogs, or gibberish-speaking 80's girls. Morgan was relieved immensely to learn that it was all just a vivid, horrible nightmare. It was when she finally took a deep breath that she observed her surroundings. She was alone, in a Cal King bed with a massive, golden bed frame complete with a gossamer canopy. Judging by the muted light peaking through the blinds, it was still early morning.

The room itself was ornate and meticulously designed, with white walls, pillars, and black marble floors with veins of smoky grey. She immediately recognized the Art Deco style and realized she had never left the Babylon. She sighed in relief, clutching the bedsheets; the last thing she remembered was getting out of the bath. Everything else was a blur. Morgan didn't think she drank that much, but then again, she wasn't used to wine. Beside her on the nightstand, an outfit akin to last night's was folded and waiting, including a new pair of almost identical shoes. She took a look at the tag attached to the collar of her shirt and realized it was Versace and the lace-adorned undergarments were Fendi, well out of her price range. She glanced around the room, looking for someone, anyone. No avail.

When she finished getting dressed, she noticed that beneath the clothing was a note penned in the same handwriting as the invitation she received. She was quick to read it.

My dear Morgana,

I hope that these supplement what was damaged and lost in the craze of last night. I apologize for not being there when you wake. My busy life knows no end, but I am certain you understand. Thank you for your exuberant services. I enjoyed myself fully. You are something not of this world, and I crave your exotic nature. I look forward to spending more alone time with you soon.

—With utmost sincerity,

Dorian Ziusudra.

Morgan chuckled incredulously to herself, musing at the fact that she had slept with Ziusudra last night. She could almost recall something of that nature, a memory of being brought to this room, but for some reason, her memory was cloudy, and her head pounded. Somehow, he found out her true name, and it didn't have any negative consequences. Morgan was confused and utterly in a daze, on top of the immense pain behind her right eye. While she questioned her alcohol intake, this hell of a hangover proved severe enough. She needed caffeine and most likely blood.

As she debated her options, a knock came at the door to the bedroom.

"Come in?" She said, confusion clear in her tone.

The door opened and a man in a black suit with freckled

skin and long, dirty blond hair entered, carrying her bulky beige purse. He was impossibly poised, his movements uncannily smooth; his face featured a permanently placid smile. At first, Morgan was taken aback by this but as soon as he bowed his head she felt a sense of entitlement.

"Ms. Scriven, I'm Oscar, Master's chauffeur. He asked me to stay behind and take you home," he said, his voice gentle. "Are you ready to leave?"

"Oh, right," she said, slipping on her shoes and folding up the letter to put into her shirt's pocket. It was at that moment she realized that Raphie and Balam would be deeply worried about her. "Yes… I'm ready."

As she approached Oscar, he retrieved a roll of hundred dollar bills from his pocket and handed it to her along with her bag. Her eyes went wide, realizing there were easily over four thousand dollars there.

"What is—?"

"Your payment for last night."

She just stared.

"Right this way," he said, guiding her out the door.

She put the money in her purse and scanned the environment once more, taking in all the rather avant-garde art that decorated the room, ranging from small statues of women with unnatural-looking anatomy to the armoire with blind cherubs framing the top. She had so many questions, questions she knew she'd find answers to. For now, she needed to report to Harding. With that final thought, she followed the chauffeur and left behind the gaudy suite.

"Well, I'll give you this, Nancy Drew," Colt Harding said, his rugged face sporting his staple 'hard-ass' demeanor. He thumbed through the stack of photos that Morgan had taken in stealth during her tenure at the Belfry. She stood behind his chair, leaning beside him and eagerly awaiting his critique.

"You've been busy. How'd you get all these?"

"I have an inside woman, helped me get into the backrooms. She wishes to remain anonymous for now," Morgan lied, trying to stay as calm as she could despite her raging stress. Just being around Harding made her nervous, but she wanted him to be impressed or at least approving enough to keep her in the program. His muted response only further fueled her panic, even still she pushed through.

"I played it safe. When I went to the Belfry, my best friend knew where I was and had the info just in case," she continued, flashing him a falsely confident grin. She leaned forward to point out some of the details in her notes worth highlighting. He smirked back, his eyes quickly darting to her chest and then back to the papers. He tried to hide the glance. In response, she took an extra deep breath. Before entering, Morgan undid the top button of her pink blouse. She wasn't stupid; she knew what men like Harding wanted.

"These photos are top-notch, and it looks like we can prove some real nefarious activity over at the Bourbon Belfry. Maybe enough that the police could get a warrant," he said honestly, "But all this other stuff about the Babylon and this 'Lounge', those are some pretty heavy accusations there. From what it sounds like, it's just a fetish club, and there are plenty of those in LA. You need to find a stronger link between it and Chrissy for me to publish this story. You're close, but no cigar yet."

She frowned, feeling better than she expected but worse than she hoped. "Okay, what do I need?"

"I don't know, Scriven, that's your job," he chuckled out of irritation "You need to more tightly knit it all together. An eye witness or a piece of solid evidence."

Like an analog TV switching channels, Morgan's brain became briefly clouded by static. The image of a bracelet being ripped from her wrist in a state of underwater panic swirled in her mind, glimpses from her horrid nightmare last night. As soon as it came, it was gone. Morgan winced, feeling a migraine following close behind. *I don't have time for this shit.* She thought, blaming it on her newly acquired recreational habits.

"You okay there? Party too much last night?" He joked. "I

have some extra-strength aspirin if you'd like them. It's not undead strength, but a few might help."

"I'll be okay, Mr. Harding," she said, pulling her hand away from her eye, thankful all she had on was eyeliner and mascara, both smudge-proof. "I honestly just want to thank you for trusting me with this opportunity to use company resources to prove myself."

"Well, I wouldn't say that just yet," Colt said, deflating Morgan's demeanor slightly.

"Oh."

Colt stood, meeting the girl closer to her eyes and taking the advantage to eye her cleavage again, however briefly. He awkwardly collected Morgan's portfolio and handed it to her, this time sure to keep his fiery eyes in contact with hers. "You're the hardest-working intern I've seen in a very long time. I reward hard work. So don't let it go to your head but… keep it up."

"So you think I might be able to stay in the program?" Morgan looked up to him with eyes like rose quartz and long, batting lashes. Her high cheeks raised in a smile and flushed a light pink.

"Ya know," Colt looked her dead in her eyes and gave a charming smile, his tusk-like fangs protruding, "You just might."

The two, chief editor and intern, were inches apart. Within their conversation, at some point, they must have slowly gravitated toward one another. Silence hung over them. Morgan felt her heart swell with undead blood, beating in an irregular flutter, like a drunk butterfly. *Oh, gods*, Morgan thought. *Eliza was right…*

"I… uh… should get back to it…" Colt shattered the tense silence, that same streak of awkwardness returning; a vulnerability that Morgan found exceedingly attractive in a man. "I've got a lot of work ahead of me."

"Me too." Morgan took her portfolio and hugged it close to her breast. She turned and crossed to the door. Colt beat her there, opening it for her. "Thank you, again… like, seriously." Those words spoke volumes about how she truly felt. Colt seemed to read some of it, his smile widening as the Vampire in a pencil skirt walked away with the natural, alluring sway of her hips. Though in her infatuation, she bumped into the door frame, laughing it off as she left.

He closed the door and held his hand on the knob for a hanging moment. His smile devolved, his eyes drooping, and mouth forming a frown. His breath became shallow and a chill feeling crawled across his green skin.

"Nope. Don't go there!" He said, holding his hands up and walking away as if surrendering. Before he made it fully to his desk, he looked back at the door the blonde bombshell came and left. He gave a heavy sigh and spoke again to himself, a lingering disappointment clipped onto each word. "Ain't worth it."

2

Apartment 161 was not what one would call a crowded place. Despite there being four occupants and a cat, Raphael hardly saw any of them. He was certain he hadn't seen Seth in over a month. Raphie didn't work, so despite his schooling, he was often home alone. Left to his own devices, he found ways to pass the time and relax. But, no one to speak with left him going a little stir-crazy. He looked forward to when his best friend would return, giving him someone he enjoyed talking to.

He sat at the Bar, a cup of hot tea in his *Black Sabbath "War Pigs"* mug, a gift from his beloved best friend. Morgan was set to be home soon, but she needed to run an errand beforehand, something that had to do with her suddenly impressive supplemental income.

He grinned and sipped the tea, sweetened with honey; the only soundtrack to be heard was the birds chirping outside. The sun reached the end of its run for today, taking the light but replacing it with vibrant oranges and brilliant pinks painted across Westlake.

The door to the master bedroom unlocked. Balam emerged to meet Raphie's unexpected gaze. "Oh hey." The Wood-Elf grimaced as he gave his uncomfortable greeting. "I didn't know you were home."

"Same for you," Raphie said, sipping his tea but still looking at Balam. "Another late night at the clinic?"

"What? Oh yeah, just woke up. Had a busy shift last night. Only on days like this do I feel any regret opening a 24/7 emergency practice," He scratched the back of his head and yawned as he spoke. "So… how's school?"

"It's been alright," Raphie replied, somewhat reluctantly. "I cut a few classes, so my workload is manageable now."

"Neat," Balam gave a flimsy smile and moved to the fridge. "So… you're dating someone new, I think Morgan told me?"

"Yeah…" Raphie raised an eyebrow, curious as to where this was going, but also somewhat engaged in the conversation. Seldom had the two talked alone, Morgan was usually there to help keep the conversation moving. It was for the best, as the two seemed to butt heads more than they didn't. "I met her last month. She's a real-life witch."

"Nice," Balam said, turning around with a pre-made salad in a Tupperware container. "So a lady… how does that work?"

"Excuse me?"

"Your… bedroom habits," Balam pushed as if nothing was wrong.

"I say again," Raphie said with a twitch of his eye, "Excuse me?"

"I'm sorry. I just don't get how you date girls. I mean, you don't have a dick right?"

"Dude, that's A) none of your business unless you're trying to get into my pants, which no, and B) none of your *fucking* business," Raphie fumed, setting his tea down for the first time.

"Jesus, sorry I asked," Balam scoffed.

"You should be. If Morgan was here she'd kick your ass. You know she's totally liberal, right?"

"Probably not," Balam scoffed again. "She's never gotten on me before. At least not that I can remember."

Raphie shook his head, stood up, and grabbed his tea, taking a long drink of it before realizing it was almost empty. "I don't know, dude," Raphie began, with irritation growing in his voice. "She's been getting more righteous since college began. Being an intern at the Chronicle has helped light a fire under her ass."

"You think you know her so well, don'tcha?" Balam scowled. "You know I'm her *boyfriend*, right? I'd like to think I know what does and doesn't upset her… Also, why are you keeping track of all this? You sometimes bother me, man."

"What?! How?" Raphie said, agitated, but knocked off his guard.

"You act like her boyfriend more than I do sometimes, it's not normal," Balam crossed his arms in a stance of masculine prowess.

"At least if I were her boyfriend, she'd be treated better," Raphie mumbled low into his mug.

"The fuck you say?" Balam argued, puffing out his chest.

"You're acting fucking absurd," Raphie said with growing candor. "I've known her since elementary school. She's been my best friend for more than half my life, and I've done a lot with her. That makes her very important to me. I care about her happiness. I always have. We've both been through some heinous shit… like her parents… She was picked on in school, too. Did you know that?"

"Why?" Balam said in disbelief.

"'Cause she's a Trueborn, you warm tub of cottage cheese. Albino and the only Vampire in our grade? Add glasses and braces to the mix, plus being an orphan. Kids are fucking mean. You might have been immune to that being an Elf. Wood-Elf or not, people see your ears as a status."

"What the fuck does my race have to do with anything?" Balam barked "I was talking about how far up Morgan's ass you've been since we moved in here."

"I hear a lot of shit-talking, but I never seem to see you around. Might as well call you Seth 2.0. For real though where the fuck have you been? Maybe if you spent a little more time with Morgan, your relationship wouldn't be so strained," Raphie began.

"She's hella overwhelmed right now, dude. She needs a stable base, someone who's going to help keep her standing when she inevitably bites off more than she can chew. Unlike me, she doesn't back down. She's like a pitbull; she bites down and that's it, dude. I only provide the emotional support she needs because she comes to me for it. I don't push anything on her. You're like ten years older than her, dude, you should have a little empathy. At least some understanding of what she needs without her saying it."

"She's her own person," Balam swiftly debated once Raphie was finished. "She's allowed to make her own choices and her own damn mistakes."

"Yeah, well, she might just choose someone else," Raphie laughed.

"What's that supposed to mean?"

"TREAT HER BETTER!" Raphie shouted. "It's not that fucking hard!"

Balam reeled and aimed to bellow back, but as he inhaled, he was interrupted by the sound of a car honking just outside their apartment. The honking repeated several times before the two finally sheathed the daggers that they stared into each other.

Just outside and down the flight of stairs sat a fire-engine-red, convertible Buick in one of the two parking spots assigned to Apartment 161. Morgan killed the engine as she saw her boyfriend and best friend exit their home. With child-like excitement, she leaped from the driver's seat, waving frantically.

"Holy shit she actually did it," Raphie smiled mostly to himself.

"You knew about this?" Balam said as they descended the stairs. Raphie was smart enough not to take the bait, Balam rearing to continue the fight. Raphie saw no reason to bring their beef in front of Morgan. Especially when she had such positive news to spread.

"I bought a car!" She shouted, bouncing in place, despite wearing heels, even wobbling a bit as she landed for the last time. She didn't seem to care, far too excited. "I did it, I bought my first car!"

"Oh my god, hon, you did. Didn't you?" Balam said with a forced laugh.

"Do you like it?" she asked. "It's a '91 Reatta. It's used.

Barely 40,000 miles on it. I even managed to barter the dealer down, too."

"Wow, Blondie, she's hot as hell," Raphie said with a grin, beginning to circle the vehicle and admire it.

"You do like it, right?" Morgan said, unsure and speaking directly to Balam.

"Batty-girl, if it makes you happy, then it makes me happy." He said with a wide smile. "Though I'm curious as to where you got the money for this?"

"I've been saving," Morgan said with a prepared response. Raphie looked up to her as she lied. "I've been setting money from my trust aside every month and building up until I had enough. I figured with school and work so far apart, it means I won't have to ride the bus!"

"Well, I can't say I'm not surprised, but I support you fully," Balam smiled awkwardly and hugged his partner. She gleefully wrapped her arms around him and kicked one of her heels up. Balam and Raphie met eyes in this brief moment, fencing with just a look yet again.

"I'm, like, *so* beside myself. I've wanted to own my own car since I was a kid, but it was just never in the cards. Everything was always conveniently located near me, and I couldn't justify it. Now I can!" Morgan began to bounce in place again, "I'm just so fuckin' tickled with myself!"

"I'm proud of you, Batty-girl," Balam said with a grimace. "Don't you need a license, though?"

"I've always had my license. I just renewed it." Morgan informed Balam with a triumphant look.

"Well, shit you thought of everything didn't ya?" Raphie joined in, still admiring the tan leather interior.

"You bet your ass I did," Morgan replied "If I was gonna do this I'm gonna be smart about it and do it right. Just like daddy always said, 'Don't half-ass anything. Full-ass everything'. Oh, Raphie, didn't you have somewhere to be later? Need a ride?"

"I'm meeting up with Demy, again, yeah." Raphie said with a smile, "And as a matter of fact, I'd love a ride."

"Well, grab your stuff and hop in." Morgan dangled her

keys with an ear-to-ear grin, a half-burnt clay dragon that Morgan had made in Kindergarten already on her keychain along with her key to the apartment. Behind her, Balam's gleeful face slowly melted away. Raphie tried to keep his eyes on Morgan. He didn't want her to use deduction and figure out something was wrong. However, he knew if Balam continued to wear his discomfort on his sleeve, Morgan would catch on with or without his interference. As he walked past the mahogany-skinned Wood-Elf, they glared at each other one last time. He couldn't shake the feeling that Balam was hiding something greater than just frustration or romantic negligence. But Raphie was nowhere near an answer.

Before long, Raphie had gathered his things and had made it back outside. Mirthfully, he buckled himself into the passenger seat; the roof began to retract, Morgan controlling it and cackling like the Wicked Witch of the West. Balam leaned in and kissed his Vampire girlfriend goodbye, watching them drive away with pop music blaring from the stereo.

He waved them off, waiting until the bright red Buick was out of sight entirely. Like the setting sun, Balam's face and whole demeanor changed; his smile altogether faded and became a vicious scowl. He marched back into Apartment 161, right past Tom watering his windowsill planter.

"Good evening, Wood-Elf Neighbor," Tom said, his deep, inhuman voice eternally monotone. "I hope all is well for you and your kin."

"Yeah, shove it," Balam muttered.

"How rude," Tom replied.

The door barely slammed behind him, and he had finished dialing the number into their phone. He stood in place, arms folded, foot tapping.

"Hello?" The groggy woman with a mild Transylvanian accent answered.

"It's Balam..." he spoke with fervor in his every word. "We need to talk."

3

As the sunset painted Downtown Los Angeles orange and pink, much of the city still struggled to escape its man-made beauty. Thousands flocked to the freeways in a desperate attempt to get home and end the grind of working in high-rise offices and massive banks. Among the bumper-to-bumper cars was a red convertible.

The irony was never lost on the driver, Morgana. Even still, the words of Victoria, her Vampire coworker, rang true. She felt pangs of guilt driving the convertible. She knew it was the privilege of her sub-species to be able to enjoy the sun. But likewise, she'd been called "day-walker" and "fake vamp" among some much harsher slurs; she'd been teased for her stark white skin and had taken years to feel comfortable showing as much as she did. If purchasing a convertible was showing off, then Morgan supposed she was showing off.

Her fingers gripped the steering wheel tightly at ten and two. The crawl of the traffic barely allowed her to take her foot off the brake. She tapped her fingers to the beat of "Rhythm of the Night" while Raphie looked down at his notebook, sketching away mindlessly. Occasionally, the sound of a Hispanic talk radio station would static in. Morgan always thought the DJ sounded distressed when she heard the station. But before any real words could be heard, it cut out. Despite her passenger's boredom, Morgan was still visibly giddy.

"I'm on the 5 freeway… in rush hour!" Morgan said, dancing in her seat. "I'm doing it, Raph!"

"Oh fuck yeah. You're in the big leagues now, bitch!" Raphie deadpanned, the two bursting into laughter. "Thank you for braving these morons for me," Raphie said with a sweet smile, admiring the light of the setting sun bathing his best friend.

"I'll be honest, I just wanted a driving buddy. I don't wanna park her just yet." Morgan was beyond happy. Her cheeks were fixed as high as they could go, forced upward by her fanged smile. "So thank *you*."

"So… elephant in the car," Raphie said. "What went down last night?"

"Well," Morgan said, grimacing as her head pounded again. "It seems like a pretty standard kink club for top dogs."

"Kink club?" Raphie said, "You mean like fetish shit?"

"Yep."

"And you… participated?"

"Yep," Morgan said, her cheeks flushing. "I think I slept with the head of the whole operation…"

"You think?" Raphie asked, looking out his window to hide his embarrassment. "Shit, they must have run a train on you for an 'I think.' Or drugged you."

"It was a crazy night," Morgan frowned, feeling guilty again. "I drank a lot and had wicked, horrible nightmares that I can't seem to get past."

"I'm sorry, Blondie. I know all about that," Raphie said, a look of revelation crossing his face. "Despite traffic, I'm still *way* ahead of schedule. I could go for tacos and a beer."

Raphie chuckled. Morgan didn't laugh, but rather raised an eyebrow and genuinely considered his proposal. She noticed they were less than a mile from the next off-ramp, and they weren't far from Pico Gemelos. "Hold on." She said, turning her turn signal on and gliding quickly between the cars and off the freeway.

"Wait for real?" Raphie said in disbelief. "I was joking."

"I know." Morgan glanced at him quickly with a flirtatious smirk. Raphie gripped his notebook tightly, hiding the profile drawing of his best friend. "But it's happy hour."

*****

For the first time since the start of the semester, Morgan and Raphie had a moment to themselves to share a beer. The two of them sat at the bar at their favorite Mexican food place, Pico Gemelos. They were always drinking buddies, but once "the Bar" was constructed back at Apartment 161, it became a ritual. Ever since the start of Raphie's romantic and magical adventures and Morgan's undercover sex romp, neither of them had the time to be together and be friends. Twelve years of friendship could never be strained by distance; it only made their time together more special.

"Okay… I got to meet her and she seems like good people…" Morgan began, taking a few drinks first. "Tell me about her… Demy… like, I wanna know what you two have been up to! You gotta have some good stories already. You two are always together now."

"Where should I start?" Raphie giggled to himself, caressing the sides of the glass, his thumb collecting the condensation. Morgan no longer felt the need to be cautious about Demy, she could see how happy Raphie had become.

"From the beginning." Morgan smiled, resting her elbows on the bar top and knitting her fingers together patiently.

"Well… from the moment we first met at the laundromat, there was something. I accidentally saw her, ya know, she was just a random who happened to be using a machine by me. And then again at the party, how could I have possibly known she'd be at the same party miles from where we met? It doesn't feel like an accident… it feels like fate."

"Guess so," Morgan said, not willing to sour Raphie's idea of destiny.

Raphie nodded, "Ever since we first hung out, she's taught me more and more about magic. How the metaphysical world works. There's magic all over this city, literal magic just bleeding from the cracks in the concrete. I've seen it. It's not Prete stuff either, she's only Half-Elf and she can do amazing things. She has so much intelligence, so much spirit to give that I feel I really can find a home in her heart. She invited me into her life despite the protest of some of her coven friends. Especially her girlfriend. Well, ex now I guess."

"Whoa, she had a girlfriend when you met?" Morgan sat up straight, similarly to how a mother would when they are about to punish their child.

"Technically," Raphie said, raising both his hands. "But they had an open relationship, so it's all good."

"So you didn't break them up to get with her?"

"No, absolutely not," Raphie shook his head "I guess she

was kinda toxic, to begin with. Not sure the details. Not my business to know or ask really. I just try to be there for her when she needs me and give her space when she doesn't. She has this generosity about her that just radiates to everyone and everything. I feel like a king when we're together. Like nothing can stop me."

"You're a really sweet guy, Raph," Morgan gave a soft smile. "You like, really care about Demy, huh? You just never talked this way about Oliver. Or anyone for that matter."

"Yeah, I guess she's the real deal," Raphie smiled, taking a drink as he mused, staring off into space.

Morgan watched her best friend's face light up with honest love. He may not be ready to say it, or maybe he didn't even realize it himself; he was in love with Demy. His heart soared when he talked about her, and that was purely evident in his eyes. Morgan's smile faded as what he said sank in. *This COULD be it for him, s*he thought.

"That's how I felt when I met Balam," she chose to say. It didn't make a difference what she said, this also brought a distinct look of sadness across her face.

"Are you okay there, Blondie?" Raphie frowned.

"B-Balam hasn't been himself lately. This whole past month, he's been… so distant. He's been acting strange, too. Like, today, for example, he was like, really stiff and awkward… It's almost as if he's trying to avoid me."

"I'm not trying to be an asshole, but I mean, where are you at night?"

She said nothing, just stared off in space and drank her beer.

"He's been way off his fuckin' game." Raphie cleared his throat. "He's gotten—"

"Weird?"

"…yeah…" Raphie paused, his hand outstretched to take hers if she needed it. She accepted his hand and held it tightly. His voice deepened, his eyes glazed over, and he dared to ask, "He hasn't hurt you, has he?"

"No. Nothing like that," Morgan shook her head, running her thumb over his knuckles and refusing to look anywhere but forward.

"Blondie… I think Balam is—"

A cell phone rang loudly. Both snapped out of it and looked confusedly at one another, then down to Morgan's purse, hanging off the chair and resting between them.

"I didn't know you had a cell phone," Raphie said.

"I don't," Morgan replied. A chilling sensation took over her as she reached down to retrieve the device that seemed to so mysteriously materialize from thin air. Her fingers reached the bottom of her large, white bag. She hadn't emptied it since last night, and someone might have placed it in her bag by mistake while it was unattended.

As her fingers brushed the edge of the hard plastic device, she felt a pang of overburdening dread— irrational and from nowhere. Morgan snapped back to reality, feeling a migraine manifest behind her right eye, the phone still ringing in her hand. With no more time to hesitate, she opened it and extended the antenna.

"Hello?" she answered, both stunned and perturbed. She gave a sideways glance to her best friend, who also looked just as disturbed.

"Ms. Scriven? It's Dorian… Dorian Ziusudra," the smooth-voiced 'benefactor' spoke, and Morgan had risen as if he were in the very room.

"Oh, hi! Yes, this is Morgan. Hold on just one moment, sir." Raphie shrugged in confusion. Morgan held up a finger as she got up to leave the rather busy interior and exit onto the patio area. Once she saw she was alone, she spoke more freely, "I'm sorry, Master. It wasn't safe to talk."

"Obviously, you received the cellphone I provided you," he chuckled softly.

"Yes, Master," she said, forcing glee. "You're too generous."

"It is merely a work provision," he said, a smile coming across clearly in his voice. "You have just begun to scratch the surface of my generosity."

"Oh? I'm eager to find out when I see you next," she said with a smirk of confidence.

"I am grateful to hear you want to return to the Lounge, my

dear. I have much planned."

At the mere mention of the organization's name, Morgan felt another wave of memory, this one with a spike of agony. She was only given fragments of moments; Ziusudra standing before her, her body soaking wet from the spa water. The image faded into a swirling mass of tendrils, too noisy to make out any great detail. In another flash, she saw her fist clenching his bedsheet, her body wracked with pleasure.

As soon as it had begun, the vision had ended, leaving her in a cold sweat, struggling to find her words.

"Um… Everything is still a little hazy from last night…" Morgan felt lost. "D-did we?… Were you and I—"

"Intimate?" He finished her sentence, with a slight sigh, he continued. "Briefly, yes. After your bath, I came to collect you. You seemed more energetic than when you had left the party space. You asked me to bed you, and I would be a fool if I resisted your beauty and charm, my dear Morgana. So I took you to my chambers. However, you were so tired that we began to make love, and your body gave out. I could not bear the thought of continuing, so I left you to rest."

Somehow, as he spoke, she uncovered all the fogged-over details. Morgan could now clearly remember the events; she remembered rising from the spa and looking up at Ziusudra. She remembered hanging her wet form on his and asking for him. She remembered his hands caressing her naked body as he took her, her back arched and mouth agape, crying out in lust. She didn't remember when it stopped, merely that she awoke in his bed at dawn. She was certain there was no way she'd been drugged, perhaps it was exhaustion and that damn nightmare muddying up the details… and perhaps she should cut back on the Bolivian Marching Powder.

She smiled, knowing now that in all likelihood Ziusudra was a gentleman. Despite this comfort her Master provided, she still could not shake that dread feeling; Morgan could not recall when she told him her real name. She deduced that they snooped in her purse and found her wallet and ID, which did not make her any more pleased.

"I'm sorry I passed out on you, Master," she admitted, sighing in relief.

"You were wearied, it was only natural for you to need sleep after what you did for the Lounge," Ziusudra said. "Which happens to be, in part, my reason for calling. What are your plans for Halloween night?" He asked, his booming voice like thunder in a nighttime rain.

"Nothing," She replied, realizing her deadline was closing in fast.

"Excellent. I need another girl for the party I am hosting. It will be co-hosted by my friends from The Keep. Are you familiar?"

"The Keep?" Morgan deduced, yet another major nightclub, this one in Little Lenora. It was rumored that the Elf mafia were its owners. "Yeah, that's like, *the* hot spot for Elves."

"Excellent, their associates have all paid their dues and are officially members of the Lounge. A step toward a collective effort for a better tomorrow. I will be honoring them at the party. I'd love for you to be present."

"I'm available," Morgan saw a flash of red inside of her right eye, the same place it always was. She thought it was strange for a migraine aura. This was debunked when images of suffering and pleasure filled her mind. Bodies intertwined in orgasmic torment. "Ugh…" Morgan groaned through gritted teeth.

"I will not bore you with the details of why your work is so important. Though it will reflect in your pay for Halloween," Ziusudra added. "You will be taking on a more passive role than before, and a costume will be provided."

"Sounds like fun," Morgan strained, holding her palm over her eye like an open wound.

"You sound tired. I will let you go. I will send a car for you on Halloween."

"I have the car I just bought. I'd like to drive myself if that's alright," Morgan managed to choke out. She had to be able to deliver her information directly after the party. Seems Raphie was more right than she thought, she would need to get away quickly.

There was a silence on the other end for a moment, until he

chuckled, "Of course, Morgana, my dear."

Morgan hung up the cell phone and entered back into the restaurant. Sitting at the bar, doodling in his notebook, was her patient best friend. He glanced up at her as she approached and turned to her fully when she sat down again. He watched her drink the rest of her beer in one go.

"What was that about?" he asked.

"It's the same head honcho that ran the event last night…" She said with a heavy sigh, "He wants me back Halloween night to perform for a bunch of Elf fascists."

"Okay," Raphie chuckled at her verbiage. "Is there no way out of it?"

"I need to go, I'm in deep, Raph." She hung her head. "There's more to this that I'm missing. I think the Belfry has more answers… and if the boys from The Keep are involved now too, that doesn't bode well."

"Why?"

"Two of the hottest, criminally run locations in LA work with this Lounge club. It worries me."

"If you're that worried about it, let me help. Demytria, too. She's literal magic and has a knack for helping. She'd probably do it if I ask."

Morgan sat quietly and thought for a long moment. She clenched her jaw and looked up at the decor, her eyes darting from the various images and trinkets of Mexican heritage. After a long pause, she gave a reluctant sigh and looked to Raphie, locked with his dark eyes.

"Okay," she admitted at last.

4

On a warm Tuesday afternoon, Griffith Park was widely unoccupied. Holding hands as they trekked across the rolling grass, Demy and Raphael scouted for a place to practice that was mostly secluded. Before long they were alone, beneath a vast maple tree. At its base, near the roots, a small bundle of withering purple nightshades swayed calmly in the autumn breeze.

"Here is perfect," Demy had said, unrolling the blanket from under her arm, spreading it across the grass. Raphie helped her straighten it and sat down with her on the purple, argyle print. He faced her, cross-legged and gripping his crimson-stained wand. He admired the Hebrew inscription again, enamored with Demy's nigh supernatural intuition. Across from him, Demy sat with her legs beneath her and pulled at her black skirt resting just above her knees.

"So today, I want to teach you some of the basics of being a spell caster from the eyes of a witch. Though technically you'd be a mage, you're being taught magic by a witch, so that's the techniques you'll learn," Demy began, retrieving a few candles, an incense plate, and a decorative tin all wrapped together in a delicate silk cloth. "It's not all just herbs and dressing like *The Craft*."

"Dope film, by the way," Raphie interjected.

"Meh, it was full of inaccuracies." Demy cleared her throat. "Real magic isn't all just wand-waving, and magic happens. Mages somewhat function like that, but even they need to connect with the ether to draw their power. You will have to learn to work with a patron."

"Okay, sweet," Raphie smiled. "First question, so this is a religion as well?"

"It can be," Demy answered, the corners of her black lips turned upward. "That's honestly the dividing line between mage and witch. Witchcraft is all based on faith, but how you interpret your patron is up to you. I know a few atheist witches, I know a Buddhist witch, you'd be the first Jewish warlock I've ever met… But I do understand if you have reservations."

"My folks were super religious, but once I hit thirteen and became a man, they let me choose," Raphie explained. "I mean, I still practice because it's my culture, but I never really gave a shit about faith or religion until I met you honestly… I didn't have true faith until I saw your gorgeous blue eyes. I figured some sort of all-powerful being must exist to create something so beautiful."

"Awww, Raphie," Demy said and looked to the ground, her

smile evolving into a grin. "I'm touched that I could do that for you."

"So what is it I need to do?" Raphie sat up straight and shimmied his shoulders in excitement.

"Well the first step is going to be very simple, you'll be communing with your patron. If you've ever meditated before it should feel somewhat similar." As she spoke, Demy reached into her bag, pulled out a small Newton's Cradle, and placed it between them and the candles.

"You keep saying patron," Raphie raised a brow and said, "What patron?"

"That's just the thing, it can be any deity from any religion or mythos. It doesn't have to be anyone in particular or the same one each time. A patron can look like anything or anyone. Just let it come naturally. Whatever form the gods take in your mind is what's meant to be for you," Demy explained.

"Sick. I tend to have a pretty fucked up subconscious so this should be interesting," Raphie said, only partially in jest.

"The Enclave, and I as an individual, have a saying. 'An' it harms none, so mote it be.' What that means is: as long as you don't bring misfortune or pain to anyone, the act is safe. It's a very adaptable phrase and can be applied to much. I try to handle all of life that way. Just by giving back as best I can and doing what my heart feels right. I implore you to do the same."

"So… what happened with the Enclave… if I may ask?"

"It's… complicated." Demy glanced away for a moment. "They are up to some dangerous shit and I can't be a part of it. It goes against our principle."

"Then I'll do my best to uphold that principle in their stead," Raphie said, determined.

"Good," Demy delighted. "There's not much good around these days. The world needs as much kindness as we can give it. If you'll stay by me, I'd be honored to spread that light and love with you."

"Of course, doll," Raphie said, taking his girlfriend's hand. "I don't see myself going anywhere in any foreseeable future. And the honor is all mine."

Demy smiled at the ground. After several lingering seconds,

she finally broke away from his hand and activated the pendulum, the metal spheres clicking back and forth at a relatively slow speed. Like a metronome, the cradle clicked left to right to left to right.

"Alright, Raphie, close your eyes. I want you to concentrate on the sound of the pendulum. Follow the noise with your eyes and ears, but do not look," she said. "Breathe like I've told you, focus on the sound of your breath and the sensation of your heartbeat. Watch the sound as it plays in your mind. Each click like a train car passing."

Raphie did as he was told. His hands held on his knees, palms toward the sky. He saw the pendulum behind his closed eyes, each impact of the balls, and how the momentum carried. The spheres raced past his vision just as Demy said they would, like a passing train. The rush of motion became a blur, barely any details capable of being made out.

*****

As the passing train became an indistinct blur, the ticking had become a loud crash like that of a gong, with just as much echo. Raphie was in a stark white room; massive and undefinable in its dimensions. He recognized this place from his dreams.

"I've seen this place before," he spoke to Demy in the waking world. "Where do I go?"

"Well, follow the safest path, see where it takes you."

There was no path. Or perhaps there was. The bright space, or lack thereof, had no definition. Raphie turned around in place for some time before deciding on a direction to head. He walked for a moment before the white void eventually began to change.

Soon he could make out he was in a corridor with blood-red doors aligning the sides. Above him, where a roof should be, was an open sky; a writhing and ever-shifting cosmos. Raphie could see the massive celestial eyes forming above and kept moving forward. Behind him was no sign of the space he had come from and was certain he had just left, instead a seemingly infinite hallway. Still, he pushed on.

He was tempted to try the doors, but something told him they weren't safe to open. He didn't start feeling safe until somehow the walls became defined, blood red, and doors of black. Feeling a sense of curiosity, he tried one of the doors. It opened to a crossroads. It seemed to resemble an intersection in Santa Monica, his and Morgan's go-to beach spot.

"Weird," Raphie thought aloud, pressing on into the crimson world. Shadows seemed more striking here, blocking out entire sections of the world around him with their sharp darkness. Above him, black and gray clouds began to form together in a spiral above the pier. Raphie felt no good could come of that manifestation and turned away. When Raphie faced the bulk of the city, his mind struggled to comprehend that half of LA had lifted itself vertically into the sky. Though this place felt abandoned, most of the buildings were intact... most... Some seemed to be at the center of roaring infernos, reaching straight out in a blasphemy of physics.

As he crossed back into the "city", he saw a tall figure block his path. They were beautiful and androgynous, their naked form covered by a series of gold and purple sashes. The being strode forward on long legs of silky, smooth, lilac flesh. Their arms unfolded to reveal four individual limbs adorned with countless rings and bangles. Their slender body was tattooed with ornate tribal designs and ritualistic scarring, which appeared to take the shape of a breeding ball of snakes. The beautiful being was suddenly standing above Raphie, though he did not find any threat in it.

"Hi!" he said softly, with a wave.

The deity said nothing and rather leaned forward close to Raphie. At first, he suspected they were going to whisper to him, but then they closed in on his lips. He froze, panicked, and was unsure of how to react. An inch before his lips, the deity stopped and exhaled an ethereal wisp into Raphie's agape mouth. Somehow, they spoke without ever moving their lips.

"Welcome home, my son."

*****

Raphie opened his eyes as he breathed in the wisp. The real world, with his beautiful girlfriend sitting across from him in Griffith Park, returned to him. His lips curled upward and Raphie chuckled with disbelief.

"That was a trip," he said, blinking so his eyes could better adjust. He told her all of what he saw; Demy seemed thoroughly impressed. While he spoke, she reached forward to stop the pendulum from continuing.

"It's not common that first-timers get such vivid images," Demy puzzled. "You truly are sensitive… let's try to see if you're strong enough to channel your life force already."

Demy gripped his hand and guided him to his feet. She turned and pointed to the wilted nightshades growing at the base of the maple tree. With her physical guidance, Demy helped Raphie steady himself with his wand at the flowers.

"I want you to bring them back," she instructed. "All you need to do is imagine something positive. Feel it draw energy from the earth to your core. Then imagine that energy as a ball of light. When you're ready, say the Elven words 'akt, flurz, akt', and send that ball through your wand. Nature should do the rest."

Raphie closed his eyes and took a deep breath, following her instructions without question. Her lips pecked his cheek softly, and his smile widened again. "Akt, flurz, akt," he repeated. His happiness glowed like a star in his mind and fired down into the wand like a cannon. Raphie lost his balance and even felt a bit weak. He stumbled forward, catching himself and opening his eyes as he did.

"Oh my gods," Demy finally spoke, in awe of the field of nightshades that now surrounded them. Beneath them, a plethora of purple flowers engulfed their feet, extending meters out from the point of origin.

At the epicenter, the original flower was now the largest and most vibrant of the bunch. Raphie held his hand to his head, looking upon his work in disbelief. "This is incredible," He spoke, his voice cracking.

"This is magic," Demy returned gleefully, leaning down to pick the massive, bright nightshade. "This is you."

She leaned up to her boyfriend and placed the gorgeous violet flower behind his ear. The two gazed into one another's eyes, surrounded by a miracle. They could only resist each other's embrace for a mere moment before they pulled one another close and, with fiery passion, kissed.

5

"I don't know, Morgan," Eliza said, scratching the back of her mop of a head, her black bangs resting around her red horns. "You're a Vampire. Shouldn't it be *you*?"

Navigating the chaos of the Chronicle, Morgan followed Eliza as she made her rounds delivering documents and final product. Morgan dodged a Giant carrying stacks of backlog copies to be destroyed. They both ducked, going unnoticed by the 8-foot-tall humanoid.

"Look, I would," Morgan pestered like a baby sister. "I'd do it, but I already pushed my luck last time I was at the Belfry."

"What exactly did you do to get those pictures?" Eliza said, her mouth scrunched up, skeptical of Morgan.

"I broke in," Morgan lied, straight-faced.

"Damn, girlie, you may be a culturally rude Vampire but you're a hell of an investigator," Eliza laughed. "Alright, well, what is it you would need me to do?"

"I need you to pose as a reporter from another paper. Yessenia, the owner, has a mean streak, but she's easily distracted by her ego. Tell her you want an interview and a photo of all the staff. You'll go in during off-hours and take photos of everyone on the main stage. Meanwhile, I can get Raphie and Demy to sneak in and search for those disks. I think I may be able to crack the passcode now."

"And we can trust Demy, how?"

"Because I trust Raphie, and no offense, I trust him more

than you. I'm coming to *you* for your skills as a journalist *and* as a friend." Morgan pouted, "Pleeease?"

"Girlie, stop…" Eliza threw up her hands. "Morgan, you're adorable. No wonder all the men here who aren't chasing me are chasing you."

"What?!" Morgan snorted.

"You hear things around the water cooler."

"Nothing but nice things, I hope?" Morgan asked cautiously optimistic.

"Virtually," she replied with a grimace. "I try to shut down most of the gross stuff. I'm not down to listen to hetero sex fantasies."

"Amen, sister," Morgan laughed. "So you'll help?"

"Yes. I will help," Eliza caved, somewhat reluctant.

"Awesome! I'll hit you up with the details. Goal is to do this before Halloween. But if I can manage to coax a small extension out of Harding I will."

"Good luck with that," Eliza scoffed.

Morgan chuckled, turning around to leave. She, for a fleeting moment, felt on top of the world. All of her plans were coming together, and like cogs in a machine, her brain was running as smoothly as it possibly could. No migraines or random flashes— only excitement for the future. As she trotted downstairs back to her next task, she was blocked by Colt's linebacker body. She flashed him a smile and moved to get past.

"Hey! Rainbow Fright…" he barked, stepping in front of her, forcing other people to divert as they blocked the primary path. "Your last draft was riddled with grammatical errors. Like Christ, do you know how to use a comma? Your sentences run on longer than you do. Also, it's 'Mission Viejo' with only one 'J.'"

"I'm sorry, Mr. Harding. I'll be sure to fix it." She walked past him, yet he followed her to the main floor, continuing to grill her.

"It's too late, I had to fix it myself to get it done by the deadline," he huffed.

"I'm sorry, sir," She said, stopping to face him again. "I

understand it was a little messed up, but are, like, a few missing commas really worth getting so upset about? I understand I need to be more careful, and I will."

"Yes. You will or you won't be here. Maybe you should focus less on your passion projects and more on assigned stories so you'll make fewer mistakes. You're an intern, remember? Not Susan Sontag. Now listen well, Transylvania Barbie, go and get your pretty little ass to work so I can focus on big-picture shit, please? Thank you." He never gave her a chance to speak; instead, he marched off back toward his lush office.

"Fuckin' bigot," she mumbled low, though not low enough.

"Excuse me?" Colt steamed, turning around slowly to face her.

She didn't know what triggered her to lash out, but she was in no way quick enough to stop herself from saying, at the top of her lungs: "I called you a gods damned bigot! You're misogynistic, you make uncool comments about me being a Vampire, and you've talked down to and demeaned me since I arrived! Do you hate all the women who work here, or is it just me who gets the special treatment!?"

For the first time, the room fell silent. All the bustling movement stopped. Morgan looked around the room. She saw Eliza baring her teeth and shrugging her shoulders. It was the best Morgan could ask for. Even she didn't know why she said it.

"Meet me in my office, Miss Scriven," Colt said with a sigh, cold like the soldier loading his weapon for the firing line.

Ah fuck, Morgan thought, sweating profusely. She followed Colt back up the stairs, this time to his office at the end of the building. She spared a final glance back down to Eliza, who mouthed "Good luck" in response. Though the look on her face didn't seem as positive. He held the door open for her, locking it behind them and pulling the shade down. Morgan felt more nervous now than when she interviewed at the Belfry or when she was first chained up by the Lounge.

"M-Mr. Harding," she said, cupping her hands together, "I'm sorry I lost my temper. I-I should not have outburst like that. I'm under a lot of p-pressure right now and… I… I'm sorry."

"Just can it and sit down, Scriven," Colt said, and she obliged. He poured himself a drink from his ornate crystal decanter, off his minibar. It seemed Colt needed something a little extra to level himself, though he drank slowly and deliberately. "Are you familiar with Phyllis Barks?"

"Yes, of c-course. She's the first female Preternatural to be on prime-time news. In 1979, I think? She's my hero! No kidding," Morgan said, swallowing her nerves the best she could.

"It was technically 1978, but good. Because I have a story to tell you about that Shifter." He sat down across from her, behind his massive desk, inherited with the title of editor.

"It was twenty-five years ago, maybe longer. Well before they came in with this frickin facade remodel," Colt took a drink but made a sour face before he continued. "I started working here, and it was a fuckin' sausage plant. Nothing but guys doing what guys do best: being foul. I'll be honest, Scriven, as a man who loves journalism first and everything else second, I never understood it. I tried my hardest to be kind to the secretaries because no one else was, and it made them more likely to stay and learn. They all got churned out with a ridiculous turnaround. You'd think it was a burger joint, not the first paper aimed at Non-Humans. However, throughout all the torment and abuse, one woman persisted. Barks. She was a bombshell, that one. I was more than blessed to be around her, to be honest. She climbed ranks like you've never seen. She saw that paper journalism was a thing of the past. Got a job with the network, working both angles and just submersing herself entirely in the world of Non-Human journalism. She got there way faster than I did, I'll tell you that much."

"We stopped working together, and we never kept in touch. It wasn't until a rooftop pool party in '88 that we'd meet again. Those parties were insanity, more blow than you will ever see in your life, let me tell you that." Colt was incapable of masking a toothy smile.

Morgan pursed her lips, stifling a laugh.

"Anyway," Colt continued, clearing his throat. "She had way more men pining for her attention than she could possibly want, and knowing her, that wasn't much. But she gave me time, a couple of hours, a few drinks. She gave me time, just like I gave her time all those years ago. When she was an intern in college."

Morgan smiled at him, noticing where this was starting to lead.

"I finally gathered the courage to ask her how she did it. How did she not break? How did she put up with all those nasty, lecherous men? She told me, 'I didn't. I just told myself it would all be worth it and that once I reached the top, I could look back down and laugh.' I asked if she did it. Make it to the top. She said to me: 'I'm at the top looking down… but I ain't laughing.'"

Colt took a long pause, like he was paying his respects to the dead. "What she said next I'll never forget. She said: 'So when you're Chief Editor at the Chronicle, promise me one thing: you won't be a parasite, feeding on the women that work beneath you. If anything, callus yourself and treat them as you would any man. Don't let them stay soft'… I don't know what happened to her, Scriven, but she was stone cold sober when she said that and a shell of who she once was by that point. I see I've gotten carried away at some points, and I admit that… but you need to know two things about me if you are going to keep working here."

"What's that?" Morgan asked, leaning forward, listening intently, and watching him with pink doe eyes.

"Firstly, I don't *like* any of you guys. But you, Morgana Scriven, have my respect. Second, I only treat you like shit *because* I respect you. Because you're fucking tenacious and you're going to knock the planet off its fucking axis when you reach the status of a decorated reporter. But I don't want you for a second to let your guard down. I don't want whatever happened to Barks and all those other girls to happen to you. If that means you view me as a shitty boss then so be it. Because at least at the end of the day, when you inevitably leave the Chronicle and move onto bigger and better things, you'll keep your eye on the side and your trust close to the vest."

"Wow…" Morgan said with a smile on her face, not brash enough to hold eye contact. Her cheeks flushed as she spoke again. "I… I don't know what to say. Thank you… as a start? I'm honored that you feel comfortable enough to share this with me."

"Well, I'm not gonna lie, I don't really see the bigot end of your comment," he confessed, scrunching his face.

"What do you mean? You're constantly commenting on my undead nature. How would you like it if I called you 'Tonka Tusker' and acted like it was a cute nickname?" Morgan protested softly.

"That's… a valid point… I guess I really *did* get carried away…" Colt sighed, standing and putting his rough hands in his slack pockets. "Listen, I'm sorry for what I said… but still… consider this a verbal warning. I can't have you mouthing off to me in front of the others, and I won't be nice about it next time."

Morgan giggled and stood up herself. "I promise it won't happen again, Mr. Harding."

"Hey," he reached down and grabbed his business card, turning it over and writing a number on the back, "My beeper. I can't always promise I'll be pleasant, but if you need something, just give me a beep. I'll try to make things move."

"Honestly. I could use a few extra days on the Donavon story. Just like five days. I'm so close I can fucking smell it," she pleaded, feeling more confident in asking this now more than ever.

Colt hung his head and chuckled a bit, "Already pushing it, I see. I guess I can do that for you."

Morgan looked down at the business card he had handed her and ran her thumb over the rough paper, her fang caught her bottom lip, and her eyelashes batted, looking up to her handsome, Orcish boss. "Thank you so much… I… Thank you, Mr. Harding."

"Don't mention it," he said, his tusked smile on display. "Seriously, keep *that* on the down-low… and when it's just us you can call me Colt."

6

Arriving at this off-the-books location on Halloween, Morgan expected a wild night. After a little pick-me-up in the car, she went inside. At the door, she practically purred a password, the one Dorian had given her over the phone: Sandu daltu.

Inside, she met two other girls, younger than her, eighteen or nineteen: Tiffany, blonde and Elven, and Diana, a Taknoling with purple skin, matching horns, and a spaded tail she kept hidden. They were both amazingly gorgeous and curvy in all the ways Morgan wished she was. Thankful for her long, shapely legs, she felt the rest of her body paled in comparison. Seeing the other girls dressed in vinyl booty shorts and tube tops didn't help the situation. Especially once she squeezed into white variants of the vinyl and fishnet. The other two had been adorned with cat ears, tails on their shorts, and masks that featured whiskers. Morgan received a similar outfit, albeit with white rabbit ears and cottontail. Morgan was silently grateful not to be wearing what equated to a Catfolk costume.

Tiffany and Diana were nothing but excited, claiming this was their first Lounge event. Morgan, now the veteran of one party, immediately took a stance of maternity. She didn't want to frighten them, but she wanted them to know that they could be safe if they were smart. She told them not to go anywhere alone, and in the scene, their consent controlled everything. They nodded and listened intently. Then she began going on about the benefits: the pleasurable parts.

After a while, the rest of the servants showed up to get their costumes, each seeming complacent and eager to serve. Unlike the new girls, all they could talk about was how amazing Ziusudra was as a master. One of them, a literal Catfolk, approached her and gleefully shook her hand.

"I've heard of you, but it's awesome to finally meet you," she said. "How come you're not living at the Babylon yet?"

"I'm only contracted for four more gigs after tonight… gotta have a day job still, ya know?" Morgan answered.

There was silence at first, then the group of more veteran

servants laughed.

"You're hilarious," a Giant man spoke."Eventually, Mr. Z will ask you to stay. He likes to have us all close and in one space."

"For his pleasure," the Catfolk added. All of them seemed unnaturally happy. Morgan felt uneasy, fearful that she might end up like one of them.

"Oh… well, time will tell." She said, trying to stay cordial despite her unease.

Theodora had been at the edge of the space for gods know how long. Animosity bled from gold eyes, leering into Morgan's with raw, impassioned loathing from a porcelain mask of false cheer. She instructed the group on their serving procedure, as well as described what Morgan and her new friends would be doing a few hours into the party. Morgan had never worked in food service, but sex work felt somehow less intimidating.

The space was wide-open, broken up by support pillars and temporary red velvet curtains designed to look higher class. It was far from empty, however; one section saw a group feasting on sushi off the bodies of naked women. Another contained a full-scale waterfall spilling wine. A third section featured sex swings in use, and a fourth hosted fencing matches. Servants with endless smiles, in provocative cat and bunny outfits, patrolled the party, waiting on the massive congregation. One thing she noticed, everyone was wearing masks this time.

Hours would pass, and she would cater to the guests. Offering champagne on a silver platter that had been difficult to balance at first. After a while, she had it down pat, gliding around the party with ease. She attended to as many of the elaborately dressed patrons as she could, their outfits, lavish gowns, or tailored suits in bright colors that matched their jewel-encrusted, feathered masks.

She was apparently not up for sale just yet, as no one asked for her services. Though while stopping at one group, masked but oddly familiar, she was offered lines to do with them. This she gladly accepted, before moving on.

She managed to arrive just as Ziusudra himself had collected a gathering of individuals who fawned over him like Christ in a Renaissance painting. She felt drawn to the main man, approaching him while attention was off for a moment.

"My friends," Ziusudra boasted. "I assure you, enlightenment comes with repetition. We struggle so that we may reap the rewards. That is why the Echelons exist. That is why we require *dues*. You have to be invested in every capacity of the Lounge for the system to work."

"Champagne, Master?" She asked during a pause, noticing his empty hands.

"Naturally," he said, taking one. "How are you doing, Miss Vaughn?"

"Doing well… honestly excited for tonight," she admitted. "I was a bit nervous seeing all the guests, but… I'm eager to please them."

"You honor me with your willingness to serve," he rumbled, caressing her cheek. "Our friends at the Keep surely appreciate your company as well."

"The Keep, huh?" she inquired. "Who are they?"

Ziusudra pointed across the space to a group of blonde, ageless Elves, all dressed in silver suits. They cackled amongst themselves, drinking wine and shamelessly revealing their faces, the only ones at the party to do so. They also didn't bother to wear outfits of any kind, choosing to coordinate in their metallic suits and their women in dresses that appeared to be of the same material.

"You see the man at the center, the short one with short hair… the one who looks like the living embodiment of Napoleon Syndrome? His name is Lionel Shaedresh. He's the head of the Shaedresh family and is a very wealthy, well-connected High-Elf."

"They seem like an… interesting bunch," Morgan said, thinking about the rumors she'd heard. The sprinkling of theories she'd heard around the office, that the Keep was a front for the Elf Mafia… a gang known for connections to the Lenoran Legion.

"Interesting is one way to put it," he said sternly, and lower than he'd ever spoken. "I am reluctant to work with them myself."

"Then why do it?"

"A matter of necessity… but only for now," he said with a smirk. "I should let you be to your duties… and I to mine. Sha hatti darisam, my dear."

Morgan, with still a full tray of champagne, made her way over to the Elves. She was masked, and as long as she didn't grin too wide, they'd never see her fangs. She could play off that she was Human as long as she needed to interact with the xenophobic mafiosos. As she approached, her Vampiric ears picked up the fringes of conversation, one that sent a chill up her spine.

"The Moth has been seen flying around lately," one of the Elves said.

"It hasn't, has it?" Replied Shaedresh. Morgan winced. "Where?"

"Supposedly, in Hollywood, he stopped a car with his wing and nearly killed a guy."

"Fucking freak," Shaedresh replied "That bitch has never had any respect for anyone. Decides to join the Feds like we forget that you're a fucking Cryptid. Don't care how many cases it solved. A fucking freak in more than one sense."

All the while, Morgan stared off into space, trying to ignore how they were talking about her aunt. How they were demonizing her in every way. Morgan never could wrap her head around it; just because M was built like a brick house and had the moniker "Mothman" assigned to her, so many assumed she was male. She wasn't and never has been. M is her aunt, and Morgan has never seen it any other way. She kept her hands on the tray and a ditzy smile on her face. She still was selling the character, but some were more perceptive than others.

"Champagne?" She said, stepping up to the circle. A few took some without thanking her.

"What were we talking about before this?" Shaedresh said, snapping his fingers. "Right! The shipments. Just because the Moth is active again doesn't mean we need to worry. We have been getting the product in at an exponential rate, even coming from Europe. So we should be good where we're at… and if the Moth comes near us, we'll deal with it."

Morgan fought the twinges at the threats they made about her aunt. She didn't realize she was loitering for so long until one of the other Elves turned to her and made a disgusted face. "Can we help you?" He scoffed.

"Yeah, toots… beat it," Shaedresh said. "This is for the big kids to talk about, not pets."

"B-but of course," Morgan replied, turning away and shaking her head. *Shipments… shipments of what?*

And so she returned to her patrol of the party, making a few rounds. It was on her passing by the curtains that she saw *him* speaking to Theodora several yards away, nearly dropping the platter when she did. He was dressed in his finest suit, with another woman on his arm, his mahogany skin hidden partially by a mask, but Morgan wouldn't miss those antlers anywhere.

"B-Balam?" She choked on the gasp.

The woman on his arm stepped out from beside him. She recognized her, too. The silver hair, the black and red eyes, the constant, evil grin. *Yessenia*. Together, they mingled at the most prestigious sex party in all of Los Angeles. A thousand questions of how and why filled her mind, nothing made sense in an instant. It was like her entire world was crumbling down around her, the sky itself cracking open and spilling with it Armageddon.

As those three mingled, ignorant of Morgan's presence, she stood frozen, unable to move. As Balam, Yessenia, and Theodora laughed together, Yessenia was the first to stop and open her eyes, staring directly at Morgan. They locked eyes, and Yessenia grinned wider. Morgan began to hyperventilate.

Anger, fear, confusion, betrayal. She couldn't pin down one emotion. There were too many. The urge to vomit came on when she watched Yessenia grab Balam's face and kiss his lips. Then came the migraine. Shocking and sudden, like a bursting electrical current; like a pick through Morgan's right eye to the back of her skull. Corpses were clear in her vision once she closed her eyes. Everything was bathed in crimson. The blood of innocents or the light from the washed-out, carmine sky, she couldn't be certain.

Morgan pushed into the nearby hall, dropping the platter with a calamitous crash. Alone in the dimly lit white corridor and drab brown carpet, she collapsed, holding her splitting head as images of sex and carnage occupied her brain simultaneously. Balam's face smiled between the images, quickly turning sinister. His antlers seemed to grow and splinter with the sound of breaking bone; his flesh split, and snakes exited his skeletal mouth. She wanted to scream, but it all seemed to subside together. She shook, soaking, albeit sweating more than she shed tears.

"Morgana, my dear, please tell me what is the matter," Ziusudra, undetected in his approach and just as uncanny in timing, slowly knelt beside Morgan, still curled in the fetal position.

"Nothing, M-master," Morgan breathed. He pulled out a handkerchief and patted her forehead, she immediately felt calmer. "Just nerves I guess."

"I thought you were excited," Dorian said, concern clear in his voice. "What can I do to make this easier for you?"

As she looked up at him, she was sent back to another image, this one a memory from the first night they met. She saw his body over hers, a feeling of insurmountable bliss overtaking her. She felt euphoric beyond comparison, craving his flesh and letting him take her body in kind. She didn't realize that in the waking world, she was biting her lip, her head now resting in his hand.

Why do I feel so safe with you? Morgan thought. *I should fear you, I should hate you. Why do I want you?*

"We're ready for the ladies, Monsieur," Theodora said, entering from an adjacent hall. "Why is she here and not out with the others?"

When Morgan looked up to the Domhainn woman, something further down the hall caught her eye. She swore she saw a young woman with skin the color of a doe's coat and curly black locks. She stood at the end of the hall, disheveled and bloodied, wearing a *Bob Dylan* tank top just like Morgan's. She shivered in place, beckoning Morgan to come to her like a wounded child pleading for help. It was the girl. It was Chrissy Donavon.

"She was just having a bout of stage fright," Dorian said turning to his assistant. "But she is better now. Right, my dear?"

"Y-yeah," Morgan replied, only half paying attention to what was said.

"Good. Then let us begin." Dorian helped Morgan to her feet as Theodora gathered the other girls.

Together they were led a different way than the one she came. Morgan looked over her shoulder, and Chrissy was no longer there as they passed, with no exit or way to pass them. She felt unnaturally cold, colder than ice. Nothing made sense anymore in her world. Nothing felt real.

7

Behind three curtains was a bondage bench, each occupied by a woman who was strapped down. Their heads and shoulders were still behind the curtain, but all else was exposed to the crowd. On the other side of a curtain, Morgan, Tiffany, and Diana waited patiently for their first clients of the evening. They were all nervous, but Morgan doubted the other girls felt the knots in their stomachs like she did.

She heard the attendant greet each of the men as they reclaimed their tickets. On this side of the curtain, a brass masked guard, looking particularly bored, reading an issue of *VOGUE*. She gripped the mount tightly, praying that she did not hear Balam's name. Glancing to the side, she saw Tiffany had been purchased already. Her squirming and giggling were a sign she was enjoying herself. Another name was spoken, and Diana was taken. For her, there were no preliminaries; her body jolting back and forth.

Morgan tightened her grip; she was the only girl yet to be purchased, or they were simply taking their time getting ready. "Thank you, Dr. Sequoia. Enjoy," the attendant said in their scratchy, guttural tone. Morgan trembled, her thoughts firing like bullets from a machine gun. *This can't be happening. Does he know it's me? Does he even fucking care?*

Balam positioned himself behind his girlfriend, her soft backside presented for him. He noticed her trembling frame.

His hands hesitantly touched her flesh. There was a bizarre silence only between them. The girls bookending them were moaning and screaming in pleasure while Balam's fingers had barely touched the hem of Morgan's glistening shorts.

A violent passion overtook Balam, his hands gripping her bottom and pulling them down roughly. He wasted no time, ripping her stockings open and revealing her g-string-clad rear and womanhood. He gave a breathy croak, trailed by the words "Oh, god, yes," mumbled under his breath. Morgan was certain he would find out it was her. Though she still tried to pretend it was just another John, she knew the closer he got to completely taking her, the sooner all would be revealed. Even still, it seemed there was a shudder in his touch, a mental block holding him from doing as he normally did as a Lounge member.

She felt him slide her panties aside. Kneeling like a proposal, Balam kissed her, his tongue going wild as soon as it made contact with her flesh. She moaned, her body defying her as it often did, making it difficult to do anything but become engrossed in sensation. Her legs tightened around the bondage horse, shaking with desire for more.

They could no longer pretend they were strangers. Morgan recognized his touch, his kiss, his lust. Her desire grew like fire, scorching the nerves she had and replacing them with blind pleasure. He gripped her hips and teased at her sensitive bundle of nerves, continuing well past any of his previous records. Morgan lost control of her eyes, rolling back and lids fluttering as he drank from her like she was the fountain of wine, becoming just as drunk.

There was barely any time to recoup before his bare hand struck her right cheek, then the left. Then right. Then left. Over and over until her flesh resembled his more than her own, with more than a few bruises. She never once called the safe words, allowing him to continuously strike her. He was brutal and relentless, only yielding when he had exhausted himself. Morgan buried her face into the leather pillow beneath her head, stammering, trying not to make a sound, just in case he still didn't know it was her. Even still, she could not fight her whimpers.

Balam unbuckled his belt, gently pulling her thong down

over her freshly bruised rump. She trembled as the cloth brushed against the raw skin. Her womanhood wept, hungry for his throbbing member. She wiggled her hips, as weak as she was, to lure him further. His hands found her waist and caressed her exposed midriff just before the curtain. With one simple, fluid motion, Balam joined them together. Morgan's climax was more immediate and far more intense than any she'd had in a long while, including her tenure with the Lounge and the Belfry. Perhaps it was who it was, the fact that she felt like one of his concubines, his high-class whores. He was treating her just as he would any of the other girls. At least then she knew, at this moment, he was invested in her.

Morgan screamed finally, her voice strained.

"That's it, scream for the Doctor…" Balam taunted. "Batty-girl."

It happened again: an orgasm that rattled the bench she straddled, her body tensing around him. He laughed as if it were a game, watching her fall apart just like he'd done to so many strangers before. But she wasn't a stranger; he knew, she knew, and each other knew. Yet for some reason, she couldn't stop herself. Despite the pain in her heart, her body was in bliss. For a brief, fleeting moment, Morgan was happy in her relationship: for the last time.

"Red," she called, the most final of her safe words. The guard looked up from his magazine, dropping it to the floor and moving with haste to Morgan's side. "Red!" She surrendered.

Within seconds, Balam was separated from her by another brass-faced guard, who reeked like a wet dog.

"Is everything alright, Miss?" The attendant on her side asked in broken English, speaking with a scratchy, high pitch. He unhooked her straps and helped her to her feet. "Are you hurt? Do you need a paramedic?"

"No…" Morgan shuddered, her body crashing down from an ecstatic high only to dump her into the depths of sorrow. "I just want to go home."

"Uhh… let me get the Master," he said, wrapping her in a blanket and then heading out to the party from the back rooms. Mere seconds it seemed, and Ziusudra was there, a look of distress awash over his sharp features. Morgan was already standing and making her way toward the door.

"Morgana, my dear. You called the safe word, and now I understand you want to leave?… Tonight was supposed to be mild. Are you okay? Did Dr. Sequoia hurt you?" he asked, a boiling choler building in his voice.

Not how you think.

"No, M-master… I-I just… I-I don't feel well," Morgan stretched the truth. "I have to go now."

"My dear, you will miss the ceremony. I planned to honor you," he said with a warm smile and gesturing out to the party. "Is there no way I can get you to reconsider?"

"Can I just get my things?" Morgan asked, refusing to look Ziusudra in his crystal blue eyes, too embarrassed to face her Master.

"I am sorry this happened," Ziusudra waved to the attendant violently, who rushed from the space in kind. "I will have security escort you out of the building, so whatever disturbed you does not bother you again. I am so sorry, my dear."

"P-please don't apologize, Master," Morgan wept, no longer capable of holding it back. The guard returned with her purse and another small cloth bag containing her clothing. "If anyone should apologize, I-I am sorry."

She marched past, using her memory to guide her out of the building, leaving the attendant in the dust. The guard followed, but not before shrugging to his employer. Ziusudra watched Morgan leave, clearly hearing the sounds of her sobbing. He cracked his knuckles.

Though some people had left the debauchery early to experience the rest of All Hallow's Eve, many remained. Dorian Ziusudra had easily convinced Tiffany and Diana to stay amongst those enjoying the festivities. He claimed his party "wouldn't stop until the witching hour." Something many of his compatriots and servants expected to be literal. Despite Dorian's disappointment about the change in plans, none noticed, many of all kinds still drawn to his light until entangled in a bisexual frenzy.

Theodora Abaddon instructed the servants as they closed down some of the more eccentric activities and packed them up to be carted out. A more clinical-looking seat with straps for arms and legs was wheeled in. With it, the servants brought a multitude of black candles, with swirling Elven inscriptions carved into the wax. They surrounded the scene with candlesticks that stretched from a few feet to well over 6 feet tall. One by one, they were lit, and the electrical lighting was turned off, setting the mood to an already heated engagement.

A stranger stood in the corner of the room, leaning on one of the posts and hiding behind a collection of candles, their face obscured by their hood. Theodora smiled and moved to the figure, in her hands, a tan envelope, sealed with the knotted snakes of the Lounge. Before she even spoke, she handed it to the figure, who leaned forward from the darkness to reveal the tips of their brick-red horns as they took it. They broke the seal immediately, revealing a large wad of crisp, clean cash within.

"I take it by this, it went well?" the stranger spoke, their voice rugged and tired.

"Without a hitch. Just as you predicted," Theodora tilted her chin smugly. "I do hope this compensates you enough. I added a bonus for such quality information."

"I told you it would work. Was it all you hoped?" the horned shadow replied.

"And more," Theodora sighed, savoring the memory. "Those two had a hell of a history. Sent the bunny scampering, and Sequoia bounced shortly after. Master thinks he did something to hurt her. He was furious. Sequoia is lucky he was only demoted by a rank and added to the watch list."

"We're running out of spots on the watch list. We only have so many eyes," the figure said without enthusiasm. They turned their head to the scene at the center again, watching the Elf Mafia elite and their gals entangled with Ziusudra in an act of lust. They scoffed at the hypocrisy of the mobsters.

"I hope you understand that I wish to keep this between us

for the time being," Theodora said, folding her hands at her waist, her golden eyes focused on the stranger with a flirtatious side glance.

"Of course. We wouldn't wish to cause Master any undue stress, do we?" The figure queried pleasantly. "What about the Donavon story? Should I intercept it again?"

"Not yet. Scriven is being trained well. She is following the code and took kindly to becoming subservient. Unquestioning even," Theodora said, looking up at her charge. "If she becomes a *real* threat, you'll be the first to know…"

Theodora stepped forward, playing with the ties on the figure's cloak, coiling one around her finger. "You are such a loyal pet. It's the effort of you and all the other watchdogs that makes all this possible."

They stepped forward closer to Theodora, holding her grey hands, and revealing their sharp-toothed smile. The stranger tilted their head to see the crowd below had changed. Instead of being dressed to the nines, they were draped in faceless red sheets; like waves of blood spilling from their crowns and falling to the floor. As the red-cloaked figures surrounded the orgy, its participants remained unfazed by the faceless ones that observed them.

"Will you be staying for the ritual this time?" Theodora asked. A pair of servants approached her, dressing her in a violet robe, distinguished by an angular hood that only covered her upper face. "As my personal pet, you're welcome to join us."

"No, thank you. I draw the line at the chanting by candlelight. Always have," the stranger withdrew their hands, trying not to convey their unease.

"Suit yourself," Theodora giggled. "One day you may find yourself wanting the enlightenment we bring… and we'll be waiting. Sha hatti darisam."

"As you say… Sha hatti darisam," the stranger replied, heading toward the dimly lit exit, looking over their shoulder every few seconds to make sure the red cloaks weren't staring at them with their featureless faces.

Diana had been strapped into the chair, her purple body

convulsing in ecstasy as Ziusudra took her. He gripped her thighs, her ankles not strapped in. She let out an animalistic scream, throwing her head back and arching her spine. The excess of their pleasure dripped into a small trough connected to the bottom of the chair. A cloaked figure reached out with hands gloved in red silk, holding a shallow alabaster bowl. Once it was full, another would approach and begin to collect more. Diana was oblivious to what was going on around her, merely enjoying the endless ravishment her new Master provided.

As she reached another orgasm, the other naked men and women began to gather about Ziusudra's waist, forming a gown of bodies. Low and in unison, the cloaks began to chant in an ancient tongue. Their hands were outstretched in prayer. As their words began to get louder in their insidious harmonies, ripples under the rich, umber skin of Ziusudra's back began to form, slithering like worms beneath his flesh. Soon, he was grunting in a mixture of indulgent pain and pleasure, the ripples collecting at his shoulder blades. As this anomaly became more prominent, the same happened with the skin on his brow.

As he brought Diana to yet another climax, her eyes began to lose their color, fading to a pale, lifeless grey. The skin of his back split and tore, a massive set of feathered wings sprouting from his shoulder blades, their darkness glittering like a galaxy. Horns pierced through the skin of his brow, long and ebon as if crafted of obsidian. Lost in his rapture, Ziusudra reveled in his transformation, heedless of the breaking girl and fervent worshipers— shrouded by colossal wings like the night sky.

8

Apartment 161's phone rang off the hook. Morgan gave up after her third attempt to call Raphie. It's Halloween night, so why would he be held up in their tiny apartment when he could be out with the love of his life? She feared calling a fourth time would either get Balam or a tired Seth, neither of whom was what she needed. Morgan struggled to dial Raphie's pager number between stoplights.

It had gotten late, there weren't many children out, but plenty of troublesome young adults. On the passenger side were her purse and bag of clothes, both having spilled out onto the floor when she scrambled for her cell phone. Too distraught to put the top up before leaving, the tip of her nose turned bright red to match her eyes. Once the page had gone through, she hung up her phone and dropped it onto her lap. Lying on the seat beside her was a business card with a number scribbled on the back. At her next stoplight, she leaned over and picked up the card. Printed on the front was the name 'Colt Harding'. Morgan sighed heavily and dialed the number.

"Now just wait," she choked out to herself, trying not to sob. "Nah, fuck this."

Without a blinker, Morgan took a hard turn as she passed a Sav-on Drugs; romping the curb, she entered the virtually empty parking lot. The inside of the building echoed with space; one cashier in the entire store. She grabbed a forty of Modelo and a quart of Häagen-Dazs ice cream before heading to the front. Getting in line, there was only one old, Human woman in front of her, and the Giant that stood behind her.

Morgan hadn't bothered to change out of her "bunny" outfit. Didn't even take her high heels off to drive. Something as inconsequential as dress was swept aside in the evening's turmoil. She didn't notice until she felt the Giant's eyes boring into her from behind. She gave a few spare glances back, each turning more and more into a scowl.

"Nice costume." The Giant tested his luck.

"Thanks," Morgan bit out, forcing politeness.

"You look like you pose for Playboy," he said, stroking his scruffy chin with his massive fingers.

"It's, like, Halloween, shitdick," she scoffed. "You said it yourself: 'costume.'"

"Whatever, bitch, I was just complimenting you."

Morgan wanted to scream. To turn around and bash him over the head with her bottle. To leap on the Giant and rip his throat out with her fangs. For the first time since her teen years, she felt the Vampiric urge to kill.

Once she was alone again, she turned her car on to keep the heat going and sat there, waiting, looking at her phone every few moments. It was unlikely anyone would call back, but she couldn't just go home. She knew Balam was probably there, waiting for her to walk in the door with that disapproving look on his face. *How dare he do this to us? How dare he? So many secrets... How could I do this? I'm just as bad.* She at least felt that there was some good in what she was doing. A girl is still missing, multiple girls that Morgan actively searched for… Balam could have facilitated their disappearances.

Some time passed. She chose not to drink in public just yet; the cops were out en masse, and she *was* a Vampire. Instead, she opted to just eat her ice cream. She didn't try to change in her car or anything; it felt pointless. She at least had her coat in the back seat, which she regretted not wearing into the store. Her body was still burning, her eyes, her head, her soul. It all finally broke loose; she sobbed into her steering wheel, furious, wanting to punch, claw, and rip. Rather than be violent, she continued to cry, sobbing the loudest, ugliest cry.

As the radio played, Morgan did her best to release some tension: doing a pathetic, solo karaoke, mouthful of cookie dough ice cream. "*We must try to ignore, that it means more than that. OOOH! WHAT'S LOVE GOT TO DO, G-got to do w-with it?*" She half sang, half sobbed. "Oh gods, Tina. How do you do it? Please give me your strength." She put her hand on her radio as if to gather divine energy from Miss Turner, almighty.

The high-pitched, digital ring of her cellphone went off, making Morgan jump in her seat. She hurriedly grabbed it, surprised it hadn't died without the charger. "Hello?" She sniffled.

"Morgan? I just got your page…" Colt said, somewhat irritated but equally concerned, his voice garbled and half-awake. "Is everything okay?"

"Um…" Morgan contemplated lying "No… I-I have nowhere t-to go right now. I c-can't go home… Mr. Har—Colt… I… I fucked up bad, real bad…" she began to sob again.

"Are you safe?" he asked, his voice changing to full alert.

"Now."

"Good. What happened?"

"I… I don't know… I…" It was then that the migraine behind her right eye flared up again, greater pain than it ever had been before. She had to drop the phone.

"Morgan… Morgan? Hello?" She could hear him say, but she couldn't reply. All she could do was quickly hang up the phone and let out a pained scream louder than anything she'd ever mustered. It devolved into a sob, tears streaking down her white face. Once the pain began to subside just a bit, she managed to lift the center divider of her bench seat and lie down across the tan leather. She surrendered and closed her eyes, a broken woman.

The clamorous bell signaled the day was ending for Medrano-Lynch Middle School. Morgan was, as always, one of the first kids out. Her mom and dad always told her, "Unless you have a club or speech therapy, meet us outside as soon as you can." She'd been called a goody-two-shoes and a loner because of it, but she didn't want to disobey her parents. Soon, the black CHP Mustang, provided by her daddy's work, would pull up along the curb and honk for her to come.

She hopped down, avoiding other kids, and sat on the furthest step down. Morgan was a bumbling and awkward preteen at her best. Braces were attached to her teeth, trying to realign her disproportionately small fangs. She wore large pink glasses, overalls, and had her hair braided into a ponytail. It would be years before Morgan would grow into herself, but for now, she was just happy she was an undead who could enjoy the sun.

Familiar grumbles came from the school's entrance. A group of kids Morgan had grown to know— against her will— made their way down the steps. Two of them were Human boys,

Kennith and Filipe. The third was an Elf girl, Sally Redstone, the meanest bully at Medrano-Lynch. For some reason, the boys flocked to her, but she was just cruel to them, too.

"Hey, Casper," Sally said, practically skipping up. Behind her preppy pink and black outfit and cheery sound, she was telegraphing her next insult. "How come you don't go to night school like the Vamp kids at the high schools? You don't even wear that rainbow shit."

"Y-you m-mean refractium?" Morgan asked.

"Nerd," Filipe hid with a cough.

"I-i-i-is it?" Kennith mocked, both laughing.

"Yeah… whatever. Why?" Sally pressed.

"Um… I-I'm a Trueborn…" Morgan said, struggling to stop her stammer while she was nervous. "Th-that m-means I-I was b-born a Vampire… some other k-kids are, too. B-b-but not at this schoo—"

"See?" Sally said, cutting Morgan off. "Told you she was a freak."

The bullies cackled and continued to talk about Morgan as if she weren't even there, pressing down the steps and onto their journey. Thanks to her Vampiric hearing, she understood everything clearly.

"Freak is right," Kennith said. "She's a Vampire and in puberty. I've heard all they want to do is fuck everyone all the time. Then they kill you after sex like a praying mantis."

"Gross, she was probably staring at my boobs," Sally scoffed.

"She probably wanted to kiss you, too," Filipe added. "And don't let her! That's how people become Ghouls."

"Do you think she acts like that because she's a Vamp or because she's retarded?" Sally suggested, all of them laughing.

Morgan felt her stomach boil. She wanted to stand and shout at them, or start clawing at Sally with her talons, dig into Kennith's meat with her fangs, and puncture Filipe's eyes with her thumbs. Instead, young Morgana just held onto her backpack like a pillow and sat, waiting for her parents. She didn't make a noise and just let the tears well up. A small, puffy, green dragon was attached to her backpack like a charm, an almost duplicate of her stuffed wyvern back home: Mr. Cuddles. Morgan held it in her hand and felt the boil vanish. For a moment, she wished she were strong enough to stand up to bad people, like her daddy and Auntie M. The sun continued to shift, and Morgan waited, growing ever nervous. Forty-five minutes passed. Most kids had left for the day, and only a few late clubs remained.

Mom and Dad are never late. She thought, pacing back and forth and swinging her arms about, having finished her homework already. As the time continued to pass, she sat back down in her spot.

"Hey, Blondie!" Raph's shrill, young voice came from behind as a few more kids exited Comic Club with her. She waved goodbye to them and stood beside her friend and fellow nerd. Raph was dressed as a tomboy as she always did, wearing a *Teenage Mutant Ninja Turtles* t-shirt, blue jeans, and short, curly hair. Morgan was admittedly a little jealous of how free Raph was to choose her nicknames and style. Though Morgan would be lost without her, being the only friend she had after moving from Pennsylvania, and that never changed. "What are you still doing here?"

"M-My parents never came. I think they forgot me," Morgan pouted.

"Maybe they're just late. My mom is late all the time to everything," Raph said, patting Morgan's shoulder.

"Not m-my dad," Morgan replied. "He's *always* strict about being on time to places. 'If y-you're on time, you're late,' he always says. That's why I have p-p-perfect attendance."

"That and you don't get sick, which is so boss. I wish I didn't have to deal with colds and asthma." Raph noticed Morgan was still lost in thought. "Hey! I saved up all my allowance and got *Metroid*! The main character is a chick in power armor! You can come home with me and play it. That way, you can call your mom from my house."

"Okay… I just don't w-want my dad to yell at me for leaving without p-permission, again."

"He can yell at me!" Raph insisted. "It'll be my fault anyway."

"Alright… let's go," Morgan giggled.

They walked down Oxnard Street toward Raph's house. Morgan watched over her shoulder with every few steps, just in case they missed her parents driving by. She held onto her backpack straps; she didn't like the way her overalls dug into her shoulders if she didn't. Raph noticed her solemn mood and reached into her shoulder bag to pull out a drawing pad.

"I drew us as superheroes in comic club," Raph said, opening the pad and showing an impressive drawing of Morgan in a pink variant of a Scarlet Witch-style get-up. Raph was done up as her version of Spider-Man, except teal. Morgan smiled and took them from her. "I call myself 'The Arachnid' and you can be the 'Crimson Fang'… unless you have something better."

"Oh my gods, Raph, these are so c-cute," Morgan said.

"Well… I mean… I guess yours can be cute. I think mine is badass," Raph said with a nod of self-assurance.

"I think it's cute that y-you drew it at all, b-butthole." Morgan laughed and smiled, softly socking Raph on the shoulder.

"I'm glad you like it."

They pressed on past a few crosswalks before the major intersection where Raph turned to go home. At the end of the street, several cars had backed up and crowded the kids' vision. As they approached, they could see the flashing lights of first responders as well as a pillar of black smoke.

"What the hell is going on?" Raph asked, standing on her tiptoes. "Is that your aunt?"

Morgan narrowed her eyes and looked for the 7-foot-tall mothwoman. She caught sight of her antennae and short grey hair.

"Y-yes, it is," Morgan said, her face becoming grim as they passed the first layer of traffic and saw the twisted masses of metal that were once vehicles lying in the center of the road. Both vehicles smoldered, smoke and steam billowing out. Morgan noticed one of the vehicles was once a black Mustang. Through its smashed windshield, within the erupting smoke, a small charm of a green dragon, half blackened by the flame, still somehow hung from the rearview mirror.

"That's m-m-my parents' c-car," Morgan said, a cold realization as she whimpered.

"No way…" Raph grabbed her head and began to panic with her.

Morgan was hesitant no longer and dropped her bag, powering through the crowd. Maxine, speaking to a paramedic, turned and saw the small, albino girl darting past police at speeds exclusive to a Preternatural.

"Morgan?" Maxine said to herself, lunging after the child. "MORGAN!"

Using all of her might, Maxine leaped and caught the girl, who too possessed immense strength. Maxine picked Morgan up off her feet and held her facing away from the wreckage, but she had still seen the burnt corpses, trapped in the crushed front seat.

"Daddy! Mommy!"

9

Morgan jolted awake when there was a knock at her car window. Her horrid dream was more a memory than anything else. Tears still streamed down her face. It was bright out already, her eyes doing a poor job of adjusting. She sat up in the driver's seat and saw a police officer standing there.

"You can't stay here," he demanded through the glass. "Get outta here."

She nodded and started her car, thankful that he didn't clock her as a Vampire, or else she might have had some serious trouble.

It was well past noon when Morgan pulled up into her parking space. She kept a spare pair of ballet flats in her car at all times and changed into her previous day's clothes from before the party. Just a pair of jeans and a T-shirt. Despite all her sensuous night work, she had never entered the next day with such a preloaded shame.

She turned the key of Apartment 161 with bated breath, opening it slowly. Balam paced the living room, a cup of coffee sitting on the center table, no longer steaming. He saw her, his motions became more animated. She looked him in the eye and gave a weak, forced smile.

"Hey," she said enfeebled.

"'Hey?'" He scoffed "You were gone all night and morning and all you have is 'hey'? "

"What's the pleasantries matter? We're both liars." She shook her head and dropped her laptop at the entry table. Without saying another word, she pushed past Balam, walking straight to the fridge and pulling out a beer. Utilizing her Vampiric strength, she popped the cap off with her bare hands, taking a big swig. Balam crossed to the only opening in and out of the kitchen, leaning on the counters and blocking the exit.

"Now you're day drinking? Who even are you?" Balam said angrily.

"Please stop, Balam," she retorted. "I'm exhausted and have a massive headache. Neither of us is on any grounds to be judging each other's decisions. We both fucked up."

"Why do you keep saying 'both'?" Balam said, playing his best stupid.

"I'm not a fucking idiot, I know what the Lounge is… " Morgan scoffed, taking another drink. "I went in because of a story. I'm undercover, under a fake name. A 17-year-old girl, C-Chrissy Donavon, went missing… she worked for the Lounge. T-to get where I am, I-I had to have sex with clients, and that was… so wrong of me… I-I've never regretted anything more than doing this without ever even trying to c-communicate. It got out of hand so fast, and I didn't know how to make it right. I'm so sorry, Balam… I truly am… but because of it, I've learned of some fucked up shit. Kidnapping, and possibly worse."

"That's no excuse for what you did."

"It's not, but… why were *you* there?!"

"Morg, I'm not like those other people," Balam deflected, still failing to be fully honest and doing a poor job of hiding it.

"Oh, so you only pay to fuck your *girlfriend*? Of course,

that's the noble thing to do. I'm so sorry I mistook you for one of *them,*" Morgan scoffed. "No… that's wrong… because you're clearly fucking Yessenia too…"

She pushed his arm off the counter with ease and made her way to their room.

"How do you kno— How long have you been working for them?" Balam asked, turning around and following her. "Answer me. How long have you been whoring yourself out?"

"'Whoring?' You're gonna jump right into calling me a whore?" She shook her head, scrunching her mouth and nose in disgust. She marched to their closet and pulled down an empty blue duffel bag.

"I really don't know what else to call it at this point ..."

"Real classy, babe," Morgan replied, looking him in the eye. "I'll leave… your name is on the lease, so it only makes sense that I'm the one to bounce. After all, I cheated too… and for that I only bear regret."

Morgan sniffled, no longer capable of holding back. She turned away to the drawer on her nightstand, pulling out as many of her socks and panties as she could and stuffing them into her bag along with a plush green dragon— which she squeezed— before moving back to the closet.

"Morgan, I don't want you to leave," he said.

"Have you seen my Bob Dylan tank top? It's like, one of my favorites," she said, not looking in his direction. "It was my dad's."

"No, I haven't…" Balam begged, "Please let's talk through this."

"What the fuck do you want to talk about? Tell me how I'm a slut for doing sex work? Which I've been making a killing in, thank you." Morgan turned to him, poking at him with her fingers as she sliced him with her razor-sharp tongue. "Then you can try to tell me you only joined for networking and things got 'out of hand', right? Finally, you can belittle me and scold me like the child you *clearly* see me as. Is that what needs to be said? 'Cause I'd rather cut the bullshit and skip to brass tacks."

"You wanna skip to brass tacks? So, what, I fuck a few servant girls and that gives you free license to get railed at

Lounge parties?" Balam blustered.

"A… a few?" Morgan choked out.

"Yeah… more than a few. And it was fucking great. Better than what we do most of the time."

"Better than…" she started to say. "You fucking bastard, so first it was because we didn't have enough sex, and now it's because I wasn't good enough at it? Pick a fucking lane, Balam, and stop trying to blame me for your shortcomings."

Morgan felt the migraine return and held her eye. She simpered and stormed into their half-bathroom. Grumbling, she opened the medicine cabinet and pulled out a white and lime green bottle labeled *"Tylenol: Undead Strength"*. She poured two neon green capsules into her hand and took them with her beer.

"Fucking migraines. Go away," she groveled to herself. She stood, invisible in the mirror before her, just a floating shirt and jeans. The images weren't coming this time, merely the pain, though it seemed to be compensating for the ease in the mental torment. "Never even got my mirrors."

"Morg…" Balam said, growing weak, approaching the doorframe of the off-white bathroom. "Look, you do have a point… There is some shady shit behind the scenes. But the world they offered me… I mean, come on, you saw how alluring Mr. Z makes his parties."

"Speaking of headaches." Morgan rolled her whole head with her eyes, tilting her neck and looking at him lazily. "Look, I don't give a fuck how allured you were." Morgan stood up straight and faced him. "Do you have any idea what these fuckers are doing? To innocent kids? Teenagers, Balam. They're pulling them into this fucked, dark world and doing gods know what to them. At least three girls have gone missing around these people since summer. Did you know? Or did you just not care where the pieces of meat you blow your load in are coming from?"

"I… I didn't—"

"Didn't what!?"

"I didn't know!" he bawled. "You're right, I joined to build connections for my clinic. I've made so many invaluable business partners that I couldn't dare back out, or we could lose everything I'm working toward. For us. For our future."

"Pfft, some future," she said, walking past him and back into the common space, looking for her tank top among the rubble.

"I should've known better… that your typical pretty, airhead valley girl with a massive trust fund wouldn't get it," Balam dismissed with a waning boldness. Morgan stopped in her tracks.

"What did you say?" She turned to him at a snail's pace. Her nails dug into the flesh of her palms, her fists were balled so tight. "My parents are dead… I'm not some fucking trust fund baby… It's my inheritance… from when they *died*." Morgan stormed back into the room, continuing to pull dresses off hangers and into the bag. "I would much rather have my mom and dad than their fucking money… asshole…"

Balam pouted, looking like a scolded puppy. "I… I don't believe this."

"I don't really care if you do or don't, Balam… I made fucked choices. They were awful things that hurt you badly, and I see that. But I've come clean, I can't justify or excuse away any of the shitty things I did, but what about the shitty things you did? Why do you get to be the shocked and appalled boyfriend when I'm just the cheating bitch?"

"You want the truth? Fine!" Balam yelled, extending his arms widely, in a desperate gesture for Morgan to hear him. "I was invited once, and they seduced me. It was that bitch Yessenia who pulled me in the first time. She knew exactly what to say, and I buckled. I was her +1, and soon I was paying monthly dues."

"Y-yessenia…" Morgan forced her confident smirk, though it dwindled almost immediately. "Well, that's something we can call a wash. You may have lost interest in me, but she liked me just fine. You got to screw some teenagers; meanwhile, I got Top Performer at the Bourbon Belfry. That will always be a crowning achievement for me… because I was *desired*. By the clubgoers and by Yessenia herself."

"That whore," Balam grouched, staring at their bed with fury.

"That word is getting a lot of mileage today, and I don't appreciate it," Morgan chastised. "That woman may be a deviant, but those parties bring out some seedy shit. I *have* seen it."

Balam stayed silent, spacing out and staring at the bed, only for a second glancing back to Morgan to see her staring at him in kind. Frustration and confusion were plain on her face as she focused on the bed as well. After a second or two, the gears began to turn in Morgan's head.

"You did sleep with her at one of the *parties*… right?" She choked out.

Silence remained constant.

"Did you fuck her here… in *our bed*?" Morgan's voice began to break, her eyes welling with tears.

Balam looked to the floor, saying nothing. Morgan held her mouth agape, tears trailing down her cheek as she said, "W-where I sleep with you every night? I can k-kinda understand going out to cheat, b-but in our bed? Did you at least wash the fucking sheets?"

"I think…"

"Gross."

"Look… the first time was an accident and I've—" Balam tried to defend himself, but was swiftly cut off.

"FIRST? You mean you fucked Yess here more than once? When the hell did you find the time to keep sneaking a Vampire in while I was gone? That must have taken some *Mission Impossible*, crack teamwork to pull that shit off without anyone noticing. 'Cause it could have only been when I was at school or work, which may I say, is *BULLSHIT* because you told me if we were less intimate because of all my studies that it would 'be fine and work out.' Your words. Now I see it's because you just pay for someone else's pussy or page Yess for a booty call."

Morgan fumed, her body tense from the nape of her neck to the bottoms of her toes. She reached into the closet, grabbed more work-appropriate clothing, and continued packing, sniffling to herself. "And what's worse… I'm trying to understand when and where you met Yessenia."

"It's not important."

"Yes, it is!" Morgan blustered. "Where!?"

"At a bar in Downtown. I was there on business and stayed late. I overheard her talking about Sanguimancy, and I got curious. You don't meet someone on the streets who knows medical practices often… We shared a few drinks, and she introduced me to the Lounge. That's the truth!"

"Unbelievable," she said, shaking her head.

"Batty-girl, listen to me…" Balam said low and forlorn.

Morgan spun on her heel, her forefinger an inch from his nose. "Don't you dare call me that again!"

"Morg…"

"Y-you wanna know the sick thing? I was intimate with you every night I was with a John because it ate me alive! It made me feel like shit because you were home alone after working your ass off, but, *nope*: he's not working hard to make a better life for you, Scriven, he's fucking older women in your bed and spending aaaall night banging strangers. Stupid me, right?" Morgan began to cry again, taking a deep breath and continuing where she left off. "I'm not even sure if your graveyard shifts at the clinic are real."

"Yeah you are stupid, pretending to be a big shot reporter so you had an excuse to fuck around. Of course you found this as your first story. It only makes sense that a slut like you would go looking in places like that. I'm home thinking you're safe in Studio City when I should have been worried about you fucking around in Vulture Capital," Balam argued, only infuriating Morgan further.

"What? Y-you knew? How long have y-you known about th-this??" She stammered, feeling the panic set in at last.

"Since you first arrived at the Lounge," He admitted, cold as ice. "That party… I was there. I showed up late and didn't stay long when I saw you, but… You were blindfolded. So you never saw me."

"You motherfucker…" Morgan fumed, tears streaking down her face. "I tried my hardest to make things work since we moved in together. It was b-beautiful for a solid moment. Then we got so 'b-busy' we never had a moment together. I care so much about you, Balam. Even throughout all of this, I still worried about how badly this was going to hurt you. In the moment, I was thinking with my pussy, but it ate at me every single day. I didn't know *how* to tell you," Morgan pleaded in her own way.

"Of course you never tried to tell me. How can you say 'I'm gonna go fuck people for a story, but I'm only "pretending" to be a whore'? I should have known. Of course if the pressure was really so bad you would have come to me but you didn't"

"And what evidence did you give me that told me you wouldn't react exactly like you are now?" Morgan shook her head, growing tired of being berated. "I don't think theres a world where you'd ever support me through this."

"Ya know, you have a point…" Balam scowled. "I wouldn't have. Broken clocks and all that."

"Therein lies the rub," she said on trembling breath, being fully honest with him and herself. "I discovered things about myself on this story… I think you found out something about yourself being a Lounge member. Part of me feels like we could have made this work if we were just real from the start."

"I doubt it," Balam said, crossing his arms. "You obviously didn't have me in mind when you fucked Yessenia and god knows who else. You probably don't even think about me at all."

"You have it so wrong," Morgan seethed. He ignored so much of what she was saying, but she still tried. "I think about your concerns and your fears, your desires, your needs, your wants. I buy our groceries and clean our apartment, and, when I have the time, I cook for you because even though I want a career of my own, *you* want Susie Homemaker. Raphie and I work our *asses* off to make sure it's that way for you… What have you done with me in mind lately? Do you think about *me* at all?"

"Of course I do," he moped, "I think about you all the time."

"Okay. What projects am I working on? What classes am I struggling with?… Who's my idol?… Where's my internship?… What's my favorite color?… When's the anniversary of my parents' deaths?" Each pause was met with silence. Morgan shook her head and scoffed at his incredulous behavior, realizing where she stood. "Wow… None of it, huh? You really don't know anything about me."

"That's not fucking fair!" Balam barked, making Morgan jump. "I tried my damndest to build a future for us! I did this only so I could connect with other doctors and specialists. It expanded my portfolio so much that it put this goddamn roof over your head! So no, I didn't enter there every night with the idea that I was going to fuck some random girl. You don't understand, Morg, once you reach a higher status, these people have a way of digging their talons into your brain, and you just lose all control."

Morgan was frozen in place, thinking heavily. Her eyes poured tears, not a sound coming from her open mouth. Finally, her voice crackled with noise, and she spoke. "W-wait… you… were a Lounge member *b-before* we moved in together… weren't you? Y-you've been cheating on me since we moved in… if not longer."

"Maybe *I* should pack my bags instead," Balam said, taking responsibility for the first time all day. "Besides… you having lived here devalues this place."

"Get the fuck out then," Morgan said, practically breathing frost. Her tears were the only sign she was feeling anything.

It didn't take Balam long to pack up; he only grabbed a few necessities, claiming he'd return for what he left. While he packed, Morgan switched into her plush pink robe for comfort. She stood patiently with her arms folded as if holding herself. As he moved about the space he slammed doors, tossed hangers, and huffed to himself every time he knew she was in earshot. Each time something would slam, Morgan would jump, forced to take a deep breath and slow the panic. He wouldn't try anything at this point, but she wasn't 100% sure, and that still frightened her. He emerged with his suitcase in his hand and a blazer hanging over his shoulder. She stood stalwart, refusing to budge or shed another tear in front of him.

"Goodbye, Balam."

He said nothing, merely turned and exited Apartment 161.

Morgan waited until his footsteps could no longer be heard

before beginning to sob again. She stood in place, paralyzed with grief. Only a few seconds passed, and she was alerted to the sound of Raphie's door opening. She turned, wiping her tears on her robe's sleeve.

"Hey," Raphie said, poking his head out. Behind him, Demy stood patiently.

"Hey!" Morgan faked happiness. "I didn't know you guys were home."

She couldn't lie to Raphie. His eyes were too kind. Morgan's knees crashed into the wood floor, exuding boisterous and ugly sobs. Raphie didn't wait; he sat down and wrapped his arms around her. Demy followed out and held her from the other side. Raphie looked up to his girlfriend, his heart breaking in empathy. Morgan gripped an arm each and went limp in her friends' embrace.

"I loved him," she grieved. "What have I done?"

10

The next few hours of the day went by painfully for Morgan. She was quiet, a trait she did not normally possess, but was overcome by silence all the same. She sat in her pink robe, between her friends. She had come to know Demy as a kind person; she knew now that Demy meant no harm to anyone. Morgan was grateful that the seeds of friendship were already sprouting.

As they sat, watching TV to decompress, Morgan could do nothing but think of her distraction from her pain: the story. She knew Chrissy was with the Lounge, and now she knew the Elf Mob may be involved with the case. She recalled the discs that were in Yessenia's office and wanted desperately to get back in. With Eliza's help, she'd have her answers soon enough… but there was more to the puzzle. Who were all these power players, and how did Ziusudra manage to pull together crime bosses from rival families? It didn't make sense. Morgan was determined to find out.

"Okay, loaded question, but are you feeling okay?" Demy asked her.

"Huh?" Morgan said, "Yeah, I mean… as good as I can."

"You just seem very lost in thought. Is there anything you'd want to talk about?"

Morgan looked to the floor bashfully; Raphie smiled. She felt like she could trust Demy, she was close to Raphie and he wasn't the kind to get mixed up into trouble long. So she told them… she told them everything.

"Fuck it," she said pounding the rest of her beer and standing to retrieve another one. "Chrissy Donavon. 17. African American. Human. Missing."

Once Morgan began her tale, there was no stopping it. For the first time in her journalistic career, she had an audience, captive at that. She told of the night she was hired at the Bourbon Belfry, admitting to lusting over strangers and dancing the night away.

"So you worked at the Belfry?" Demy confirmed, her brows scrunched.

"Is that a problem?" Morgan snapped back with a bit of her buzzed attitude. Raphie held his breath.

"Not in the least bit," Demy replied, shaking her head. Raphie sighed in relief. "I'm just glad you got out… The Tyrants, particularly Yessenia, are nasty people."

"You've met Yessenia?" Morgan queried.

"Once. Unfortunately." Demy appeared distracted before snapping back to attention. "Please, continue."

Morgan went into detail from there about Chrissy and her disappearance. How she climbed the ladder. How Morgan did the same. The tale of the Lounge seemed to most intrigue her friends, the lustrous and mysterious private lives of some of the most elite and respected individuals in the city piqued their interest. She didn't give names but the descriptions painted pictures.

A light lit up within her face when her story reached the first party, her body shifted, and her eyes dropped to the floor. Her finger traced the cool, wet exterior of the bottle as her lips formed a subtle smile. Without warning, she gripped her eye, wincing in pain before she finally took another drink and continued her story.

"So I stopped by the library and searched on the web…" She said, moving to her laptop bag to withdraw a set of black and white prints of the webpage.

"Man, the internet scares me," Raphie scoffed. "You watch, that shit will be everywhere by the turn of the millennium."

Morgan returned with the documents and plopped them on the coffee table.

"I looked into Ziusudra as a name, cause I wasn't sure where he was from. I didn't find anything on him, but check this out," she said and pointed to the spots she'd highlighted. "His name is Sumerian, like real ancient. Like… creation myth old. It's a derivative of the name… Utnapishtim? I'm probably butchering that. He's a king from an old myth in the Gilgamesh epic."

"Yeah," Raphie said, recognizing the second name. "I learned about that in my Mythologies class. He was like… the Akkadian equivalent to Noah."

"Right. Finding the name, I looked into the greeting. 'Sha hatti darisam,' which I didn't recognize when I heard it, but it's also Ancient Sumerian. Translated as 'To sin forever.'" Morgan continued.

"Kinky, and totally not spooky," Raphie said with an anxious sigh.

"And fascinating…" Demy spoke after hearing the crime drama unfold like a teleplay and just as intrigued. "How can we help?"

"I dunno… this is really dangerous," Morgan sighed.

"Blondie, we've got you," Raphie spoke up, and Morgan felt uplifted.

"Well, what I need is information," Morgan stated apprehensively. "Or rather, I need information that can't be obtained by normal means. The Tyrants and the Elf Mob are working together, and the Lounge is the glue holding it all in one piece. Chrissy is tied up somewhere between all of it. When I was at the Belfry, I found a floppy disk that was password protected. If they're working together, the Elves should have something like it. I saw some suits in refractium deliver a portable lockbox to Yessenia's people— my theory is that the suit works for the Lounge, and whatever's in that lockbox is something they don't want anyone seeing… that lockbox is at the Keep in Little Lenora… but I'm a Vampire and an Elf Mob run club would definitely be a risk for me."

Morgan felt the signals of a migraine strike her directly behind the eye, pulsing across her skull like sonar. She placed her hand over her right eye and grunted in pain.

"That sounds like where we come in, right?" Raphie said to Demy, before turning and noticing Morgan in more immense pain. "Blondie?"

Morgan proceeded to double over. "Sonofabitch! Motherfucker!" She screamed, stomping her foot and startling them both. "Fuck this hurts."

She rubbed her eye and stopped at the inner corner. She scratched at it with her long, red nails. A jolt of pain shot to the back of her head and ricocheted about. "I-I think th-there's something in my eye," she hissed.

"What? Do you want me to take a look? I know it's not necessarily something you could do easily without a mirror," Demy offered.

Morgan shook her head at first, then switched to a nod, whimpering like a wounded puppy. "Yes. Just look, okay?" She looked at Demy, who held her chin with just a touch for stability.

"I think there is something in your eye. Like a hunk of eyeliner or something," Demy said, leaning closer. "Do you have a magnifying glass?"

"I think I've got something, somewhere," Raphie said, running to his room.

"You have gorgeous eyes, by the way," Demy said, flashing a kind smile.

"Th-thank you. So do you." Morgan smiled back, blushing slightly. Before she could fully appreciate what was happening, she winced, having to close her eyes firmly.

"You okay, sugar?" Demy said, frowning grimly.

"I don't know. W-whatever it is, it fucking hurts," she said, letting her head rest in Demy's hand out of reflex, who gave her chin and cheek a gentle pet in an effort to soothe her.

"Found something!" Raphie said, entering the common area with a small magnifier he used to perfect some of the finer details in his art.

"Thank you, babe." She took the magnifier and looked in Morgan's eye. "Oh shit that's… a big something."

"Fuck just get it out! It hurts so bad!" Morgan cried.

Demy turned to Raphie, her voice shifting to a center of command. "In the side pouch of my bag, there's a pair of tweezers. Please, could you grab them for me?"

"Gotcha." Raphie nodded, jogging over to her purse at the entryway, only for a second before returning with the small black tweezers.

"Okay, sugar, you're gonna have to hold still…" Demy leaned in, holding the magnifier with one hand and the tweezers with the other. The sharp, angled tips touched the small, dark mass. It felt hard. "What the fuck?"

Demy finally managed to get a solid hold and pulled slowly. Morgan flinched, pulling away and causing Demy to also lose her grip. Demy was swift to reel back, fearful of scratching Morgan's eye.

"FUCK! GODS DAMNIT! I don't like this, Demy. This feels fucking awful."

"Maybe we should go to a doctor then?" Raphie said, looking to Demy, who nodded in approval.

"NO! No…" Morgan said and took a deep breath, flashes of swirling masses of calcified flesh, covered in eyes, polluting her mind's vision. "Just do it. Whatever this is it's b-been giving me fucking hell."

"Okay… only if you're sure," Demy said, not confident in what was being asked of her. She released the magnifying glass as her tattoo of clouds began to glow, lifting the tool in the air, freeing up Demy's hand to hold onto Morgan's face. "Morgan, sugar, I'm going to go slow, but this is some sort of build-up in your tear duct. It's going to hurt but if you can't take it or you feel like it's fucking up your sight you gotta tell me and I promise I won't touch it again. But, we'll need to see a doctor if that's the case."

"Okay," Morgan whimpered, pounding her fist on the arms of the couch. "I-I fucking hate things near my eyes."

"I get it, sugar," Demy said, moving to grab the mass again. She planted the tweezers on the dark hunk and gave a slight tug. Morgan replied with a grunt of pain. "Okay, it moved."

"FUUuuuuck" Morgan groaned.

"Going back in," Demy said, grabbing the now rice grain-sized piece. With a slightly longer tug, the mass extended more, and then more. Morgan screamed and dug her nails into the couch, tearing the fabric. Demy pulled it out far enough so Morgan could see it in her vision, revealing more of the hard black and forest green mystery.

"Fuck! Just stop!" Morgan waited for Demy to back away and jolted up. Now that it was out of her skull, she could see it. She marched with purpose to the bathroom across the way, nearly tripping on a dining chair as she went. In the mirror, just a robe was visible. Floating above it, a rough, inch-long spine, that seemed to glimmer in the light, protruded from her tear duct. Morgan wasted no time, leaning into the mirror and grabbing the now semi-flexible substance with her naturally pointed nails.

"One…" she began "t-two…fff," she pulled again, clenching her teeth sharply and grunting through the pain. The spine moved again, extended another two inches, causing merely a second of hesitation. She felt it in her sinus, in the back of her throat, shifting through her pallet and digging into the soft tissue behind her eye. After a final yank, the spine was free of her duct, and in the sink, along with it came minor droplets of blood. A single crimson tear trailed down her face as the tendrils and eyes engulfed her vision. The last thing she saw before she fainted was the world turning crimson.

11

Brilliant strobing colors polluted Morgan's mind like she'd

taken a powerful hallucinogenic. Eyes and tendrils spiraled around her, each a different shape and color. The eyes twitched, eternally darting about the shapeless, immaterial void. She felt as though she was falling infinitely through space. Before long, it became a tunnel, leading to a subway terminal. In an instant, she was sitting patiently, alone, waiting for a train. The reality of it all, however, was that there was no train. Rather, a series of images whizzing by, each an isolated memory. Morgan would blink and would find herself viewing an entire film's worth of content played in reverse, all centered around her life over the past weeks.

She saw herself mourning over her breakup with Balam, curled up with Demy and Raphie on the couch while she sobbed to a *Lifetime* movie. She was brought back to last night, at the lavish party where her relationship faltered; she thought she saw Chrissy Donavon beckoning for Morgan to come to her from across the hall. She saw herself in Colt Harding's office, an unseen tension between the two as he handed her his business card.

It did not take long until she arrived at the night she first became charmed by Dorian Ziusudra, and the images began moving forward. She watched herself be debased by the Upper Echelon of the Lounge, used as a plaything. Despite what she experienced elsewhere, this was a memory she cherished.

She could vividly watch herself swimming and bathing in the astonishingly deep spa. Dread overtook the eroticism that the previous memory had provided. All that she saw before was the truth; she could not deny these memories as anything but. Without warning, she was thrust into Dorian's penthouse hallway, stretching infinitely, seeming to flex and waver as if the Big One struck Los Angeles. She tried to keep focus as the world bent and bowed, seeing herself standing down the hall dressed in a white bathrobe.

Morgan chased herself down the hall, desperate to understand what she was experiencing. Somehow, she was in front of herself again, seeing the fear in her own eyes— and that *thing*. A living exercise in disproportionate anatomy and a face that seemed impossibly stretched over a blank surface. The thing chased Morgan, like a marionette of its own volition. A primal hunger was in its black, empty eyes, a speck of white as an iris, like a white dwarf star on the backdrop of the void. She could now see more of its scaly skin beneath the fleshy face mask. This only further disturbed Morgan.

She was suddenly alone in the endless hallway. From both ends, the paint began to break away and weather, crumbling upward to give way to red walls and black doors. Her fear became paralyzing, incapable of seeing either end of the hall. Another blur of reality, and she was beneath a crimson sky, clouds of ash swelling on the horizon past the ruins of LA; half the city was lifted in one solid piece and left to sink into the ocean, as if the very tectonic shelf the city sat upon had buckled and raised vertically.

Before her, hundreds of people of all kinds were being dragged into a colossal, rusted tower that pierced the heavens. They screamed for mercy, effortlessly carried by fleshy abominations into the infinitely spanning tower. Morgan tried to gaze up at the top of the spire, only to see it stretch far beyond what her vision would allow. Morgan followed the horde upon seeing one girl, dressed in lingerie and begging for her life. A girl who looked like Chrissy Donavon.

Beyond the iron gates of the tower, Morgan wept upon seeing a mountain of defiled and mutilated bodies, many of which had been blinded or their mouths sewn shut; they possessed bodies with twisted limbs or surgical piercings that could only cause agony. All, however, appeared to be in rapturous pleasure as they worked their art of pain and flesh upon thousands of souls.

Within the endlessly tall tower, Morgan's past self was held high, hoisted by a living throne, and bound to look upward through a massive opening at the black sun. On legs like coiled snakes, a gargantuan, four-armed goddess appeared, identical to the one seen in her terrible migraine visions. *Impossible.* Morgan thought, baffled at the impotence of her memory. She watched in horror, unable to act, as the monstrosity rose, its head adorned with six goats' horns. It bore multiple eyes that flashed a plethora of colors, rather like glowing beams of light.

Beyond her, watching from balconies along the inner wall were figures, donning sharp and sleek full-plate armor and brandishing ornate glaives. Perched on cloven hooves, with curling horns, and feathered wings like galaxies, they watched. The armored observers did nothing to assist the abominations; they merely surveyed with their glowing white eyes.

Neither her past nor present self could do anything as all four talons of the titanic deity touched her body, their razor-sharp edges cutting into the bare flesh of her past self. Layers of skin were removed, piercings adorned in nightmarish places, and her face scarred. That was nothing to say of the more carnal acts, the abominations performed. Both present and past wept, praying for a swift end to the torment.

"*Not today...*" A voice seemed to echo through Morgan's very mind, past and present.

A blinding flash of green light and an immense gust of wind forced Morgan to avert her eyes from the memory. She heard the entity screech in agony, a baleful wail like nothing Morgan had ever experienced. The hurricane winds caused Them and Their subjects to scatter into the dark ruins. Morgan lifted her eyes to see her past self adorned with lacerations and piercings across her body.

Naked and whimpering, her past self tumbled; ash fell from the sky. She felt anguish for herself, experiencing the abuse firsthand, twice. In her fall, something suspended her, holding her above the endless, forge-like spire that defied logic. A man in the mask of a plague doctor and a cloak of raven feathers approached Morgan, wielding a staff of green light. With a wave of his staff, her wounds and involuntary piercings seemed to heal and dissipate. The glowing lime-colored light of his staff faded as his hand outstretched to help guide her to the platform he stood upon.

"You must leave… before He finds you. I can return you, but only once." The man said, his robes like wings of a dark feather. She took his hand, and at that moment his eyes flashed green; from them blasted a black and green cloud, funneling its way into Morgan's eyes and nose. Her past self was knocked to the ground. Rather than crash into the steel, she fell into water, tumbling upwards to the surface.

Another blur of images, and she was in the bathhouse again. Dorian Ziusudra and Theodora Abaddon stood at the side of the pool alone as some mysterious red figures made their exit. Before Morgan could gather any details of their conversation, her past self emerged, once more, from the pool.

"Well, you certainly are full of surprises," Ziusudra mused, bending down to aid her climb from out of the pool.

"What the hell?" Theodora hissed.

"I'm sorry, Master, I must have dozed off in the water and sank…" Past Morgan said, confused. "Good thing I don't breathe."

"You do not remember anything else?" he said, looking to Theodora, who seemed just as intrigued.

"No?" Morgan said, raising a brow in suspicion, "Should I?"

"Naturally not," Ziusudra said, a remarkable smirk across his lips.

"I was actually wondering if you had a little time for me, Master." Past Morgan flirted, incapable of remembering what she had just experienced, and her present self helpless to warn her. "I still have some energy reserved and I'd like to expend it before I go home."

"Absolutely!" The corners of Ziusudra's mouth turned up as he pivoted to face Theodora. She had already retrieved a bathrobe for him to wrap around his new charge. "Theo, the bed chambers are already prepared, correct?"

"Yes, Monsieur, but she's—"

"Utterly unique," he finished, taking Past Morgan by the hand. Past Morgan smiled, looking up at him with naive eyes and flushed cheeks.

"But, Monsieur—" Theodora pressed, the concern prevalent in her voice.

"Theo, you can take the rest of the night off." He smiled down at Past Morgan as he ushered them to his bedroom, ignoring Theodora's pained expression. "Let us go to bed, Ms. Scriven."

That was the last slide of memory that was shown to her. Morgan sat alone in the train terminal, tears streaming down her face. A presence had snuck up on her, sitting beside her in her stupor. She turned to see the same mass of black and grey feathers, with a mask like a plague doctor, that saved her.

"In the liminal space between joy and sorrow comes the dream," He said.

"Dnatsrednu t'nod I." Morgan asked, clasping her hand over her mouth as she spoke. The room began to shake violently, rocks tumbling from the roof. Morgan could not scream before the tremors brought the tunnel down upon them both.

*****

"Ready?" Raphie said, sweating profusely, "One. Two. Three."

Demy and Raphie lowered Morgan's unconscious body onto the couch. Immediately, Raphie paced in dismay, his hand running through his curly black hair.

"What the strawberry fuck?" He finally said with a trembling breath. "What the fuck is happening to her? What the fuck is that thing in the sink? What the hell is going on? We gotta call 911. She's not waking up!"

"You're right," Demy said, looking at Morgan. Demy had sat directly beside the pale woman, caressing her head, the drop of blood still streaked down her white face. Without breathing naturally, it was incredibly difficult to tell if she was alive. Demy took the risk and opened her closed eyes, seeing Morgan's pink iris darting about back and forth. "She's in a REM state. I don't know if that means she's seizing or she's dreaming. But she's non-responsive."

"Okay then, I'm doing it," Raphie said, running up to their wall-mounted phone. He dialed the first two digits a split second before Morgan sprang up, more akin to the dummy from *Ferris Bueller* than a living creature. "Morgan?"

"Morgan, don't move, you just passed out," Demy said, placing a hand on either of Morgan's shoulders with a feather's touch.

Morgan gasped for breath, not a reflex she normally felt

unless she felt suffocated or enclosed. She panted, holding her hand over her chest, feeling her slow heartbeat. She laughed manically, running her hands over her face, smearing the dark red blood against her skin, staining her robe, and leaving a pink stain on her flesh. Her body violently shook as she scanned the room, wide-eyed, her insane laughter deconstructed into uncontrollable sobs.

"I-I remember… everything," Morgan stammered, breaking out, again, into a peal of frightening laughter, snorting as she did.

"What happened?" Raphie ran over, kneeling before his best friend, and cupped her hand in both of his "I swear to God if that Ziusudra motherfucker—"

"I'll be fine…" Morgan insisted, a broken smile plastered across her tear-streaked and bloody face. "But, I think I know where Chrissy is…"

12

The Cryptid Chronicle was as buzzing as ever the day after Halloween. It was a new month, a new day, and work had to resume. The news waits for no one, as Colt had told Morgan. She entered the office space off the floor with a timid step. She gripped her laptop case so tightly her knuckles ached and her hand shook.

"Hey, Girlie," Eliza leaned back in her chair and smiled at the Vampiress as she approached their shared cubicle. "What's the good word?"

Morgan kept silent, standing there before Eliza for a moment, frozen. Her mouth hung open in a desperate attempt to form words, "I…. I need to talk to Harding."

She said sternly, not looking at the woman in her

heterochromatic eyes. Instead, she just kept forward and marched up the stairs, gripping the rail firmly as she trudged. Once she reached the editor's door, she hesitated, knowing that this meant having to recount what she'd encountered… what she'd experienced.

She knocked.

"You may enter," Colt said from the other side, robust as always. When Morgan opened the door, she saw him sitting over his desk in a rather sharp blue suit, wire-frame glasses on his nose, eyes scanning document after document sprawled out across his desk. He glanced up at Morgan and spoke, "Hey, Scriven. Everything okay? You worried me on the phone."

Morgan stood there frozen again, looking at Colt in his fiery orange eyes and shuddering.

"I-I-I…" She struggled, lifting her laptop case. "I… have m-my story…"

"Okay…" he said, suspicious. "Let's see it then."

Morgan gripped the case tightly, her words caught in her throat, which felt as though a crushing fist had been wrapped around it.

"I…" Morgan began, but couldn't get another word out. Instead, it was just tears. She crashed to her knees and let out a banshee wail. Colt stood up, his face shifting from hard ass to genuine concern.

"Woah… what the hell, Scriven? What happened?" He said, approaching her and kneeling beside her. Still, she sobbed, incapable of catching her breath as the racing thoughts took hold. She became overwhelmed with all she'd learned. All she'd *felt*.

"I… I'm the inside girl," she said finally, through her bawling. "I went underc-cover… I… oh gods. Oh, gods… I guess…I let my guard down…"

She knelt in the fetal position and cried some more, begging gods she didn't believe in for an answer of some sort. He tried to console her as best he could, with a professional pat on the back.

"Th-there's so much to this, C-Colt…" She sat up, turning to him with a thousand-yard stare. "This is deeper than anything

I c-could have imagined. We're t-talking magic. Real fucking magic. Powerful shit… something… I… they…. Know things… The Lounge… they're behind it all."

Colt went still, his tone chill.

"Who else knows about this story?" Colt said.

"Eliza, my best friend Raphie,…" she sniffled, "And his girlfriend."

"Okay… this is heavy, and if it's as dangerous as you say, it's not smart to talk here. The walls are very thin," he said as stern as an ox. "You should come to my place tonight. We can work out all of the details of this story, and you can talk about whatever you need to, okay? Whatever you went through was…"

"They t-t-tortured me…" she said cold as ice. "Among other things…"

"The Lounge?"

"No…" Morgan said, her eyes welled with tears, but a primal survival instinct was alight. "So…so much worse."

*****

Demy paced about Apartment 161 as Raphael lounged and played on the PlayStation. He watched his girlfriend wander their small space, occasionally passing by the TV when Raphie wasn't in combat. She would look out the window, feeling a pendant of an animal scale that she kept around her neck. It was new. Ever since that rainy night, she came to Raphie, that night her relationship with Amy fell apart, she's worn that pendant.

Something happened that night, something more than just a breakup. Raphie had yet to deduce what it was. But something told him that wasn't what was on her mind in this instance.

"Penny for your thoughts?" He said, pausing his game.

"Hmm?" She said, turning to him, her full facial features illuminated by the light. "Oh… um… I'm just… worried about Morgan."

"You too, huh?" He placed down the controller and rubbed his face, fatigued emotionally. "I… I can't even begin to imagine what she went through if it was all true."

"You believe her, right?" Demy asked, more begged.

"I mean… I think she experienced something, or else she wouldn't be acting this way," Raphie said, weaving his fingers together and slinging them between his legs. "I'm just confused, is all. If she did find another world, then she may have uncovered magic more powerful than even your coven has, no offense."

"None taken. Whatever the Lounge is dabbling in is like nothing I've ever heard of. Demonic beings, apocalyptic landscapes, and erased memories? That's all new to me. I'll do some research, but that's some high-level magic we're talking about," Demy foreboded, sick with worry. "There's only one group I know who would have access to that kind of power."

"What is that?"

"The Legion," Demy uttered the name like merely speaking it would inflict a wound upon Raphie. "Or more specifically, they're sympathizers… the Elf Mob."

"What makes you think they have the power to do something like this? The Mob is under the same restrictions as everyone else."

"And it's not like we can't practice magic just fine," Demy protested. "Raphie… if we can find a link to the Lounge and the Mafia, we can help Morgan find some answers. We can help her answer the questions she can't."

"And how do you propose we do that?" Raphie said. "What you wanna go to their clubhouse and just walk right in?"

Nightfall had overtaken the silvery streets of Little Lenora. Magically charged illumination combined with the latest in fiber-optic technology created images on buildings and hanging off signs that moved like living beings. Countless bars and clubs lined the main street, each trying to sell their brand of the best time money can buy.

None stood like such a beacon of intemperance as The Keep. Taking up nearly half a city block, the movie studio turned nightclub stretched stories above the smaller businesses that surrounded it. Floodlights moved across the sky as giant girls made of light and dust danced atop the roof. Stones built around the old building truly created the illusion of being an ancient Elven structure, complete with elaborately carved and impossibly smooth masonry. From its gaudy "drawbridge" entrance to the backside of the building, a line stretched. Among the front, Raphie and Demy began their infiltration.

Raphie anxiously watched the lights and colors around him, having never gone to Little Lenora at night. He was truly amazed at the magic and tech that was always exclusive to the Elves. Though he knew now that what he had considered to be magic before was just parlor tricks compared to what was possible. He scratched his ears, now bearing a pointed illusion with mass that his lover Demytria had crafted. His hands moved to his ornate, branch-like antlers. He understood her choice to make him a Wood-Elf, given his skin tone. Demy might have an easier time glamoured as a High-Elf, but she explained it should be fine, as that was half her heritage. Even with all the lights and fanfare around him, Raphie still found himself staring at her.

She looked gorgeous, dressed in a short, spaghetti-strapped dress and a pair of chunky black heels. He had tried to find something more "club-appropriate" to wear in his wardrobe. Slacks, nice shoes, and a grey button-up shirt that he rolled up the sleeves of. He already felt stifled and was dying to unbutton it. He looked up, pulling on his collar and unbuttoning the top few buttons. He hated how starchy dress shirts felt. Up past the floodlights, Raphie swore he saw a massive bird of a peculiar shape flying from within the clouds. It was impossible to tell for sure, but it looked almost like a giant moth. He mused that it might be Morgan's aunt, out and about doing her PI thing. She was known to use her method of flight when necessary, often springing for that or public transportation.

"Hey, I got a question," Raphie said out of the blue.

"What's up?" Demy said, looking out into the street, ever

vigilant.

"If you've got a car, why do we walk and bus everywhere?"

"Can you afford parking in LA? Cause I can't." She replied.

"Fair enough." He laughed.

"My Bronco's also not the most reliable. If I'm with someone I don't wanna get stuck."

Demy was looking about discreetly as if she was trying to keep a 360 view while they waited in line together. Raphie scrunched his face and cocked his head.

"What's wrong, doll?" he said.

She pointed with her nose to a car across the street, a black Monte Carlo. Within, two people could be seen watching the long line into The Keep.

"What's with the creeps?" Raphie scoffed, noticing the two occupants.

"Don't know," Demy narrowed her brow, "But I smell bacon."

"Cops?"

Demy nodded once, a look of concern held firm on her face. "Don't know why they're here, but I don't trust them."

"I am not a fan either. Cops only came around our neighborhood to harass us." Raphie added shuffling forward in line. "Two-faced, whack ass mother fuckers."

She shifted her weight to face him. "This town is all about misconceptions. No one is as good as face value."

"You are," Raphie said, taking his girlfriend's hand.

She looked to her feet, the fingers of her other hand grazed over his knuckles. "I'm honored you think so highly of me. I'm not perfect, though."

"I never said you were," Raphie replied, "But I think you're real. Even if you have a cloudy past, it doesn't mean anything about who you are today. You dropped your coven because you smelled Gruel's half-baked bullshit from a mile away."

"'Half-baked,'" Demy laughed. "You can say that again."

Before they realized it, they were at the tall, Elven bouncer, dressed in a slick silver suit that had a sheen-like battle armor.

"Are you on the VIP list?" He asked

"Nope. Just casual," Demy said right away, stepping slightly in front of Raphie. She reached into her bag and withdrew two playing cards. With a quick flick of her wrist, they appeared as California IDs. As soon as she put them back into her purse, they returned to their normal shape and design. Raphie blinked and felt he had missed the whole transformation.

"Go right in," the bouncer said, after a moment of pretending to listen to his headset, and opened the velvet rope that barred the entrance.

"Thank you," Demy said, sickly sweet.

"Um, how'd you do that?" Raphie asked low, as the bombastic dance music began to overtake all sound.

"It's a perspective illusion. I only wanted people within 10ft to see it, so rather than cast the illusion on him and risk him disbelieving it, I cast the illusion on the cards, making us all perceive exactly what we think we should be seeing."

"That's brilliant." Raphie smiled, squeezing her hand and moving with a spring in his step.

The two crossed a faux drawbridge that was built over a koi pond designed to look like a moat. Suits of ancient-looking Elven plate armor, crafted to look like mithril, lined the "portcullis" into the explosively loud club. They were in.

Hundreds of people filled the massive multi-level nightclub. Much of its structure was smooth and geometrical, creating pillars like ancient obelisks for dancers to take up stage or large platforms that acted as VIP balconies. It truly felt as if they had stepped into medieval Ile de Lenora. Demy pulled them both toward the massive bar she had seen when entering the building.

As they proceeded deeper, they found themselves closer to a center stage, before a giant screen, projecting images that could only be described as abstract underwear ads in neon. Raphie's eyes wandered to the highest point in the club, just above the center stage. He saw the veiled-off and empty VIP section that seemed to radiate a heavenly glow, standing like an ornate, multi-person throne.

"Betcha that's where the boss likes to hang out," Raphie said, over the roar of the music.

“I’m inclined to agree with you,” Demy replied, reaching the edge of the bar and grabbing the bar top between a pair of separate men. “You want a beer or something else?”

“A beer is fine.”

The two Elves looked somewhat annoyed at first, but Demy batted the lashes of her pacific blue eyes, and they backed off. Raphie had to hold up the rear; they wouldn’t let him in because he’s a dude. He smiled, feeling validated as a byproduct. He observed while she ordered their drinks, quick to realize how out of place he was seeing the many High-Elves doing the Macarena un-ironically. Security seemed to be sprinkled about, focusing like the guards of Nottingham Palace.

Demy thanked the bartender, paid, and spun around to deliver the glass of cold Dwarven ale, called *Ironstout*, despite not technically being a stout. A light, Elven sour for Demy, always springing for a mild, sparkling flavor.

“I hope this is good,” She said. “You see where the employees are coming from yet?” She put her glass to her lips as she spoke to hide the sight of her talking.

“Not yet,” He said, searching about less discreetly.

“Keep your eyes on one hemisphere at a time,” she said adamantly, but kept her soft smile. “Don’t let them see you looking. They might get suspicious.”

“I think my melanin alone might cause that,” he chuckled, sipping his strong, bitter ale.

“I’m serious,” she said through a juxtaposing smile. Demy scanned just past Raphie’s shoulder and saw a door with a red label marked ‘Staff’ in Elven and, in much smaller print, English.

“6 o’clock,” she said through a sip again. Raphie began to turn around. She gripped his wrist, pulled him down to her, and planted a rough kiss on his lips. “Don’t look,” She yelled in a whisper as they parted.

“Sorry,” Raphie smirked. He was about to ask if looking again would get him another kiss, but he noticed movement in the lofty VIP balcony. Several people were filing up the steps and into the lushly furnished section. He saw the elaborately dressed Elves and recalled how Morgan described the leaders at the party. Fine silvery suits, blonde hair, smug entitlement: it was all there. This was Lionel Shaedresh, owner of The Keep and, in all likelihood, a mob boss.

"Well… I bet the main office is clear, if we're gonna go now's the time," Raphie stated.

Just about then, the lights dimmed and the main stage lit up. A troupe of acrobats dressed in their skimpiest clothes began to perform a sensual and elegant dance with one another. It was traditionally High-Elven, eloquent, deliberate in every motion, and practiced by only the most dedicated of artists.

"That's our cue," Demy declared, took two small vials from her bag, and dropped them open into their beers. A softly glowing blue ink spilled from it and began to pollute the drink. Demy proceeded to pound her beer and slam it down empty on the bar top. By the time the glass touched the surface, she was no longer there.

Raphie, distracted but still holding Demy's hands, jumped when she vanished from his sight.

"Drink your beer!" She said, pushing at the bottom of his now glowing glass. "Before someone notices."

He began pounding his drink quickly, turning invisible with his partner. He looked at his own hands, seeing nothing and feeling incredibly uneasy. As he pondered his current reality, he felt a tug at his sleeve.

"C'mon," she said, almost laughing as they pushed through the focused crowd, a few people were bumped, and drinks spilled, but nothing got on them, so in Raphie's mind, no harm, no foul. So far, they were without a hitch. *Don't jinx it.* Raphie thought.

13

Colt unlocked the door to his Studio City condo shortly after 8:30 pm. Morgan stood there, less than confident. She was still dressed in the day's work clothes. They were dirty when she put them on, not having done laundry due to the whole Halloween fiasco. Neither had she bathed since last night. Her nose and eyes were still puffy and red, having cried the entire drive. Her laptop case seemed to never leave her hands since the day started. She held onto it with all her life. It was the only thing she had at this moment that was still working: the story.

"Hey," he said, his voice low and gentle.

"Hey." She trembled in place. He stepped aside to create space. "Um… y-you have to invite me in."

"Oh! Right… uh… Come on in."

She did not assume Colt Harding lived in squalor, but his condo was ornate, designed, and decorated like a model home. The downstairs was mostly one open space, kitchen, living room, and dining room with a door to a guest room beneath the stairway. Upstairs was a loft-like space that was Colt's master bedroom.

"You have a beautiful home," Morgan said, void of emotion.

"Thanks." He turned to her. He was in casual wear, a white T-shirt, and jeans. He rubbed the back of his bald head, scratching behind one of his pointed, moss-colored ears, unsure what to say or do at this point, so he just asked. "You didn't come here to talk interior decorating, Scriven. What happened?"

"Well… for starters. I think I know where Chrissy Donavon is. But I don't know if you're going to believe me," Morgan stated, not looking him in the eye.

"Try me." He crossed his arms.

"That night… the night I went to the Lounge," she began. "Something happened that I couldn't remember… After the party, I was alone in the halls and shit got weird. Like, nothing made sense. There was this girl with dirty fucking feet that spoke in tongues, a horned dog, and… that thing…"

"Thing?"

"It was… how do I even fucking describe it?"

"Come on, we should sit down," Colt said, guiding her to his dining room table where he pulled out a chair for her and took her laptop. When he took the case, he nearly dropped it as he misjudged the weight by how effortlessly Morgan toted it around.

“Okay… so this thing,” he asked.

“It was… short, but bulky. Scaly. It had… this… face. I c-can’t even begin to describe how it looked. Like… a mask. A latex mask that had no eyes or teeth…”

“It might have been a Cryptid,” Colt said.

“Huh?”

“A Cryptid,” Colt repeated. “These all sound like Cryptids.”

“Oh… I… never thought about that. I’ve never seen anything like it.”

“Some Cryptids are one of a kind, some of them there’s no other being on the planet. Like Maxine Mothman.” He said, completely ignorant of who her aunt was. She kept that to herself as she often did. M preferred it that way.

“Well… that makes me feel a little better, but… what happened next…” She froze again, tears forming in her aching eyes. “Ziusudra… the whole head of the operation was there, and he found out my name. Took me to his bathhouse, and there were these, like… c-cloaked figures, not a face shown among them. He t-tossed me into the pool and… oh gods…” she broke again, remembering the torture she endured.

“Is that when it happened?” He asked, doing his best to console her by caressing her shoulder.

“Y-yeah…”

She went on to describe the entirety of it. The monsters, the giantess, and her cloak of bodies, the brutality they committed against her. She described everything about it in graphic detail. So much so, Colt appeared visibly ill at times, only muttering the words “Jesus Christ” over and over.

“Why… why didn’t you tell me any of this sooner?” Colt said, finally, “I could have helped.”

“Because of this,” She said, reaching down into her bag and digging out a small mason jar with the black and green spine encased in it. Along with the laptop, this was her most important possession. “Was in my skull.”

“In your what?” he said, leaning over to look at the glass. “How did you find that?”

“I pulled it out of my tear duct.”

“W-what is it?”

"I don't know."

"What. The. Fuck?" Colt sputtered in disbelief

"So you believe me?" Morgan pleaded

"I…. I don't know what to believe… can I see your notes?" he asked.

"Yeah, sure," she replied, pulling her entire laptop out and all of the paper documents she had. She sprawled them out across his table and opened her bulky laptop to her digital corkboard. It was as she reached across the table that her currently unkempt hair fell about her face. Its soft and silky texture was gone due to a lack of care.

"Gods damnit," She muttered.

"What's wrong?"

"I-it's embarrassing," She said, timid. "I haven't showered since last night… I had performed at a party and, gods, I feel disgusting."

"Do… you… want to use my shower?" he croaked.

"Holy shit… that would be awesome," she said tearfully.

"You know what, you go for it. There are soaps, towels, and a robe in the master bath. No conditioner though." He gave a charming smile and swept his hand over his bald head. "But if you did half of what you said in your initial report, you need and deserve it. I'll put on coffee and go over these notes."

"Thank you, Colt… you're something else," she admitted, standing and running upstairs to finally get clean.

Morgan took full advantage of his kindness, spending well over half an hour crying off and on as the water poured across her face and body. For the first moment in a while, she felt a sense of safety; she felt that being so vulnerable was natural. Now she could be honest with Colt moving forward, yet she still feared what he would say once he saw all her debauched details. Part of her hoped he was into it. With how everything went down, one would have thought she'd want nothing to do with sex for a long while. And yet here she was feeling a desperate longing that she couldn't fight. On top of it all, she knew it was wrong to burn for your boss, but being wrong hadn't stopped her this far.

She finally stepped back down the open staircase, holding

the banister. Colt had spread out all her handwritten documents and was now scrolling through her laptop. Wire-frame glasses sat on his hooked nose, the image of her digital corkboard reflected in their lenses. He noticed her as she rounded the stairs and headed into his dining area/kitchen, not that different from Apartment 161's, just nicer.

"Hey!" he said, standing to pull a chair so they could look together. Once she was sitting, he went and retrieved a cup of steaming hot coffee. "How do you like your Joe?"

"Shit ton of sugar, please," she said with a weak smile "No cream."

"I respect that." He nodded.

Once it had been prepared, he approached with a mug whose design long since started to wash off. Something to do with New York City. "So… I've been reading, and I'm not going to lie… I'm impressed."

"Thank you?" Morgan blushed, hiding her face as she drank. "Wow… that's a damn fine cup of coffee."

"French press, baby. The only way to go," Colt smirked, sitting down beside her. "I do have to say: you did a lot of stupid shit, too. You put yourself in the line of fire over and over again, it's no wonder you got hurt… but you did this all on your own?"

She leaned back in her seat and put her mug to her lips, steadying with both hands. She nodded.

"I looked at your notes about the Lounge and their allies. If you're talking about Elf Mob and T-Town Tyrants working together, you're getting yourself in the middle of a centuries-long feud-turned-alliance. Do you have any idea how bad this could blow up in your face if you stay involved?"

Morgan looked on in horror, clasping her hand over her mouth. "I can't back out now, I'm a part of this. Do or die. I-I just hope that this story is enough to keep me in the internship," she said, her voice tired.

"Scriven… I was never going to kick you from the program," he said with a sigh, one hand rubbing his temples.

"W-what?" She said, turning to face him.

"You were just so bright-eyed and bushy-tailed, I had to

teach you a lesson… after the hard work you've displayed, I'd be a heel if I fired you now," he confessed, not looking at her for the whole while. "I would have only kicked you if you found *nothing*. I never once thought that would be the case."

"Well, at least I didn't nuke my life for nothing…" She appeared stunned, blinking rapidly and trying to parse what he said. After a moment, she slouched in her chair and gave a weary sigh.

"I saw, um… I saw that your boyfriend was involved," he grimaced. "Do you want to talk about what happened?"

She looked up at him with watering eyes. "Yes."

*****

Demy and Raphael snaked through the staff entrance, narrowly avoiding security, tech staff, and cocktail waitresses alike. Raphie held onto Demy's hand tight, keeping pace with his invisible lover as she led him to the manager's office. Demy kept a close eye out for any magical wards. She said she didn't suspect these urban Elves were smart enough or in tune with their history enough to know anti-magic spells, but she wasn't going to take chances. She reached into her small, stitched bag, retrieving a skull-shaped key, a visual pun that doubled as a Mystic Lock Pick.

Once they approached the oak door, etched into the frosted glass was the name "Lionel Shaedresh: Owner." She stepped forward and found the keyhole, wiggling her fake key into it and then proceeding to mutter incantations, too soft for even Raphie to hear. He looked over his shoulder as a waitress in a silver dress nearly collided with him. He stepped forward into Demy, bumping her slightly.

"So… these guys are like… Elf Mafia, yeah?" He whispered to her.

"Mhmm," Demy said, somewhat irritated that she was bumped and had to start over.

"Shouldn't we be armed or something?" Raphie's voice

began to crack from anxiety.

"We'll be fine. We've got magic," Demy said, unlocking the door finally and letting them both in. She was swift to close it behind them and locked it from the inside.

"You're right. We're invisible and it's not like… they're…" Raphie's confident tone disintegrated as he entered the polished, apartment-sized office. Along all of the walls, within glass cabinets, on side tables, littering the main desk, and even invading the floor space, were Lenoran Legion artifacts. They ranged from swords and uniforms to an entire Steel Phoenix flag held proudly aloft behind the desk; a relic from a time when Ile de Lenora was a fascist state and Great War Axis power. "Actual…Legion…"

"Yeah," Demy replied as if it were obvious. "We said that multiple times."

"I THOUGHT YOU WERE HYPERBOLIZING!" Raphie squeaked, struggling to breathe and not pass out from panic. "I can't be here, Demy. I'm Hispanic, queer, *and* Jewish. If they find out what we're trying to do here, then we're fucked!!! You're a witch. I'm a *warlock*. We're fucked! Oh, my God, they're gonna kill us!"

"Hey!" She said sharply but melted into a calm and endearing tone. Somehow, she knew exactly where to move because she kissed him square on his invisible cheek. "Keep it together. We can do this."

Immediately, his worries faded somewhat. With a heavy sigh, he and Demy got to work scouring the office adorned with Great War-era propaganda. Additionally, there were a distinct number of artifacts dating back to 10 BCE when a sect of High Elf Dragon Slayers made landfall in England. Raphie scrunched his nose as he came across a case beside the main desk of "trophies" claimed from the ruins of Transylvania in 1940. He looked back at her, scanning through a closet she had found, large enough that she almost disappeared inside it.

"This dude must masturbate to the History Channel," he joked.

Demy gave an amused chuckle as she approached the desk, sparing only a moment's glance at the wood-carved Steel Phoenix statue beside the computer monitor. She searched through the drawers, having no difficulty with the lock again. Supplies, weapons, and drugs, but nothing that fit the description Morgan gave. She looked up at his computer, beside it were several blank floppy disks.

"Hmm..." She pressed the eject button on his tall, tan tower, pulling the black floppy disk out. She scanned the environment and noticed a stepladder hidden behind a display case.

"What's up?" Raphie asked.

"If you were gonna use a disk to store secret information, you'd probably hide it, right?" Demy spoke up, the question somewhat rhetorical.

"I would assume so." The two looked up at the large flag hung on the wall behind his desk, framed with pride.

Demy levitated up to the flag, pulling the massive frame from the wall.

"What do you see?" he asked.

"Our answer," she said, her voice beaming with epiphany, seeing a small safe set into the wall. Unfortunately, there was no keyhole. "I can crack this open, but it might take a second."

"Do what you need to do, doll. I'll stand watch," Raphie replied.

Demy got to work, placing one palm on the safe and gripping the dial with the other. She began muttering incantations in Elven, a dull blue glow coming from the space she should be. Raphie glanced over and watched as she worked her literal magic. At one point, a group of people gathered outside the room. Raphie got on guard, alerting Demy to hurry, only for the group to break apart with laughter. Both Demy and Raphie sighed in relief. After a few moments more, the safe was open. Within, as Morgan predicted, was a small metal lockbox. Demy grabbed it, stuffed it in her bag, closed the safe, and fixed the fascist flag.

"We really should burn this place down," she thought rather loudly.

"What?" Raphie asked, "You're not serious, right?!"

"Of course not," Demy assured, though it was best he wouldn't be able to see her contradictory expression. As she landed beside him, they became visible again. "Shit, we're out, I'll get the other doses ready. We're gonna have to do these plain though, it's gonna suck… and stain your tongue blue."

"Good to know," Raphie said with a raised brow. Something caught the corner of their eyes, and they whipped their heads around. It was two figures outside the door. They then heard voices as the key hit the lock. The knob began to turn.

14

In the dark closet, gathered amongst the many coats and boxes, Raphael and Demy hid and waited for an opportunity to attempt their escape. Through a crack in the door, Raphie observed none other than the owner of the Keep himself, Lionel Shaedresh. On his arm was one of the exotic dancers from before, dressed in a skimpy, metallic leotard that barely covered her. He, on the other hand, was in a white suit of the finest silk money could buy, quick to shed his jacket and show off his rather stout form for an Elf.

"God, you're so beautiful," Shaedresh said like a lech. "Your skin is so creamy. You're like a porcelain doll."

"Th-thank you," she said, unsure of how to take the compliment as her body was caressed and manhandled. The dancer was guided to the elaborate office chair, where he pulled her into his lap.

"You have those Invisibility vials ready yet?" Raphie asked in a hushed tone.

"I…I can't find them!" Demy panicked.

"What?" Raphie tried not to join in the panic.

Demy looked at her bag and noticed, at the very bottom corner, a hole small enough for the vials to slip through. "Fuck, they fell out. My bag must have ripped on the dance floor. Fuck."

"So we just gotta ride this out?" Raphie looked back out to the criminal overlord, who was positioned perfectly to see the door. If they so much as opened it a sliver more, he would notice.

"That's it, right there. You know exactly what you're doing, don't you?" Shaedresh, the Elven creep, said as he admired the dancer's body, his hands drawn to the tie at the back of her neck that kept her top up. As he unstrung it, she shifted in her spot and got in a more optimal position, thus spinning the chair around.

"I think we just got our window," Raphie whispered with a burst of premature joy.

Demy poked her head beside his and scanned the room. Lo and behold, the bright blue vials were there on the floor, twenty feet from the door. "Shit, there's the potions.'

"I'm gonna go for them," Raphie got low and sneaked his way across the floor.

"Raphie, wait!" Demy protested in a shouted whisper, but he was already gone.

He stretched his arm out and swooped up the vials, ending up directly in front of the desk. The office chair moved a bit as he grabbed the liquid spells. His heart skipped a beat. He could hear the dancer giggling and talking like a valley girl, unknowingly preventing the High-Elf from spotting them. The chair stayed facing away. With narrow timing, Raphie managed to reenter the door, Demy closing it behind him slowly.

"I could have just used Spirit Hand to grab it," Demy whispered.

"Spirit what?" Raphie responded.

"Telekinesis," Demy reminded.

"Oh fuck… right…" He yelled in a whisper. "Why didn't you say that!?"

"I tried to."

Shaedresh spun the chair around, standing and becoming increasingly lecherous in his treatment of the dancer. He bent her over the desk and ran his palms down her back. She was noticeably uncomfortable. Raphie held the Invisibility fluid in his hand, Demy taking one and downing it immediately.

"Come on, drink it," Demy said with a disgusted face. She stuck her tongue out once she was done, becoming transparent in a second. Raphie hesitated, still watching out the door with the urge to intervene; he only took his after a moment of pause. When he did, his nose and mouth scrunched at the disgustingly sour and pungent fluid, like drinking straight balsamic vinegar.

As he leaned back to drink his potion, his elbow brushed one of the many coats, pushing it into a box, which pushed another box, and another, until an entire stack of containers came crashing down. Raphie cringed, "Shit."

"Who's in there?" Shaedresh said, holding up his pants. "Who's spying on us?" He reached into the pocket of his coat on the chair, withdrawing a 9mm pistol.

"Stay still," Demy breathed, pushed up against Raphie, and whispered as softly as she could, as close to his ear as she could manage. "Hold your breath, even."

Raphie made his breath shallow, beads of sweat formed on his face, invisible as he was. He prayed that the Elf Mafia weren't mages or could see through magic. Even still, he knew they could handle him… as long as they got the first move.

"I don't think it's anything," the dancer said in her ditzy tone. "It was probably from outside."

"No! Shut up!" he barked as a vicious precept. "I heard a voice. Stay there and be a good girl."

Opening the door, Shaedresh aimed his weapon around the closet space, and the two lovers remained still. They sweated bullets as the weapon was waved around inches from their faces. Shaedresh seemed to be calmer, not seeing anything, but the confusion was clear on his ageless face. He leaned his upper body in and looked at the pile of spilled storage and its miscellaneous contents. Demy and Raphie took a step back, synchronized, trying to avoid touching him. Shaedresh's eyes narrowed, and he took a step forward.

Rather than try to avoid him, Demy's arm lit up with blue light, revealing the limb and only the limb as she reached forward to jerk his wrist down, so the gun was aimed away. Before he could pull the trigger, Demy pressed her glowing palm against the mob boss's face.

"Shassa," she said, an Elven word that Raphie had yet to learn. Immediately, Shaedresh's eyes rolled back in his head, and he collapsed unconscious to the floor like an accordion, landing in an awkward position in the door jamb. The dancer screamed.

As Demy stood there, her body slowly began to fade back into visibility, starting from her hands and flowing along the lines of her tattoos. "Great," She hissed, looking up at the woman screaming.

"Oh gods, what happened to him!?" the dancer said, clearly seeing the Half-Elf witch in the closet. Raphie was lucky enough to remain cloaked. "Who the fuck are you?!"

"Woah, woah," Demy pleaded. "Please, we're not here to hurt you. Keep it down."

"Did you kill him?" She screamed, naked and afraid, grabbing a letter opener off the desk and aiming it at Demy. "Stay the fuck away from me!"

Demy raised her arms in surrender and reeled back. "Look, we're just leaving."

"We?" The girl pressed. Raphie didn't give her any more time to act. In his invisibility, he had marched slowly around her, ignored entirely. Once he was in position, he reached around and gripped both her wrists. Not harshly, but enough to control where the knife went.

Demy strode with ethereal speed, moving so fast that Raphie barely registered the movement. With her glowing arm, Demy touched the face of the dancer gently.

"Please just, shassa." Like Shaedresh, the dancer collapsed into Raphie's arms, who carefully guided her weight to the ground. Once she was down, he gently released her and kicked away the knife. "We need to go."

"Right now," Raphie completed.

The two rushed from the room as quickly as they could, and as the door to the room slammed, Shaedresh stirred.

The back door of The Keep slammed open and spilled hot

club air and blaring music into the dank alleyway. Demy and Raphael scurried down the short collection of stairs and to the ground level. Raphie had only now regained visibility mid-stride, gathering strange looks from two Elves smoking a cigarette. They quickly dispersed, leaving the lovers alone for a moment, panting and blood rushing from the sense of adventure.

"That was crazy," Raphie said, unbuttoning his overshirt. "Fuck, I'm hot," he muttered under his breath.

"You mean crazy awesome!" Demy jumped. "If this is the kind of stuff Morgan gets up to, I see why you like her so much."

"She has a habit of getting into trouble. Shouldn't say it's always been this way… but it has." Raphie laughed weakly, resting on his knees.

"A little winded?" Demy giggled.

"Just a teensy panic attack," he said, waving her off, "I'm okay."

He took a deep breath and stood up straight, running his hands through his hair, "I'm okay," He repeated. "Hey… you didn't, ya know… hurt them, did you?"

"An it harms none, so mote it be." Demy recited "It's a Sleep spell. They'll wake up with a tiny headache and be fine. Better than Shaedresh deserves."

Raphie had just noticed that at this moment he no longer had pointed ears or antlers, figuring the glamour had worn off already or was perhaps overridden by the continuous invisibility. The door above them burst open, and a group of roughly five people poured out of the club, looking about the alley. "Hey! What are you doing back here?" One of them barked.

"Uh…" Raphie choked out.

"We were just leaving," Demy chimed in. She gripped his wrist and led him down the opposite end of the alley, away from the main street. "Come on."

"Hey, I was talking to you punks," the man shouted before saying something in Elven to his mates.

"Just keep walking," Demy said, squeezing Raphie's hand. "We'll be fine."

As they approached the mouth of the alley, another group

of Elf Mafiosos rounded the corner. Demy and Raphie looked behind them and saw the other group closing in. "You sure it was these two?" the first Elf had said, his voice deep and booming.

"Oh yeah… I know it." A stouter man in a white suit pushed through the crowd. His voice was instantly identifiable. It was him. "I feel it in my blood."

"Yeah," added the bouncer who checked them in. "The man was a Wood-Elf beforehand, and now he's not."

"You trying to make fun of us, punk?" The man in white said. "Don't you know who the fuck we are? Who the fuck *I* am?"

"You're Lionel Shaedresh, club owner, mob boss, Legion wannabe, and fucking fascist. Did I hit all the marks?" Raphie spoke up, glaring at the man.

He chuckled back. "You're amusing, in the way a snail covered in salt is amusing." One of his cronies handed him an Uzi and an extended clip. He loaded his weapon. "If you two punks think you can attack me and make it out scot-free, you're fucking wrong. Why don't we go back inside and we can discuss this further?"

The other men started revealing their various pieces, each armed uniquely. Demy's eyes darted around to each of them, the flame tattoo on her arm glowing faintly. As she squeezed Raphie's hand, the hand he swore he'd keep safe, he would be able to feel the air temperature rise. Raphie was furious, panicking inside, but projecting it as rage. He was not about to bow down to a racist or an anti-Semite, let alone both. Demy, all the while, stared up at the sky.

"What the fuck is the halfie looking at?" One said, looking up.

With a rush of wind and the sound of concrete crushing, a creature that filled the alley dropped from the sky and landed hard behind Demy and Raphie. Both fell back into the creature's arms, large and strong. Its massive wings wrapped around the two sheltering them in scales like plated armor.

"Have a problem here, boys?" Maxine Mothman said, lifting them back to their feet "Just picking up my kids, hope you don't mind."

"The fucking Mothman," Shaedresh said, the others all backing up and whispering to one another. "Naw… we don't have a problem."

"Good, 'cause know I could rip you all limb from limb if I wanted to," She grinned. "Luckily, don't want to… right now. Tootles."

Maxine flapped her wings and gripped Demy and Raphie tightly, taking flight with them and carrying them high above the city within seconds. Once she was away from The Keep, she finally spoke.

"Got a lot of explaining to do, Raphie," Maxine spoke in a grim, gruff tone. "You know those guys are Elf Mafia, right?"

"Yeah," Raphie said, hanging his head like a scolded child.

"And you," Maxine said, turning to Demy. "Gotta quit meeting like this."

"Y-you know each other?" Demy stammered, shocked, and holding on as they soared a mile above the City of Angels. She kept her eyes shut tight as the lights below whizzed past them.

"Yup," Maxine replied.

"She practically raised me," Raphie explained. "This is Auntie M, you may have heard Morgan or me mention her."

"Aunt M is Maxine Mothman?!" Demy was stunned.

"Yup," they both replied.

"How do you know her?" Raphie asked, wildly confused.

Before Demy could respond, Maxine began diving, causing Demy to scream a bit. Maxine swooped down and opened her wings wide, landing on a high-rise rooftop in West Hollywood. Demy was stumbling. Raphie, having flown Air Mothman before, was able to stick the landing.

"Why are we on top of a building?" Demy asked.

"Questions," Maxine demanded, her full seven-foot self imposing with her thick arms folded impatiently. "Why were you in that building? For starters."

"We were just checking it out. What harm is there in that?" Raphie looked at Demy, who understood that they needed to keep this on the down low.

"Neo-Legion Elves and gangsters. No harm, indeed,"

Maxine scoffed. "What would you have done had I not been there, Raphie? Guy had a gun."

"All those guys had guns," Raphie added.

"More reason to stay away," Maxine said, flustered. "Morgan doesn't have anything to do with this little stunt, does she?"

"What? Morgan? At an Elf club? You gotta be joking," Raphie said with a chuckle.

"I'm serious."

"No," Raphie said with ice in his veins, using his ultimate poker face. "She's not."

"Then why are you sweating so badly?" Maxine challenged.

"Because I just had a gun pointed at my face?" Raphie deflected honestly.

"So she's not involved?"

"No," Demy intervened. "She's not… just us."

"'Cause I raised her to know better. Ashamed you didn't pick up on that," Maxine scoffed at Raphie. "Wanna know why I was there?"

"I have a feeling you're gonna tell us no matter what," Raphie popped off.

"Got a lot of sass tonight for someone who named himself after a *Ninja Turtle*." Maxine cocked her head and widened her already massive eyes.

"…The cool one," Raphie said, kicking his feet.

"Anyway," Maxine cracked her neck and took a deep breath. "Following a case, think I might have stumbled upon something bigger. They have a bizarre and complicated shift routine. Haven't found much pattern, but know they're moving more than just drugs. There's a whole warehouse next door to The Keep that men keep coming in and out of. Only do it on nights they're open and the crowds conceal the alleys. Why?"

"Do you think it has to do with the missing teens?" Demy spoke up with her hand to her mouth.

"Yeah… I do." Maxine looked at Demy, her eyes spoke an elaborate tale between them without saying a word. Maxine arched an eyebrow and continued, "What I've uncovered… Someone is trying to restart a war between old enemies. Elves and Vampires have a rickety alliance and want to know why. Reality is, they've been working together for a few years. Have evidence that connects Tyrant logistics working with Mafia storage, just don't have a way inside. Yet."

Silence fell over the rooftop. The wind at this elevation, blowing much colder, was the only sound for a moment. Maxine was dressed in a black long-sleeve turtle neck, with holes for her wings, coupled with track pants, making her the only one comfortable. Neither Demy nor Raphie knew what to say. Demy kept her purse tight to her, feeling the box inside to make sure it was still safe, which it was; her other hand played with Maxine's scale hanging from her neck by hemp string and bound in wire. Maxine looked to the floor and sighed, seeing both of them getting visibly cold.

"Was hoping you would have seen something in that shit pit. Just going for fun," Maxine said with a disgruntled groan. "Just don't understand why they were giving you trouble."

"I cast a Disguise spell on us," Demy admitted. "I thought it would land us better chances of getting in, and it did."

"Until it wore off?" Maxine finished for Demy.

"Exactly."

"Be glad those cops didn't see you. Glamour is stupid illegal," Maxine scolded. "Who are you even?"

"She's my girlfriend, but how do you know her?!" Raphie stressed, having never been answered. Demy smiled at her title being mentioned.

"She saved my life," Demy admitted. "She stopped a car from hitting me."

"Wait… *YOU* were the mystery girl?" Raphie said, becoming consistently more exhausted as the night carried on. He remembered hearing about it on the news that Maxine had brought herself back into the limelight by saving a Jane Doe from certain death at the hands of a reckless driver. But for it to be Demy was beyond coincidence. It was uncanny. It was magical.

"Explains why I saw you in my vision… if I'm not careful, you might be family," Maxine said calmly.

Demy couldn't maintain eye contact and turned her gaze to

her feet.

"Let's get you home," Maxine said, having each of them grab onto an arm before taking off into the cloudy night sky.

15

It would be hours and an entire two batches of coffee before Morgan and Colt would look at the time and realize how close to dawn it was. For the first hour, she spilled all the gory details of her failing relationship and decadent exploits, breaking down a half dozen times. Each time, Colt got a little better at consoling her. At one point, she leaned into him, and he lazily wrapped an arm around the back of her chair. She craved the affection; it'd been so long since she'd felt safe and warm in someone's arms.

By the end of the second hour, Morgan was no longer as downtrodden. He'd managed to change the subject naturally, as expected of a good reporter. She talked about her studies and her friends, Raphie in particular. Diving into her high school adventures, they even laughed a few times. Never once did he pressure her to talk about the story or the events that had transpired. Morgan received his politeness, feeling more comfortable the longer they spent together. At some point, she found her hand near his and traced the side of his thumb with hers. Out of instinct or lack of sleep, he held it briefly before realizing what he was doing and distanced himself again. It was then he saw the clock.

"Shit. It's fuckin' late," Colt said, standing up and stretching with a yawn. "I've got a spare room, it's small, but you can crash here tonight. I don't like the idea of you driving so late. I also have some of my ex-wife's clothes still here. She's been gone over a year. Anything that fits is yours."

"Ex-wife? Didn't know you were married," Morgan said with a smirk.

"Never really came up, but yeah, seven years. We just never got along, I suppose. The split was mutual. I got the condo, she got the car, the dog, alimony, and 50% of my retirement… Not the best deal when I say it out loud…" He crossed to open the guest bedroom and turned the lights on.

"Have you been seeing anyone?" Morgan wondered, approaching Colt while his back was turned.

"Not really," He chuckled while scanning to make sure she had blankets and at least a pillow or two. "The dating scene has changed a lot since I last tried it. Besides, who wants some old newspaper editor—"

He turned to face Morgan, now nude at the center of his condo, the robe in a bundle behind her. She seemed to tower over him despite being a foot shorter. She sauntered up to him, cheeks like pink roses.

"Scriven… what the hell are you doing?" He managed to get out, frozen in place.

"I dunno, I'd say you're alright for an old newspaper editor," she purred.

"I know you've been in some crazy situations, but this isn't necessary. You're gorgeous, but you know, my employee?" He was trying to keep it light, enjoying the sight but not wanting to stare.

She approached close to him but stopped just out of reach. "It's not tit for tat, Colt. I've had a real shit week. I don't know what's going to happen when I leave here. My relationship is over… I feel like I'm losing my mind over this story… All I'm looking for is comfort from someone I can trust to know it's just that. Please touch me."

He reached forward experimentally, and she leaned her cheek into his callused palm. Their eyes met in understanding. It didn't have to be any more than that. He seemed to breathe in acquiescence and closed the distance, reaching for her cool softness.

She gripped the cloth of his shirt, her bottom lip quivering. For the first time, he allowed himself to touch more than just her shoulders or hands. He held her waist softly, looking down at her with his own needs clear in his eyes. She leaned up, lifted her heels a bit off the ground, and kissed him. His grip tightened, and her arms wrapped around his neck. They kissed for several moments in the doorway; their tongues danced together, and Colt gripped her by her thighs, fingers cupping the bottom of her pert rear. For a moment, they parted from this kiss. Morgan giggled, disbelieving what had just happened; he smiled back. Their eyes met, a lingering pause; smiles faded. A primal fire lit in their eyes.

With reckless abandon, they made their way to the master bedroom, slamming each other into furniture and walls as they proceeded. Morgan moaned into his lips, aroused by the scent of his aftershave lingering even still. Lost in his touch and musk, Morgan had not registered the bedroom until he tossed her onto the deep indigo sheets.

She giggled, quick to catch herself on her hands and knees. She looked up at him in the dim light; his pants were tented, and his breath was heavy. Crawling forward, Morgan pulled his pants down as he lifted his t-shirt off, revealing his solid body. Morgan audibly gushed, kissing his belly and working up to his defined pecks and then jawline. She placed her lips on his neck, suckling hard, causing him to fully rise to attention against her stomach. Morgan lowered herself again, taking his head past her lips and then swallowing his length without contest. She'd imagined this moment for months, dismissing her feelings as nothing more than fantasy. Now that she was here, she felt as if it was a dream, like a pain-free version of the hallucinations she'd been dealing with. She half expected it all to be gone every time she blinked, only to still be on her knees servicing her boss.

After a few minutes, rather than let himself loose so early, Colt pulled his hips back and leaned down to shamelessly kiss her again. Gripped by her hair and forced to meet him halfway, she mewled at his touch, her lips curling up into a half-smile as they kissed, drunk on the moment. His weight was soon on her as she was guided to her back. Morgan looked into Colt's fire-orange eyes with desperation, holding contact as they made the ultimate connection. Her eyes rolled back, her mouth agape in a silent scream. She gave lewd, voracious moans with every movement, as sensual, strong, and tactically spaced apart as they were.

"Th-thaaaank youuu," she whimpered, arching her back and

rolling her hips into him as she built towards release.

"The pleasure's mine, baby," he crooned, kissing her neck softly and teasing with his tusk-like fangs pressed firmly against her skin. She laughed sweetly, transforming into a cry of lust halfway through. "Just keep giving me those cute moans."

Morgan, eager to please, stopped holding back her sounds of pleasure. The moans seemed to stoke the flame in her almost as much as they did him, raising in volume toward a crescendo. It was as if her true sensuality and eroticism were kept under lock and key, escaping only temporarily when someone else gave permission. With his hard, emerald flesh against her pale figure, she had been set free and would now take her pleasure. Seizing the use of her Vampiric strength, her palms pressed on Colt's shoulders, and despite their width and mass, she pushed him onto his back as easily as he did to her. Wide-eyed at first, he adapted the moment Morgan's hips collided with his, their bodies having never fully parted.

They moved as one in primal lust; her hands wandered up and down his chest while she repeated his name in breathy whimpers. Even in his prone state, he was anything but passive, meeting her passion with rare ferocity. Her nails gripped the sheets of his bed as she leaned back. In her moment of ecstasy, the memory of Ziusudra doing the same to her invaded her mind. The parallels couldn't be ignored, but in Ziusudra's arms, she was fearful, and that fear aroused her. With Colt, she felt secure, guarded. It allowed her to let loose, to fully be herself without any masks.

Morgan fell forward, lying on his chest but still moving her hips out of instinct. His masculine hands gripped her to facilitate the motion; her blue butterfly peeked through his fingers as they traced her body. Colt, far from done, withdrew himself and gently laid the petite Vampire on her belly, face into the plush down pillows. He lifted her rear into the air, kissing her long legs and plump cheeks before tasting the nectar directly from her flower.

She finally gathered the strength to speak once he had moved his lips away, standing on his knees behind her. "Fffuck… how are y-you single?"

"Because I love the freedom to do things like this…" He

smirked, gripping her hips and pulling her onto him.

She gasped a fraction of a second before he began, forcing her body flush with the blankets. She turned her head to look back at him, her eyes at half-mast, barely capable of focusing. His fingers wrapped around her neck, guiding her body to its crescendo and back as if he were playing the world's most sensual cello. Even in her current state, she did her best to remain active.

His body began to spasm. Morgan smirked, confident in her actions. She knew she'd conquered him with the sway of her hips. Knowing Colt's story, hundreds of women could have pined for this position, and tonight she was the one to be honored with his passion. As far as she was concerned, his increasingly sporadic thrusts were the equivalent of being crowned Queen of Vampires. He tightened his grip on her neck with one hand and the small of her back with the other. He was losing steam, but not without a finale.

"Fuck, baby," he moaned, placing his hands on either side of her for stability as he prepared to withdraw again.

Morgan, much to Colt's surprise, gripped his wrist with shocking vigor. "Do it."

"But—"

"DO IT!" Morgan growled.

Colt didn't need any more convincing. With the last of his fervor, he poured his essence into her, his body convulsing with hers. They collapsed onto their sides, keeping their bodies close. Morgan took a deep breath and gave a satisfied sigh while they cuddled together, Colt planting soft kisses on her ivory neck.

"Oh my god, that was amazing," Colt muttered out as almost a single word, panting heavily. "I can't believe that just happened."

"You're not regretting it, are you?" Morgan said, worry in her voice.

Rather than speak, Colt pulled her partially atop his chest, kissing her soft, pale lips and holding her blonde head with his rough Orcish hands. "Naw," he said with a warm smile.

Colt's arm immediately wrapped around Morgan. She

curled up into him with a perpetual smile, her problems miles away. She was happy, for a moment. She closed her eyes, drifting out of consciousness during the brief respite. Maybe, just maybe, if she fell asleep, this moment could stay a little while longer.

*****

The shadows on the streets of Transylvaniatown began to fade away as its people's natural enemy emerged: the sun. Vampires and Ghouls scrambled to their homes and vehicles, with windows coated in layers of refractium. Those who walked hurried to get on their opaque, rainbow masks and gloves, made of the same light-reflecting material— all before the sun touched their skin.

As the light began to peak on the eastern horizon, the space outside the Bourbon Belfry was all but abandoned. Its staff not long ago finished closing the place down, barely released in time to flee to their refractium. For the first time since Halloween weekend began, T-town was peaceful and quiet. No passing cars, and only the sounds of tweeting birds.

The first vehicle to appear for a while was a blacked-out van, screeching to a stop right outside while another black vehicle, a pickup truck, pulled into the backside of the club. From the vehicles emerged a collection of silver-suited individuals, each wearing a plastic "monster" mask, based on the fairly racist Universal movies. In the hands of the largest, an Orc hidden behind a Frankenstein's Monster mask, was a plastic crate of glass bottles full of glowing red liquid; most of the others carried tanks of gas.

The one who didn't stepped forward, an ancient-looking, jagged knife in their hands. They stood close to the brick wall, breathing deeply behind a plastic mummy mask. With a swipe of the blade, it sparked purple, creating a gash-like portal in the wall big enough for them to fit through. A few kept watch while the rest entered the building, the glowing gash closing behind them.

"We have 5 minutes. Move." A gruff voice ordered from behind a zombie mask over refractium.

At once, they began working in a synchronized pattern, pouring gasoline on predetermined areas throughout the club. Gasoline covered the stage, the dressing rooms, the office. Once their tanks were empty, they gathered in the main basement hall.

Before the first bottle was tossed, a black Crown Victoria pulled up, parking with one wheel on the curb. From the driver's seat, a High-Elven man emerged, gun in hand. "LAPD! DROP YOUR WEAPONS!"

"Shit. Sound the alarm," a woman, standing watch in a werewolf mask, said to a woman in a skeleton one. She raised a baseball bat, firing a magical burst of flame from its tip. The Firebolt scorched the hood of the unmarked cop car, causing the radiator to burst and steam to pour from a newly formed hole in the hood. The other in the skeleton mask ran to the back door of the Belfry and pounded three times, the sound echoing through the empty club and alerting the witches inside.

"Time's up," the zombie said.

The cop dove into his car and gripped his radio, shouting frantically as his windshield and roof were each hit with another Firebolt, causing chunks of burning glass to land on him. "Shots fired outside the Bourbon Belfry on North Euclid and Greydon! Need immediate backup! Magical shots fired. Repeat. Magical shots fired!"

The officer fired on the woman with the magic bat, missing her each time but hitting the truck behind her.

"Fuck this." Without hesitation, the 'werewolf' ran. Within seconds, she had taken magical flight and landed on a nearby rooftop, leaving the cop in the dust.

"Did you hear that?" Another woman said from behind a *Creature from the Black Lagoon* mask and clutching her cane-like wand. "Those were gunshots."

"Then we go through the walls," the mummy said, diving over the bar and slashing an opening in the wall with their magic dagger.

“Everybody scatter, they can’t chase us all,” the zombie commanded, tossing two alchemical firebombs and igniting the inferno. Others did the same, causing the dance floor to become an instant blaze.

The monsters in silver all emerged from the other end of the building, dispersing like cockroaches when the light came on. The mummy took their knife and cut through the neighboring wall across the side alley, creating temporary doorways to allow their mates through; they tossed the dagger to ‘Frankenstein’s Monster’. The skeleton and the Monster disappeared through the buildings, the *Creature* took flight and scaled a wall, and the mummy made it to their van.

Once in, Adrian pulled off their mummy mask and took off with the sound of screeching tires. Moving fast, they reached for their dashboard and popped the cap on an intake labeled “Evasive Maneuver”. From a bag between the two front seats, they pulled out a vile of bright blue fluid, pulling the cork out with their teeth and pouring the contents into the port, letting the bottle drain. As squad cars powered down North Euclid, the van had vanished.

The zombie found himself crossing the street, cursing in his guttural tone. He heard the officer shout “Freeze,” but didn’t stop. His clawed hands began to dig into the brick wall of a building, pulling him up with ease. *BANG!* A searing hot pain struck him in his arm, causing him to reel back and consequently lose his grip. He fell hard, crashing onto his back.

“STAY ON THE GROUND, MOTHERFUCKER!” The cop ordered, just as more squad cars rounded each end of the street. “You’re under arrest!”

The cop grabbed his cuffs, etched with glowing Celtic runes, and rolled the man over onto his stomach. Once his wrists were cuffed, he pulled the zombie mask off, taking with it the refractium hood. Gruel groaned as his face was exposed to direct morning light, blinding him and causing nausea. The cop began to read Gruel his rights, but he didn’t care; he grinned like the devil as he looked on at his handiwork. The Bourbon Belfry was entirely engulfed in flames; from each blacked-out window, fire licked upward. Black smoke billowed into the air, blotting out the sun for the people of T-Town. Some emerged from their homes wearing their protective garments only to watch the immolation of the iconic structure.

"Fuck," one officer said, talking into his radio "Suspect is apprehended. Others at large. We're gonna need fire department stat." He lowered the radio and cursed a few more times, watching the inferno eat away at the neon bourbon bottle that was its historic sign.

Gruel ignored them, laughing like a madman, even when threatened and kicked. He couldn't help it. All of the effort and money that Yessenia and her people had invested was destroyed. Two stories and a basement engulfed in an indomitable fire, melting all of Yessenia's home videos and detonating her office computer. The last room to be fully engulfed was the top-floor dressing room. Flame licked the vanities in the back, burning off the plastic and paint with a sickly smell. In the far corner, two Polaroids, one with Morgana Scriven, the other with Chrissy Donavon. Each picture warped and melted away, scoured from existence.

M's Journal

November 2nd, 1996

Fuck. Just... fuck. Bourbon Belfry in cinders. Took only a few minutes for the flame to engulf all 3 floors. Can't believe didn't see it coming. That place had secrets still. Need to start thinking outside the box. Start playing dirty.

Persons responsible haven't been identified yet, save for one Ghoul captured fleeing the scene. He's not gonna talk. Police don't have the means to interrogate an undead. Can't scare them with prison time. Got all the time in the world. That's where the DSA comes in... Now Yessenia has insurance money to play with. Worries me.

Somewhat related, think about immortality a lot. Some Cryptids can live for centuries, others decades. With as much as I stress, I'm not sure if I'm gonna be one of those "immortal" Cryptids. Have less to stress about if my niece called me every once in a while.

Know I sound like the cliche annoying aunt, but I love my little princess more than the beat in my chest. She survived for years, with me as a guardian. Until I quit the Feds in '89, would be gone constantly. Even then, was far from present. That kid thanks me regularly for helping raise her. Latchkey kid. Raised herself. That's why she moved out at 18. Had her life in order before I could lift a finger to help. Couldn't stay in that giant house alone. Followed suit thereafter. Downsized to here.

Not saying I'm not proud. Opposite, she's all my pride.

10th anniversary is coming up. Not sure how either of us are gonna handle it this year. Miss them both so much... Got a call from B. Wants to have lunch. Think I'll take him up on it. Be nice to see an old colleague.

-M

Act 4: Everyone Dies in the End

1

Infinite void... crushing darkness beneath the seemingly endless depths so unknowable and massive... Suffering and lust... in rapturous harmony.

Morgan's eyes jolted open, haunted by the same nightmare that plagued her with migraines. As the vision faded, she didn't feel immediate panic, but rather relaxed and refreshed. She stretched her arms about on the massive bed with a deep blue comforter and matching sheets. It didn't even dawn on her that this was Colt Harding's bed until she chose to look around, seeing the wide-open, pristinely white walls and carpet, the nice furniture, and high-class decorating.

She sat up, alone in the bed, holding the sheets tightly to her chest and looking about with wide-eyed amazement and guilt. The sun shone through his creamy white and purple drapes; she blinked, her sensitive eyes fuzzily adjusting to the morning light. She ran her hands over the emptiness on the opposite end of the bed, the blankets having been left pulled back. It was cold. Her eyes caught Colt's alarm clock. Simple, metal, digital. Its red numbers read 11:24 a.m. This was when Morgan panicked.

"Fuck." She hissed, ashamed. She saw a woman's t-shirt and gym shorts laid out on an ottoman just past the foot of the bed. Getting dressed to the sound of a sizzling pan and clanking cookware, the smell of cooking meat filled her nostrils, and she followed.

Morgan poked her head out of the room. This being her first time seeing Colt since last night, she wasn't sure how to approach him. She had never intended to stay so late, nor what came after. She didn't even have a reason for what she did, only that she wanted to feel free of pain and worry. He provided her with that freedom and then some; now she had to deal with the morning after.

As she crested the stairs, she could see him in his kitchen, diligently at work, dressed in a yellow shirt, jeans, and a blue apron. On two separate plates were small piles of white mush, likely eggs. In the pan, he held two steaks, still pink outside. As he cooked, he caught her in the corner of his eye.

"Oh hey, you're up! Guten Morgen," he said with a charming giggle.

"Good morning," she smiled back, far more awkward than when she was aroused.

"I was about to check on you," he said, flipping one steak and taking the other off early. "I made steak and eggs. I read egg whites are good for Vampires, and your steak is ultra-rare, so if it's too much for you to eat, you can still drain it." His tusky smile was infectious. Fortunately, Morgan was immune to 99% of disease.

"Um… I th-think I should get back. I have a long day ahead of me," Morgan closed her laptop, gathered her papers, and slid them loose in her bag. She packed up in seconds, looking about for her car keys, finding them on the counter near Colt. She grabbed them and scurried away, too embarrassed to look him in the eye.

"I should have realized you'd need to get going." He said, shutting off his electric stove and turning to face her, drying his hands on a dishrag. "Do you need help with any of your things?"

"No. I-I've got everything," she stammered, finally looking up to him to see his compassionately warm eyes. She gave him a forced smile and turned to the door. She was getting accustomed to these types of smiles, and she hated it. He followed her, stopping at the dinner table where they sat and spent hours connecting. As she opened the door, she stopped, frozen in the doorframe. "I-I… I'm sorry."

He waved goodbye as the door shut behind her, she didn't look back to notice. In front of his condo, her red Buick sat waiting for her. The condensation of the Fall morning still built upon her windshield, glistening as the sun reached the center of the sky. She was barely clothed but didn't bother with her coat. She just needed to get out of sight. She looked up at Colt's front door, part-wishing and part-dreading him coming after her. Why would he? It was just a casual work fling. As she turned the ignition of her vehicle, she swore she heard someone speaking.

"Rood eht nepo. Dnatrs eht peek." Morgan scanned frantically, looking to where the unintelligible sentence came from, but there was no one. She wrote it off as just that Spanish station breaking through on the radio.

As she put the car into gear, she spared one last glance at the condo door. Still nothing. She was smarter than that. At least she thought she was.

She drove off, trying to keep her cool until she was out of the complex. *Nagrom, srood kcalb eht dnif.* The gibberish intruded into Morgan's brain. Her car rolled out into the open streets, stopping at a 4-way stop alone. With a sudden fury, she pounded on her steering wheel, causing the horn to blare. "FUCK!" She screamed through the stress, incapable of maintaining her chill any longer. When she was done, she gripped the wheel and let her forehead rest on the top. She laughed. She laughed hard, leaning back into her seat and running her hand through her hair. "Fuck, Scriven… what are you doing??"

A glimmer from the passenger seat caught her eye from her current position. She leaned back, fascinated by the source. There, sitting on her seat, were two significant items. One: a pocket knife that had belonged to her father, normally kept in the glovebox for safety; and two: a small silver charm bracelet. She reached down hesitantly, lifting the metal jewelry into the light. Two letters dangled at the bottom: CD. A horn startled her into pulling over.

She stared back at the charm, the light reflected, shining green in her eyes. Morgan was brought back to that night at the Babylon. The girl in the hallway, the charm bracelet, the crushing darkness of the pool, flashes of memory rushing back in an instant. She felt dizzy, confused, and hurt. Nothing added up, and every time she felt she uncovered an answer, progress was pushed further back.

"What the hell is happening?"

*****

The adrenaline rush from The Keep had finally subsided. Raphie and Demy had been graciously delivered by Morgan's aunt, something Demy still to this moment had a hard time believing. They watched the massive woman fly off into the distance at a speed far greater than when she carried them. *You might be family.* Raphie remembered, trying to understand what all of it meant. Morgan still wasn't home, despite how late it was… so naturally, the two sat at the Bar and waited patiently for her return.

He served her a gin and tonic and stood across from the Bar. The two were somewhat quiet for a while before Demy finally broke the silence, an awkwardness lingering over them with a moth-shaped elephant in the room.

After a while, the ice broke and they began chit-chatting, deep in their mixed conversations. But Raphie had questions, and the small talk was just a way to prolong the inevitable. Who were the Corvus Enclave? What were they planning? Why did Demy leave them *and* her girlfriend? They were alone, and there was no reason for her at this point not to give him an answer. Ironically, it was Demy who would bring her questions first.

"Why did you lie to M?" Demy asked. "She seemed to be on our side."

"Morgan already made me promise that I wouldn't tell Aunt M anything." Raphie sighed, looking distant and chewing his lip. "I told her to tell M, but Morgan seems to think it will only complicate things further. I don't personally understand how; she's already lied to her boyfriend, sorry, *ex*-boyfriend, through all this and only now brought us into the fold. Adding in a former fed-turned-PI on a similar case? That's just too much bullet-dodging for one person."

"It's not smart," Demy said bluntly.

"I know."

"Why does she think she has to do this all on her own?" Demy said, exasperated.

"I don't know," Raphie continued, taking a swig of his beer.

"Blondie likes to think she's bulletproof, that she's been through too much to be hurt. The truth is, I'm scared to death that she's gonna just not come home. That she walked out there to do this crazy fucking story and just disappeared… just like Chrissy Donavon."

"You are worried about her, aren't you?" Demy said softly as if to coax him into full honesty. "It's clear you have her best interests in mind."

"She's my best friend. I've known her longer than I haven't… I don't know what I'd do if something happened to her," Raphie confessed. "Which makes me wonder," He changed his tone sternly. "Why would you abandon your friends?"

"I didn't abandon them," Demy said, lousy with offense. "They abandoned the principle and I said fuck that."

"How?"

"I don't want to get into it." She excused.

"That's BS. You're trying to protect me from something," Raphie deduced. "Or at least keep me in the dark for some reason."

"I don't *want* to, but it's safer for you if you don't know. Plausible deniability and all that," Demy enforced.

"Okay… then explain to me what they did with my blood that had them all so spooked. They were trying to conjure something that night, and it failed. What happened?"

Demy paused, staring into her drink and trying not to get too emotional, but it was clear she was breaking.

"Doll, you can talk to me," Raphie reinforced.

She looked up to him with watery eyes.

"It was a binding ritual… That music shop had been a go-to dead drop location for the T-Town Tyrants… we were trying to curse any objects that were left there willingly... But something about your blood disagreed with the ritual and caused it to backfire. If anything, Gruel lost power that day… He has it out for you, Raphie… The day I gave you your wand, we had a meeting. It went sour quick when I told him."

"Demytria, I told you I wasn't worth your friends."

"You don't get it… they were going to move forward on

magic of my design that would lead to some shady shit happening. Something that would draw in major power players that we don't want to deal with. So I backed out… that's when… Amy…"

"What happened?" Raphie pushed. "Demy… what did Amy do to you?"

Demy rubbed her hand up her arm.

"She hit me."

"What?"

"She grabbed my wrist and kept me from leaving, and when I protested, she slapped me across the face. Citing, 'Grand Priestess or not, you're my girlfriend, and you'll do what I say.'" She finally admitted, the breath seeming to return to her lungs. Raphie could only imagine what weight that secret would bear upon the poor Half-Elf.

"Hey… you don't have to say anymore," he said, seeing her visibly uncomfortable. "I hear you… I see you, and I swear to God that I will never lay a hand on you that you don't want. I swear it."

"Raphie…" she trembled, leaning over to him, he met her halfway and kissed her plump lips. He took her in his arms, his hand waving through her short teal hair and grazing her pointed ears. "Let's wait for Morgan in your room." She smiled, beginning to stand.

"Gladly," Raphie replied, grabbing his beer, leading her into the bedroom, and sealing the door until dawn.

The next morning, they arose, expecting Morgan to be back already. She wasn't. Raphie tried her cell phone a couple of times, to no avail. He began to panic.

"This is exactly what I was afraid of…" He bit his nails, racing thoughts. "Do you think I should call M?"

"Don't stress, love, I'm sure she's okay," Demy said, her tone less sure than she wanted it to sound.

"If it hits noon and she's not back, I'm calling it in," he said sternly.

"I thought you didn't want to bring in M," Demy questioned.

"I don't," Raphie answered. "But I care about Morgan

enough to know when *I'm* in over my head."

"That's fair." Demy scratched the back of her head and grimaced, sitting down on the couch with her tattooed legs folded beneath her. Raphie was about to continue on his diatribe when he heard the front door rattle. He sprang up to meet Morgan as she came through the door. He ran and gave her a huge hug, nearly knocking her over and her laptop from her hand.

"Holy shit you're okay!" He cheered.

"Woah there, big guy!" Morgan chuckled, patting him on the back. "Yeah, I'm fine."

"Where did you go?" He asked, stepping back and putting his hands on his hips like a disappointed parent.

"Colt's," she said, fighting a smile.

"Colt?" Demy asked, leaning forward.

"Wait… Colt *Harding?* Your boss?" Raphie said, the corner of his mouth starting to curl up. "You… slept overnight at his place?"

"Yep," Morgan said with a tight-lipped smile, slowly turning into a giggle. "Though not a lot of sleeping involved."

"Fuckin' rad rebound, dude," Raphie said, raising his hand to high-five Morgan, who reciprocated the gesture. Once the first high five was completed, they repeated the move as a low five before switching to a slide of their palms, finishing it off with a fist bump and flourish. Demy watched the exchange with amusement. "Wait, I thought he was off limits."

"What can I say? You changed my mind," Morgan grinned. "So what have you two been up to?"

Demy and Raphie looked at one another.

"Well…" Raphie began hesitating a bit with a choked-up voice.

"We remembered you mentioning the Elf Mob and the Keep…" Demy continued, standing to retrieve her bag from Raphie's room. "So we went looking of our own volition."

"We found something…" Raphie added.

"You what?" Morgan looked confused and partially hurt. As if she had been encroached upon by the act. "You… infiltrated the Keep?"

"Yes," Raphie said confidently.

"That's stupid, you could have gotten killed," Morgan scolded.

"Correct," Raphie said just as confidently.

Demy had returned, tossing a pair of floppy disks to Morgan, who caught them with ease.

"I knew it!" She said, squinting as she looked at them, "Where did you find them?"

"Inside a lockbox, like you said," Demy grimaced, pointing over to the open container. "In a safe, behind a framed Legion flag, totes obvious. Shaedresh's hubris is his downfall."

"Tell me about it. Alright, let's check 'em out." Morgan quickly set up her laptop at the Bar, climbing on the stool and putting on her pink, square glasses.

"Okay… what have we got?" Morgan popped the first disk in. Immediately, it pulled up a password-protected window, the same one she saw on Yessenia's computer. She paused for a minute. There could only be one universal password. "Sha hatti darisam."

ACCESS GRANTED

"Alright, Blondie!" Raphie cheered. In an instant, the screen sprang to life in black and white and revealed a spreadsheet with two distinct columns. The first was grid coordinates paired with small numbers in the second. Some of the coordinates had an additional column. When Morgan clicked to the next screen, it showed columns with no labels, these more sporadic. In all, there were roughly 80 rows of numbers. The trio was puzzled, quiet, and simply trying to take in the information.

The next disk yielded just as confusing results, though rather than grid coordinates, they were dates, and each was labeled with first names. Without even a middle initial, it was impossible to tell who some of these were. Paired with the names were two letters: EE or UE.

"Elite Echelon," Morgan said aloud. "Upper Echelon… these are ranks within the Lounge. They have this weird caste system in place… I guess technically I'm Middle Echelon?"

"What does that mean?" Raphie asked.

"Different privileges, I guess… I only met Upper and

above… I have no idea what he offers people of lower ranks, but I get a feeling they function as servants," Morgan puzzled.

"Like a modern-day serfdom," Demy added.

Further in the file were columns full of small, sometimes single-digit numbers.

"What do you think those are?" Demy asked and pointed, "They look like shipments, maybe. Units of something."

"Units of what?" Raphie chimed in.

"And why are there drastic variations from location to location?" Morgan added, "All I can think of with these dates are Lounge parties. It's obvious from what I've overheard at the parties, they're moving 'products', but most of what was said was in Elven. Maybe if we compare the dates with the corresponding columns, we could find out when and where these parties were being held and who purchased what?"

"It's all so confusing," Raphie leaned against the Bar, eyes baggy and shoulders slumping. "It's almost like there's information intentionally missing. Maybe the Tyrants possess that information?"

"The teens who have gone missing have worked at either The Keep or the Bourbon Belfry," Morgan said. "So that may be what was on that disk in Yessenia's computer."

Morgan switched her screen to her digital corkboard. Demy raised her brows, impressed with the attentive construction of her story's path. She clicked open several notes before grabbing a pad of paper off the far end of the Bar.

"Raphie's right, so we have to cross-reference the data," Morgan said and began writing down the different locations she'd noted in her investigation, all the hot spots for gatherings, including the Babylon. "I'm curious as to what could convince the Vampires and Elves to work together. They're historical enemies."

"Well… A little birdie told me that the truce between the Tyrants and the Elf Mafia was uneasy." Raphie said, glancing at Demy before speaking again. "Somebody is making it hard for them to stay allies."

Morgan sat up straight."Where did you hear it?"

"Aunt M…" Raphie confessed, incapable of lying to both

halves of his extended family. "She swooped in and saved us at The Keep. Just in the nick of time as always…"

"Fuck… she was at the Keep!? Why?" Morgan said with alarm.

"She was investigating the Mafia… has something to do with her case," Raphie added.

"I don't like that… that means the LAPD was right to think there was some major kidnapping ring if M's case is overlapping with mine," Morgan replied, opening a new file and labeling it 'Tori Franques'. "This story is so fucking strange."

"You wanna know strange?" Raphie added. "Do you remember the mystery woman that M saved the other day?"

"Yeah."

Raphie pointed to Demy, who still looked to the floor, frozen with guilt.

"Well, that's a hell of a coincidence," Morgan said, blinking rapidly.

"I… don't believe in coincidence… not ones like this," Demy said, feeling her scale pendant. "I had no idea you two were related, and that's something I can't ignore."

"She adopted me when I was still in middle school," Morgan informed. "I'm just glad she always seems to be there to save the day… Kinda amazing that I avoided her this long."

"True dat," Raphie said, rolling his eyes. "There's no way for us to get back into the Keep now, especially after M made a scene."

"True. If these were at the Keep, there's a strong chance there's still one at the Belfry." Morgan deduced. "Also, I have reason to believe that Yessenia keeps home videos of her and her girls in a locker in her office."

"How do you know that?" Raphie blurted before realizing and blushing fiercely. "You know what, never mind. I'm good."

"Yeah, maybe I should keep that to myself," Morgan said with a grimace. "Anyway, I think it's time we execute our plan on the Belfry. Once we get there, some of these pieces will come together."

2

"Fuck."

Once a staple of Transylvaniatown, the Bourbon Belfry was now a blackened ruin filled with the ashes of its former glory. Yellow police tape did a poor job of blocking trespassers. Not that anyone would have a reason to enter besides tagging: the insides and all of its contents only recently stopped smoldering.

Morgan, Raphie, and Demy stood before the catastrophe that was once the Bourbon Belfry. Raphie sketched a pseudo-blueprint as he paced the perimeter, to have any kind of reference.

Morgan sighed, defeated. "There went any chance of us finding anything Yess had on the Lounge…"

"Well, not quite," Demy replied. "We know the Mob and Tyrants have an alliance going on. Talked to some friends over in Inglewood and East LA. Turns out they've seen Elves and Vampires do deals. Have an eyewitness say some hooded, crossbow-wielding gangbanger has been interfering with those deals."

"A hunter," Morgan said as if she'd said a curse. "I'd heard a similar rumor. A story a colleague was working on. We've got a real live Vampire Hunter in LA."

"Yeah… It's frightening," Demy replied, covering her mouth.

"Whoever burned this place down couldn't have known what was inside," Raphie said.

"Or they know exactly what it held and wanted it wiped from existence," Morgan finished.

"None of this makes sense, it just feels like anarchy," Raphie said exasperated.

Demy sighed at their conversation. "Yeah, I just don't know who it could be."

"Wow…okay," Morgan said, offended.

"What?" Demy played dumb.

"You're lying to us. You've been lying to us for some time, and I didn't wanna pry, but you seem to be involved with this,"

Morgan went, marching right up to her. "What do you know?"

"I don't know what you're on about," she defended, visibly sweating.

"Demy…" she said, looking her in the eye, the exhaustion clear on her face. That broke Demy.

"I know who caused all this," she said, squinting in the morning sun as if she was going to be pummeled. "His name is Gruel, not sure what his real name is. He runs a coven called the Corvus Enclave. My coven… At least they were my coven. I haven't seen them in a while."

"Why are you just now telling us?" Morgan stressed.

"I'm kind of wondering the same thing," Raphie said, concerned. "Why were you trying to start a gang war?"

"I was hoping you wouldn't ask that..." Demy sighed, wanting to bury her face and hide. "It wasn't my idea."

"But your magic," Raphie interjected.

"Yes… I thought I could do some good by causing a fight between two groups. You know, bad taking out bad? One of which made it personal, okay?" Demy took a deep breath, trying to get her heart rate back to normal. "I…I don't want to get into it right now, but… just trust me when I say the Tyrants are no better than the Elf Mafia…"

"So this *is* about revenge," Morgan raised her chin, a bit taken aback by Demy's confession. "What about all the innocents that could have gotten hurt? If this war starts?"

"Why do you think I stopped? But it wasn't enough to stop Gruel." Demy cried, her body weak from stress. "I didn't think he could pull it off without me, but he's got the Enclave wrapped around his finger."

"Shouldn't we still try to stop him anyway?" Morgan asked.

"It's complicated."

"Try me," Morgan said, losing her patience.

"I don't…" Demy said with a sigh, "You both might as well know. My family didn't die in an accident… they were killed by a clan of Vampires back in Romania known as the Exiles of Night… Known as Tyrants in the New World. Gruel helped get me out of there, and he lost more than I did."

"Oh, my god." Raphie clasped his head and approached his

lover, “Makes sense why you wouldn’t want to stop Gruel.”

“But I don’t want to help him either. This isn’t the retribution I asked for. It’s a stain on my soul,” Demy said, her voice wavering.

“No, it’s not… you’re better than Gruel,” Raphie said, putting a hand around her shoulders.

As they spoke, a figure in a windbreaker jacket and track pants, with a long, striped tail protruding, approached the rubble. She snuck in the opposite end while they talked, Morgan catching a glimpse of the girl.

“I just saw a Catfolk enter the building,” she said.

“Catfolk?” Raphie replied, raising a brow and looking for her.

“Fuck it, I’m going in,” Morgan huffed following the stranger into the desolate remains of the Belfry.

"What?" Raphie said as she ran past, unable to stop her. Even still, he followed her directly up to the building.

“Just wait here. I’ll call if I need backup,” she said, climbing over the rubble of the outer wall.

“Be careful,” he shouted with a whisper.

Most of the inner walls were decrepit and ruined. The floors had all but given in on themselves. At the center point, the main dance floor had collapsed, blocking any would-be space. Morgan carefully guided herself in heels through the destruction; she picked a bad day to wear a pencil skirt as well. Upon almost tripping, Morgan caught herself just before falling into the basement. She took a deep breath of relief. Elsewhere, the sound of clamoring in rubble echoed from where the main office used to be. Morgan followed it.

“Hello?” She asked, crossing over the waist-high debris and into the collapsed room. She navigated her way along a somewhat flat surface forming a ramp to the bottom level, where the Catfolk was. Hearing her approach, the woman’s soft black ears perked up, and her tail flicked. The woman stood up rapidly and took a boxer's stance. Morgan knew her. “Tabby?”

“Chastity?” Tabby said, stepping closer, putting her hands in her jacket pockets, Morgan took a step back in caution. “I never would have expected to see you here. Especially after you got swooped up by the upper crust."

"Well, I was hoping I could find some answers." Morgan professed.

"Answers to what? They caught the guy, I heard," Tabby replied.

"About Chrissy…" Morgan stated firmly, her face furious for this poor girl. "Chrissy Donavon is missing, Tabby. She has been for months. If we don't find a way to her soon, she's going to be dead… if not already."

"You're not a hooker are you?" Tabby said with a grimace. "So that makes you what, a cop?"

"No," Morgan shook her head, her eyes heavy. "I work for the Cryptid Chronicle. I'm trying to find the truth about what happened to Chrissy and what the Lounge did to her."

"At least you're not a cop, I guess," Tabby said, disappointed nonetheless. "You want the whole story? I told you all I know about Chrissy. But I didn't tell you all I know about the Lounge."

"I'm all ears," Morgan said, pulling a pad and pen from her bag.

"Their currency is people," Tabby confirmed. "They get everyone to consent. Somehow. It's worse than trafficking: it's a cult. They worship… what's-his-name."

"Ziusudra," Morgan answered.

"That bastard. He's got them thinking he's an untouchable god. He's not." Tabby fumed as she spoke.

"Did you work for him, too?" Morgan asked.

"Once and only just… if you're smart, you'll make yourself scarce from those people, 'cause once they've got you, it's too late." Tabby began her climb out of the dangerous ruin, scaling it with feline grace.

"I came out just fine," Morgan said with unjust arrogance.

"That's because they wanted you to be free, baby… just… skip town… if you're smart." Tabby made her way out of the building. "Hey…" She turned around one last time. "What's your name?"

"Morgan. And you?"

"Nichole." She smiled, her teeth just as fanged as Morgan's if not more. "Take care, baby."

Morgan smiled back and watched Nichole leave her sight. As soon as she was sure she was gone, she walked over to see what Nichole was scouring for. When she arrived, she saw a lockbox, covered in soot, but otherwise unscathed. The lock had already been picked, bobby pin still inside, and its contents taken.

"Shit." Morgan did her best to leap out of the scorched building and jogged out into the street. She scanned all around her in a tizzy. Nichole was gone.

"Everything okay, Blondie?" Raphie asked, approaching as soon as he saw her.

"That was a former dancer at the club," Morgan said with frustration. "She took something from the office. Something from a lockbox. Where did she go?"

"We didn't see anybody leave," Demy replied.

"It was floppies, wasn't it?" Raphie asked rhetorically.

"I don't know," Morgan sighed, exasperated, "I don't know who to trust."

"You can trust me," Raphie said with a handsome smile.

Morgan met his charmingly scruffy face and glanced back down, becoming sheepish from nothing. "Thank you," she peeped.

"Also," Demy piped up. "I've got no reason to do ya dirty."

"Yeah, Blondie, you've got people in your corner," Raphie beamed.

Morgan gave a little chuckle, looking into his amber-brown eyes and getting lost for a time.

"I've been thinking," Demy added, cautious not to interrupt the moment. "If you're willing to meet one of my coven mates… There's *one* among them I trust to bring this to…I don't know how soon they'll be available, but I think they may be able to identify the spine that was in your head."

"Really?" Morgan contemplated, getting tangled up with actively practicing mages would be dangerous. Any more dangerous than what she'd done so far? "I guess so… what have I got to lose?"

3

A week had passed; the day of dread had finally come. Ten years. Ten long, confusing, and painful years. Morgan was eleven when she lost her mother and father. Of all things, a car accident is what took their lives. It was the 80s, and seat belts weren't even required to be worn, let alone refractium. The windows were tinted. The car was a tank. There was no reason her parents should have died, and yet they were unceremoniously taken from her and her aunt.

Aunt M was far from a perfect parent, but she was lucky to have her. If Maxine didn't exist, Morgan would have entered foster care, been forced to move, and would have had no one. Maxine saved her as she saved so many people in her tenure at the FBI.

At least, that's what she heard from the stories. Stories of triumph and glory. Stories like pulp action heroes, derring-do, and adventure. Morgan never wanted to be an agent; she didn't want to have to carry a gun. But she did want to be like her father. She wanted to help people. So far, all she's done is destroy her own life. In one whole month of searching, she had more questions than answers.

Morgan entered Lunar Light Investigations as the sun began to go down, the cloudy sky blocking the beautiful California sunset. She hesitated before unlocking the door fully and knocking.

"Auntie M, it's Morgan, please don't point your gun at me this time," she said timidly, at last entering the apartment turned office.

Once she was in, she'd see the place was empty, save for the dozen or so moths fluttering about the place. She locked up and proceeded into the cluttered apartment. She shook her head, seeing that many of the haphazardly plugged-in lamps were still on, and a cigarette was in her ashtray that was not properly snuffed, judging from the long ash trail. Morgan approached the desk to make sure nothing was burnt when she saw the complex web of her aunt's current story.

Morgan's skin went cold as she noticed everything in her corkboard present on this one. The only difference was that the center of it all wasn't the curly-haired Chrissy Donavon but the grey-fleshed Domhainn, Tori Franques. Morgan knew the investigations paralleled one another, but she had no idea how many near misses she'd had.

The Bourbon Belfry: Maxine had a history with Yessenia and managed to get information out of her that Morgan couldn't. The Keep: Maxine found a warehouse full of candles that ultimately led to nothing. One of said candles was on her desk, black and etched with Elven script. Morgan wished she could have Demy identify it. Upon smelling the candle, her nose scrunched. It was musky and rather pungent.

Moving forward through Maxine's investigation, came to a chilling conclusion. She noticed on the desk three floppy disks. One labeled "locations", another "clients", and a third "product". It seemed these disks were the last stop on the trail of Tori Franques. Whatever method Maxine used to acquire these, Morgan was ignorant of, but it seemed as though it was the roadblock Maxine had hit… the same for Morgan. The information on those disks was tantalizing. Morgan gulped. *Product.* She thought *That's the disk that was missing from the Keep…* She froze, thinking long and hard about what she was considering.

After moments of contemplation, she found herself at the wall of Maxine's triumphs. Maxine had been documented for decades saving lives and attempting to warn the masses of disaster. To the world, she was something of a superhero, fighting criminals and violent Cryptids alike. A particular photo stood out, Morgan took it off the wall, and stared longingly at it.

"Morgan?" Maxine shouted, coming through the front door, its window pane rattling as it opened and shut. "Morgan, are you here?"

"Yeah," Morgan answered from the main room, not glancing away from the framed memorabilia. In her hand, Morgan held a photo of Maxine and her august father, a rare candid photo of him without refractium so she could see his sharp jawline, terra-cotta flesh, and perfectly straight, fanged smile. The two sat clinking beers together after their successful mission in the Ozarks. Both of their badges, inscribed with "FBI", were on display in a glass cabinet beside the photo. She set it back in its place beside yet another photo of her whole family: Maxine, Noah, Odessa, and a 5-year-old Morgana.

"I'm sorry I didn't call, Auntie M," Morgan said, only glancing away from the photos for a second. "I promise I haven't been loitering long."

"Don't worry about it, kid," Maxine said softly, crossing the office-like apartment to get to her kitchen. When she arrived, she plopped her grocery bags on the counter and crossed to Morgan, giving her a long, tight hug. "Just glad you're here. Been almost a month since I've seen you. How… how are you doing? How have you been taking… life?"

"Um… I'm holding on," Morgan said, her eyes fixated on the photo of them all, her eyes wandering to her mother; she was a spitting image of Morgan, albeit a bit shorter, ginger, and with more flushed skin. "This is the first year since, like, middle school that I've been single on the anniversary. So that's a thing… Do we still have to call it that? I always fucking hated that name: anniversary. It makes it sound like a celebration, and it's just not."

"Uh, of course not, sweetie." Maxine stepped back and began to put her ice cream and lunch meats away as she spoke. "Well… what would you normally do on… today?"

"Get drunk… sleep and fuck the day away," Morgan realized how freely she spoke and hid her face, on the brink of tears. "I'm so sorry, I-I don't know why I said that."

"Well…" Maxine laughed awkwardly and pulled the whiskey out of the bag and uncorked it "I have a big ass bottle of cheap booze. I'd be honored to share it with you and have girl time. Kinda like we used to when you were little."

"You mean our tea parties?" Morgan said with a sniffle and a smile. "That sounds amazing."

*****

Less than a quarter of the bottle remained, the woody brown liquor rested at the bottom. Maxine saw some remaining and poured herself more, throwing a few half-melted ice cubes in from a bucket. Morgan was mid-giggle fit, flushed pink, and trying to tell a story, underscored by *The Who* album played low on Maxine's dusty record player. Both of them had to take off their coats ages ago, becoming warm in their drunkenness, with Maxine down just to her pants and white tank top, a rare sight of Maxine's feminine bust. Morgan took notes from Maxine's book and unbuttoned the first few buttons of her blouse, her cheeks flushed pink from drink and laughter.

"When Mom came home, my hair was the shortest it's ever been before or since. Like, full pixie. We were both drinking milkshakes, and there were Polaroids of me with a mohawk on the counter," Morgan said with a snort and giggle. "You should have seen Mom's face. She just stood there and was all 'What the fuck, Noah? We're supposed to go out to dinner with *your* boss in twenty minutes!' She was fuming. I swear, Auntie M, I thought she was gonna go feral for a second there."

"That's a riot," Maxine laughed, cocking her head when she noticed there was only a bit left in the bottle "Your Irish accent is great by the way. Sound just like your mom."

"Thanks. I used to practice all the time," Morgan said, looking off as she fondly remembered. "Daddy defended shaving my head because he said I looked like Annie Lennox."

"And that was the first time you heard Dessa swear?" Maxine laughed, "You were what, eight, you said? Before she got pregnant, your mother swore like a sailor."

"As if, she was Mrs. Hyper-Tense-Catholic-Therapist. She said 'fuck' like ten times in her life, max." Morgan couldn't stop giggling but felt a rush of regret when her Aunt poured the rest of the whiskey into her once-empty glass. "Noooo. No more, please. I have to drive." She gave a weak plea.

"Not while you're drunk, you can't. Plus, you have a full glass. How rude is that to leave a full glass of whiskey?" Maxine chuckled, "And no, hate to break it to you, but that's false. Your mother was a fucking foul mouth, especially on the receiving end of her anger. Never seen such a sweet little woman string together a sentence out of mostly curse words. Where you got your mouth from for sure," Maxine grinned and winked.

"That's unreal. I can't see Mom doing that." Morgan did as the Romans and leaned forward to retrieve her glass, topping it off with Coke from a can before she drank it.

"Oh, you better believe it… she smoked like a chimney and was crass, but still maintained this femme image. Never out of a dress and heels, again, where you get your style." Maxine said, gesturing to Morgan's very professional attire, still dressed in her work clothes. She reached for her cigarettes on the table, needing one due to the mere mention of smoking. "Inherited her grace, too. See her so much in you. Would be so proud of how strong and independent a woman you've become."

"I hope so," Morgan said, her eyes lowered.

"Know so," Maxine looked up at the many lamps flickering, moths gathering around several of the brighter ones, and took a draw. "Ironically, she was the one who convinced me to embrace my femininity *my* way. Sat me down and said, 'You look how you want, dress and act how you want. Don't let anyone else define you.'… Irish accent isn't as good as yours."

Morgan felt a pain in her heart as she noticed the tears appearing in Maxine's dark eyes.

"And your dad," Maxine continued, wiping her tears away. "You got his heart and his fucking tenacity. You Scrivens are like steel traps when it comes to doing the right thing. You'd have to pry him off a case if he knew someone innocent could be saved. I owe everything to your mom and dad. To the opportunities they gave you. They loved you so much… Noah would have given all the blood in his veins for you. Hell, he made sure that your future was lined up years before he d—…died." She looked down, solemn. Morgan did the same.

"Shit. Doing bad job at cheering up." Maxine shook her head.

"No, I love this… I love hearing about Mom and Dad. You knew them so much longer than I got to. I have a relationship with them through you…" Morgan also began to feel herself lose it, watching tears stream down her aunt's face. "And I've not been appreciating you for it."

"What are you talking about?" Maxine shifted and gave her a stern look. "Was with B the other day. Remember Albert, right?"

Morgan nodded. "How can I forget Bigfoot?"

"Some people still think he's a hoax, so I don't fuckin' know." They both chuckled. "Anyway, was bragging to B about you and how proud I am. Think you're doing amazing. In school. Holding up an internship. A job, I assume, since you got a car."

Morgan felt her stomach knot for still lying to her Aunt, sipping her drink through the awkward silence. "Yep, I've been moonlighting as a cashier," she managed to make up.

"See!? That's what I mean, you're amazing. You're just… Ah, proud of you. Truly am." Maxine said, caressing Morgan's shoulder.

"Th-thank you…" Morgan said, beginning to sob. "Y-you have no idea what it m-means to me to hear that: th-that I'm enough."

"You're more than enough." Maxine turned to fully face her niece and held her hands. "You're my whole world, princess."

Morgan leaned forward and hugged her aunt, both crying tears of mixed happiness and grief. Maxine just squeezed her niece, no longer the little girl she watched grow up. The further Morgan leaned forward into the hug, the further she nudged her purse back with her foot. Within, a black floppy labeled 'Disk 3: Product."

Demy rapped on the door of Apartment 161, waiting patiently for her boyfriend or his best friend to answer. Before she could knock again, Raphie opened the door, already joyful just to see her. He stepped forward, kissing her before ushering her into his abode.

"Hey, doll, thanks for coming over so soon. We thought you

might wanna see the breakthrough Morgan had." He said, closing the door behind his woman and looking at her rear in the dress before following her in.

"Hell yes, I'm invested in this now," Demy said, placing her bag down at the entry table, glancing at a jazz band trophy with Raphie's name on it. She turned to Morgan, rubbing her hands together and grinning, "What did we find?"

"Well, I didn't find it," Morgan confessed, not looking up from her laptop, pink glasses set on the bridge of her nose. "I kinda stole it… from my aunt."

Demy looked to Raphie, her thoughts of concern broadcast. Raphie simply shrugged and shook his head. "I can't do shit," he mouthed.

"It's the final piece," Morgan declared. "For whatever reason, there was a disk missing at The Keep. But this seemed to be it… or close enough. I'm gonna be honest… the product is kinda disturbing."

Morgan leaned back and gave Demy enough space to read the next piece of the puzzle. Morgan had a copy of the numbers from the other floppy taped to the screen of her laptop. With each number, a name coincided: mostly girls' names. Among them, the name "Larsson, Joana", dated a week before she was found dead. On one date, the night of the first Lounge Party was the name "Vaughn, Chastity." Beside each person's name was a ratio. Judging by both her and Joana's numbers being larger, she assumed this was something to do with their likelihood of being recruited to the Lounge. These details confirmed exactly what Morgan and her peers were thinking: that the product was people.

"My first thought was that the Belfry and Keep were transportation, and there seems to be some of that," Morgan began. "But, these clubs are recruitment centers… for indentured servitude. Sex trafficking, under the guise of consensual BDSM."

"That's beyond fucked," Raphie chimed in.

"Beyond fucked is right. These people are being recruited into… into a cult… they're being convinced that their lives will be better if they submit to Ziusudra, then he passes them around to whoever he pleases…" Morgan deduced, her mind moving like a bullet train, switching tracks over and over with expert precision.

"So why did he send Chrissy away?" Demy asked, "Why not just recruit her to one of these parties and just use her that way?"

"Maybe she knew something… maybe Tori Franques knew something. Joana Larsson too… Something Ziusudra didn't want getting out."

"Like what?" Raphie dared to ask.

"I don't know… but if we don't find Chrissy soon," Morgan turned to her friends, taking off her glasses and speaking like a grave omen, "It'll be too late."

4

Morgan strolled across the green, rolling Avalon campus, following the paths that stretched across the open courtyard. The sharp, polygonal structures of the school were designed to reflect the awe-inspiring feat of a university made for and by Non-Humans. Morgan loved coming onto campus, seeing Orcs and Elves, Medusae and Vampires, Giants and Dwarves, Shifters and Ghouls, Taknolings and Valkyries, Humans and Catfolk, all on the same campus, intermingled and being raised to be the leading generation. Now that fall was in full swing, and the normally sunny California skies were grey, hardly any students at all were out on campus. All of them were in class or studying for the upcoming finals. Morgan was here for more somber reasons.

She glanced up at an overcast sky, smelling the moisture in the air, grateful to be dressed in a large, white, and gold Avalon University sweater and fleece-lined jeans that kept her normally cold body warm. A pair of ballet flats was possibly not the best footwear for walking across campus, but it's no worse than when she's worn heels. She always remembered her mother in high heels and professional dresses or pencil skirts when she was a little girl, a shining example of what Odessa *imagined*, embodied womanhood. Morgan tried to achieve that, but as of late, she couldn't put on any more masks.

She'd finally reached the library. Half of its perimeter faced the public street; the building itself was colossal. Her eyes followed the towering front extending into an almost church-like turret into the sky. She saw it as a metaphorical middle finger to Human clergy, though many acted like it was only Humans and not Lenoran High-Elves that subjugated so many other Non-Humans for centuries.

She pressed on through the glass double doors, the massive, multilevel library sprawled out in an intricate, symmetrical pattern. Dividing the massive super library down the center was a row of mostly occupied study desks and hefty beige computer monitors. If the archives of the Chronicle were no help, this library could hold the answers. A few feet from the entrance was the librarian's desk. She was a well-preserved Ghoul, meaning she wasn't particularly old, though her skin still possessed a sickly green hue to it like many Ghouls. The librarian had big, frizzy, red hair, emerald green eyes, and a hooked nose. In Morgan's opinion, she was quite pretty, if not possessing a minor, perpetual scowl.

"Hi," Morgan said with a fanged grin, "I'm looking for articles or books on old Los Angeles buildings. Particularly in Beverly Hills."

"Oh, Isle 144 would be your best bet for books, but you're more than welcome to check the archives. Have you used a microfilm reader before?" The librarian said.

"Yes, I have, thank you!" Morgan gave her two thumbs up and made her way down to the ground floor, where the bulky viewing machines awaited her, bumping into the railing as she did.

After searching the archive for old news articles, she sat herself down at one of the center machines, placing her bag down only to bring out a small notebook with some of her more in-the-moment scrawling. Once she'd placed her pink-framed glasses on her face, she was ready to begin. Her inquiry into the Babylon Tower yielded results almost immediately, leading to several articles that all mentioned the building, but none seemed to carry any significance other than its strange architecture. She took notes on its involvement in any major socio-political events, including those exclusive to high society. Many documents confirmed that while it has always been there since the founding of Beverly Hills, it was once a hotel instead of high-rise condos. From what she'd gathered, the name Ziusudra dated back to its founding.

She scanned further into her finds and found an article that dated back to 1955, ten years after the Vaydark Accords and the Branson Act that ended the use of magi-tech warfare and banned magic respectively in over one hundred nations. The name featured: Sol Ziusudra.

"Dorian's father?" She noted, reading deeper. She was disturbed to find out that a similar scenario to what had happened with Chrissy and Joana happened to a Trueborn Vampire woman named Velva Sabien. She was a singer at the bar that appeared to be the same den where Morgan performed. She frequented the lavish parties that were held in the penthouse, singing for the biggest wigs in LA at the time. Her body was found mangled in Griffith Park. She was only 18. This story was blamed on the serial killer, Wilber Earl, who had stayed multiple times at the hotel. Morgan sensed it was a convenient scapegoat.

An article from 1989 told of a girl named Kate Carper, a girl who went missing but had a room at the hotel. Reports say witnesses heard her in the halls muttering to herself in an 'incomprehensible gibberish'. She was 19. Morgan recognized the big blonde hair in the girl's school photo: it was the girl she saw in the Babylon the night hell broke loose.

She reached an even older news article, dated 1934, where she saw a picture of a man captioned Luciel Ziusudra. He looked much different than Dorian as far as style and dress, but the resemblance was present. Morgan was puzzled by the aspect.

"He'd be over 100 years old…" she puzzled to herself. "That's impossible, he's Human."

She was hushed.

Though this article was the most horrifying bar none, a major elite party was broken up by a group of disturbed "American-Elf Legionnaires." They cornered most of the patrons, all the dancers, and entertainers, and executed them with wands and Incineration spells. Curtains caught fire, and an entire floor of the building was burned to ash with its occupants inside. Allegedly, Luciel was one of the survivors. The article suggested he was horrifically burned and, thus, was never seen publicly again.

The Legionnaire who was caught alive due to a bad cyanide pill called upon the reasoning, "There is something unholy in that hotel." History would claim the deranged Elf was most likely talking about interracial sex or homosexuality, but Morgan knew it couldn't possibly end there.

In 1913, apparently, the Babylon was a place that represented peace and freedom. Elves and Vampires alike could enjoy the company of the most beautiful women in LA. The descriptions of the parties sounded like a precursor to what would eventually be contorted and twisted into the Lounge. When Ile de Lenora entered the Great War as an Axis Power, that peace ended.

Morgan dug deeper into local news from the '30s and '40s. In addition to the horrific murders within the Babylon, multiple massacres took place around Beverly Hills and Hollywood during this time. Wealthy Legion Sympathizer families in Little Lenora and impoverished Vampire clans fleeing genocide formed into splinter groups that acted as the first Elf and Vampire crime syndicates. Many of the Vampire clans became rolled into what is now the T-Town Tyrants, and a few others remained higher on the pecking order, including the Exiles of Night. Demy must have been wrong to think that the Tyrants and the Exiles were the same… but Morgan didn't doubt Yessenia's involvement with her family's deaths.

The Elf families became rivals for a similar cause, disappearing into the shadows when the War ended. LA became the factions' battleground for years to come… until Dorian Ziusudra signed the treaty. If Morgan's research lined up right, the treaty was signed 5 years ago… roughly the same time the hotel was turned into condos.

Morgan took to the next source, Isle 144, and looked for any books involving the Babylon and its early years. She found a single book: *Historic Hotels of LA*, published in 1978. It not only spoke of the Babylon but went into full detail about the grim events that took place. Morgan followed the trail of Velva Sabien, seeing her as the closest relation to anything she was searching for. It was a tragic story, a young, talented woman turned violent murder victim. A crime still unsolved to this day. Morgan feared that if she continued this path, she might be a twisted corpse somewhere.

If I get Chrissy out... come what may. She thought. With it came a memory of something she heard her father say, "Scrivens don't live long." Her mother scolded him for saying that in front of her. In her gut, Morgan knew he was right. She just wanted to make sure Raphie or Demy or Aunt M weren't harmed by her actions. They deserved better than that. In a few hours, she had much of what she needed and checked the book out. She took a deep breath; it was time for VanderGraf's class.

5

All communication with Ziusudra or the Lounge had gone dark. Morgan hadn't received a single phone call or new assignment. As an added relief, there hadn't even been a peep from Balam. Raphie and Demy had done a wondrous job of keeping Morgan stable and grounded the past couple of weeks, and she felt she had developed a bond with Demy. After all, she was the only person Raphie dated that she ever 100% approved of. Together, Raphie and Morgan sat, intently listening to VanderGraf's lecture.

"...the Great War began in 1912 and ended in 1945. It wasn't continuous fighting, however. In 1918 and again in 1930, a cease-fire was called that would last for years at a time. That said, the Axis and Allies would begin fighting proxy wars in the South American and African theatres during that time, which culminated..." He rambled, manually changing the slides on the projector as he did.

Morgan looked to Raphie as he took notes, or possibly doodled. She knew her overprotection of him was unwarranted. He could more than handle himself, as could she, but they both cared enough to ask one another, 'Do you need help?' Morgan was stubborn, not wanting to do things any way but hers, and it could be a bit disquieting. Somehow, through all of it, Raphie decided to put up with Morgan, and in her mind, she could never properly repay him.

Morgan sat up straight as she noticed Professor VanderGraf look their way, a habit she'd developed as of late. She gave a soft sigh of relief as his eyes moved to another student nearby who was speaking to him. It had been so long since her party with the Lounge, and he hadn't given her the slightest inkling of suspicion. With or without his direct suspicion, she felt on constant edge in his class. Though she was certain with the amount of time that had passed, he didn't recognize her, and with any luck, won't ever.

After the short lecture, VanderGraf left the students to work in their duo groups for their final project. Low murmurs had formed as a calm white noise in the background of Raphie and Morgan's conversation. It was loud enough that both felt they could safely talk about the hidden state of the city.

"So, question," Raphie asked, "You think the reason everything has gone quiet is because of the Belfry going up in smoke?"

"Absolutely," Morgan replied, typing away on her laptop. "The Lounge has frozen their assets and halted all activity because they're trying to figure out what the next move is. They're, like, afraid someone is gonna start shit."

"Shit might already be started," Raphie said with a short chuckle of disbelief. "Have you heard about all the Vampire attacks in East LA? It's insane."

"You wanna know insane?" Morgan leaned on her desk and turned to Raphie, "There have been attacks in Little Lenora, too." She shook her head and clicked to open a document. "Word is it's all Tyrants."

"That shit's gonna set Elf/Vampire relations back to the '50s, dude," Raphie sighed.

"That Gruel guy is gonna get his wish… a gang war," Morgan moped.

"Hey… You're not mad about the whole Burned Belfry business? Are you?" He asked softly. "I mean… at Demy, specifically."

"No, she had nothing to do with it…" she smiled and looked him in his eyes as dark as the autumn leaves. "From where I'm sitting, Gruel manipulated her into helping, and she got out before it got dangerous."

Raphie raised his brow, trying to grapple with the irony of her statement.

"Okay, seriously, we have to focus on this project… Um, do you remember when the Scourging of Transylvania was?" She said, oblivious to his concern.

"Shouldn't you know that?" Raphie teased. "Aren't you from Transylvania?"

"I'm from *Pennsylvania,*" Morgan said with an eye roll. "I'm Irish and Cherokee, for fuck's sake."

"I was just joking," Raphie giggled, thumbing through pictures and notes in his notebook. Morgan raised a brow upon seeing an image of her scribbled on the pages. She became even more intrigued upon seeing a second. "Uh, 1941?"

"No, that's when The Vampire Nation officially joined the Allies." Morgan glanced back at his notebook. "I don't have any notes about it… can I see yours?"

"What makes you think I have it if you don't?" Raphie continued to laugh. "Besides, you know I just listen and it sticks."

"Oh, that's right, your weird-ass photographic memory," She said with a sassy smirk. "Let me see."

"No. It's private," he pouted, slamming the notebook.

"A history notebook? On a partner project?" She said, her tone getting pushier as she reached for the notebook. "Come on, let me see it."

"No!" A few students turned to see Raphie's stifled shout. He laughed nervously to play it off.

"What do you draw porn or something?" Morgan joined in the laughter. "What's that stuff you get from Little Tokyo? Hentai?"

A few other students looked their way. Raphie, in turn,

became noticeably flustered.

"That is *art*… and no… It's not that." He grumbled, "Here, just look."

Morgan took the notebook with a boastful "Thank you". She thumbed through and saw strange and vivid doodles that would look at home on any stoner's wall. Psychedelic but frighteningly realistic. The longer she stared, the more she was pulled back to the nightmare she experienced at the Babylon; she turned the pages faster to get past the more dizzying artwork. She came across a few more graphic and disturbing images that could only be described as "body horror". In all, it was frighteningly similar to the otherworld.

"Shit, Raph, you doin' okay?"

"I draw my nightmares sometimes," Raphie said, watching the floor.

Morgan looked at the embarrassed Raphie before turning the page to see more realistic drawings, some of nature: trees, birds, and skylines. The only people who weren't stylized or monstrous were pictures of Morgan and Demy. She was grateful to see he also drew pictures of his girlfriend, but just as many of her, and often it was both of them. Raphie was completely turned away by that point, luckily so, as Morgan's cheeks became bright red. Each was a complimentary angle, flattering in every regard but never sexualized. Some of her sitting and reading with her glasses on or working on her laptop with her hair up, others of her laughing and happy. He paid special attention to her facial details: high cheeks, doe eyes, heart-shaped face. All of them, especially close-ups, were photo-realistic.

"Raphie? Why are there so many pictures of me?" She said, calm, but off guard.

"You make good practice," he confessed. "You're a part of my daily life, so I just draw when I see something pretty I want to replicate. You don't think it's weird, do you?"

"I don't know…" Morgan gave a half-smile. "I like them. I mean, they're well done. You're not being creepy, they're just, like, your notebook doodles, right?"

"Right," Raphie said, his skin feeling the cool rush of

relaxation after panic.

"Besides, you're my best friend," Morgan placed her hand on Raphie's shoulder to reassure him. "I don't think there's much you could do to chase me away at this point."

They must not have heard VanderGraf excuse the class, as everyone around them stood up and began gathering their belongings. Morgan packed up her laptop, handing the notebook back to Raphie. When he took it from her, they touched fingertips. An awkward silence suspended for a moment, letting the feeling linger, unwittingly allowing it to evolve. Before either became conscious of the sensation of their fluttering hearts, they both looked away and focused on getting out of class.

"I do have to find that answer. I wasn't lying." She stood, still looking away and blushing.

As she walked away, a weak smile broke out across her lips. Worry was clear in Raphie's expression, following her with his eyes, down the steps until she reached VanderGraf's desk. Morgan turned around and waved to him, signaling that she'd be right behind him.

"Excuse me, Professor VanderGraf, I had a question about when the Scourging of Transylvania took place?" She said, shifting her weight. "For some reason, I'm missing that in my notes."

"May 27th, 1940." He said without looking up from the papers he was grading, "After the Legion's fusion bombings."

"Awesome! Thank you!" She said in a high-pitched tone, then turned to walk away. Something about it grabbed VanderGraf's attention.

"Hey, wait a minute," he said, studying her. Morgan's demeanor shifted to immense discomfort. "Come back here… You never said 'Please.'"

Morgan stared back in his direction. Never before had he been a stickler for manners. She had difficulty holding eye contact as he leered directly into what felt like her immortal soul. "Um… p-please?"

He craned his head, listening to every inflection carefully. Suddenly, a devilish smile formed across his bearded, limestone-textured face.

"Okay, my turn for a question," VanderGraf said, running his tongue against his inner lip

"Okay…"

"Do you have a blue butterfly on your ass?"

Morgan froze, ice running up her spine and frosting over her brain. She looked at Raphie from the corner of her eye, too far away to hear anything with Human ears.

"On m-my hip…" she said soft and broken, still avoiding looking at him.

He stood up and approached her, his expression mutating into sleaze. Even a foot and a half shorter, he was intimidating, his bulk suggesting he was just as strong as her. "You have an interesting taste in extracurricular activities… Ms. Vaughn. Perhaps you can earn some 'extra credit' on your project. With the partner you chose, you could use the boost… You could pass by just doing what you do on weekends."

"I'm c-confused. I don't know what y-you're talking about." Morgan stood there paralyzed, feeling eyed up like she was naked despite wearing merely a sweater and jeans.

"Of course not," VanderGraf slyly walked past her, leaning up ever so slightly and whispering. "Sha hatti darisam."

Morgan gasped.

"That's what I thought." He chuckled, "We'll talk more soon, Morgana. Consider my proposition."

She wasted no time and stormed out of class, looking at Raphie with a thousand-yard stare. He furrowed his brow, glanced at her, then at VanderGraf, glowering at him.

"Everything okay?" he inquired.

"Let's just get out of here," she insisted, her voice strained.

The two friends charged out of the building and into the open green courtyard. Students had already cleared the main walkways and dispersed to the rolling hills of the campus. Morgan pushed on, holding her laptop case to her breast. Raphie stepped in front of her, stopping her in her tracks.

"What did he say to you?"

"Nothing, he was just answering my question… 1940," Morgan said, polite and in denial. She tried to push past him.

"Bullshit, I know my best friend… so, please… Don't hide shit from me, too, dude." Raphie held her shoulders and looked her in the eye.

Morgan sighed, trembling in fear, "He's a Lounge member. He was… a client, and didn't recognize me until now, I guess."

"What the fuck? What did he say?" Raphie said, blinking rapidly in disbelief.

"I don't know… he—"

"Morgana Scriven?" a man in a chauffeur's uniform, white gloves, and wavy, dirty blonde hair called to them as he crossed the courtyard. Morgan recognized this man as Oscar: Ziusudra's driver.

"Who's asking?" Raphie said in his deepest voice, stepping between them. Morgan felt no qualms about hiding at this point and gripped her friend's sleeve.

"Miss Scriven, our mutual employer sent me to gather you from class," he said professionally, ignoring Raphie. "He'd very much appreciate an audience with you."

"He's here?" Morgan asked in a panic, Raphie took her hand, running his thumb over hers.

"Yes, Miss Scriven," Oscar said, keeping his distance but remaining ever placid. "He was in the area, and when your phone was off, he figured you were in class."

"It's okay. I can go," Morgan whispered to Raphie, stepping out from behind him with her head held high. "Take me to him."

Morgan was led to the parking garage elevator and taken straight to the top floor. Above, in two spots, sat a white Lexus with blacked-out windows. As she got closer, she noticed the holographic elemental symbol etched into the corner of the windshield, an indicator that the glass was layered with government-mandated refractium; it was a detail Ziusudra kept so as not to be bothered about the tint. Oscar stepped in front of her and opened the door, gesturing for her to get in. She gulped and made her way inside the white and maroon leather interior.

"Morgana, my dear," Ziusudra said with a damnably good-looking smile, dressed in a sharp scarlet suit. "I hope my presence at your school does not alarm you. I do not have your schedule. I was merely in the area, and you did not answer any of my calls."

"I was in class, Master, I'm sorry—" Morgan tried to explain, but was cut off.

"Do *not* apologize for receiving higher education, my dear. You are too brilliant a mind not to," he said genially.

"Of course, Master." She could not contain her smile, his being so highly infectious. "I do have a question… It may be bold for a servant to ask this… could you learn my schedule if you wanted to?"

"Well, first off, you are one of my dearest servants. I do not know if that word fits you anymore, to be honest," he looked away in what Morgan deduced was bashfulness. "But if I so wanted to, yes… I suppose I could… but I want you to know that I trust you, I do not feel like I need to have a watchdog follow you."

"Watchdog?" She asked.

"The eyes and ears of the Lounge. The unsung heroes of the Bottom, Lower, and Middle Echelons," he said, plain and content.

"Why did you ask me to come see you, Master?" she inquired. "And why can't you see me yourself?"

"I am not fond of crowds I do not control. It makes me uneasy. But I am being honest when I say you are my dearest servant. And please, when it is just us, Dorian." He admired her with his haunting stare. Morgan felt a chill. "I wanted to ask if you would come to the Babylon again, in a few weeks. I am having renovations done, and I do not want you to have to deal with anything but the best I can provide. However… I merely wish to have you over for dinner."

"Dinner?" she smirked. "As in—"

"A date? I suppose so." He smiled and gave a satisfied little laugh. "I want you to know there is no obligation to do anything, other than having dinner with me… if you so choose to accept. I will also make it count toward your party quota."

She thought hard and long about Colt— the nights they shared since. She deliberated the dangers of the Babylon Tower and how risky just going back could be. She knew that the only way to this otherworld was through Dorian's pool, as she couldn't find anything like it in her research. She had to make a choice, for Chrissy, Tori, Joana, and all the teens who'd gone missing since summer. She had to be the one to break the chain… and she had a way.

"I hate to be this way, but I must be off to my next appointment soon. I need an answer, my dear," he relented, his hand trailing down her arm toward hers.

"Yes, I'll have dinner with you," she said, took his hand, and wove her fingers with his.

"Excellent, I will have my chefs prepare a Vampire's meal," he said with a white smile. "One last thing, my dear. May I trouble you for a kiss?"

"Absolutely." She closed her eyes and leaned into him, his warm lips locking with hers. She absorbed his aroma, earthy and woodland, a juxtaposition to his clean, pristine attire. She parted from his lips and gasped, fighting the urge to go back in. Something about him, his aura, drew her in even with all she knew.

He kissed her hand as the door was opened. "I will be in touch soon with the date and time. I know it is a ways out, but I am a strong believer that distance only makes the heart grow fonder."

"I couldn't agree more," Morgan uttered, unintentionally telegraphing her arousal. "I'll see you soon, Dorian."

She climbed out and within seconds, Oscar was in the driver's seat and taking off down the ramp. Once she was free of Dorian's galvanic scent and charm, she shook her head as if to free her senses.

"What the fuck?" She laughed aloud and ran her hand through her hair. Somehow, she just landed a date with the leader of the Lounge. She planned to see it through.

6

Feverish typing, constant chatter, and fluttering papers created a soundtrack for the Cryptid Chronicle. One that told the story of diligent Non-Human reporters working tirelessly to bring the news to people of their kind. Eliza and Morgan were two such souls tasked with writing an article on affordable housing and healthcare for the undead related to a falling crime rate. Being a Taknoling, Eliza was no stranger to disenfranchisement. She lived her young life an outcast on the edge of society, misunderstood and broken. It wasn't until her senior year of high school that she realized she could turn people's hate into fear. Morgan was the first victim of her new personality, attracted to the "bad girl" persona she put off.

Morgan scanned through drafts and other news clippings to reference. She looked up from her documents, Eliza still typing away. The Vampiress sat on a file cabinet, sitting just high enough for her feet to dangle. Morgan thought of the first time they kissed; she was young and at the time, according to word of mouth, 'only recently hot'. While Morgan would later become a cheerleader, date jocks, and would graduate high school with honors, Eliza was anything but. Eliza was dishonest and impossible to read, on top of cutting corners in her academic life. They couldn't be more diametrically opposed. It was better that they were just friends now.

With a deep breath of focus, Morgan returned to reading. Her thoughts, however, couldn't be less grounded today. As her memories of relationships in the past that didn't work left her mind, those that currently did entered. She gazed past her pink glasses, up at Colt's office, and bit her lip. After a moment, she slid off the cabinet and tapped Eliza on the shoulder.

"Hey, I gotta ask Harding which sources he'd prefer us to cite, cause we could use a lot of these." She said, holding the folder close to her chest and backing out of the cubicle into the chaotic world of the Chronicle. "Be right back!"

Eliza rolled her eyes and returned to work, not having the chance to answer for him. Just as she got back into her stride, Colt Harding appeared in her cubicle.

"Hey, Wagner," he said in his abrasive and loud voice. "Where's your lackey?"

"Morgan? She just left to ask you something," Eliza said and clicked her cheek. "You two seem to talk a lot now. I mean, it's usually just you bickering… but…"

"She's *my* intern, remember? I only distributed her to you because you complained you didn't have enough help," Colt said, becoming defensive.

"I'm just sayin' you spend a lot of time together, it seems. I'm not gonna say shit, you know my motto, 'Loose lips sink ships.'"

"That's a horrible motto for a reporter," he replied, shaking his head. "What's with the 3rd degree? I spend a lot of time with Dalkom too, does that mean we're grinding beards behind the press?"

"Uh… I don't know what to say to that," Eliza said. Before she could give a proper reply, Morgan returned, announced by the sound of her heels clicking hard into the concrete.

"Harding! Thank the gods." She jogged up, looking exasperated, her eyes welling with tears. "I need you in the basement. I made a mistake with the print you had me handle. Now we have copies printing out of alignment. I don't know how to tell Dalkom."

"Fucking hell, Barbie, what the fuck did you do?" He barked, marching toward the basement.

"I'm sorry!" she said and followed.

"This is the second time this week you've fucked something up. I'm not gonna bend over backward for you anymore!"

*****

Morgan propped herself up, bent over a dusty, long-forgotten desk. She moaned, growing louder with every passing second. In the underbelly of the Chronicle, tucked back behind a bulky, out-of-service printer, was a paper supply closet that was relatively untouched— even by the basement-dwelling print and photography types. It became a perfect spot to disappear among the chaos upstairs. Colt reached from behind her and clasped his hand over her mouth.

"Fu-fu-fuck!" she managed to gasp before he did so.

"Shhhhh," he said, kissing the length of her neck, slowing the movement of his hips. "Don't get too loud, baby... we're almost there."

He noticed her start to squirm, gripped her ponytail tight, and tugged ever so slightly. Her eyes rolled back.

"You might already be there." He laughed, removing his hand slightly from her mouth, only to have her lips wrap around two of his fingers and suckle on them. "Damn, you're too fucking cute."

He pumped faster, both of them now giving muted moans until he delivered those sharp final thrusts. Both of them went limp where they stood.

"God damnit you almost told the whole basement we were down here, Scriven." He said stumbling back into a rack with old paper rolls.

After buckling his belt back up, he pulled a cigarette pack from his shirt pocket and handed one to Morgan. She staggered to an upright position, pulling her panties and stockings back up and lowering her miniskirt. She smiled softly at Colt, took the cigarette from him, and leaned against him.

"Sorry, bossman," She teased, her words slurred somewhat. "Maybe don't fuck me so hard while we're on the clock."

Colt smirked when he was called 'bossman', maybe because all of this went so far against his morals. He admired her lips around the small paper tube and raised his Zippo to light it. She was aware that he was infatuated. She just wasn't ready to bring those emotions to a dialogue, yet. She took a draw and passed it to him; neither of them was an avid smoker, but doing this a bit regularly had made it somewhat difficult to return to the grind without it.

"You're something else..." he scoffed.

"I get that a lot," she said with arrogance, the smoke escaping her lips in a plume beneath the single lamp.

“We’re gonna have to drum up better excuses or people are gonna start thinking you’re incompetent,” Colt replied, taking a draw and looking up at the swirling smoke, casting phantom-like shadows across the room. He passed the cigarette back to her.

“Don’t worry, we’ll think of something,” she said. “Maybe we can just start meeting here at designated times.”

Colt sighed. Morgan was immune to his obvious dilemma.

“I’ve been thinking about why the Lounge has gone quiet.” She said, drawing on, then returning the cigarette to him.

“Oh yeah?” He said, distracted, and passed the smoke to her again.

“I’m good,” She waved at him in dismissal, buttoning her blouse back up. “Like, they’re afraid of getting found out. A fire at one of their main hubs draws a lot of attention right?”

“Mhmm.” Colt took one last hit and put it out on the bottom of his shoe, then began to fix his shirt and tie.

“And Dorian told me their network of information sits on the backs of these ‘watchdogs’,” She continued, blinking as details rushed to her “He also asked me out to dinner.”

“Wait, what?” Colt said growing irritated.

“Yeah, can you believe that shit?” She laughed.

“No. Who’s Dorian?” Colt said, gesturing for her to continue.

“Oh. It’s Ziusudra’s first name. I guess he just got comfortable around me. Like, he’s way into me,” she said looking for someplace to view herself. “So these watchdogs.”

“Right,” Colt had to know he wasn’t the only man in her life. If not, he rather quickly needed to realize that she was, as long as she was working this exposé, a woman of the night. She may be in a lull now, but she’d be called back to Ziusudra’s side soon enough.

“If you don’t want to talk about it you can just say work talk is off-limits in the metaphorical bedroom,” she pouted, pulling out a tube of red lipstick and reapplying with her reflection in a spare metal panel.

“What the hell are we?” He asked, shooting straight.

“A Vampire and an Orc having sex,” she replied.

"I know that," he chuckled and shook his head. "I'm just… I'm about to run out of digits to count how many times we've done this little dance. I wanna know where we stand."

"Look," she said as she turned to him. "I'm not trying to put labels on anything right now. I mean, I thought we were supposed to keep this all on the down low."

"Part of me says we should, but barring the sleazy publisher getting pissy, I don't think that much backlash could hit us… if that's your worry."

"It is, but I also just got out of my longest relationship. I like… need some time." She looked away at first until the light of insight overtook her face. "Hey, isn't the Christmas Party coming up?"

"Two weeks." He said raising a brow "Why do you ask?"

"Well… let's say if nothing changes —and I'm not saying it will, but it could—," she said, playing with his blue tie. "Maybe you can come pick me up that night? And maybe we could like, go together?"

Morgan was not herself. She was conflicted. She felt she was asking for a reasonable accommodation. Thankfully, Colt was in all honesty a generous man.

"Alrighty then," he nodded. "That's a deal."

He held out his hand to shake hers. After the first two shakes, he pulled her into a close embrace, kissing her lips. She held his side in return, kissing him back.

7

In the back of a white Mercedes, windows blacked out by refractium-infused tint, Theodora Abbadon rode. She sat with her grey legs crossed, her body wrapped in all white: pencil skirt, blouse, and jacket, even her patent leather pumps were stark white. The darkest thing about her was the black shades she wore that cost just about as much as the interior of the car she rode in. Being Dorian Ziusudra's personal assistant came with many, many perks.

As the car pulled into a parallel parking space near T-Town, the driver, Oscar, piled out as quickly as ever. "Be right back, Madam." He said as he exited. Theo looked at her clipboard in her stormy hands, observing the notes she had taken about this particular individual. The strings she had to pull to get him out of lockup were beyond anything she'd had to do before. She had to sit on more desks than ever, and her knees weren't together for some of it. But alas, that is the duty of a Lounge Servant. No matter the rank, you exist to serve the cause, using any and all resources available to you.

It was then that the back door had been flung open, Theo looking up, unamused as the raggedy Ghoul was pushed into the car. Oscar may come off as having impenetrable patience, but his treatment of the undead man made clear that was not the case. The door was shut, and Theo was alone, face to face with the decrepit Ghoul, flesh greenish and adorned with veins. Theo loathed working with this kind of undead, finding them abysmal… and odoriferous.

"What the hell is going on… who are you?" The Ghoul asked in his guttural tone, brushing his moppy black hair from his eyes. Rather than answer, Theodora began reading off her notes.

"'Gruel the Ghoul.' Born Zagiri Avakain. Turned in 1971. Moved to the States in '79. Founded the Corvus Enclave with a Ms. Demytria Moon in '91. Burned down the Bourbon Belfry last month… you have been a busy bee, Mr. Avakain."

"Wait… I know who you are… You're that Abaddon chick from Beverly Hills…" Gruel said, fully displaying his disgust, which shifted to concern when the car began to move. "Why… how did you boost me?"

"My organization has done quite a vast amount of work trying to build a reliable network of informants and allies within all crooks and crevices of any movement. From the gangs of LA to the police: knowing things is our business. In all, it's our secondary product," Theo said with prudent dignity. "It wasn't easy getting you here, Mr. Avakain. You're on the DSA watchlist for the use of magic. The only reason I got you out was because the officer who arrested you committed a hate crime by removing your mask. So I'd consider yourself lucky."

"I guess so," Gruel said. "And I assume your primary export is 'people'?"

Theo chuckled, "You're an intuitive man. Do you know what a person will pay for a willing slave? Much more than we could make kidnapping. So yes… people are our product, but in a much grander sense: We sell obedience."

"Not that you didn't dabble in abduction," Gruel said and cocked his head. "You see, I make it my business to know things, too. I've been selling guns, drugs, and magic to the fine people of LA for years. People say the name Mr. Z like he's some sort of boogie man. He's a ghost story to them, an undiscovered Cryptid. Something to be feared and respected. But I know you've had to get your hands dirty… and it's not been years or any shit like that so don't come to me like a legitimate businesswoman."

"I am a legitimate businesswoman, you cretin!" Theo scowled and lurched forward. "The insinuation that I am anything but is insulting. Now, if I were where you are sitting, I would show the woman, a stranger, who paid my 150k bail and got my vehicle out of lock-up, a modicum of respect."

Gruel stayed quiet.

"Thank you," Theo cracked her knuckles. "To make matters abbreviate, you have caused my Master and his companions a great deal of grief. I understand that you have a vendetta against the Tyrants and the Elves. Your attempts to incite violence among them are starting to take hold. Yessenia's boys are attacking Humans and Elves alike. The system is hemorrhaging. As it is your fault, I want you and your partner to piece it back together for us."

"Well, to start, your info is outdated: Demy isn't my associate anymore, she's been out for a while now," he scratched his scruffy chin. "And to be frank, I don't deal in peacekeeping, so I don't know how much I can even help."

"That's just it, Mr. Avakain. My Master needs someone to help him deal with his less savory allies. In recent years, his clientèle has expanded to the wealthiest and most powerful people in the country. Hollywood, music producers, politicians. People have begun coming from across the world to experience true spiritual vitality. To be truly free from the fear of sin and the shackles society puts on us."

"The Lounge," Gruel completed.

"Since you seem to know so much about us," Theo said, intrigued. "Unburden yourself with that knowledge."

"I know that you signed the truce between some of LA's oldest enemies."

"That's true." Theodora nodded. "But as you can see, even rumor and hearsay are enough to break down that truce. We can no longer trust that our allies will follow through. If the Vampires continue to get out of hand, they will need to be dealt with. As well, we'll need someone to reel in the Mafia when they inevitably try to break off the leash. For now, they're only regulators and logistics. They trust my Master. We can use that to our advantage. But that Yessenia, she's unpredictable. At some point, she's going to have to disappear."

"I'm honestly not sure why you're asking me to do this when you have such a vast network," Gruel glowered.

Theo leaned forward, lowering her glasses and looking at him with glowing white eyes. Her voice was low and furious. "This is as much your mess as it is mine. So your options are: work for the Lounge or the check I wrote for your bail bounces. Your choice, Zagiri Avakain."

"You make such a tantalizing offer…" Gruel said, his voice thick with sarcasm. "I can't promise I can get Demy back on. If she says no, what's the deal there?"

"We'll cross that bridge when we come to it…" Theo leaned back and calmed down. "As for the rest of your Corvus Enclave, I think they would benefit from Lounge employment, as well."

The car came to a halt, and seconds later came Oscar, opening the door.

"For now, we'll consider you 'Bottom Echelon'. With any luck, that standing will change." Theodora said, placing her hands in her lap. "We'll be in touch, Mr. Avakain. Sha hatti darisam."

Gruel stepped out into the morning. The car peeled off with haste, leaving him alone in front of the impound lot.

8

As time pressed on, returning to class proved difficult for both Morgan and Raphie. Both of them were troubled by their separate reasons. She typed away diligently as VanderGraf spoke, translating 3/4's of whatever he said into shorthand text. Raphie tore a piece of paper from his notebook and wrote on it, passing it to his best friend before returning his gaze forward.

Did you bring the thing?

Morgan took the paper and gave a single chortle.

You make it sound like I'm smuggling drugs or a gun. Yes... I got the "thing" She wrote.

We're goin to see Demy's person after class, right?

Yep.

You okay?

Trying to focus.

I'm just worried about you... I'm sorry if I'm being annoying.

Before Morgan could finish what she was writing, VanderGraf excused the class. The body of students gathered their things and shuffled their way out of the raked seating. Morgan turned to Raphie as she packed up, giving him a weak, unconfident smile.

"You're not annoying," She said with conviction. "I'm not in any danger, okay? If Dorian thinks I'm completely under the spell of that...place... Well, he's got another thing coming."

"I'm sorry you had to go through what you went through..." Raphie said, his eyes showing nothing but sorrow. "I'm here for you. We'll make it, together."

"Morgana," VanderGraf said, his voice echoing as they stood to exit. "Can you come speak with me for a moment? It won't take long."

"Son of a bitch," Morgan said baring her fangs. "Just go to the car, I'll be right there. I'm gonna get this over with."

"Are you sure?" Raphie said weakly, attempting to assure her.

"Yeah. I'm good."

"Okay…" he said with a sigh, his face ill with uncertainty. "I'll… see you there."

Morgan trotted down to the bottom level and held her laptop bag to her chest. VanderGraf smiled at her from behind his salt and pepper goatee. It was obvious he was admiring her, undressing her with his eyes, despite much of her body being hidden. Somehow, he still made her feel disgusting in one of her most casual outfits.

"Yes, Prof. VanderGraf?" She asked, trying her best to obscure her stress.

"I just wanted to see you again," he said with a wickedly lecherous grin. "To see if you thought about my offer at all. Not many Avalon students are servants of the Lounge. You're the first one I've ever seen. So why not take the benefits of the Lounge into your academics?"

"I'm not fucking you again. That was a coincidence, and you got lucky." Morgan said, scowling.

"Oh, that's kind of cruel, isn't it?" VanderGraf feigned hurt and slowly began to approach her. "Considering I paid for that fucking car you're driving. You *do* know I'm being awfully generous here. You can bend over my desk now, or I'll have a word with your Master. I'm sure he'd *love* to hear how his new prized bitch is being a disrespectful little tramp. Probably get you expelled from the school."

She stood there, shaken, angry, and tearing up at his berating. Her brow furrowed, hissing slightly behind clenched, razor-sharp fangs.

"Don't be like that, 'Chastity'. After all, this was the job you chose, right? Besides, it won't take long, just a few minutes of your day, and you won't even have to do your final project. You and your queer little friend are off the hook. A+ for each of you." He stood beside her, grinning slyly and reaching up to caress her face. "What do you say?"

"What do I say?" She barked, slapping his hand away. "I'm more than a 'new prized bitch', I'm *the* prized bitch. I have a direct line to Dorian with me at all times. I could pick up the phone, call him, and tell him what a disgusting, tactless pervert you've been, and I'm sure he'd gladly reconsider your status within the Lounge." Morgan smirked, noticing the stunned look on VanderGraf's full face. "Oh, what's the matter? Shocked that I'm telling you no, or that I'm on a first-name basis with *Dorian*? All I did was fuck him and now he adores me. And here you thought some shit-tier college professor had weight. Go ahead. Cry to Ziusudra. Tell him all about how I 'misbehaved' when you tried to blackmail me for sex. He's made people disappear for less, so please, Eliott. Make. My. Fucking. Year."

"I—…You…" He reeled, his eyes full of terror at the woman who towered over him.

"Sha hatti darisam, motherfucker," Morgan spat, flipping him off as she marched out of his classroom.

*****

Raphie paced behind the red Reatta, fidgeting with one of his pencils, spinning the wooden utensil between his fingers. Every few seconds he would glance out to the campus, hoping his friend would enter the ground floor of the parking garage each time he looked. Each time he was left wanting, and sighed. He stared out at the grey sky of the gloomy December morning.

Morgan had changed. Something like a switch flipped in her, and a fire of determination unlike anything she'd had before had been lit. She kept the details of what had happened to her sparse. He knew asking, again and again, wouldn't solve anything. The only fact he knew was that Morgan was adamant about returning to the Babylon. VanderGraf wasn't helping the situation, thankfully, he'd kept his mouth shut until now, but Raphie knew he'd say something eventually. All of this caused him anxiety. He had to know it wasn't something that she couldn't handle alone. But should she?

Before long, he heard the sound of soft footsteps, seeing his best friend stride up to him with a new air of confidence. He smiled up at her. "How'd it go?"

"Walk in the park," She grinned, unknowing that her smile was what Raphie found to be the most attractive thing about her.

"Oh, thank god," Raphie beamed back.

"Hey, did Hanukkah start already?" Morgan asked.

"Yeah, I have to go see my folks sometime this week. I'll take the metro down to see them so you don't have to drive me or anything." Raphie said.

"Nonsense, I can take you whenever you're ready. What's the point of having a car if I don't use it?" Morgan said. "Speaking of which, I've got something for you."

Morgan hit a button on her keys, popping the trunk of the car. She moved around to the back of the vehicle and retrieved a box wrapped in blue paper printed with Menorahs and dreidels.

"*Cute* paper," Raphie chastised with a short chuckle, almost like a scoff, reading the tag aloud. "'To: My Favorite Ninja Turtle, From: Blondie.'"

"Open it!" Morgan said, gesturing to the box eagerly.

Raphie gave a muted laugh and did as he was instructed. After ripping through the box and its wrappings, he revealed a leather-bound art book with a green gemstone encrusted in the center. Its surface was ornately embossed with spiraling designs, not unlike the ones in his notebook. Remaining in the box was a refillable charcoal pencil with a marbled green handle to match the color of the stone. He unlatched and opened the book. The paper was pressed and rough, each thick enough to paint on. Printed on the inside of the cover, in gold ink, was the inscription "Property of Raphael Shapira."

"It's mixed media, so you can paint or draw or do whatever you want… do you like it?… you're awfully quiet."

"Morgan… this is gorgeous… I don't know what to say. I don't have anything for you. I wasn't even thinking about Christmas." Raphie stammered, utterly flabbergasted by his gifts.

"You don't have to get me a Christmas gift, Raph," Morgan said with a smirk. "Gift-giving is my love language."

"I can't do *nothing* for you," Raphie simpered. "I've always gotten you something. I'm just… strapped for cash this semester."

"Don't worry about it. If you feel so bad about it, then paint me a picture. Something extraordinary," she beamed.

"Okay. I can do that." Raphie smiled and tightly hugged his best friend in this or any universe. "Thank you so much, Blondie, I love you."

"I love you, too, big guy." Morgan held him back, immediately relaxing into his arms. "Happy Hanukkah."

"Happy Hanukkah," he replied.

9

The Reatta pulled up to the backside of an isosceles-shaped commercial building. The red Buick came to a halt just outside the back of one of the narrower suites. Hanging in its boarded-up window was a 'For Lease' sign well weathered and sun-bleached from months of sun exposure. Exiting the vehicle, Raphie looked up at the papered-up windows up to the third floor. Morgan exited as well, moving to her trunk to retrieve a camo-green ammo box, a relic from her dad's old stuff, and the best way to keep the specimen 'contained'. He waited patiently with his hands in his flannel jacket pockets, his eyes darting about the surface of the building and taking in the exciting new graffiti. The most prevalent one, off-center from the door, was a crow's skull.

"So this guy's an alchemist?" Morgan asked, rounding the other side of the car.

"Yes, they are," Raphie answered. "Allegedly, Adrian is the best in town."

"Let's hope that's not just a boastful advertisement," Morgan sighed.

She approached the caged door, ringing the rusted doorbell. The two waited patiently, no response at first, but even without the help of Morgan's Vampiric hearing, Raphie could hear the bass of music blaring on the other side. After a few more seconds of waiting, Morgan reached to hit the doorbell again. Before her finger touched the button, the youthful Ferrah opened the inner door in a fishnet top over a black bra and short shorts.

"Yo," she said over the technopop blasting behind her.

"We're here to meet Adrian?" Morgan said.

"We're friends of Demy," Raphie added.

"I know who you are," Ferrah deadpanned, unlocking the three bolts that kept the cage door closed before inviting them in. Raphie sensed Morgan's discomfort.

"Ladies first," he said, giving a courteous smile.

She nodded back but still entered with a timid look about her. Raphie touched her elbow to show he was still there, and he immediately felt her relax at the gesture. The three walked down a relatively long hallway to the mouth of the open space that was the alchemist's workshop.

Entering the dark and cluttered room, the sound of "Ready to Go" shot out from speakers jury-rigged together and strewn out across what could only be described as a laboratory. Massive chemistry equipment, gas tanks, intricate beaker systems, and plastic tubing were just a few of the things Raphie spotted as he entered. There were no uncovered windows save for the four propped open at the loft level above, matched with four industrial fans hanging in different locations.

Adjacent to them, Adrian stood in a tank top, cargo pants, and welder's goggles. They worked diligently, in time with the music, bobbing their head as they turned valves that released drops of clear chemicals onto carefully laid out sheets of paper. Raphael looked around with amazement. Morgan did the same, if not with a sprinkling of unease. Demy sat on the other side of the complex equipment, on a sunken couch, eating a bag of Corn Nuts.

"Hey, guys!" She said, leaping up to meet the duo. Adrian saw Demy react and sped up their process. Demy snaked around the lab and gave Raphie a hug and a kiss before turning to Morgan to hug her as well, taking her by surprise. Though Morgan seemed far from ungrateful.

"How are you both doing?" Demy asked.

"I'm peachy," Raphie shrugged with his hands back in his pockets. He turned to Morgan, his voice changing to concern,

"Not here for me, though."

"I'm doing alright, I'm not in any real pain, and I haven't gotten a migraine since this all went down. So at least there's that." Speaking to the aqua-eyed witch seemed to immediately shift her demeanor. Raphie was enthralled by the equally beautiful women, smiling and thankful for each other's company. He could barely contain his heart from breaking free of his ribcage and soaring about the room.

"Terribly sorry 'bout that," Adrian said, taking off their protective eyewear and wiping off their hands on a rag. They tossed it aside and took Raphie's hand immediately, gripping it firmly. Raphie pushed through, despite his much smaller hand being crushed in Adrian's vice grip. "Raphie, always nice to see you."

"Same," Raphie said, smiling through the pain.

"Speaking of nice to see." Their attention turned to Morgan. Adrian's pupils, already dilated, became more so. "You must be Morgana. Adrian."

"Morgan is fine. A pleasure to meet you." She smiled and outstretched her hand to shake theirs. Adrian swiftly took her hand and brought it, subdued, to their lips. Never once did Adrian look anywhere but into Morgan's pink eyes, their own a glimmering russet. Morgan, in return, could not help but visibly blush, sparking a scowl to form on Raphie's face, already at a baseline of 'grumpy'. All of this, Demy observed and absorbed.

"Please, the pleasure is all mine, Morgan," they smoldered. "I wasn't aware Raphie and Demy kept the company of supermodels."

Morgan's face flushed brighter. "Oh... Oh my... I'm just a journalist."

"Of course, I merely mean that you give this city new meaning to its name, angel." They turned away, completely ignorant of Raphie's growing rage, and guided Morgan back to the more casual space. "Walk with me. Talk with me, mi rosa."

Morgan turned back to her friends, mouthing "mi rosa?" She still seemed to have trouble understanding how desirable she was— without being made up as a sleazy vixen. Raphie was there through every one of the image issues she developed over the years of being ridiculed for her looks. Now she can barely believe that people are fighting for her attention. Even if the suitor was right beside her. He couldn't help but feel the knee-jerk reflex to protect her, even when she didn't need or want it.

Morgan was always coming up with some crazy endeavor. That's why he took a more passive role between the two of them. Being neutral was easier than constant worry. However, since Balam and her split, he did a poor job of remaining neutral.

"You okay there, babe?" Demy asked, her concern still prevalent on her face.

"Yeah… I'm fine. Why wouldn't I be?" Raphie said, forcing a smile.

"Well, you look like you're about to burst a blood vessel, for starters." Demy began to follow the others, taking Raphie by the hand. "You can tell me ya know… if you have worries or concerns, even about friends, I can do my best to sate them."

"It's not that… I'm just not feeling well." Raphie was being truthful: he felt sick anytime someone came from nowhere and started flirting with Morgan. *Am I jealous?* Raphie thought, *I can't be… I love seeing Demy be affectionate with Morgan.*

"So I heard you could find the chemical composition of just about anything, living or not," Morgan said, sitting down on an old couch across from Adrian and Ferrah.

"You heard correctly," Adrian said, leaning back and putting their arm behind their apprentice, Ferrah, who at this point was busy rolling a joint.

"Well, I hoped you could help me discover what exactly *this* is." Morgan unlatched the ammo box and pulled out a small mason jar. At the bottom, curled in a crescent shape, was the black and green spine. Adrian raised a brow at the sight, just in time for Raphie and Demy to join Morgan on the couch.

"Interesting," they said. "Where'd you find it?"

"It was… in my eye," Morgan said, attempting to swallow with a dry mouth. "Tear duct to be exact."

Adrian's expression changed, and they sat forward to take the jar, examining it closely. "Do you think you were cursed?"

"I don't believe in curses," Morgan said, completely guileless. The only movement was Ferrah beside Adrian, lighting her joint. Morgan scanned over to Raphie and Demy, the evidence of the faux pas clear on their faces. "Uhh… I-I do know that there is some validity to their existence, though. In the w-way of lethal magic?"

"You should try to understand the rules of your own existence," Adrian said, side-eying Morgan, still keenly observing the specimen. They were handed the joint and took a puff from it. "You're a Trueborn Vampire, yes?"

"Yes, I am," Morgan said with a nod.

"Do you have any powers?" Adrian asked.

"Trueborn don't have Vampiric powers. We just get to stand in the sun and eat stuff occasionally," Morgan chuckled.

"Oh no, mi rosa." Adrian passed the joint to Morgan. "Trueborn can access the ether much easier than those who aren't. Unless you're Wonder Boy over there." Adrian gestured to Raphie.

"No, thank you." Morgan waved off the pungent herb, to which Raphie graciously accepted.

"What do you mean Wonder Boy?" Raphie asked.

"I told a few of my close friends about your magical success," Demy said with glee. "You're one of the fastest learners I've ever seen."

"So does that mean I get to learn how to cast Firebolts?" Raphie smirked, feeling suddenly more confident as he exhaled the smoke.

"We'll see," Demy said, taking the joint from him and hitting it herself.

"Lethal magic is like using a gun. You gotta know whatever it is you're aiming your wand at is potentially gonna be maimed, burned, and/or obliterated. You gotta be responsible with that choice… unlike some people…" Adrian lamented

"Who?" Demy asked with a sharp change in her voice.

"Your ex cast Firebolts at a cop the night you were… absent." Adrian looked over to Morgan suspiciously.

"She knows," Demy said with a nod.

"Okay, good, then we can speak freely," Adrian added.

"Your coven is a mess without you, Demy. Ed and Rhonda are gone… Ferrah and I are most likely going to follow. I can't speak for Trina or the out-of-towners. But I hope they wake up, too. Gruel has gone off the deep end. Talking some conspiracy theory shit and I'm just not down for it."

"You do whatever you feel is necessary, Adrian. I've known you a long time and I trust your judgment," Demy replied, a small smile on her lips, but her eyes were wounded. Raphie sensed the pain the destruction of her beloved coven caused her. He couldn't imagine putting years of work into a project for it to fall apart on someone else's watch.

"You're not gonna narc on me, are you?" Adrian said to Morgan.

"Not at all." She waved her hands again. Unprompted, her signature smirk took hold. She leaned forward, placing her hand on Adrian's knee. "I wouldn't dare. Will you be willing to examine this specimen? I'm desperate to find out what happened to me."

"Well," they smiled back. "If you know *the* truth, then you need to tell me all about how you found this thing."

"What do you want to know?" Morgan asked.

"Start from the beginning."

10

The sounds of construction echoed through Dorian Ziusudra's penthouse. The vaulted ceilings and marble flooring made sure the sounds of labor echoed throughout every chamber of the seemingly endless floor. Dorian paced about, adding commentary and opinions to the golden fixtures and immaculate stonework he was having installed. He observed to make sure every detail was manicured to the best of mortal ability, all to be finalized before his date.

He was tailed by a whining Eliott VanderGraf, pacing a few steps behind and blowing endless hot air. Dorian rolled his eyes as he proceeded to complain about his new favorite servant. On the sidelines, Theodora waited patiently, thoroughly documenting all the costs and adjustments she'd need to make for each of Dorian's alterations to the current decor.

She too stirred in her thoughts, pondering how she would manage to tell her Master the truth about Morgana Scriven. She could tell by the irritation in her Master's face that he hated how VanderGraf spoke about her. She knew she couldn't let it stay quiet forever. As much as she was enjoying tormenting her, the little harlot was trying to infiltrate and report on the deepest innards of the Lounge: the Elite Echelon. But Dorian, having invited her over, without Theodora knowing, made matters all the more complicated. The ultimate reality of Theodora's dilemma was that she had waited too long and now Morgana Scriven *was* a very real threat.

"You should have seen the way she disrespected me," VanderGraf said, following Dorian like a lost puppy. "I've never been so insulted in my life, which she threatened! Could you imagine? Threatening my life? She acted like I was beneath her."

"Well, technically you are," Dorian said artlessly, half ignoring the blustering man. He leaned down to one of the workers, focusing on the base of one of the many marble pillars. "That grout is going to change color when it dries, right?"

The man nodded.

"Excellent. Just checking."

"What are you talking about? Are you even listening to me?" VanderGraf scoffed, "I'm her professor *and* I'm a veteran Lounge member. I'm Elite Echelon! I get that she's the fucking talent, but those girls are a dime a dozen right? Remember that little blonde Elf or the black girl with the real pretty face? You threw them to the wolves almost immediately. I don't get why this bitch feels she has the right to walk around free *and* talk down to her superiors."

"What did you call her?" Dorian said, turning around and looking VanderGraf in the eye for the first time.

"She's a bitch! What? Why is this a bad word all of a sudden?" VanderGraf shrugged.

"EVERYONE OUT!" Dorian ordered, and all but

Theodora stopped where they were in their projects and cleared out of the elephantine dining room. "Do you know why Morgana Scriven walks free? Because I will it so. She has a powerful resistance toward magic, and I am infatuated with the idea. She has had nothing but respect for the Lounge and me. You tried to get some off-the-books action. No wonder she shot your punk ass down. And no… You are NOT Elite Echelon. You're UE, you don't have what it takes to be any higher."

Theodora grabbed a servant on his way out, "Grab a glass of the '89 Sauvignon Blanc for Master." He nodded and went on his way.

"Oh you talk a big fucking game but you forget who got you access to Avalon University. What did you say, some 20% administration are Lounge? That's pretty fucking spectacular returns if you ask me. So, please remind me how I'm not Double E, again?"

"Because it is actually 30% recruited, and while yes, you opened the door, that is where your usefulness ended. From there, I gathered each contact on my own. I charmed my way to the Board of Education. Do you think Avalon is the only university I have a stake in? I built my empire on my own back, and you were merely a stepping stone to achieve it. So kindly fuck off out of my house."

"No," VanderGraf said, literally standing his ground. "You're gonna stick up for some hooker over me? Just 'cause the cunt is a pretty, blonde, white girl with pink eyes and bats her lashes to get what she wants? Naw. She told me she fucked you. So what is it? Is it just because she can survive fucking you without going zombie like the rest of these fucks? Admit it Mr. Z, you're just addicted to pussy like the rest of us and that bitch isn't worth protecting!"

Theo looked away, no longer capable of enduring the embarrassment by proxy.

"Did you manage to call Miss Scriven a hooker, a cunt, and a bitch all while insulting me and my servants?" Dorian said, his tone reflecting disbelief more than anger. He marched directly up to VanderGraf, looking him in the eyes. Dorian's iris and pupil vanished as his eyes began to glow. Soon the color, too, faded from VanderGraf's."Eliott VanderGraf, take down that pillar with your forehead."

"Yes, Master," VanderGraf said without life in his voice, walking slowly over to the pillar he gestured to and standing before it, staring at it with adept concentration. Theo approached with a glass of white wine, giving it to her Master. His eyes also stared off into nothingness, glowing white and deep in his concentration.

KRACK

"Are we gonna have to replace that pillar?" Theo asked.

KRACK

"Dwarves only have a thin layer of stony flesh," Dorian said, fully concentrating. "We can handle a few chips."

KRUNK

"Of course, Monsieur."

THUD

Theo winced at the sound. Glancing over to VanderGraf off and on, incapable of looking away entirely.

THUD

"Is something on your mind, mon cheri?" Dorian said, taking a drink. "You've seemed distracted all day."

THUMP

"I'm..." *THORP.* "I have some bad news," Theo said, physically uncomfortable at the awful sound. This did not go unnoticed by her Master.

SHLORP

"Tell me," Dorian said, unfazed by the gory display, and rather perturbed that she was. He grabbed her chin and forced her to look up to him and away from the carnage. "Feeling a bit squeamish today, mon cheri? That is so unlike you."

SCHLORP

"It's a bit distracting... but no, it's about..." *SSSCHLEP.* Theo jumped as VanderGraf's lifeless form hit the floor, too terrified to look away from her beautiful Master. So she diverted. "The Moth... she was seen at half a dozen of our locations in the last couple of months, including the Belfry and the depot at the Keep. She's going to eventually come looking in this direction. That Cryptid is famous for her intuition and investigative ability. Her sense of time and space."

"I have always admired the Moth… I would be honored for her to accompany us one evening." As Dorian spoke, a horned rottweiler entered from the hall and began devouring the remains. He released Theodora and glanced over at the beast. "Good boy."

"Master, between The Moth and the Tyrants, we have a lot of fires to put out. I need your attention," she said, keeping her eyes on her clipboard.

"You always have my attention, Theo," he said, his eyes returning to their crystal blue state. He gripped her by the waist and pulled her into him. "Please don't worry, my love. Thanks to you, Gruel is going to take care of the Tyrants… with his and the witch's magic, they'll be no match."

"As for the Moth?" Theo said, her body now feeling safe and bursting with warmth. She looked up at her Master, knowing that she still had a place in his heart, and leaned into him, letting her arms wrap around him. "Is it time to pull out the big guns?… She's gotten close to finding us before, but never this close."

"I will consider it," he said, finishing his wine and breaking from their embrace. "Until then, I have a date to prepare for."

Dorian strode without care from the dining room, leaving Theo and his feasting dog as a second-horned beast entered. Tears of heartbreak began to stream down her face. In her anguish, she clutched her clipboard until it splintered in her hands.

"Fucking bitch," Theo cursed, left alone with the mess yet again.

11

When Colt arrived at Apartment 161 on the night of the Chronicle Christmas party, after getting lost looking for the mislabeled second-story apartment, he stood at the door in an all-black suede suit with a forest green silk tie that matched his emerald skin. His beard sculpted and head clean-shaven, he was as handsome as he'd ever been. The robust cologne he wore enraptured and aroused Morgan, not that either was a hard state for her to achieve around him. She took his hand, and he led her to their ride.

She was in a long red gown with a single strap and glittering thread woven throughout. Two long slits went up to either side of her legs, revealing the blue butterfly on her right hip. Her legs were clad in her most sheer pair of tights, and she lifted herself with her favorite red pumps. Her hair was curled and styled meticulously, making her look like what her aunt called her: a princess. Her eyes were shadowed with a dark, defined crease, a contrast to her pale skin; her lips were as red as the blood she drank.

The town car Colt rented was already more than what Morgan was expecting: spacious, lush, and capable of closing off the front seat with tinted glass. They sat in the quiet for at least half the drive, a certain childish meekness fell over them. Morgan didn't mind; she simply held his hand and smiled. Most of the time, he was smiling back.

"I'm really glad we're going tonight," she said at last.

"I am, too," he smirked. "I'm not entirely sure why you like me, but I'm grateful for it."

"There's a lot to like about you," Morgan said. "Are we going to, like… make the step tonight?"

"I think so," Colt said, scratching the back of his head.

"When?" She asked eagerly.

"Well… unless someone sees us get out of the same car, I don't think we'll have to tell the news the moment we walk in the door," Colt said, looking onward.

"You *do* want to take that step, right?"

"Yes… I do," Colt said, with a brief smile before returning his gaze out the window. Something about him was off. Morgan knew it, but she couldn't begin to understand why.

"Okay," Morgan said, leaning forward to roll up the partition glass. "I've been putting more thought into the story… I have a theory about Chrissy."

"Should we be talking here?" Colt asked.

"I don't think we'll be safe talking at the Chronicle either…" Morgan said, "Ziusudra has eyes and ears everywhere. Remember the watchdogs? It goes deeper than that… I'm more concerned about these disks, honestly."

"Damn girl," Colt scoffed "When do you sleep?"

"I'll sleep when I'm dead," Morgan said matter-of-factly. "My work ethic is going to find us Chrissy Donavon. Maybe even all of these girls. Those disks I found? I've been mulling over them for weeks now. I think the reason Chrissy was cast out was *because* she knew about the disks. She knew that there was more going on. A bigger operation beyond what we're seeing. Something to do with the cult and their rituals. I think they're breeding lambs for the slaughter."

Colt remained silent for a moment, bewildered. "You think if you find Chrissy—"

"I'll find out what Dorian is really planning," Morgan said.

"How do you plan to do that?"

"Dorian is unaware that I know all of this. He thinks that my amnesia is still keeping me from acting on reason. I'm going to use that to my advantage when I go on this date… I'm going to go back," she said with the determination of a paratrooper about to drop from an airplane.

"Scriven…" Colt said, rubbing his brow. "If you go in alone, there's no telling how you'll get back."

"Some entity helped me get out before… Something tells me Chrissy isn't so lucky." Morgan said, glancing up to see the lit-up Chronicle approaching. "If I can remember properly, I can find my way…"

"Entity?"

"A man wearing a plague doctor mask and a cloak of feathers… I think he was the one who wiped my memory…" She said, noting the puzzled look on his face. "He told me I needed to leave and then said this phrase… I can't get it out of my head."

"What was it?"

"'In the liminal space between joy and sorrow, comes the dream,'" Morgan quoted, "I can't wrap my head around it."

"Interesting."

"You believe I can do this… right?"

"I do… But this is a lot to take in… if this Ziusudra guy is using magic to kidnap people, he could be put away for life," Colt said, unbuckling his seatbelt as they pulled up. "I think we should call it a night for talking… We'll visit this later, but if you can find proof… You have yourself one hell of an exposé."

The chauffeur exited the car and walked around to Morgan's side. She smiled wider the longer she digested what Colt had just said. She bit her knuckle trying to hide her enthusiasm. She was so close to Chrissy, she knew it in her slow-beating heart. Her door opened and the young driver reached for her hand. She stepped forward, glancing up at the structure; its exterior was trimmed with white Christmas lights, trailing down about the polygonal structure to form a softly glowing canopy. Colt slid out of the vehicle and gave the driver an excellent tip.

Morgan admired the strands of red ribbon that were layered between the lights, ending in ornately tied bows attached to the fronts of the planters. Morgan didn't hate the holidays, even if she used to. Especially as she's grown older, she's learned to appreciate the beauty of the time of year for what it is.

Colt stood beside her, alone on the steps. "Are you ready?" He asked.

"Are *you* ready?" Morgan said with a smirk.

"Let's go," he said sharing the smile with her, their little secret only staying the status quo for a few minutes longer.

Colt opened the door for her, as he often would. She aimed her smile at the floor and entered. As she turned her gaze upward, she was amazed to see how transformed the central space of the building had become; most of the desks between the walkways were rearranged intricately to leave room for a sizable dance floor that was crowded with employees and their dates. While they were still on the raised portion of the entryway, Morgan could see the conference room had been set up for a full caterer. The DJ was playing a good mix of dance music and the inevitable upbeat Christmas tune. Just beneath his setup, a massive Christmas tree had been erected, its bulbs of green, gold, red, and silver were evenly distributed as well as long strands of gold and silver garland that wrapped around it and extended to the roof. The display couldn't help but fuel the smile on Morgan's face. She needed this.

The crowd was much larger than a day at work, with at least double the number of people normally here. Her chest started to lock up as they began to brush shoulders with strangers; her nerves began to wrack, squeezing Colt's hand tightly.

"Okay, baby?" Colt said softly, caressing her knuckles with his thumb despite her viselike grip.

"Just nervous," She said trying her mock breathing exercises. "Little c-claustrophobic… right now."

Colt opened his mouth to try and sate her worries before spotting a group of Human males he'd been hoping to avoid. "Shit, it's my publisher, he never shows up to these things. What the fuck?"

"What's that mean?" Morgan said, her panic ramping up. He cupped her hand with his other and placed a key in her grip.

"If you can't find Eliza or anyone else, go up to my office. Unlock the door and turn on the desk lamp nearest the window. Pour yourself a drink from my private supply and we'll chill out together." Colt stepped away, heading to the group of executives. "I'll be right back."

"Okay." Morgan nodded, uncertainty clear in her voice and on her face.

She hung her head and walked the perimeter of the party, feeling like a private shame. On her way around she came across the full, open bar they had set up, grabbing herself a Whiskey Sour, double, with extra cherries. It didn't take her long to get to her normal workstation. Not far from there, she could see a small gathering of suit-dressed individuals, with a gown or two sprinkled in. She noticed one of the suits belonged to Eliza. The others were also reporters or photographers. She kept walking toward the stairs, feeling somewhat unwelcome.

"Hey, girlie!" Eliza waved at Morgan. "Come hang with us!"

"Sure," Morgan said with a grimace, joining the party. "What are you guys talking about?"

"The gang war," One person had said.

"Word has it there's not only a hunter on the prowl but a

group of mages were behind the Belfry fire as well," another joined in.

"LA is about to get real hot," a third woman joined, she was a Vampire, and Morgan immediately recognized her voice. "Gonna be rough to be undead."

She was beautiful, with long raven hair, smooth ivory skin with lightly freckled cheeks. She had bright red eyes, like most Vampires, revealed now that she was free of her daily refractium. Morgan had never seen her face, but it was Victoria, Morgan knew that without a doubt.

"Yeah… The Tyrants are making us all look bad and the Elf Mob is only going to perpetuate the problem," Morgan said, looking her in the eyes for the first time. There was an understanding between them, something that wasn't there before.

"Hey, speaking of Tyrants," Victoria said, circling the rim of her glass with her forefinger, "Eliza told me you broke into the Bourbon Belfry before it burned down. Is it true?"

Morgan laughed a bit, not out of humor but stress. She felt so on edge about everything since her memories returned to her, but she was at her home base. She was safe here. At least as long as she kept the details of the Donavon story to herself.

"Yep. I was following up on a story and infiltrated the Belfry to get photos," she spun, partially telling the truth.

"Damn, you went up against Tyrants," one of the others in the group said, the Giant she often had near misses with when walking the floor. "That's ballsy."

"No shit," Victoria added, looking at Morgan with a hint of respect in her eyes. "You could have gotten seriously hurt. You sure you're just an intern?"

Morgan chuckled, this time more real. "Yeah… I'm just an intern."

"Unless you ask Harding," Eliza said in a snarky tone, taking a sip of her drink.

"What's that supposed to mean?" Morgan said her face becoming stern.

"You two spend a lot of time together. Supposedly collaborating on a story but… I mean… I can't imagine that's all you're doing when you and him disappear for, what? Twenty—thirty minutes at a time?" Eliza replied, looking Morgan up and down and grinning like the devil. "Who did you come with, again?"

The group fell silent.

"Whatever," Morgan said and rolled her eyes. "Even if we were together, would it fucking matter? He runs this place."

"Well, we won't care… his boss might though," Eliza said, continuing to sneer. "Unless he put him up to it… heard sleeping with the interns is a historical occurrence for Chronicle editors. Guess you got lucky to be Colt's first amoral shag."

"Man, fuck you," Morgan choked, turned around, and left before she could be berated any further.

"Eliza… what'd you do that for?" Victoria asked with a frown, her voice quiet yet scolding.

"What can I say?" Eliza replied in kind with a snicker and swirled her drink. "It's my chaotic nature, my friend."

12

Night blanketed the streets of Echo Park in darkness and shadows cast by the lights of businesses closing up for the night. It wasn't incredibly late, but as Raphie and Demy stepped off the late bus, they were aware that this was one of those places you had to always be cautious. Raphie used to hate walking alone at night, always in fear of being clocked and attacked or just straight-up mugged. Now that he knew magic, he felt more confident in his ability to defend himself. With his beautiful Half-Elf girlfriend beside him, anything that would challenge them would have to resort to mundane means. He liked their odds.

As Raphie and Demy rambled on about virtually nothing, as usual, they turned onto a side street between two apartment complexes.

"So this is how you get to your place, on foot yeah?" He said looking about his surroundings to be hyper-aware.

"It's a shortcut, yeah. Sorry, we have to cut through an alley but we'll be good," Demy replied with a bright smile.

"I don't doubt that." Raphie nodded, putting his hands in his pockets, a smug look sprouting across his face. "So what do you want to do when we get back to your place?"

"Well," Demy bit her lip subtly. "I have a few ideas."

"DEMY!" A familiar voice called. From the mouth of the alley sprang a Ghoul in a tattered duster. "It's been a while."

"Gruel…" Demy said, halting in her tracks. Though she spoke jovially, her face was unmoving, sizing Gruel up as he approached. "Well, this sure is a lucky encounter."

"It's not luck this time, Moonstone," Amy said, blocking the alley from behind them. In both of her fingerless-gloved hands, she brandished the enchanted baseball bat.

"Amy? What's going on?" Demy said, her eyes narrowing. When she looked back at Gruel, his wand was drawn as well. The crooked branch of yew, carved to a narrow point, was wrapped with hemp as a handle. "What is this?"

"Demy… what should we do?" Raphie said, prepared to move, his desire to keep Demy safe overriding his anxiety at this moment.

"Your little boyfriend here is a problem," Amy said, a cruel look in her eyes.

"He ruined that ritual. We would have been so much further ahead had he never shown up," Gruel barked. "But in all honesty, Amy is here for him… I'm here for you, sweet Demytria."

"For what?" Demy blustered.

"You turned your back on the Enclave… and without your magic, it's fallen apart. So I'm going to give you one last chance to join back up…" Gruel threatened.

"Or?"

"We kill you… right here. Right now." Amy answered.

"Like hell you are," Demy said, placing a hand on Raphie's chest. "You're not going to harm anyone today."

"Uh, Demy…" Raphie protested, watching several of her tattoos begin to glow. Glancing over at Amy, he saw that the core of her bat radiated a magenta light.

"So is that a no, Demy?" Gruel cracked his neck, and his

eyes sparked with electricity. "Are we doing this?"

"You think you know magic better than me?" Demy said with a determination that literally set her eyes ablaze. The turquoise rings that were her irises glowed like her tattoos, a raw power in the air around her. A fell wind began to blow. "Fine then… show me what you've got."

"Hmm," Amy scoffed, "Pathetic."

She raised her bat and arced it with a mighty swing. Demy simply pushed Raphie into the wall, her palm glowing bright. With a rush of energy flowing around him, the world seemed to ripple. Immediately, a burst of purple and red light slammed into Demy, knocking her from her feet with a painful thud. As Demy's tattoos faded, Amy cackled. Raphie tried to move forward but was prevented by an invisible wall of force.

"Demy!" He cried, banging his fists on the barrier.

The two other mages approached the fallen witch. Both were still brandishing their wands and ready for combat. As they encircled the still body, Raphie watched on helplessly.

"Damn… downed to a Bolt of Force…" Amy mocked. "Some High Priestess."

"Well, amigo. Hope you're happy, cause her protecting you is what killed he—" Gruel tried to say, but the very ground split with a thunderous crack. A chunk of floating asphalt struck him hard on his chin and knocked him back into a car. Amy went into a battle stance, aiming her wand, only to be pummeled by smaller chunks. Demy rose, levitating herself to her feet, her short hair billowing as the wind seemed to spiral around her. She pounded her fist into the ground, that same thunder echoing through the alley. Chunks of road levitated around her, circling her body in a helix before launching at her foes.

Amy dodged as best she could and swung her bat, knocking pieces out of the air, her pompous demeanor dropping. Even still, her wand glowed bright pink, storing her spell energy the longer she waited, allowing her to cast stronger blasts. She saw Gruel's eyes, and she nodded. Without a noise, Amy swung her bat in a wide arc, sending a searing hot flame in her direction.

A wall of frost, as if from thin air, blocked the blast. The excess of the Firebolt spread across the invisible barrier, though Raphie could still feel some heat, thus hiding his face and yelping. This dissolved the ice into steam and water at their feet. Demy stood with a hand out toward Amy, her eyes glowing vibrant blue.

"Firebolt? Damn, you are so fucking lame." Demy sneered. About Demy's head, three chunks of asphalt spun around her, firing in their direction one at a time. Amy managed to swat one away, Gruel took another to the torso.

From the sky, a bolt of lightning struck down, gathering in Gruel's wand held aloft. With a downward arc, he threw the bolt from his wand while Demy's eyes were on Amy. Without looking, Demy caught the lightning with her bare hand. She turned, growing more furious as the encounter continued, the energy she caught still pulsing in her hand.

"Harness Thunder? I taught you this spell, Gruel," Demy said, tossed the bolt back, and knocked Gruel prone into the street. She turned back to Amy just in time to dodge her second volley. This one hit Raphie more directly, reflecting around the invisible wall and temporarily encasing him in flame. Still, he remained unharmed.

"Sit down," Demy scorned, her left leg glowing bright. With a wave of her hand, Amy was lifted and thrown into someone's hatchback. The back of her head slammed into the window, causing a crack to form in the glass.

Marching toward Gruel, Demy pushed the sharpest point of her Moth scale onto her thumb until it bled. She reached into her bag and pulled out small strips of parchment. Gruel lay just on the edge of the sidewalk, getting to his feet, his hair standing on end and charged with static electricity. He stepped forward and lifted his wand. Demy sprinted to meet him face to face before he could finish muttering the words of incantation.

She stuck the sheet to his forehead, a Mandarin character written on it in her blood. Gruel's body was wracked with pain, and he tried to swipe at her with his Ghoulish claws. She danced around him with haste, placing more parchment with separate characters on his hands and chest. He spasmed and collapsed to the ground, half-paralyzed and tucked between the building and a truck tire.

"Wht-wht thfck." He twitched and sputtered.

"Undead Hold seals. A simple but quite effective spell," Demy said, her eyes and tattoos returning to their original color. "Ya know if you tried to learn more magic instead of trying to use me to start your stupid, senseless gang war, you might have bested me… maybe… Leave town, Gruel… Or I'll make sure your next paralysis isn't temporary."

She stomped back deeper into the alley, past Raphie, who looked on with awe, and swooped up both Gruel and Amy's wands. She approached Amy, who was just beginning to regain consciousness.

"Are you okay?" She asked sincerely.

"I'm fine," Amy huffed.

"Good." Demy lifted the wands. The arm she held them with glowed brightly as they were engulfed in a blue-green flame. The arcane fire obliterated both wooden objects. Demy was still holding them and maintained eye contact with her ex. She let the smoldering wood fall to the wet asphalt, the embers hissing like snakes. "Don't ever speak to me again."

"That's reasonable." Amy nodded, wide-eyed at her ex's power.

Demy then returned to her boyfriend, waving her hand and dispelling the barrier. Raphie finally could move freely and ran to her.

"Holy shit. Are you okay?" He asked, looking at the spot on her side that was struck.

"I'll be alright, but let's get out of here before the 5-0 show up," Demy pushed, taking him by the hand and leading them both out of the alley. Raphie glanced over his shoulder and met eyes with Amy. There was no arrogance in them anymore. These were the eyes of someone who had been humbled… and possibly concussed.

"Have a good life, bitches," Demy said, flashing a peace sign.

13

The party was just ramping up into full gear, the majority of the guest list had arrived at this point. Colt's direct supervisor, Lloyd Butcher, had Colt as a captive audience for what felt like an eternity. Reality would be somewhere closer to thirty minutes. He rambled on about the successes of the Chronicle and he even credited Colt for some.

Colt drank his bourbon and smiled through the cringeworthy small talk and forced back-patting, pretending to genuinely enjoy the conversation. Lloyd Butcher, or "Butch" as he asked people to call him, was an insufferable pig, one of the last remnants of the old Chronicle. One of the predators.

"So, I saw that arm candy you brought with you, word is she's your intern," Lloyd said, a cigar between his teeth.

Colt felt his body freeze up, not expecting a comment like that and having nothing prepared at this point. "I'm not sure where you heard your information, she's—"

"A fine piece of tail, Colt," Lloyd cackled, speaking low so only they could hear.

"Uh... yeah... she's something," Colt mumbled, rubbing the back of his head.

"Nice job. What'd you do? Promise her a 'big story?'" Lloyd said, thick with smugness.

Colt's entire world froze as he felt the pat on his arm from his boss. He'd worked his entire career to suck up to these people, jump through their hoops and do whatever trick was commanded. Becoming like his boss, however, was his worst nightmare. He felt his skin crawl. He felt predatory.

I'm sorry, Phylis... he thought. *I'm so sorry, Morgan.*

"Something like that," Colt said, remorse breaking through his fake grin. "Hold on, sir. I've gotta go talk to an employee real quick. I need to ask them about something for tomorrow's print."

"There he is, Colt .45, always gunning for a story. You're the most dedicated man in Los Angeles," Lloyd said, nodding his head in approval, too drunk to notice the mood change. "When you come back, I've found an organization that I'd love to introduce you to."

"Sure thing… I'll be right back, Butch," Colt overacted, still playing off his disgust with his boss and himself "Oh! Dalkom has his own party downstairs. I wouldn't want to miss whatever Dwarven kegs he brought this year."

Colt stomped away and pounded down his drink, baring his tusks at the thought of kinship with Lloyd Butcher. He glanced up, just past the DJ, and saw the light was on in his office. Grateful for the excuse to get away, Colt snaked through the crowds and into his office, closing the door quickly and releasing a long exhale.

Morgan stood with a glass of brandy poured from his crystal decanter. When he entered, she was gazing out his large window at the full moon, just beyond the glamorous lights of the city. She sipped her liquor, gliding around his office couch to grab the second glass off his desk.

"God damn, Lloyd can shove his nasty attitude up his holly jolly ass," Colt said upon entering. "How are you feeling?"

"Better," she said, taking another drink. "So schmoozing didn't go well? You were talking for a while."

"It was alright," he admitted. "But I… don't know how soon we'll be able to make our announcement if I'm being perfectly real with you."

"We're not going to make it official tonight… are we?" Morgan sighed.

"I never said that," Colt said, taking off his velvety jacket and setting it aside, down to a vest and white dress shirt, both form-fitting to his muscular frame. He took the drink from her and stood before her, not quite looking her in the eye. "Thank you, baby." Behind her, he saw specks of white on his desk beside a curled-up 20-dollar bill. He raised his brow, now choosing to look her in the eyes. Dilated.

"You call me baby, and ask me where we stand..." Morgan began, her irritation unequivocal. "Yet I'm ready now, and you're not? What do you want from me?"

He stared into her pink orbs and spoke, "It's complicated."

"Of course it is," she said, placing down her now empty glass. She started to teeter a bit and wrapped her arms around his shoulders, drawing him closer for stability. "At least we can still hold each other, I guess."

"Absolutely," Colt replied, unsure himself if it was forced or not. "Are… are you okay?"

"I'm just peachy," she said, sarcastically.

"I mean like… never mind." He said, shaking his head. "It's nothing… honestly. Just my imagination."

Her doe eyes glistened in the moonlight, creating an alien refraction of color in her roseate irises, as narrow as they were. Be it the innate, charming ability Vampires possessed or the natural allure of her beauty, he couldn't resist. As he kissed her, his hand found the back of her head, touching her delicate hair with hardly any pressure, beholden to have the golden strands touch his rough skin. She tightened her grip around his shoulders, his hands about her waist, locked in an amiable embrace. She used one of her own hands to guide him to her bare thigh. Her kiss became ever inviting, her intentions becoming clearer. Colt had no desire to deny her.

His hand cupped her buttocks, lifting her onto his desk, her legs dividing for him. She pulled the long fabric of her dress aside, further leading him to undress her. Her skin felt like satin at every point and fragrant with the aroma of rosewater. It didn't take her long to free him from his stifling cloth cage either, already delivering soft moans into his kiss from the anticipation alone.

"You know," she giggled, biting her lip and reaching down to guide him. "Despite everything, bossman, we've never done it in your office before." He leaped at her touch, never quite used to how cold her hands got. Though her body always seemed to warm up as soon as they started.

"Merry Christmas to me," he smiled, looking into her eyes as he moved his hips into her.

Like flipping a switch, she shuddered; her bottom lip trembled. She held onto him tightly, moaning his name into his ear. As she started to get louder, she left lipstick marks along his neck and undid his vest, tie, and collar. Her lips wrapped around his bare shoulder and suckled, her teeth pushing against his skin but never breaking it. The rush of her nearly biting him yet again drove him into a frenzy, leaning into her and forcing her to lie back on his desk. His hand swept off the papers and desk widgets as he laid her down, sending them tumbling to the floor. Her spine arched, her head thrown back and silently screaming, only to croak out a weary "Gods yes."

A sudden burst of light and Christmas music halted everything, both of them sporadically rectifying and covering up.

"Sweet, it's unlocked, no one should be—" the Catfolk intruder said as he entered, another employee by the name Freddy Gutenberg with his pretty Orcish date in tow. No doubt their goals aligned with Colt and Morgan's. Colt stood there, holding his pants up, staring like a deer about to be flattened by a Mack truck.

"Oh… my bad," Freddy said, seeing how indisposed his boss and the intern were.

"Get the fuck out!" Colt barked.

"Right." He slammed the door and could be heard snickering with his date as they left.

"Come on, bossman, we're not done yet," Morgan cooed.

"I…I don't know if I can—." Colt said, weak and broken.

"I can help you get back there. Trust me," Morgan flirted, sliding off the desk and licking her lips suggestively.

"I mean…" Colt sighed.

"It's just Freddy if that's what you're worried about. No one cares about what he says. That's why he arranges the funnies," Morgan said, starting to reach for him, beginning to kneel. "Besides, I wanna give you a little Christmas present."

"No, Scriven. Stop!" Colt said, stepping back away from her. "I can't do *this* anymore."

Morgan fell back, her butt landing on the desk with a solid thud. She couldn't move, speechless as well.

"W-what?" She finally squeezed out "Wh-what do you mean?"

"Come on, Scriven… I'm your boss. I'm over twice your age." Colt began dressing, pacing a bit as he did. "This can't work… one way or another, it's just inappropriate."

"It never stopped us before," Morgan said, growing more furious as she spoke. "Why are you just now saying this?"

"Because I've been mulling it over for a month and a half,

and I've been weighing the pros and cons. We have a connection. A *real* connection and I'm not going to pretend like we don't but… you've been through a lot since this whole Lounge bullshit began. Some troubling shit. At the end of the day, no matter which way you dice it… I'm not the answer to your problems."

Morgan blinked a few times, sat upright, and said, "Oh… I see."

"I'm sorry." Colt hung his head low.

She stood, pulling her skimpy panties back up and rolling her shoulders. Morgan silently walked over to his mini bar, where she found the brandy in an ornate crystal decanter.

"Look… I don't want you to think I don't like you. We just can't pull this off like I thought we could… I can't pull it off… I feel like a monster, ya know?" He said, incapable of even looking in her direction.

"Mhmm," Morgan grabbed the decanter of brandy and formed a U-turn out of the room.

"I just don't want you to hate me, and I definitely don't want you to go anywhere… you're the best intern I've ever had." Colt finally looked up as the light from the party spilled back in, and Morgan exited. "Scriven? Morgan!"

Morgan stormed her way past the DJ, down the stairs, and through a few groups of people, taking the crow's flight to the front. Colt followed not far behind. "Morgan! Morgan, wait!" he called. She either couldn't hear him or chose not to; considering Vampiric hearing, most likely the latter. Some eyes followed the scene, but only those immediately disrupted. Among them, Eliza and Victoria watched as they saw their coworker and boss one after the other.

"Told you," Eliza smirked, inebriated. Victoria lightly smacked her arm.

Morgan was already at the curb, hailing a taxi, by the time he got outside. The driver saw her and signaled he would swing back around and park. Morgan gave him a thumbs up, acting as if her would-be boyfriend wasn't coming in hot behind her. "Morgan, please, just let me explain."

"I'm good." Morgan only slightly turned her head to see him

coming down the steps.

"Will you please just listen to me?" Colt panted, catching up with her. She held an index finger up to make him wait as she proceeded to drink gulp after gulp of brandy straight from the decanter. Almost losing a drop, she stopped and dabbed her lips on her hand.

"What? You said it. You're not the answer to my problems. What else do I need to hear?" She practically groaned.

"I didn't want it to go down like this," Colt said, his heart bleeding. "Please, don't leave."

"I don't want to stay. I just kinda thought, having sex with you, like, what? Two dozen times? I just thought you actually liked me. But I'm just trying to solve my problems through a man, and you wanted to fuck the young blonde intern." Her words were frozen. "Guess we both got what we wanted for a minute."

"You're so much more than that," Colt said, reaching for her hand only to have it pulled away. "You're hurting, confused, lost. I get that. There's someone out there who is truly going to be what you need. But it can't be me… I shouldn't have let it go on this long. It wasn't fair to you."

"What the fuck does fair matter? Nothing is fair. Some people get everything like Ziusudra, and others end up like Chrissy Donavon. Or Joana Larsson… in hell." Morgan shook her head and sneered. As the taxi pulled up, she took another long swig from the decanter and handed it back to Colt. "It's been real."

"Come on, Scriven… you don't have to go."

"I truly believed you were something for me… maybe this is me just paying my dues. According to Phylis Barks, right? Did that story happen, or did you just use my idol to butter me up? "

"Please understand…" He shook from her barrage, "It wasn't like that."

"Goodbye, Mr. Harding," she said, getting in the taxi. "I'll see you after the date with Ziusudra."

She slammed the door. He stood there hoping she'd open the door and change her mind; knowing well she won't. He looked at the tires, watching them roll away with a one-of-a-kind woman. He was too busy wallowing in his shame to see the Taknoling reporter, whom he now shared an ex-lover with, approach.

"Girl trouble, Mr. Harding?" Eliza said with a drunken, miserable snark.

"Please tell me the *whole* party didn't see that," Colt said, a defeated Orc. "Especially not the men who write our fucking checks."

"I think you'll be much more interested in what my other employer has to say," she said with a sinister smile.

"What other employer? What are you on about?" He turned to face her, frustrated and not here for her bull.

"You know exactly who, Mr. Harding." Colt's veins turned to ice. She raised her glass to him. "Sha hatti darisam."

*****

Morgan trudged her way up the stairs of the apartment complex, making her way to her home. Her eye makeup had run, she cried the entire ride, a bit drunk from the excessive amount of brandy she drank solely on principle. Standing outside the apartment next door, looking up at the full moon, was the horrifying-looking Cryptid known as Tom. He did not turn to even look at Morgan as she passed, but he did speak.

"Good evening, Vampire Neighbor," he said. "Blessed Yule."

"Blessed Yule, Tom." She said, pulling out her keys and snuffling.

"You are unwell," he said. "Did your night not go as planned?"

"Not at all, Tom… " She chuckled at the absurdity. "Not at all."

"My sincerest condolences. You seemed to be quite elated when you left with the green-skinned man," he said, finally turning his skull face toward her. "Would it ease your suffering to expunge details of your experience?"

“I don’t…” she began, turning to him and thinking for a long moment. Maybe it was her drunken state or the disturbing Cryptid’s hospitality, but she changed her tune. “Do I seem… like, gullible? Am I like, dumb?”

“You speak like the youthful women of the valley, who are not commonly known for intelligence,” he said plainly. “And I have seen you dress like a prostitute.”

“Gee, thanks,” she scoffed.

“You’re welcome,” he said, turning to her fully. “I will also include, I sense a latent kindness and honed intelligence. You are a student at a prestigious university, no?”

“Avalon U…” she said, looking down her nose, unsure of where he was going with this.

“Precisely,” he prattled. “I do not know the context of your anguish, but I know that pain is temporary. As all things are until the cold embrace of death.”

“Right…” she nodded. “But people like us—“

“Are eternal. Oblivion does not come for us unless it is thrust upon us,” he said, looking up to the moon again. “It is a beautiful moon, but the energy of this Yule is different… I diverge. I think, as the mortals put it, you have a ‘good head on your shoulders’. I do not understand how one head could be better than another, as they are all filled with the same meat, but I understand the expression means you are balanced and capable. You accomplish many tasks other Preternaturals would not. You should not think lowly of yourself, Vampire Neighbor. You will destroy your enemies and dance upon their graves.”

She chuckled, glancing down for a moment. “Thank you, Tom.”

“No thanks are necessary. I merely answered your question.” He replied, focusing again on the full moon.

“Seriously, I… actually appreciated this,” she smiled.

“All doors are merely thresholds. It's the doors we choose to enter that matter,” he said. “Rest easy, Vampire Neighbor. The moon is divinely charged tonight, it will guide your dreams.”

“Goodnight, Tom,” She said entering the apartment, feeling a modicum better than she had.

“Goodnight,” he replied, as the door shut. “What a strange

woman."

14

"And the fucker just stood there, acting like a hurt child," Morgan vented, getting herself ready in the mirror, preparing for yet another date. This one, however, was destined to go sideways.

"What a fucking tool," Raphie said, not looking away from his video game. "Is this going to affect your story?"

Demy leaned against Raphie and watched him blow zombies away with his cop avatar. She always found it odd how zombies were the grey area of undead sub-variants that the media had no problem portraying as monsters. Maybe it was because there wasn't such a thing as a zombie with a brain. If you weren't a Vampire, a Ghoul, or a Lich, you were just a feral animal. According to Morgan, feral Vampirism is an uncommon occurrence that still happens in fully 'rehabilitated' Vampires. So much so that the CDC has plans for an outbreak of any one type of feral undead. Regardless, shooting virtual zombies made for fun entertainment, she supposed.

"I don't know… it better not. Even if it does, I'll go to the Network with it… Though odds are they won't believe me. I have to get proof of this otherworld first. I have to find Chrissy. I just feel it in my gut that she's there. Like, she's calling for me," Morgan urged, focused on curling her eyelashes.

"I'm not saying you made this up, but I've had dreams that look exactly like this otherworld you described," Raphie said. "Do you think they're related?"

"I don't know." Morgan sighed. "I hope not."

Demy traced her hand up and down the design on Raphie's *Alice In Chains* t-shirt, an image of a three-legged dog. She looked up at him, knowing that these otherworldly visions don't come to just anyone. For both her boyfriend, and the fast friend she made in Morgan, to be potentially spiraling deeper into danger worried her. She was just grateful she could be around to intervene if things got even stranger.

"I'll be fine, Blondie. Even if I'm getting strange visions, then maybe I'm just like your Aunt." Raphie said.

"Maybe," Morgan said with a weary voice. "I just want everyone to be okay."

"We're going to be fine, I wouldn't let anything bad happen to us, you know that… and that's only if Aunt M doesn't swoop in and do her thing," Raphie chuckled. "Seriously… are you going to tell M about all this or what?"

She didn't reply.

It was clear to Demy that Raphie cared exponentially about Morgan. She admired his bravery, how open-minded and laid-back he was. She needed him more than she could have ever possibly known. But the chemistry between these two best friends was undeniable. Demy wasn't afraid of Raphie leaving her for Morgan: that would be thinking too small.

After a few moments of silence between them, Morgan exited the bathroom to reveal she was dressed as best she could in what she imagined Dorian Ziusudra would like to see her in. A black spaghetti strap dress with a high hem clung to her form. Her arms were kept moderately warm by a gossamer black overshirt. Small accents of red adorned her entire outfit, from her lips, to her rose-shaped earrings, to the blood-red on the sole of her heels, to the inner fabric of her dress. Raphie's eyes lit with life when he saw her exit. Demy felt his heart flutter and grinned. *Oh, you've got it bad, sweetie*. She thought.

"How do I look?" She asked, twisting and showing off different angles of the outfit. "It's not too much, right? Do I look acceptable?"

"You look… great, Blondie," Raphie said with a wide grin.

"Seriously, Adrian was right to call you a supermodel," Demy added.

"Like, for real?" Morgan blushed. "I wanna make Dorian drool. The longer I can keep him like putty in my hands the better."

"Absolutely. You know I can't lie to you," Raphie said, his smile hindered after a second. "Are you sure there's nothing we can do? Dude… we've got magic, we can make shit work."

"I appreciate it, Raph… but the only way to pull this off without anyone getting hurt is if I play his little game and pretend this is a date… but I like, know how worried you are." Morgan gave a touched smile and outstretched her arms for a hug, her hands making a grabbing gesture. "Come 'ere."

Raphie got up and obliged her. "Of course, Blondie. I just want you to be safe," Raphie said, holding her hands after.

"And thank *you* for everything you've done so far, Demy. You're really awesome… I think you're just perfect for Raphie," Morgan said, curving her neck to Demy to speak to her. When she looked back at Raphie, her eyes changed.

Holy shit they both got it bad. Demy thought, herself blushing at the compliment. "Thank you, Morgan, you're too kind."

Morgan walked over and went in to hug Demy. "You come 'ere too! I have so much to thank you for." Demy stood and embraced her friend, taking in her fragrance, smelling of roses and the ocean air. She exhaled, feeling an immense peace, an unintentional energy transfer that seemed to sync them spiritually at that moment. Though it was strange, she felt as though her connection with the ether wavered as long as she was in her arms. As if the ethereal energy that surrounded all lifeforms halted and hung frozen in place. She credited it as care for her friend, but took a mental note even still.

"I owe you…. A lot," Morgan whispered to her, as if from nowhere.

"Just be safe," Demy whispered back. "We'll call it even."

Off to the side, Raphie stood back, looking confused at what was happening when the two girls parted from their embrace and looked into each other's complementary eyes. In that second, Demy felt a sensation she couldn't possibly describe at that moment in time. She believed that the Moth scale pendant around her neck seemed to be more than just a token of a miracle. Rather, she felt it was a beacon that led her to Raphie… and Morgan.

"It's time…" Morgan said solemnly, turning around and gliding to the front, grabbing her purse. She spared a glance back at her friends.

"For the love of God, be careful," Raphie said, following her closely.

"Please trust me when I say I can handle this." Morgan insisted.

"I've heard that statement before, Blondie…" he said, taking her hand one last time. "Come home."

"I will. I swear." Morgan returned a weak smile before leaving Apartment 161.

"I don't like that we can't get involved," Demy said after a few seconds of silence, once she was sure the door was shut.

"I know, me neither." Raphie gave a heavy sigh and walked back over with a sudden lack of energy as if the abrupt interaction had sapped him of all his positivity. He trudged over to the coffee table and took his beer. "She's going back into this otherworld, and I don't even know how to wrap my head around this… plus she's not doing well. She's not herself. That bastard Colt did her dirty. God If he wasn't 250lbs of pure muscle I would kick his ass… can we turn him into a toad?"

"We'll talk about Polymorphing next lesson," she chuckled, not entirely joking. "He was… her boss and significantly older, so… big surprise it didn't work out."

"Well, I mean Morgan's always had a thing for older partners," Raphie stated. "In freshman year of high school *and* college, she dated a senior. She met Balam when she was nineteen. Just her type, I suppose… I just hope she doesn't fall for this Ziusudra joker."

"How come you guys never dated?" Demy boldly said.

"Um… we're best friends. I've known her since I was a kid… pre-boy mode. It would be… weird." Raphie took a sip of beer.

"Weirder than you having a bunch of photo-realistic drawings of her?" Demy asked, forthright.

Raphie choked and spat out his foaming beverage. He managed to catch some, briskly walking to the kitchen to retrieve a towel.

"I know you're not gonna dump me for her, but I mean… It's stranger that you kinda play it off and act like you're not absolutely in love with her," Demy said, picking up the controller and continuing the zombie hunt for Raphie.

"I-I uh, I'm nnnot in… love with… Morgan." Raphie said, his voice squeaking to a higher pitch momentarily. He coughed, clearing his throat.

"Or neither of you has ever been single long enough for you to make your move," Demy said with certainty, bordering on giggles. "Right?"

"Why is this so funny to you?" Raphie said in his defense, putting his hands on his hips and letting the beer bottle hang loosely from his fingers.

"'Cause you're a terrible liar and I think there's something wholesome about that," she said, smiling. She paused the game and patted the empty seat beside her. "Let me tell you something."

Raphie moved to sit beside her, trepidation overtaking his other emotions.

"First off, don't worry, I'm not mad. I know you like me a lot. I like you, too. I've honestly… fallen pretty gods damned hard for you. But I'm not gonna pretend like I don't sense the energy change when Morgan walks into a room. You look at her the same way you look at *me*."

"Demytria… I don't… I'm not going to—" Raphie tried to speak, but he kept tripping on his tongue.

"I'm not done," She continued. "Morgan looks at you the same way… I saw it just now. Your eyes change… she's not as stealthy as she likes to think she is. But she loves you, Raphie. Ziusudra doesn't stand a chance."

"I… love *you*, Demytria," Raphie said, his fear of rejection, of what happened with Oliver, clear in his actions. He took her hands, staring into her eyes to show her that truth.

"I love you, too," she confessed, reaching up and touching his stubbly face. She pulled him close and kissed him. Partially hesitating to fully embrace her as well, he soon kissed her back, his brow furrowed. "What's wrong?" She eventually said.

"Uh… you just accused me of being in love with my best friend and vice versa?" He said, "I'm just… a little…"

"Lost?" Demy giggled. "I forget Amy and I were your first experience being a part of an open relationship… Look, you can date people all you want. I haven't been looking because I recently just got over Amy. That doesn't mean I'm not still keeping an eye out for potential partners. And if I'm being completely honest, she was here first."

"What? Morgan? She doesn't have dibs on me," Raphie debated.

"You weren't seeing what I saw when we met at the party. She was sizing me up. Then she stared at you… And there was that look again." Demy stood as she spoke. "Here's the sitch, I have to go home to water my cats and feed my plants. When she gets back tonight, she's going to have seen some shit. She's going to need someone to lean on. Who better than her best friend?"

"So you're going to leave now?" Raphie said, standing with her, his eyes hurt.

"Yeah, it's already getting dark."

"Exactly! What if Gruel comes back after you?" Raphie stressed.

"What if he does?" Demy scoffed. "He has no wand and his only friend is my ex, who is still too busy cleaning her shorts."

"That's… fair…" Raphie said, scratching the back of his head.

"If I'm gone when she gets here, it will be less awkward. Just think about what I said. She's single now, and in desperate need of a good man in her life… maybe bring polyamory up to her when the timing is right."

"Are you sure?" Raphie said with a frown of uncertainty.

"Yes! You two would be so fucking cute together," Demy admitted. "If she gives you that look, and the mood is right, you kiss that girl."

Raphie grabbed her and returned the kiss in full this time. They held each other in devotion until they ended the night together on that famous trio of words. Demy felt she made the right choice; she couldn't deny love in any form it took.

15

Sundown had long since passed by the time Morgan pulled up to the Babylon Tower. She felt strong wearing black accented with red. Pink may make Morgan feel pretty, but red made her feel empowered. If there was ever a night she needed a boost, it was tonight. Exiting her vehicle, she was met with the same curly-haired valet that greeted her the first time she visited this vexing place. Then she did not know what she knew now. This building was a dark pathway. Morgan was certain Chrissy Donavon was somewhere in that pathway.

She handed off her keys to the valet, watching him drive her car into the underground parking garage. She closed her eyes and centered herself, opening them again with a fire that she lacked any other night. With gusto, she strutted into the Babylon.

She felt especially uneasy riding the loud and shaky elevator; she reached into her purse and looked for her dragon pill container. Upon popping it open she saw there was not a grain left of her stash. She tilted it, to see if some was hidden: nothing.

"Fuck." She hissed to herself, loathing the idea of going into this sober. A sudden rush of anxiety and added claustrophobia caused her heart to race. She began counting from ten, using the buttons of the elevator to count. As she examined the buttons, she couldn't help but wonder if the missing number was the burned-out floor. As soon as the doors parted she reached into her purse and felt inside a ziplock bag full of spare buttons that she'd collected from her many blouses. She took a small handful and, starting from the elevator, dropped one every few yards.

"Miss Scriven," Theodora had swooped in from out of nowhere as she always does. "You're late."

"I'm sorry, there was traffic," Morgan said, feeling justified.

"You should just thank your lucky stars he enjoys your company. For some reason," Theodora scowled, turning and leading Morgan onward. "This way."

Morgan wanted to stop where she stood and ask her what

the hell she'd done to make her dislike her so much. It was not the time nor the place, as much as Morgan wished it was. Through her inner monologue against Theodora, Morgan kept the pattern of dropping buttons and even took mental notes of which colors were dropped where. Despite her strategy, Morgan felt at any moment, even with an escort, she could come into contact with the unnatural scaly thing or find herself in the hellish otherworld. She saw nothing of the sort, albeit, at one corner, she swore she heard the howling of that strange horned dog.

Finally, they passed the double doors that Morgan indubitably remembered as the bathhouse. She dropped a stack, two orange buttons, one green, by the corner of the doorframe. She would have to return here before she could even consider making a break for it. It wasn't much further and she was at the dining room where Dorian waited. Once Theodora and Morgan were out of sight, the horned dog followed behind. It sniffed a button that Morgan had dropped, picking it up in its mouth, and moving onward.

Theodora guided Morgan into the massive, open dining room. Polished, brown granite flooring and ornate, marble pillars framing the perimeter gave the vaulted room a sense of spaciousness. At the dead center was a dark wooden table that stretched several yards. A bouquet of red and pink roses and cherry blossoms sat in the center. She felt a tinge of paranoia that he knew her favorite flowers.

At the head, Dorian sat with his elbows on the table, hands folded, resting his mouth on them. He immediately became animated as she entered, his sky-blue eyes lifting with happiness. Swiftly, he stood to his full, statuesque form. He was dressed sharply as always, in a white-on-white suit, complemented by a deep blue tie. Morgan smirked, humoring the concept of her being his very antithesis. Conflicted, she savored the thought.

"Morgana Scriven," he said in a gentle voice, stepping forward with coattails flowing behind him, and pulled out her chair on the opposite end of the table. She thanked him and sat, allowing him to push the chair back in. Morgan looked as confused as she felt, the night already beginning to exceed her expectations as well as fuel her concerns. As he returned to his seat, her eyes were drawn to a suit of armor, one that reminded her of the armor worn by the horrid, winged observers in the otherworld.

"You look beautiful tonight, my dear." He said, moving his way back to his chair. "I have to be honest, I was a tad bit worried when you were late and did not call. I feared maybe someone else had captured your attention."

"No one else right now, Master," Morgan said. She saw motion in the corner of her eye and whipped her head over her shoulder merely to see a servant approaching with a bottle of champagne, pouring it into her glass.

"Leave the formality for the parties. Dorian, please," he insisted, his eyes never wavering from Morgan's.

Theodora rolled her eyes and snorted, leaving the room with an echo of her heels stomping against the floor. The two were alone, the only sound other than their speaking was the crackling of the newly installed fireplace against the adjacent wall.

"Okay, Dorian. I'm just honored to be here, if I'm being honest," Morgan replied, lifting her glass full of the golden, sparkling spirit. "To a brighter tomorrow."

"I can toast to that." He raised his glass with her. "To a brighter tomorrow."

Despite entering the building overwrought beyond all sense of the word, Morgan managed to relax somehow. He asked questions about her daily life, simple things, like what she did in school and why she chose to study journalism. She briefly explained her father's history but ignored any details of Auntie M's true identity. She was certain Dorian would use that information against her. For all the same reasons, she omitted any involvement with the Chronicle. Though at this point, Morgan was confident he already knew.

After a while, he noticed Morgan repeatedly glancing over at the armor. It was sleek, form-fitting, possessing both masculine and feminine traits. The very interlocking plates were sharp and angular, just like the helm itself, almost entirely encased by the ornate visor. At the brow of the helm were two holes, large enough for Taknoling horns or Wood-Elf antlers to fit through.

"Do you like it?" Dorian inquired.

"It's certainly… beautiful," Morgan said, reminded of the pain she endured.

"It is unlike anything from this world. The armor is made of an unearthly metal alloy that, allegedly, is organic material," Dorian began. "It is said to belong to a powerful entity known as an Incubus…"

"A demon?" Morgan laughed incredulously.

"Do not scoff at what you do not understand, my dear," Dorian said with a shaming waggle of his finger. "It was discovered by… my grandfather, Luciel Ziusudra, in the ruins of Babylon. My family can trace at least half of its lineage back to Ancient Akkad, you know. We were once godlike kings, with infinite wealth and power. I seek to restore some of my ancestral heritage here in the States."

"Is that what the Lounge is meant to be?" Morgan added, "A kingdom? You know, Vampires had a secret, global kingdom… it didn't turn out too well for us."

"Kingdom is such a crass term. To lead a meaningful philosophical movement is honestly my grandest goal. To be at the helm of a way of life that changes the world. That is the Lounge."

As the conversation went on, Dorian had managed to switch chairs three different times before ending up directly beside Morgan. He sat, a smile adorning his face, listening intently to every word she spoke. It was not long before Morgan was provided a delightful blood bisk as her main course: O positive. She feared the source, though she was certain he wouldn't try to drug or poison her. She opted to simply enjoy the coppery, cool dish and not think too much about it. Dorian did take a few bites from the fillet mignon he was served, but barely touched it otherwise, too involved in the discussion.

Their genuine interactions were layered with a tension that, until now, went ignored. At least on her end. Morgan knew who this man was, and what he did to her and Chrissy Donavon… to all the people he conned into servitude. Even still, she found it hard to look away from him or to receive a compliment without blushing. At this moment, Morgan found it hard to resist him. This feeling, however, was not exclusive to her.

Dorian was enamored with her; she knew this to be true. She, too, knew that she should be guarded in this place. Between his perfect, pearly smile, rolling-thunder voice, and the earnest way he looked at her made it difficult to suspect she was in any danger at all. It wasn't every day she'd felt admired like an art piece and not just for what she offered with her body.

As she began to entertain the thought, the overwhelming nature of her love life in cinders hijacked her free thought. Just as it all seemed bordering on suffocating, Raphie's drawing of her driving at sunset crept back into her brain, soothed it, and wrapped around it like a heated blanket. Everything centered again.

Dorian must have noticed her change in demeanor as his face shifted to one of contemplation. He stood without a word and moved to the wall closest to his original seat. There, sitting on a stand made of dark oak, was an antique record player, complete with a horn sculpted of brass. In the cabinet of the stand, Dorian retrieved one of the vinyl disks beneath, examined it, then reached for another instead. He placed the newfound record and moved the stylus. The melodious sounds of a classical symphony echoed throughout the chamber.

"This is exactly what I imagined you would listen to," Morgan chortled before sipping from her champagne. She kept a steady pace with him but refused to be caught at anything but her full capacity.

"You could say I am a very old-fashioned soul. I do not dislike modern music, but nothing hits the mark quite like Mozart does." He strode up to her, his stance nonthreatening. "Do you waltz, Morgana?"

"I haven't in a very long time; I was in Swing Club in high school," Morgan said. "I don't know if I'm any good anymore."

"Then you already possess the skills of a dancer. I have also seen your live performance, so do not sell yourself short." He said and held out a heedful hand to her. "If you would be so kind as to humble me with just one dance."

Morgan felt her cheeks flush, a fanged smirk formed on her face. She nodded, taking his hand and rising, quite a bit shorter than him. A sudden high of comfort overtook her the moment she looked into his ice-blue eyes, a stunning contrast against his skin. His razor-sharp visage struck her like a bullet and caused her body temperature to rise. He took her free hand and positioned it on his shoulder, then finally his hand on her waist.

"Just follow my lead, alright?" He said with a smile, leading her into a basic box step, "See? There you are."

Morgan watched their feet, becoming increasingly sheepish as the night progressed. She focused on watching his footwork to better follow the steps. Soon enough, they were making more progressive moves. As swoon-worthy as he was, Dorian was still a criminal overlord. One with befuddling habits and a nightmare of a home; none of that was strong enough to thwart her desire as a whole.

"You are a natural, my dear," Dorian said with triumph. Morgan finally looked up to him again, her brow furrowed. "What is bothering you, Morgana? It is clear on your face."

"You confuse me," she said with utmost sincerity.

"How so? Am I going too fast?" He said their pace was not changing in the slightest.

"Not at all," Morgan said as he dipped her, her long blonde hair sweeping near the marble floor. "You're a gentleman, I can't deny that. But I can't pretend to be blind to your lifestyle. I'm not talking about the one we share either. You run an organization that recruits the wealthiest and most influential people in the city. Meanwhile, you help facilitate gang treaties and run organized crime rings. You practically run this city and can have anything you want with the snap of your fingers… why me?"

"Why you?" he replied, picking up the pace as the song changed to one of a faster tempo. "If we are being honest about each other, most men and women are just a conquest. Something to have, play with, and abandon for the next. They simply do not last…"

"So I'm a challenge, am I?" Morgan said, raising one of her brows. She yearned to dissect his mind. Somewhere in that gorgeous cranium were the secrets to everything she needed to know.

"No, my dear," he crooned. His face thawed, as did his voice like ice on a summer morning. "I am too intimidated by you to try and conquer you. I am encapsulated by your beauty, your infectious, fanged smile, your brilliant mind; I *did* manage to find out your GPA. 3.8, despite all of this. Amazing. Truly remarkable. I do not want you as a trophy, Morgana. I want you as a partner. My equal."

"Are you asking me to be your girlfriend, Dorian?" Morgan said with rosy cheeks, playing it off with a smug grin. The reality of what this meant was somewhere lost in the dreamlike atmosphere Dorian created.

"I am, in fact." Dorian dipped her again, albeit lower this time and with more upward momentum. "At my side, the world will open up like you never thought possible. You will have freedom and wealth, unlike anything you may have previously experienced. You said it yourself, I snap my fingers and what I want becomes reality. You would gain that power by proxy. Simple as that. You would be the bride of a god, a goddess by right. A title you are already deserving of without my presence."

"'Bride of a god?'" Morgan repeated, her mouth agape, stunned by his ego but aroused by his verbiage. A tornado of emotional conflict stirred inside her. No one had ever offered her *godhood*.

"Well, metaphorically speaking," Dorian chuckled to himself. "Forgive my grandiose speech, it is as if my heart bursts when I touch you. For you to so honor me with an audience tonight is… it is better than making love."

"That's a powerful statement, Dorian. We've barely even done that much. How could you know what it compares to if we've only just begun?" Morgan slowed the dance, gazing into the sparkling diamonds that were Dorian's crystal blue eyes. He dipped her one last time.

He held her there for a long moment, and he guided her leg to lift along his side. He genuinely wanted to court her. He'd done everything he could to make her comfortable, to make her feel safe. What if he wasn't behind Chrissy's disappearance? At least perhaps it may have never been his intention. Perhaps whatever otherworldly vices are in place could be controlling him and his decisions. There's only one place Morgan would find an answer for any of this, and she knew she couldn't leave here without going back.

"I look forward to changing that, my dear Morgana." He said, holding her up in his arms. They were so close, and his lips were taunting her. She let him kiss her, wrapping her arms around his shoulders *Perhaps I can enjoy the byproduct of deception just a little longer.* She thought.

Theodora cleared her throat, suddenly standing beside the dining table without a single sound of her approach. A sneer painted on her face as she spoke, "Monsieur, Mr. Anderson is here. He's very eager to begin."

"Damn, I must have lost track of time," Dorian stood up, still holding Morgan to him. "Invite him in."

Theodora, for a split second, locked eyes with Morgan, striking at her like golden spears. In Dorian's arms, Morgan was shielded. She smirked, creating an exchange of underlying aggression. Theodora turned around and invited a man from the doorway. Morgan's face was drained of joy, made uneasy and confused by what was happening. A short, portly man entered, one of Dorian's black-suited and masked security guards at either shoulder as he was escorted in.

"Mr. Ziusudra, it's a pleasure as always," He said, striding directly up to them, with his hand outstretched. Dorian shook it. The older man crossed eyes with Morgan, and he gave her an excited smile. Oddly, his breath smelled strongly of fruit. "And you must be Ms. Vaughn. I've heard such great things about you. I'm very eager to begin."

"What's going on, Master?" She said, pulling away from Dorian, the distrust in her voice was prevalent. "I thought you said this was just dinner."

"It is, you are not going to be sleeping with Mr. Anderson. You see, Mr. Anderson is not a healthy man. He is not keen on doing what the doctor ordered. I, as a businessman, saw a unique opportunity to offer him an alternative," Dorian said, his smile not faltering despite Morgan's obvious discomfort at the new guest.

She noticed behind Dorian, through another hall, more finely dressed servants wheeled in what looked like a dentist's chair with straps. Morgan's eyes began to grow wide as towels were laid about its base, and Mr. Anderson took his jacket and shirt off. She turned back to Dorian, as he spoke again, Morgan was stricken ill by his words. "You'll be turning Mr. Anderson into a Vampire tonight."

16

"W-what did you say?" Morgan couldn't believe what she'd heard. Her skin crawled at the idea of biting an actual Human. She'd lived her entire life without. She remembered the horror stories she heard growing up, about Vampires that don't come back from tasting fresh Human blood. Her mother always said it 'unearths something in us'. Morgan knew in her heart that Odessa was a hell of a lot tougher and wiser than her daughter. Somehow, Dorian seemed nonplussed by her reaction, with an infinitesimal smile.

"You're going to turn Mr. Anderson," Dorian repeated. "Just a brief bite and a droplet or two of your blood, and he will be turned. I am sure you have room for dessert anyway." He leaned in and whispered in a mocking tone directly to her. "Anderson is a poorly regulated diabetic, so he should be a delicacy."

"I-I c-can't do this," Morgan stammered.

"Yes, you can, my dear," Dorian assured. "I understand you are worried about the legality, but I assure you there is no way that any recourse could be enacted against you. Mr. Anderson already had a meeting with my legal team and has signed a non-disclosure agreement. He has no plans to turn on us now… so to speak."

"You don't understand what you ask of me: Vampires are linked to who they turn. His blood will be mine and vice versa."

"He will not be enthralled to you, my dear," Dorian continued, his patience beginning to wear thin. "We have already planned precautions and intend to keep him here a few nights to regulate him."

"A few nights?! T-try a few weeks. He'll be a k-killing machine for a month straight, feeding on anything, and if he goes unchecked, he could go feral. He could literally become a m-monster, what half the world already sees us as. After that, what life does he have?" She turned to Anderson, shirtless and strapped in the chair, and grabbed his hands. "Mr. Anderson, please, I know what you're thinking, but this is not what you want. I'm not like other Vampires, I'm privileged enough to live like a normal person. You won't gain that ability. You'll have to live your life behind refractium. You'll hesitate to fall in love because you'll outlive everyone you care about, and inevitably that means watching your friends and family die. You *don't* want this."

"B-but I do," Anderson replied.

"Ms. Vaughn," Dorian seethed through his teeth, "Please just bite the man and be done with it."

"No. You don't want this, Mr. Anderson." Morgan turned back and glowered at Dorian, seeing his spiteful gaze only confirmed her suspicions about what he ultimately cared about: the bottom line. The whole while she stared her suitor dead in the eye. "…and I refuse to do it… it's not in my contract… none of tonight is…"

Morgan stomped away, grabbing her bag off the chair on her way. With her fists clenched tight, she turned back to Dorian and spoke with regret, "I'm sorry, Master… I'm not the girl you think I am…" As she exited, she almost brushed shoulders with the ever-lovely Theodora Abaddon. The sour Domhainn moved out of her way and flashed an arrogant smile at the Vampire's expense.

"What the hell is this?" Anderson blustered.

"I'm sorry, Mr. Anderson, I will make sure you are compensated for your wasted time. This should not have happened, and we will find you a Vampire willing to do the procedure."

"I'd certainly hope so with as much as I paid you,"

Anderson said as he was unlatched and redressed. "Try and find someone as cute as that one, please. I was looking forward to this."

"Naturally, I will do my best. Please take care, Mr. Anderson," Dorian sighed as the man huffed and puffed his way out of the dining area. His security escorts followed. Soon, the servants had wheeled the chair away, leaving Theodora and Dorian alone.

"She disobeyed you again. She's trouble." Theodora said, approaching Dorian.

"You may be right. We will have to keep tabs on her now," Ziusudra said, looking to the floor where Eliott VanderGraf lay dead days prior, a small crack in the marble pillar where his head collided. He rubbed his temples and sighed heavier this time. "I have made a decision about The Moth. We need to summon Maria: It's time."

Flustered and disturbed, Morgan stormed down the halls, free again of anyone's watching eyes. She scanned the corners and looked behind her, expecting some method of sinister creatures or people. She brought pepper spray and her father's pocket knife this time. She felt safe. Or at least as safe as one could feel wandering an endlessly convoluted penthouse occupied by frightening entities and, in all likelihood, containing a portal to someplace unlike anywhere on Earth.

At last, she spotted her buttons and did her best to follow the trail she laid out. As she did, she became ever certain she didn't take this many turns coming into the place, but still found her buttons to be where she remembered leaving them. *Is this place... changing?* She thought, entertaining the idea that the very building is alive. She took another corner and spotted the double doors at the end of a T-shaped intersection.

This same configuration was where Dorian found her begging for her life, cowering from the thing. Or at least where she ended up. Morgan approached the doors, seeing her stack of buttons. She looked around, noticing she was still alone, and set foot in the bathhouse. As she entered, a door behind her cracked open so the scaly thing could watch.

Within, the elaborate bathhouse looked just as it did from her memory, a vastly deep and eerily dark pool took up most of its space. Her body was wracked with panic; the thought of going underwater in such a daunting space was almost debilitating. The only thing that gave her any spark of bravery was the idea that Chrissy Donavon may be trapped with that beautiful, monstrous creature and their nightmarish cohort. To ensure she didn't have any more time to chicken out, Morgan stripped down to just her red bra and panties, now clutching her father's knife. A waterproof disposable camera was dangling on her wrist by a blue strap, cinched tight.

With a focused breath, she closed her eyes and chanted. "It's just water… It's just water… It's just—" Morgan dove in, swimming down to the bottom as fast as she could, keeping her eyes closed in the crushing darkness. Further and further Morgan swam, wanting to open her eyes to see how far she'd gone, but fully knowing she couldn't or she'd panic. She had to trust that the fleshy beings were not there, waiting to strike.

Just as the pressure of the water became too unbearable to her senses, she reached the bottom. She emerged into the open air, breaching to observe an endless sea against a black horizon. Her momentum carried her out of the water and into the dead space, falling upward until she crashed into what felt like solid wood. She fell again, horizontally, merely a few feet to the warm, crimson floor. She blinked rapidly, disoriented by the constant shift in gravity. After a few seconds of stillness, she sat up, looking onward into a wall of dark water. She stood and closed the door, feeling a rush of anxiety just looking at it.

When she spared a look around, she noticed she was in another hallway. At least, it resembled a hallway. A better description would have been a series of black doors on either side of a dimensionless red void. Morgan couldn't see where the walls met the floors or where either end led. It seemed as though both ends stretched forever. This did no favors for her claustrophobia. She cracked the door she came from and chose a side to progress. She expected to feel cold from the air, as she was still soaking wet, but it almost felt as if there wasn't any air at all. It made her fear Chrissy's fate. It felt like an eternity since she was last here, since she first met Dorian Ziusudra and found his homegrown nightmare.

The corridor continued forever, and Morgan followed. She tried to press on until she could no longer spot the open door behind her. It was to no avail. After an impossibly short distance, she had looped back around to the first door. Never once did Morgan sense she was going in a circle. She stopped and looked at the doors on either side, all identical, all black as night. She approached one, looking into it, and she was immediately hit with a blast of freezing Himalayan air, turning a few of the droplets on her to ice. She glanced out into the white abyss for merely a second before she had to shield her eyes and slam the door. She brushed the frost off her body, shivering a bit.

She moved to a door across the hall and tried that one. A dark, swampy environment revealed itself on the other side. Morgan assumed a swamp by the smell; however, the flora was unlike anything she'd ever seen. Sprawling tree roots with knots like eyes, vines that hung from the tree canopy, and seemed to pulse with bioluminescence of impossible colors. Naturally, Morgan began taking pictures. She would have braved the path of stones protruding from the murky water, were it not for the sets of golden, glowing eyes growing larger in the darkness.

She slammed the door and put her back to it. Glancing to her right, she tried the next immediate door. Within, a simple pie on a stand in an empty room with defined white walls; a welcome change of pace. She opted to leave the door open, just in case. Morgan approached the pie, seeing a sign propped up beside it that read "Eat Me", with a knife left to cut into it. Though while far from willing to eat it, her curiosity had her gripped. Grabbing the knife, she plunged it into the thick crust. As soon as a wide enough slit was cut, Morgan saw the blood oozing from the pie and drew back the knife. From within, two dozen blackbirds burst from the crust, scattering about, scratching and pecking Morgan as they flew out into the empty hall.

Morgan ran back out as the birds swarmed around her. She slammed the door and covered her face as the ravens flew upward into the undefined space. Finally feeling stable, Morgan dared to look up. She collapsed in terror; like a thin veil, she saw past the crimson ceiling and into the void. She stared dissolute at a trillion eyes sprouting from leathery tendrils, forming a sky of black flesh, woven together and staring back with their multi-colored horrors. Her mind shattered, and she began sobbing, remembering these exact images in Raphie's drawings. She forced herself to stare at the floor, standing to search for doors out of desperation. Without looking, she snapped a picture of the 'ceiling'.

Trying another door, she found the land of the red sky at last. What she saw was what appeared to be the streets of Los Angeles, the place that's been her home for more than half her life. What was drastically different from her home was the lack of people and the smell of fire. A sound of a woman wailing from down the hall echoed, from a source Morgan couldn't see. Not taking any chances, she walked through the door, into the crimson light. She immediately gazed up at the dead, dark sun that hung in the sky, robbing light from around it like a black hole rather than projecting light itself. It was impossible to miss and seemed to take up most of the sky at any given time. She scanned the environment, seeing that the door she came from was no longer there.

Instead, to her horror, would be the ruins of the city. Like a surrealist painting, the streets and buildings seemed to bend and fold into the sky at impossible angles, plunging into the heavens with skyscrapers like the rungs of a ladder. Flames burning in the Downtown area, at some points, reached as high as the skyscrapers themselves. Buildings and freeways had collapsed, leaving ruined cars in the rubble. She felt the need to weep, but did not have the time to even consider it. Instead, she chose to take as many pictures as she could. Morgan barely even thought of herself being trapped here. This realm was a complex game of chess, and she had no choice but to play it.

Across from her was a department store with its windows broken in. She approached, avoiding the glass with her bare feet the best she could, and climbed into the shop. It didn't take her long to find shorts, a T-shirt, and shoes her size. It was strange to her, nothing was looted. She checked the registers, the money was still in the till. There were no signs of any life as if everyone simply vanished into the dust that was layered on everything.

"You're stuck here," a voice said, causing Morgan to leap and spin in place. She was blonde, dressed in a leotard and leg warmers. She looked sickly, but somehow spotless, save for two dirty feet. She sat on a counter beside a register, holding her knees and rocking in place. Morgan was uncertain how she could have snuck up on her, but deduced that nothing made sense here.

"You're Kate Carper," Morgan said.

"Haven't heard that name in a while..." She said, giggling and playing with her curly locks "I don't answer to it anymore."

"What do you answer to?" Morgan said.

"I don't answer to anything. I'm not here. Or there. Or anywhere. And neither will you be," Carper said, giggling profusely.

"What do you mean?" Morgan asked, approaching the register slowly, the knife extended in her hand.

"You can only leave if They want you to…and no one leaves…" she said, looking to Morgan with her sunken eyes. She began laughing so loud Morgan was startled again. Like a wax sculpture or a scoop of ice cream on a hot day, she melted. Carper became little more than a viscous fluid, the color of blood and flesh. Morgan screamed and stumbled back into the clothing racks as it seeped into the cracks of the floor. With haste, Morgan fled the shop.

She wandered the outer ruins for merely a moment, finding herself at the Santa Monica pier, where Raphie and Morgan would spend their summers, and have for years. She could no longer contain her tears. Seeing the pier itself half-collapsed into the Pacific Ocean, framed by the giant, dead sun, broke her heart. Facing down and letting her tears fall, Morgan saw something peculiar in the layers of ash. Shoe prints, most likely a male's dress shoe. Morgan followed the path parallel to the coast.

The trail arched around and led to an open door of a beachfront house. Morgan had seen this house before, and often joked at the possibility of buying it when she was a "big shot reporter". Raphie never thought it was a joke; he always told her to go for her dream. He once said that Morgan could be a prime-time anchor, just like her idol Phylis Barks. Morgan took a deep breath, reminding herself of Raphie kept her mind focused and gave her purpose to push on and find Chrissy.

She entered the beach house, the footprints continued inside, tracking ash and sand on the wooden floor. The smell of fire and molten asphalt transmuted to that of burnt tobacco. She followed the footprints past the large entryway and elaborate, lowered living room, complete with a massive entertainment system. Seeing all the expensive gear still present, yet again, caused Morgan deep distress. She held her knife with a vice grip as she approached the archway into the kitchen and dining nook. Wisps of cigarette smoke curved around the corner and tickled Morgan's nose.

"Hello?" She asked, the sound of her voice becoming distorted in the impossibly distant echo. "Is someone there?"

"You're early. You shouldn't be here… yet." As she turned the corner, she saw a man in the half-lit room, his face concealed by shadows. His voice was deep and jagged, evidence of a pack-a-day habit as if filtered through velvet. A cigarette burned in his hand, smoke constantly billowing from his mouth as he spoke.

"Early for what? Who are you?" Morgan said.

"If I told you any of that, you might not come back, will you?" He spoke with a Southern drawl, possibly Texan. He took a draw of his smoke, the light of the cherry glowed softly to reveal his face. His head and hands seemed to be constructed completely of rolling ash clouds contained within a grey suit. His very face spiraled like the cyclones she'd seen in the crimson sky. Morgan felt a chill up her spine at the sight of this faceless being.

"I don't understand… where are we?" Morgan continued to inquire.

"Los Angeles," he said.

"Bullshit."

"It's true… this is just *one* Los Angeles… not yours." The man made of ash said.

"Where is everyone? What happened here?" Morgan continued to question.

"You ask a lot of questions," he rumbled. "Why don't you be honest and tell me why you're here, first? What brought *you* to this gods-forsaken plane?"

"I'm looking for a girl. Chrissy Donavon… I think she's stuck here," Morgan said, her voice echoing out into the ruins. She looked about, confused at the science behind how sound moved in this world.

"There we go… truth is: nothing gets trapped here… just displaced from reality for a while." He laughed, taking another hit.

"She's just a teenage girl. She's lost, and there might be others like her. Please, can't you help at all?" Morgan pleaded. "How do I get her out?"

"Follow your instincts. Find the black doors. Stay away from red ones. You'll be free." His body began to disintegrate, blowing out into the ruins in fragments. "You'd best be going, They're here for you…"

"Who's here?" Morgan panicked. The rest of the man, including his suit, vanished into smoke and blew out the open window. Within seconds, Morgan was alone again.

"Gods damnit," she hissed. Another door was open behind where he was sitting, cracked, and looked as though it was leading to another dimly lit hall.

Just outside the entryway behind her, she saw the silhouette of the four-armed deity. Horns like a headdress blotted out what impossible light escaped the black star. Morgan darted through the door, desperate to stay ahead of the demonic being that followed her, and exited out into a stretching hall.

Through the blue, shadowy corridor, Morgan pushed, the next door seeming farther and farther away from her the longer she ran, like a living nightmare. Her feet stomped into the tile flooring, pushing her forward with as much Vampiric might as she could muster. Behind her, just on the edge of her vision, the shadow of the demonic beast extended far beyond any reasonable source of light, as if the shadow itself chased her.

Sparing a glance back, Morgan witnessed the colossal four-armed creature filling the space, moving on a series of coiled snake tails for legs and using her long, skeletal arms to propel her locomotion. Each serpentine "leg" possessed needle-like spines along its sides and agonizing piercings across the purple scales. Upon looking at her face, Morgan's mind felt as though it short-circuited, incapable of comprehending what she'd seen, feeling only indomitable terror.

As she approached the door, it became solid black, as if it were corrupted by shadow. The terrified reporter pushed through the door and was brought into the crimson hallway from which she entered. Morgan figured the longer she speculated the longer it had to catch her. She bolted down the hall looking for that first door. But it was to no avail, she couldn't see the door she'd come from no matter how long she ran.

A door swung open before her. She froze. Out from the other end, a massive, gaunt hand adorned with rings and bangles of solid gold reached out into the hall. A hiss that could only be described as a call to Morgan sent her reeling the opposite way.

Down, far at the other end of the hall, were the fleshy monstrosities that tortured her so many days past. Chittering and writhing as they piled over one another, they trampled their own mutilated kin in an effort to reach Morgan. She could see the glint of their piercings and surgically attached weapons. If these monsters caught her, it would mean her eternal torture.

There was no hope. None other than to keep going deeper. Back through another random door, Morgan found herself tumbling to the earth below.

17

Immediately out of the red hall and into the next world, Morgan tumbled, falling down a dirt cliff for some time, bouncing off branches and rocks. She cried out with each collision, eventually falling on her face— on something hard. She would weep, slowly trying to pick her injured body up. The first thing she'd do when she opened her eyes was observe whatever it was she fell on. She was met with the empty eye sockets of a bleached skull. She yelped, leaping back as dusty bones were kicked up.

Finally, Morgan scanned around her: flames, ruin, and desolation as far as the eye could see. She was no longer in the city, standing on rolling hills, scorched black and void of life. Though the sky was still crimson, this was due to the fires burning across the charnel field. Littered across the space were skeletons and corpses left to decay for what appeared to be ages by their state. No square foot was without a piece of humanoid remains, the remnants of a vile war that took the lives of everyone involved.

The distant sounds of battle could be heard past the hills around her. She could see the flare of cannons and feel the base of their firing. Morgan dreaded getting closer, but to her detriment, the combat would come to her. The roaring boom of a tank's cannon was only followed by the rumbling of the earth. Seemingly from nowhere, the tank, ancient and rusted, powered over the bones of the dead, crushing them to dust as it fired again, deafening Morgan; it powered on, ignorant of any life other than its target. Yelping in panic, Morgan dove to the side, nearly being crushed by the vehicle's treads.

As she rolled, she found herself in another ditch with fewer bones. She kept her head low, looking up at the spinning treads as they passed. She panted, narrowly avoiding death. She observed the war machine, seeing it as a massive, rusted contraption, adorned with rivets, bolts, and pieces of scrap welded onto portions. Not only did it look worse for wear, but its structure was unlike any tank Morgan had ever seen. Simplistic and practical but somehow uncanny and alien.

While she was distracted, out from beneath a toppled and burnt-out tree, a humanoid hand grasped her wrist. Morgan screamed. Leaping up and painfully gripping her father's knife, Morgan prepared for the worst. Instead, she was met with desperate brown eyes and a dirty Human face obscured by a scarf.

"Get down!" the Human said, gesturing for Morgan to join them. As the sounds of combat grew louder, she decided she had no choice and dove down with the stranger.

Once under the tree, Morgan turned to the stranger, still aiming her knife.

"Who are you?" Morgan said, unable to make out features in the shadows. "Where are we?... Answer me!"

The stranger began to unwrap their scarf, showing their soft, round face and flesh like a doe's coat.

"C-Chrissy??" Morgan said. "Oh my gods. You're alive!"

"Morgan!"Chrissy said, leaping forward and wrapping her arms tightly around her. Morgan was stunned, wide-eyed, and beyond confused.

"H-how do you know my name?" Morgan said, pushing Chrissy off and placing a hand on either of her exposed shoulders, the poor girl in only a tank top and jeans. She was filthy, caked in dirt and dried blood, so much so that it was impossible to tell the original color of her shirt. Her hair was matted and formed into thick locks; she looked emaciated and weathered, as if she'd aged decades.

"Because I know you," Chrissy said, wild-eyed and utterly delirious, "You followed the locus and found me! Just like you said you would."

"What?" Morgan puzzled. "What... what are you talking about? We've never met."

"Not yet, we haven't," Chrissy added, with a wide smile, even her teeth worn and faded.

"You... Chrissy, I need you to focus. How do I get you out of here?" Morgan said, shaking the girl lightly. "How do we leave?"

Chrissy's smile faded.

"No one leaves."

"Bullshit," Morgan barked. "This isn't my first time coming here. We've got to find a way out."

"If you don't know how now… then you have to go back… you're not ready."

"Ready for what!?" Morgan cried. "You're not making any sense. Chrissy, you've been in hell for ages. You're not thinking straight."

"I've *only* thought about this, Morgan. Don't insult me," Chrissy replied with a sudden clarity to her voice. "You don't know how to navigate the Threshold yet… You need to go back."

"I don't know how!" Morgan begged. "I'm trying to explain that. You have to know something."

"You don't need me, Morgan… It's all in you," Chrissy said, her eyes welling with tears, tears of anger. "You get to leave as freely as you want… that's why They want you."

"Who wants me?" Morgan shuddered at the thought of something pursuing her, musing about the eldritch horror she had just encountered. "That creature?"

"They all do… The Watchmen at the Gate have big plans… and Dorian Ziusudra is a pawn in their game," Chrissy added. "Ziusudra… that name.. I haven't said it out loud in… how long has it been?"

"Five months."

"Is that all?" Chrissy said, broken. "Is that all I've been gone?!"

"Yes. And I'm going to take you home. Now."

"You can't."

"Watch me."

Morgan stood, looking about to see if any more tanks were nearby. From the sounds of things, the combat moved away. Ever rolling battle, unceasing and unrelenting. No respite or remorse for life. No factions. No flags. Just war. Morgan wasn't even sure if the vehicles were manned.

"I just need to find the black doors," Morgan said, gripping Chrissy by the hand and lifting her to her feet. "Come on… we're going home."

Chrissy began counting, muttering the numbers at

inconsistent volumes. She stumbled as she walked, visibly weak. Morgan held her hand the whole time, helping her over the skeletal remains and burnt trees.

It would be hours of traversing the battlefield, narrowly avoiding shelling, and occasionally ducking for cover. Their best strategy was to avoid the war machines entirely; keeping away from them only assured that the crossfire would not accidentally obliterate the two girls. Before long, they found the only structure among the fields, a single bunker that was left dusty and unmanned. The two girls found themselves inside, tired.

"Fuck… there's got to be a way out." Morgan racked her brain, tapping her head on the concrete wall she leaned against. Outside the bunker, the distinct sound of footsteps could be heard, crunching through the burned brush and remnant bones. The scraping, clamorous, and sickly sounds of metal on concrete harmonized with the foreboding footsteps.

"You have…106… to go…107," Chrissy whispered, "You need… 108…to get…109… out of here."

After some deliberation, Morgan and Chrissy ran deeper into the bunker. It wasn't until they'd go into the bathrooms that they'd see it. The restroom door was solid black. Morgan ran to it and flung it open. There she was met with a wall of dark water some feet out. She recognized this as the underside of Ziusudra's pool. All she would have to do is fall forward, and gravity would take her home. Their way out.

"Come on!" Morgan said, gripping Chrissy by the wrist.

She didn't budge.

"Chrissy!" Morgan yelled in a whisper as the trudging stomps grew closer, and the grinding became clearer that it was a blade being scratched into the side of the bunker wall.

"It's no use," Chrissy said hopelessly.

"There's no time for this, Chrissy!" Morgan used all her Vampire strength to drag the teen girl against her will to the door. Chrissy, weak and tired, could not fight anymore. Morgan dove through the door, only to have her arm go taught. She lost balance and fell, hanging by Chrissy's arm and dangling down above the water. She looked up, seeing that Chrissy, tears falling from her eyes, was perfectly positioned in the center of the doorway. She was unmoving as if some intangible force prevented her from crossing the threshold.

"I told you… I can't leave… stop Ziusudra," Chrissy said, dire. "It's the only way to prevent Them from winning."

"I'm not leaving you!" Morgan screamed.

From behind the teen girl, a Giant-sized humanoid in an executioner's mask entered the hall. He was armored, his breastplate designed to look like ribs, his face concealed, and his muscular, scarred arms were exposed. In his hand, was the largest axe Morgan had ever seen. As he approached he held it with both hands, stomping painfully slow to Chrissy. Morgan's veins turned to ice when she saw its skinless face beneath the mask, eternally grinning.

"Yeah, Morgan," Chrissy smiled. "You are."

"NO!"

Morgan's protest was ignored as Chrissy let go of her, letting her slip out of her grip and tumble into the water. Reaching up, Morgan saw that sweet smile for the last time before Chrissy was yanked back into the bunker and the door slammed. Morgan's back hit the water.

Sudden and crushing, the water enveloped Morgan as she fell forward and into its deep, inky darkness. She tossed and turned, tumbling through the abyss before finding herself floating upward, losing her knife to the depths. She opened her eyes to see her father's tool fall into the darkness; she witnessed the horrifying, ghastly castigators just outside her vision.

Outlines of eerie light illuminated their naked figures, revealing the pierced, stretched, and tortured flesh they possessed. Morgan pushed harder and harder to the surface as one reached her, grabbing her wrist with fingers like scalpels. It cut through the camera strap on her wrist and sliced into her skin. Along with her father's knife, the camera with all of her evidence tumbled into the depths, beneath the horde of nightmare creatures. Morgan couldn't go back and had to push on, bursting from the water like a siren.

Her chest heaved from the pressure and strain. Coughing up water, she pulled herself out of the pool and onto the floor of the bathhouse. She lay on her back, eyes closed, terrified to see what would be there when she opened them. At last, she turned her head to the side, opening her eyes and seeing the water jostling in the pool from her disturbance. Before long, the water calmed, no four-armed monsters or mutilated fiends. She closed her eyes again and lay flat, sighing in relief. When she decided to open her eyes again, she jumped at the sight of Theodora standing above her, now impatiently tapping her foot.

"Ahh! Jesus Christ! Stop doing that!" Morgan leaped up, immediately turning to confront the Domhainn.

"Enjoying the pool, Ms. Scriven?" Theodora snarled. "Or is it supposed to be Ms. Vaughn? I can never tell with you."

"I wanted to freshen up. I don't think Dorian would have been too agitated at my use of his pool again."

"Don't test me, worm," Theodora said, gritting her teeth. "Get out now. You've caused enough trouble tonight."

Morgan struck her with a look of doubt that utterly deflated Theodora and her intimidation tactics. She took off her wet t-shirt and squeezed back into her dress, carrying her shoes with her fingers. Theodora glared at Morgan her entire way out.

"Take a right and follow the path until you see the elevator. And don't stop until you do," Theodora said with a scoff and roll of her eyes.

With a sigh of contempt, Theodora stepped forward, unveiling a small cloth doll from her hand. Looking down at the doll, Theodora saw the horned hound approach. The hound lowered its head and deposited at her feet a small stack of buttons from its mouth.

"Good girl," Theodora said before turning to the dark water. She focused, knowing plenty of otherworldly things awaited within, and used her energy to call forth a particular presence. Theodora outstretched her hands and dropped the doll into the pool, letting it sink into the darkness. "Despierta, hay trabajo que hacer."

The water was still for several moments before steam rose off the surface. Soon, a thick mist formed above the spa, and with it came the woman in white.

18

Ever challenging direct orders, Morgan followed the path until she was certain Theodora was no longer within line of sight. She saw one of her buttons and took a second right. Morgan glanced down at her phone, flipping it open and pressing a button so the simple display would turn on and reveal the time. *Impossible,* she thought. She'd been gone for hours… how was it still saying that it's only 1:15 am?

The consequences of her actions never seemed to wait either. Halfway down the hall, the scaly thing stood, staring Morgan down as it had on that horrid night. A tremor of panic overtook her body. She slowly reached for her purse to retrieve the pepper spray. It smiled at her, its empty toothless mouth spread wide, with dark eyes that seemed to glow under the wall sconces, like a cat in the bushes caught by headlight reveries.

Slowly, she backed away, jumbling for the pink tube. She felt a *BludBitez* bar she had thrown in her purse in case she didn't get a chance to eat throughout her hectic daily life. She felt a gamble would be worth it and knelt, pulling the bar out of her purse and unwrapping the savory, sweet treat.

"Hi," she said, trying to hide her nerves. "Are you hungry? It's chocolate flavored."

It waved and bounced in joy, making its way toward her in a gallop. Her first instinct was to run, but she'd begun to think this thing may be one of the least frightening aspects of the Babylon. Just as it neared her, it halted in its tracks, a frown spawned across its hideous, yet once merry face. Without warning, it turned 180°, ran on misshapen legs to a room with a cracked door, and slammed it shut behind it.

"Wait!" she called to it. "I won't hurt you!"

"Jurupa is an unusual creature," Dorian's voice boomed from behind her. "I hope he did not disturb you."

Morgan stood and turned to him, holding her heels in one hand and an energy bar in the other. Her hair was still soaking wet, and her body adorned with scrapes, bruises, and cuts. She stood ready to run, certain there was no one in the building she could trust. "No, he didn't… what is he?"

"A Cryptid," Dorian said, "I am a bit of a collector, one might say."

"He's your… pet?" Morgan said with disgust.

"Do not be so offended, my dear. It's not like I do not keep people as 'pets' either," Dorian laughed.

Morgan stayed silent.

"Morgana," he said, his eyes pleading. "I beg you, reconsider my offer. Think of what we could be if you agreed to join me. Of what *you* could be."

"I told you," she said with a sigh. "I'm not the girl you think I am."

"Then tell me who you are for once. If you claim you are this different person that I have not found out about, then show me," he said, throwing his hands up in frustration.

"I don't owe anyone an explanation," Morgan said, stomping off in her pink sneakers, down the hall in the direction the Cryptid named Jurupa had gone. Dorian paid note of her footwear change and wet hair, shaking his head and running his hand over his low-cropped hair.

"That is true," he stated. Against all logic, he rounded the corner at the end of the hall, now blocking Morgan's path. "Knowing secrets is my business, Morgana, yet you somehow maintain some of your own… go for a late-night swim?"

She stopped in her tracks, looking behind her to see exactly what she imagined, no one. "What the fuck?" She said under her breath, turning around and going the way she came, the hall now stretching further than before.

"Please talk to me, Morgana." He said, appearing beside her as she ran, never entering from any real space she could see.

"I don't know what's happening, but I don't have to say shit to you." She said and stomped away, "You don't own me."

"You are right. You do not owe me anything… but your

services. I did not want to pull this card, but you are still under contract," He said, exiting from one of the rooms before her with a look of contempt. Her eyes widened, and she stopped in her tracks, screaming at him at the top of her lungs.

"STOP!" Morgan yelled, realizing what he said. "I'm not under dick. I signed a coercive contract, no way that will hold up in court."

"If that is what you choose to believe… I think you underestimate the length of the arms of the Lounge," Ziusudra stated plainly.

"You… you would really use that against me?… Only a monster would offer the safety of consent, then revoke it." She trembled.

"Then I suppose I am a monster… and you merely what… a reporter?" He glared down his nose at her, and unperceived by Morgan, his eyes began to glow. "Tell me what you know, Morgana Scriven."

Morgan could not hold back the tears flowing down her face, snarling in rage and standing her ground. "I remember… everything, Dorian. I-I know about your sick c-carnival of horrors… The otherworld… I remember what they did to me. I was t-tortured… and you put me there."

She was sickened. Yet willing to fight for her life, her distressed tone shocked Dorian from his trance.

"Morgana… I truly did not want that. You must understand. I only cast you out because I saw you as a risk. I know now that you are so much more important—"

"Chrissy Donavon, 17," Morgan interrupted, leaving Ziusudra taken aback. "Joana Larsson, 19, T-Tori Franques, 18. These are all girls who have gone missing from your parties, and now two of them are *dead*! And the list goes on! That's not mentioning the past. Like Velva Sabien or K-Kate Carper? You *are* a monster, Ziusudra… and I'm going to bring you down."

Ziusudra stood there, his expression frozen. Then he emoted in a way that frightened Morgan further than any act of violence would: he laughed. An emphatic, hearty, belly laugh at that. "Is that all? Morgana, those people are not anyone."

"They were all teenagers! One underage… do you not think

that's a fucking problem!? Or is it why you got rid of Chrissy in the first place?" Morgan challenged, "No, I get it, you did whatever it is you do that controls minds, and it broke in Chrissy… didn't it?"

"Are you saying I am brainwashing my servants? That they are mind-controlled?" Ziusudra scoffed. "These people are volunteers, no one does not want to be here but you!"

"You're right," she said in a tizzy, speeding up her walk. "I'm leaving."

"You can not run, Morgana," he said, appearing from another room before her. A collection of other doors flew open, and figures dressed entirely in flowing red fabric from head to toe emerged, appearing like crimson ghosts. Occasionally, one would reach out to grab her, to which she would narrowly avoid. She stared back at one, haunted by their expressionless gaze. "The Lounge is everywhere. We exist to enrapture and control."

"Our goddess lives within us all," he continued, appearing from another door of his own. "She is the rightful inheritor of the earth, the Lounge Her flock, I Her herald. The only reason you are here today is because She wills it. Now, you do have my fascination, Ms. Scriven… you greatly underestimate what that represents, and it is agitating."

"FUCK OFF!" She cried, breaking into a sprint. More red-cloaked figures appeared, or more of the same, however, wielding knives. A few slashed at her, one cutting her shoulder and the strap of her dress. She let out a bellow of pain as the icy slash was forced into her back. Regardless of where she ran, the cross corridor, her buttons were nowhere to be seen, and the hall seemed to stretch forever.

"You cannot deny that you love this life, Morgana. That you want to be here." Ziusudra yelled to her, appearing at the end of the hall. For the first time, she noticed something wrong with his eyes, an ethereal glow, and stopped in her tracks. The two locked eyes for a long moment, Morgan too afraid to look away. "Are you going to abandon the sins you have come to love? The spiritual awakening the Lounge provides? Tell me the truth, Morgana Scriven."

The cloaked figures blocked her path behind her. She had

to answer him, she felt compelled to. She closed her eyes and winced, imagining herself driving home, free of all this madness. Without looking up she went to the closest unblocked door and charged through.

Immediately, Morgan nearly fell as the door revealed nothing but the sheer side of the Babylon Tower, about halfway up its fifteen story height. She stared down with vertigo at the street below, a rush of confusion and panic overtaking her. Behind her, Ziusudra, the cultists, and now his brass-masked guards brandishing pistols, approached her.

"Morgana…" Ziusudra said, "This is your last chance. There's nowhere to run and nowhere to hide. The Lounge has you, and the only way out… is death."

"Then you're going to have to kill me," Morgan rumbled, her damp hair blowing in the wind and scattering about her face. She flashed Ziusudra a look, a look so lethal it would be banned under the Vaydark Accords. Something must have hit him, as his expression changed entirely to something beyond disappointment. Morgan would have deduced it as heartbreak if she didn't think the man was a sociopath. She didn't wait any longer. Before the gun fired, Morgan made the only choice she had; she took two steps back and broke into a lightning-fast sprint.

"Shoot her!" Ziusudra ordered.

Just as she heard the pop of the pistol, she was airborne, taking the bullet in her shoulder as she launched herself with all her Vampiric strength to the much shorter buildings across the street. She yelped in pain as the bullet pierced through and through in a cloud of red mist. This destabilized her, causing her to tumble and kick a bit before landing on the opposite roof.

Landing was a loose term, as she more collided with the concrete, landing right on the ledge and landing on her chest and fracturing a rib as she hung off the side of the structure. From broken bones to bullet wounds, she didn't have the strength to hoist herself up, forcing her to fall three more stories and crash into the roof of the car parked on the street.

Ziusudra and his minions leered off the side of the building, observing Morgan's motionless body for several seconds. She remained still as the alarm of the car she landed on rang out.

“She alive?” A guard asked.

“Find out,” Ziusudra ordered.

“No!” The valet shouted from in front of the Babylon. “Why *my* car??”

As he blustered, running up, Morgan gasped to life, coughing at sputtering as she rolled off the roof of the car. The valet hit the lock button on his fob and shut off the alarm.

“Keys. Red Reatta…” Morgan demanded. “NOW!”

“Y-yes ma’am.” He stuttered, turning around to grab the keys and sprint across the street. Morgan followed, and by the time she reached him, he presented her with the keys.

“Thanks…” She coughed, limping her was as fast as she could to the garage. “You uh… might wanna find a new job. This one’s a dead end.”

Around half a dozen of the brass-masked guards would pour out of the Babylon to retrieve what they presumed was a corpse. The red Reatta peeled out of the driveway, horn blaring and middle finger out the window. The guards watched her drive off, not willing to open fire on a public street. Morgan gripped her steering wheel and drove like a maniac the entire way. She might get pulled over, but in her current state, that could be a blessing. Either way, she was out… empty-handed and without Chrissy, but that at least meant she got to sleep in her own bed tonight.

Home alone with the lights off, playing video games, was one way Raphie traditionally spent his alone time. Tonight, however, he was alone with his thoughts as well. The concept of what Demy had said continued to confound Raphie. It was clear she wanted him to be happy… and she genuinely wanted him and Morgan to get together. Could this work? Could he have them both, love them both? Would they all love each other? Raphie was rather shaken that it could happen with his best friend. He feared for her: this date with a criminal, her journey to this otherworld. It was all too much. He just prayed she'd come home. To him.

There was another concept that confounded him. He had no idea how Morgan thought balling her boss would turn out well, especially being so soon out of her longest relationship. He hated what she was put through, what Balam did, and how little he cared about her in the grand scheme of things.

Raphie was cleaving through zombies with a shotgun, in-game, his focus on escapism and stress relief turning into an outlet for his frustrations toward her exes. Maybe Demy was right; he would treat her better than Balam, or Colt, or Ziusudra… he would know exactly what to say and when to say it. They practically shared half a brain already. He didn't get his hopes up, sinking all his attention back into the game.

Even in the virtual world, he seemed to falter and make the wrong choices, his poor little cop avatar getting mauled by the most frightening and animalistic type of undead. He tried again, and again he was mauled. Over and over. He couldn't focus, no matter how much he tried. He only saw Demy and Morgan sitting at the Bar, laughing and sharing stories. After another death, he dropped the remote and slouched. He rubbed his eyes and groaned, he couldn't think about anything else but Morgan's eyes like pink diamonds and the supposed "look" that she gave him— that he gave her. *Does she really love me, too?* Raphie thought.

He felt his skin become clammy, his heart pounding in his chest, thinking about all the times she'd done sweet, kind things. Since they were kids, Morgan has always been affectionate. They grew up together. Morgan was there when he transitioned… and was there when he woke up from top surgery. She only ever wanted to protect him, and he felt the same. *She always said she loved me,* he thought. *But she's IN LOVE with me?*

The phone rang just as he started up his last save. He didn't pause the game, letting his character die again. He sighed and got up to answer the phone, glancing at the clock on the microwave, almost 2:30 am. He answered anyway, in case it was either Demy or Morgan.

"Yo," Raphie answered unenthusiastically.

“Raphie? It’s Adrian.” They replied, their voice distressed. “Is Morgan or Demy with you?”

“No, Demy is at home and Morgan’s out, what do you need?” Raphie said, suddenly getting concerned.

“It’s about the specimen…” they said, taking a draw of a freshly packed joint.

“Do you know what it is?” He shifted his weight to lean on the supporting wall, listening intently.

“That’s just the thing, mijo… I’ve never seen anything like it.” Adrian began, “It’s an organic metal; it’s like nothing I’ve ever come across. It grows like a fungus, but it possesses similar properties to iron. Here’s where shit gets creepy: it's still alive. That means it was growing inside your homegirl’s skull.”

“That… might as well be happening,” Raphie said, rubbing his face and groaning.

“I sent a small sample to one of the out-of-towners. She’s far enough disconnected from LA so she should be clean. Even then, I told her little of the source. Just that it was found in someone’s skull,” Adrian took another hit and coughed, speaking through it. “However… I do know why it was planted there… shit… for drilling into the hippocampus… like a leech with blood… it was temporarily absorbing Morgan’s memories.”

“That’s why they all came back when she took it out…” Raphie puzzled.

As he spoke, he heard the front door open; Morgan was home.

“Hey, I gotta go,” Raphie said, immediately hanging up the phone.

“Wait, there’s mor—“ Adrian tried to say as the phone slammed on the receiver.

As soon as Raphie turned the corner, he was met eye to eye with the most terrifying sight he’d encountered on this entire journey: a wounded Morgan.

“Holy fuck!” He called, quickly running to Morgan and embracing her, who in turn collapsed in his arms. He held her up with all his strength, keeping her balanced. “What… the fuck… happened?”

“C-can I sit down first?” Morgan coughed.

“No, we’re taking you to a hospital,” Raphie demanded, guiding her to the couch.

“No… we’re not…that’s exactly what Ziusudra would expect… just… get me some of the Ace bandages from the cabinet…” Morgan retorted. “I’ll… spill all the glorious details.”

The next hour would be spent patching Morgan up. Raphie refused to leave it at just bandages, retrieving silk thread and a needle. Using what he learned in his anatomy class, he sterilized the needle with a lighter and began stitching her up as best he could. Each poke was met with a hiss and grunt, her fist wrapped around the neck of an expensive bottle of bourbon. It was a 21st birthday gift from Maxine; Raphie and Morgan had vowed to only drink it again when they were both married. Tonight seemed like a better occasion.

“I…I don’t know what to think of it,” Morgan hissed, taking a swig of bourbon as Raphie went in for another pass. “I still don’t understand any of what Chrissy was saying… she was so far gone, Raphie. I… I tried to save her and I couldn’t… Now she’s…”

“You did all you could. Sometimes…” Raphie sighed, “Sometimes you do everything right and still fail. You can’t blame yourself for that.”

“I guess,” Morgan said, shallow. “I just wish those beings gave me more help. Maybe then I could have done something.”

“‘Beings?’” Raphie tried to wrap his mind around the incredulous idea.

“One was this… unspeakable, serpentine creature… with an army of torturers. They were the ones that captured me the first time… I managed to narrowly escape them this time,” Morgan said. Raphie held his hand over his mouth. “… and then this… all I can do to describe him is, like, a man-made of ash. He spoke to me.”

“What did he say?”

“‘I’m too early’ and that I wasn’t safe. Then he vanished when *it* came… that serpentine ‘goddess’…” she said, with finger quotes on one hand, her other too bum to use at the moment. “I don’t know what to make of all of it, and that’s not even getting into what Ziusudra said. It's making me sick talking about it."

"That's a reasonable response," Raphie said, scratching at his aquiline nose and looking out the window. "I think you're all patched up."

He finished wrapping her shoulder in alcohol-soaked bandages to keep the infection down. She was immune to almost all diseases and illnesses, but he wasn't taking the risk.

"Thank you," Morgan said, trying to move her arm a bit. It had some mobility again, but it was limited. "I… fuck… appreciation is not a strong enough word, Raphie…"

It was at this point that Raphie began smiling, an idea sprouting in his mind.

"Hey… wait here… I have something that may be able to lift your spirits just a bit."

Raphie ran to his room and shuffled about. Morgan sat in their living room and held herself. Within seconds, Raphie returned with his new art book.

"It's a work in progress, but I figured it might make you feel better if you saw." He handed it to her. Within were the beginning sketches of her photo-realistic portrait. Morgan's eyes welled with tears as she admired the art. She was drawn in a flowing Victorian-style gown with a corset. In the picture, she looked off into the distance, in deep contemplation, her hand gently caressing her chin. Resting on her other index finger, an infant wyvern perched. The longer she looked at the more attentive details, the more she noticed how regal he drew her.

"Do you like it?" Raphie asked.

"I love it!" Morgan threw her arm around him, weeping and clutching his leather-bound book tightly. "Thank you."

"Of course," he said, petting her good shoulder. "Hmm… Then how's about you pour that in a glass and we'll drink the problems away." Raphie looked at Seth's massive recliner, fit for two, practically unused. "I have a stupid idea."

"I'm no stranger to those," Morgan laughed.

Raphie joined her in that. He stood and took her by her good hand. "Come on, you need fresh air."

19

Under a heavy comforter, that Raphie's mom had purchased from a vendor in Venice, the two friends lie. It featured three wolves in front of a full moon, howling together. Morgan and Raphie managed to stack their balcony chairs and fit Seth's large recliner in their place. It was soft, as the blanket or as Morgan's bare legs against his arms. She curled up against him, draping her legs partially over his. When he first rested his hand on them, she didn't protest. Her body was cool to the touch at first, as it always was. However, their collective warmth caused her to heat up the longer he sat with her. Soon they were both cozy beneath the heavy blanket.

It was the perfect time of night, the lights of the city just visible past the trees of the complex, like the frame of a painting made by nature herself. On their small table, Raphie brought out his boombox and had it set to something that wasn't Christmas. They spent all night, well into the morning, drinking and talking about everything and anything.

Morgan had already removed what was left of her absolutely destroyed makeup, taken the pins out of her hair, and blow-dried it. After, she wrapped her ribs in what remained of the bandages, hopeful she didn't break any that badly. She was grateful that her advanced healing would have her back to normal in a few days. In a white maxi dress that she used as a nightgown, she dressed over her wounded body.

He was loving this; so far "the look" was nowhere to be seen and he was in no hurry to change things. Morgan merely needed someone to be affectionate with. Whatever that entailed, he would make it happen.

Raphie joked with her, making her laugh as much as he could to keep the mood chipper. She would smile in a way that showed off her small fangs, something Raphie thought was the cutest; he felt his heart skip when she would tilt her head back in laughter. Occasionally she would drift, talking about Dorian Ziusudra, and the horror show that was his home. She would stare off into space as she spoke, trying to put into words the things she'd experienced. Raphie believed every word but wanted to pull her back to reality, forcing her to tell him a story from their past. Some he knew, but loved to hear retold.

"We had to go to the dentist to unlock our retainers," Morgan cackled.

"Ohhhh, my god," Raphie cupped his hand over his mouth and inspected his own teeth, still giggling. "That's so fucking scary."

"I felt awful because I thought Nate was a sweet guy, but I just couldn't look him in the eye after that," she chuckled.

"That makes my teeth hurt just thinking about it," Raphie said.

"On the ride home from the dentist, M yelled at me for making out with him. She was all, 'You could have ruined your fangs!'" Morgan said, smirking as always. There was something so precious about it that Raphie unwittingly held her tighter.

"Poor Nathaniel Duff… that kid couldn't catch a break. I honestly forgot you had braces. Your teeth are so perfect," he said, from the chest.

"I'm kinda embarrassed to say this, I guess?" Morgan continued. "I think my fangs are, like, cute. I used to be all insecure about them because of mean kids, but I… think they frame my smile?"

She looked up at Raphie and batted her lashes, only twice. Enough to let him see it: the look. He couldn't help but smile. Neither could she. Raphie wanted to keep fighting, but he knew it would be pointless.

"I think they're adorable." Raphie said, "Though I might be biased because I think you're hella cute."

Morgan buried her blushing face in his chest. "Thank you… you're so fucking sweet. Oh, my gods."

"Of course," Raphie said, taking a deep breath.

"Your heart rate is up," Morgan wandered up to him again, her eyes begging for him to act. "Is everything alright?"

"Can I ask you a question?" Raphie said, doing his best to keep his very uncool anxiety cool. He felt a chill as the winter breeze blew over them, turning the sweat on his brow refreshing. "Why have we never dated?"

Morgan was quiet at first, her hesitation making Raphie's

heartbeat spike more, afraid he had made the wrong choice. "I don't know… I guess I always thought it would be all… can I be perfectly honest?"

"Always."

"It's because you're Human," she looked away from him.

"Wait, what?" Raphie shook his head. He'd been discriminated against for a lot of reasons, but not because he's Human. "Why is that?"

"I'm a Vampire, Raph… just 'cause I'm a Trueborn and age like normal doesn't mean it will always be this way. As a woman, I'm likely done with any aging for the rest of my life… which could be a very, very long time. I *will* outlive you. Guaranteed. Y-you… I c-can't… I don't… I'm already going to have to watch you grow old without me… I can't imagine what it would be like if you were my partner," her voice was under duress, cracking as she spoke. "I don't wanna watch you die… the rule is for Vampires, especially in the worlds I've chosen to take part in: everyone dies in the end… except you…"

"Then I won't die," Raphie said with an invincible grin. "I'll stay alive until I'm a hundred, and by then we'll be able to put my brain in a robot. If you won't date a Human, then why not a cyborg?"

"What the fuck are you talking about?" Morgan chuckled. "First off, you're insane. Secondly… you… What are you trying to say?"

"So you only date people that are going to live as long as you or at least longer than the average Human…" Raphie pitched, "I know turning people is off the books for you. What if I learn how not to age? Do some magic spell to elongate my life. It doesn't matter. I'll do whatever it takes."

"What about Demy?" Morgan excused away, blushing bright and desperate to hide it. "You gonna leave her for me?"

"Have you ever heard of polyamory?" Raphie felt a rush of confidence, the power of truth taking hold.

"Yes," Morgan blushed the brightest pink he'd ever seen. She looked up with those same, wanting eyes, wandering to his lips. Before the feeling fully took hold, she shook her head and scrunched her face. "Raph… Being my partner is drastically different from being my friend. I'm a mess. I'm a neurotic perfectionist and I always drag everyone around me into the shit with me, no matter what."

"You think I don't know that?" Raphie added. "If I'm your partner, I'd be able to help you get past it."

"What if we can't? What if I'm always like this? What if dating me results in the Lounge or the Tyrants or the Mafia or, gods, anyone trying to hurt you because of my story? Present or future…" She looked at him with conviction in her eyes. "Are you sure this would be a good decision?"

"When have we ever made good decisions?" Raphie chuckled, causing a smile to break on Morgan's face. "I can say one thing… I'm about to make the best goddamn decision of my life."

Nothing more was said between them. Morgan and Raphie stared into each other, lust nowhere to be seen. Maybe it was the booze. Maybe it was the lights glimmering in each other's eyes. Maybe it was the cover of *"Hallelujah"* playing on the radio. Maybe it was the fear of their time together being cut short by any of the nefarious elements they've crossed. Whatever it was, they embraced it.

Raphie leaned into Morgan, who in turn wrapped her arms around his neck. Their lips pressed firm against one another, holding for a lingering, silent moment before they both backed away.

"You have no idea how long I've wanted you to do that," Morgan giggled, looking away.

"Me too," Raphie smiled back. "Since—"

"Middle school?" Morgan finished, glancing back at him, "After my parents died… You were there… I guess I always worried you thought I was a gross monster or something… then I just got in my head about the future…"

"I've always thought you the most beautiful Prete on the planet since I first saw you…" Raphie blushed too. "I've tried to tell myself otherwise, but… you're my muse."

"Gods, please kiss me again," Morgan said with a half breath.

Raphie pulled her close, his fingers weaving into her long, blonde hair. They became impassioned by their touch, kissing deeper and caressing each other's bodies. Morgan exhaled sharply at his touch, placing several pecks on his lips and cheeks, wandering to his neck. She kissed him along his sepia skin, suckling on his neck and leaving loving marks. He moaned at the attention, understanding how easy it was for a Vampire to bite down on his vulnerable throat. How minor a bite needed to puncture his skin to turn him. He wouldn't mind if she did bite him; he'd give up being mortal for her without question. He'd give his life for her.

He ran his hands down the sides of her waist, following her curves to the slit in her cream-colored gown. As if cued by this, she straddled him. His hands followed back up her side as she planted her lips along his jawline, eventually reaching his plump bottom lip. Eyes closed, they continued to kiss each other, trying to retrieve the time they lost during all of their adolescence. As they invoked their infatuation, Raphie's hand lifted off her dress, careful of her shoulder, freeing her pale body, bathed by the moonlight. He was incapable of speech or movement, mesmerized by her beauty.

"You can touch me, ya know. Like, *if* you want," she joked, gripping his hand and placing it on her breast, the other directly over her butterfly tattoo.

As he explored her, she gasped, leaning closer. He could feel her pulling his breath from his lungs. He often wondered both in jest and in theory if breath-stealing was her hidden magical ability. She too felt his face, holding him close, her hands caressing him delicately. He gazed up at her, bemused at his current reality, things he had not even dared to dream of. He fought the cravings for her body for years. Never once did he imagine he'd be allowed to act upon them. Not until he met Demy. These two women, both of whom he'd fallen for terribly, had made him into a better person and had shown him purpose outside of mundane daily existence.

To him, Morgan looked like something of an ethereal deity, eclipsing the bright, full moon. From the illumination of the night, her hair seemed to glow like polished gold. As his hands explored her naked body, so did hers to his. Her hands wandered under the shirt and felt his chest and abdomen. With fingers and palms enjoying his every curve, she began to lift his shirt, pulling forward. Before she undressed him, he kissed her bare chest, his lips and stubble tickling the supple skin. He knew by her noises that she enjoyed every bit of it, that she craved him just as badly. Once he was shirtless, she bit her finger and smiled with her entire face. For some reason, people seemed to forget that Raphie was fit, that he skated or walked everywhere, on top of surfing, when the tides were right.

"You can touch me, ya know," he said with a sarcastic grin. "Like… *if* you want."

She rolled her eyes, not being able to give an equal response. "Let's go inside," she said, standing and wrapping the blanket around her shoulders like a regal queen in winter— or a moth.

"Absolutely, Your Highness," he said, ensorcelled by her inhuman grace.

He followed her to see her enter the master bedroom and drop the blanket. Crawling onto the bed, her back stretched like a mountain lioness climbing San Gabriel. From across the apartment, she subdued him with a crane of her neck, the corner of her mouth curled upward. She batted her lashes, as she did whenever she wanted to get her way, and his heart was done for. Too enthralled by his lover, he didn't see or hear the doorknob of the front door rattle for a few moments.

Raphie slammed the bedroom door as he entered, leaving his pants at the foot of the bed. She turned to him, standing on her knees. Her arms coiled around him, kissing him the moment he was within reach. His hands found her hips, slowly drifting to her plush buttocks. Out of nowhere, Raphie swept his hands behind Morgan's knees, shifting his weight onto her and lying her down, leaving him between her legs.

"Ow, fuck," She coughed.

"Fuck, I'm sorry!" Raphie whined, worried he wasn't being gentle enough with his wounded beloved.

She broke into profuse laughter; her laugh was an aphrodisiac to Raphie, her smile a love spell.

Lost in their kiss for a few more moments, the two lie

together. Eventually, they pulled themselves further onto the thick bedding, rolling together for a time, fueled by the wild abandon of their love. Their hands became tools of pleasure, quickly learning their partner through a sensual massage. It was when Raphie's hand made its way between her legs that she became more vocal.

'Oohh gods!" Morgan mewed, her body trembling at his attentive touch. This made it a struggle to keep up with her lover.

"Just relax, Blondie," he said, kissing her neck, hovering above her so the flesh of their bare chests touched most minutely. "I've got it."

"Oh, my gods," She said, covering her face and wide grin with her hands. "Okay."

He grinned back with satisfaction at her reaction, clearly seeing her bright smile behind her hands. "One rule," he gripped her wrists and pulled them off her face, pinning them to the pillows beside her with a strength that fully astounded Morgan. "You've gotta watch."

"Y-ye… okay." She trembled, her entire face flushed crimson, her smile aching her cheeks.

He traced her body with his hands, kissing her lips before letting his mouth follow the curvature of her frame. She observed him, as she was told, kiss her entire body. She made a sound of desperation once he'd finally reached his destination. She fought to hold still, biting her lip and entangling her fingers in his long, curly hair. He merely indulged more.

Raphie repeated his process, gorging himself on her lust. She had to cover her face, beyond bashful, as her legs squeezed Raphie's head. He looked up and stopped, rising to meet her eye to eye.

"No," he said, merciful yet scolding, quickly pinning her down again. She moaned still, caught in the roil of her ecstasy. "You. Have. To. Watch."

"I-I'm sorry," she gasped.

"Do I need to tie your hands to the bed?" he threatened emptily.

"Yes, Master," Morgan answered without thought.

Oh damn, Raphie thought, his jaw and grip slacked.

"Oh fuck," Morgan said, she clasped a hand over her mouth, eyes wide. He gripped her wrist again and freed her mouth. "I… I didn't mean—"

"Say it again," he demanded.

"Y-yes, M-master." She replied, a sense of freedom as she spoke.

"Yes, what?"

"T-Tie me to the bed, Master," she said, her voice frail. "There are belts and ties in Balam's old nightstand. Use them."

"Gladly," Raphie smirked, enjoying the poetic justice.

Within a few moments, her wrists were crossed and tied tightly by a blue silk tie, and a black belt was secured around her wrists before being strapped to the bedpost. Raphie returned to his post, getting to work, and transforming Morgan back into a squirming mess. Morgan told Raphie everything. *Everything*. He knew what she wanted, how to treat her. His enthusiasm to do so was suppressed since his youth, now unleashed upon her in a single moment.

She arched her back in his grip, her voice breaking, mouth agape in a silent scream. The wood of the bed frame creaked with her reflexive efforts.

In the darkness, unseen by them, ripples in the flesh of Raphie's back would form, like snakes on a dune. They gathered on the tips of his shoulder blades, pushing against the skin. Raphie ignored it, thinking it was just the scratches Morgan had left. Just before they had reached a large enough mass to poke through the skin, they retracted and vanished.

"Master!" she finally called. "Fuck, Raph… Gods!"

He couldn't help but smile at her climax, kissing her womanhood sweetly as a way of saying "You're welcome". He released her to fall back. Her skin was hot to the touch, the closest she's ever been to being out of breath in her life. His lips pecked her soft, twitching flesh, working his way up to her gorgeous face, still frozen in orgasmic pleasure. He kissed her lips again and cuddled up with her.

Raphie was generous enough to untie her from the bed frame, allowing them to cuddle one another properly. They refused to not have their bodies intertwined now that they had gained this previously forbidden carnal knowledge. Their smiles were unbreakable whilst in each other's arms, their happiness inscribed in granite. Morgan ran her bound hands over Raphie's fit form, kissing his muscular arms as she did. Her head lay on his chest as he combed her soft, wispy hair with his fingers. He was certain she'd fallen fast asleep. He, too, began to drift off when she spoke.

"Raphie…" she said. "I don't know if I should say this…"

"It's okay," He said, certain of what was on her mind. "Say it anyway."

"I love you…" Morgan said, her voice muted, though not for lack of trying. "I know it doesn't mean the same as when we were just friends. But, fuck, Raph. I'm going to lose my mind if I have to pretend like I'm not in love with you anymore."

Raphie replied by gently holding her chin in his thumb and forefinger, tilting her head up, and planting a deep kiss on her lips. Her hands reached up to meet his face; her tears, incapable of being held back, escaped.

"I love you too, Morgan," Raphie backed away and looked her in her sparkling, pink diamonds she called eyes. "I've always loved you."

"Thank the gods," Morgan sighed, nuzzling her head under his chin. "I don't know what's going to happen, Raph… As much as it pains me to say this, I think I bit off more than I can chew this time."

"Then we can do this as a team. You don't have to be a one-woman army anymore." He vowed, "I swear on my life that I will never harm or let harm come to you."

"I'm not just worried about me," she wept. "This otherworld, Chrissy and the others. The Lounge and Ziusudra… What if th-they try to get to you? What if I put you in danger just by being with me?"

"I don't think that will happen," Raphie tried to say.

"W-where does Demy fit into all this?" Morgan said, still somewhat stressed. "Am I intruding on you two? She was here first."

"Demy encouraged me to begin with," Raphie said

assuredly, reminded of the same words that Demy had said. "Besides, I'm pretty sure she thinks you're cute… but that's between you two."

"I-I… are you sure?" Morgan said with a trembling voice. "I-I don't want this to ruin your relationship, or w-worse, our friendship."

"Blondie," he laughed. "Dude, you gotta breathe… I know that's hard for a Vampire. But please, don't worry. I'm not going to be in any jeopardy… And whatever dark things you're frightened about… whatever you uncover, whatever we have to face, we will do it together. And we'll be ready for it. All of us."

"This is exactly why I fell in love with you," Morgan kissed him once or thrice more. The future was uncertain, but all together, like the holy trinity, they could stand the test of time.

*****

In a grayscale world, before the sky was overtaken by crimson, the plane of shadows churned— like a nebulous amoeba, ever-shifting in shape, dividing and recreating itself, ad infinitum. Cityscapes would be wiped away, and hills from the past would take their place. Then an arctic tundra, in a moment a temperate mountain, to an alien jungle, to the heart of LA. It is a miracle for one to traverse these planes while still maintaining their sanity. That is the nature of the Threshold.

A young woman sat cross-legged in her rather pristine jeans and *Bob Dylan* tank top. Her bushy black hair was held in a bun. No dirt had sullied her skin. No cuts on her flesh. No blood stains on her shirt. Only her hair was a bit unkempt, a sign she hadn't bathed in a while. She counted, taking deep breaths and glancing at the silver charm bracelet around her wrist and the wood-handled pocket knife in the other hand. She couldn't believe they found her, despite having to fight one of those depraved torturers for them. Two loci. An anchor to the real world. An anchor to the Null.

She held her bracelet up, watching it dangle loosely, the

initials "CD" the two primary charms. Around her, the white hall was a deafening silence. Not even her heartbeat or breath. She watched. Creatures of all forms found their way into these halls. Due to their infinite expanse, it's possible to see but never interact with these creatures. Still, she watched.

In the silver finish, she saw the color of the reflection shift, and from behind the current door came a knocking sound. "Aces." She said aloud, opening the blood-red door to the greyscale. Unlike the crimson wastes, the sky was indigo, and rather than clouds, endless black spirals were covered with stars and distant galaxies. She looked about her; she was on the ground floor facing the outside of an apartment complex. Past the wrought iron, she saw the Buick. Even robbed of color, she knew it was the right vehicle.

The girl began counting again, climbing the stairs and looking for the next door she needed, one within the confines of this reality, not the next. She found the door labeled "161". She continued her count, smiling and charging up to the door. She tried it: locked. From her knapsack, she withdrew a ring of three keys of old black metal, the emerald green spots on their surface visible even in the greyscale.

CLICK

The door opened, and one key disintegrated into dust. She moved into Apartment 161 and scanned: a small apartment kept in mediocre shape. She was here, in her apartment. She'd studied this place in so many timelines; she knew everything there was to know about the place and the people who lived in it. She had to. It was the way the Threshold worked. She saw the recliner outside on the balcony and knew.

"Yes. Fuck yes I did it!" The girl bounced, returning to her count, the sound of muffled voices on the other end of the master bedroom door. She ran for the door, realizing she may be breaking into an intimate moment, but it had to be. It was the closest to what she perceived as the active present back on Earth. As she stepped, the door got further away, the apartment stretching to an impossible length. With a look of dread across her face, the door turned blood red just as she managed to reach it.

"NO! NOT NOW! I HAD TIME!" She glanced around

her, seeing she was back in the white hall. She heard the call of the Profaned One not far off, but well out of sight. She had to keep moving. That serpentine beast was ever hungry for souls, hers in particular. She would never have it. Chrissy Donavon was going to get out of here. She began counting upward this time and envisioned the place she just was. "Come on. Come on." She said as she counted. Once she reached two minutes and forty-one seconds, she opened the door and sprinted back into the grayscale.

"DAMNIT!" She hollered, finding herself at a completely separate condominium complex on the opposite end of town. The sun was absent in this world, as it always was, replaced by a massive, eternally full moon in the spiraling, blue sky. She looked up to it, flipping it off, hoping its patron was watching. As her eyes fell she saw the Buick, parked in front of someone's house: she found her again.

"Keep the strand. Open the door. Keep the strand. Open the door," She chanted, sprinting to the car. With the aid of the black keys, now only two, the door was unlocked. The sound of static fizzed in her brain as she entered the vehicle, knowing her time in this plane was limited. She placed the bracelet and pocket knife in her car, locking and closing it again to ensure the balance was kept, just as the Thaumaturge instructed her; though, she hardly trusted anything native to the Threshold.

"Find the black doors, Morgan," Chrissy said, just before she was lost from this time and sent to another. As she was teleported away, Morgan exited Colt Harding's condo, dressed in his ex-wife's clothing. Somehow, Chrissy was brought close to the black spirals, seeing not galaxies and stars, but a hundred trillion eyes, ever watching with infinite knowledge. Chrissy screamed at the abyss, and the abyss screamed back.

Find the black doors.

Epilogue

Moths fluttered about Maxine Mothman's apartment, turned office, gathering on the many lamps in various stages of wear and tear that were scattered about. A lit black candle with Elven etching blended in with the decor and filled the room with a musky scent and the lingering aroma of sandalwood. The Mothwoman entangled herself among them, a phone cord stretching from behind her as she scanned around the abode. Her blood pressure was well over what it should be, and slight sweat stains appeared on her grey halter top. Her massive, glassy eyes scanned through the bags beneath one of her tertiary desks. She bumped her head on it from beneath and cursed. Above her, one of her lamps, wrapped in a phone cord, nearly fell. Maxine leaped up, quick to catch the wobbling ceramic light and place it back.

"I'm okay, yeah…" she said into the phone, scrambling about "I know I was given three disks, thought I had them all together when I gave them to you… Have my notes. In my journal and my noggin… Well, can't you just compile what we have?… Good… No, there was nothing. Just a candle that smells like sex and wood chips…" She laughed, "Maybe working with Bath and Body Works… Thank you again for doing this at such short notice, B… So, um… can't have anything linked, magical or otherwise, to those disks. Need you to destroy the masters once done. I'll take the burned copy. Keep it safe… No, like to keep this between just us, for now… No big deal, B. Don't think it's time to bring in g-men, is all… Alright, B… Keep safe, and whatever you do, don't speak to *anyone* about this… Say hi to the wife for me."

Maxine unraveled herself and hung up the phone, placing the device back on her primary desk. She noticed the stack of papers jostling in her search and organized them, picking them up and tapping them against the desk. She took off her jacket, removed her shotgun from its inner pocket, and placed it on an empty space, neglecting the slugs in the pocket of her jeans.

She glanced up at the picture of the Domhainn: Tori Franques, the dead High-Elf girl: Joana Larsson, and a new girl that came under her radar: Chrissy Donavon. All of them were weaving like a spider's web with red and yellow yarn and thumbtacks to the pictures of a different Lounge hotspot for each girl. Among them, the Bourbon Belfry, the Keep, the Babylon Tower, and two abandoned places, one in the Arts District and the other here in West Hollywood: the very street corner that Chrissy Donavon was spotted on the last night she was ever seen.

She gave out a sigh, grabbing another stack of files off the table and moving them to her "archive", which was just a fancy way of saying "closet". As she passed, she looked at her front door, seeing that the deadbolts were all still locked; she could never be too careful.

Within the closet was a filing cabinet. She placed the documents in their corresponding homes, thinking about all the cases that were in this one place. All the people she'd saved, and all the ones she hadn't. She was losing herself; her migraines were constant these days, but the visions were senseless. Just more red halls with black doors. They seem to be random; they certainly never led to anything of value. Just senseless chaos. She wondered if maybe she was just getting old… maybe she was getting washed up. She knew Franques was most likely dead, Donavon too. All of them were. Something sinister was going on in Greater Los Angeles. She could sense it. She couldn't see it, but she could feel its presence, breathing down her neck.

Maxine pulled the smoke she had tucked under one of her antennae and put it between her lips. She grabbed a lighter from a nearby desk and lit it. She looked back at her previous works and groaned, rubbing her constantly aching eyelids. Letting out a puff of smoke, she turned back to walk to her main desk. She was almost to a point of manageable stress when a figure in the corner of her eye caught her attention.

A lanky woman in white stood there in her entryway. She was soaked, her white gown clinging to her frail form. Water dripped from her torn and dirtied clothes about her filthy bare feet. Her features were obscured by long, spindly, black hair. Like the rest of her body, her arms were unnaturally long, ending in fingertips that better resembled talons than humanoid fingers.

"Ma'am, don't know how you got in here," Maxine said, standing firm as if she were staring down a wild dog. "But we're closed. You need to leave."

"Pensé que tendrías mejor seguridad," the woman croaked, her voice a constant wail.

"No hablo Español," Maxine replied, her eyes darting to the shotgun. The woman saw it first.

Grabbing one of her lamps and tossing it at the woman, Maxine made a burst for the gun. The ghostly woman was quicker and shattered the lamp by slashing with long claws before Maxine could reach the opposite end of the room. Maxine deflected the blows with her wings, pulled over her face to block each attack; sparks flew off the ornately patterned appendages. Maxine was knocked off balance and was pushed into her secondary desk, knocking much of its contents down. She finally found a moment to strike back, swinging like a boxer: right then left hook. One after another. The woman dodged each with fae quickness, causing Maxine to take a chunk out of the entryway wall with a single blow of her mighty fist.

In a dance of avoidance, the woman countered with a single powerful strike into Maxine's bicep to disarm, then an equally powerful uppercut into her jaw. The edges of her knuckles cracked hard against Maxine's chin, causing her to bite the butt off her cigarette and stumble to the side. Maxine crashed into her primary desk, knocking the shotgun to the floor. The woman kicked it to the center of the room, protected by the maze-like desk structure. With a baleful holler, the lurid woman lept, slashing downward at Maxine.

Maxine had enough foresight to duck and avoid the attack; the info web was shredded, months of work destroyed in a single swipe. Maxine began to pummel the woman's midsection, despite her bony appearance, her body felt like punching solid concrete. Deciding to tackle her instead, Maxine grappled the woman and carried her to the adjacent desk, smashing into it and the wall behind it with force; two more lamps shattered on the floor. Maxine violently punched away at the woman, her spindly arms blocking the blows to her core and face, allowing a few to her abdomen to go through.

The ghastly stranger wrapped her legs around Maxine and swung her body around in a feat of acrobatics, clawing at Maxine's scalp and back. Maxine body-slammed the creature before she could properly get the advantage again. Both of them landed on their backs, the woman breaking most of Maxine's fall— the centermost table broke the woman's.

Maxine's eyes darted underneath an old oak desk and rolled over quickly, pulling out the top drawer. Taped underneath it was a Beretta, already loaded. She pulled it off with ease, cocked, and aimed it at the woman. The woman managed to get to her feet already and stomped down on Maxine's hand, splintering the floor. Maxine yelped in pain, looking at her bruised hand to see that the barrel of the gun was bent.

"Fuck." Maxine said aloud.

Long, sharp talons wrapped around the bulk of Maxine's wings. The ghostly assailant lifted Maxine to her feet by the appendages, causing her to cry in agony. With minimal effort, the creature tossed Maxine into her kitchen, knocking over pen holders, paper stacks, and lamps onto the floor with her. She slid a few inches upon landing, her back colliding with the fridge, knocking cereal boxes from atop it onto her.

"FUCK!" She gave an exasperated call.

Without the sound of footsteps, the gruesome woman was already in the kitchen, an eerie mist clinging to her, still soaked, form. She slashed like a wild animal, aiming for Maxine's dark red and vulnerable eyeballs. Turning away and hiding her face, Maxine raised her wings and caught most of the damage with them, merely taking a single slash across her cheek. Maxine stood, using her wings as shields, grunting in pain, scales falling to the floor about the spilled cereal and broken ceramic. With one hand, she grabbed the knife block sitting on the counter beside the fridge. Taking a step back, Maxine pulled out a knife. It was quickly knocked from her hand by a slash at the meat of her arm.

She pulled out a second knife, slashing at the creature, who in turn bit her arm with razor-like teeth, forcing Maxine to drop it again. She reeled her head back and cracked her cranium against the caustic creature. With her arm free of the woman's mouth and a bleeding forehead, Maxine pulled out another smaller knife. With a rapid jab down, the blade plunged into the woman's shoulder. She gave a banshee's wail, like a baboon's cry underwater.

Maxine brandished a fourth, serrated blade; she stabbed it immediately into the woman's side. This time, the woman didn't react at all. Rather, she gripped Maxine's wrist and forced the blade out of her, painstakingly slow. Maxine struggled, her thick arms bulging to the absolute peak, veins protruding and throbbing. Her eyes widened as the woman managed to turn her own hand on her, forcing her to drop the knife block and fight with both hands, as did the woman. The serrated knife sluggishly stabbed into Maxine's shoulder, making her release an agonized scream. She tried desperately to turn the woman and pin her to the innermost wall or fridge, but this merely gave the specter more momentum.

The ghostly woman tossed Maxine into the wall with such force that she crashed through it, leaving Maxine bloody and beaten on her bedroom floor, groaning in misery while lying on her back. She rolled over and pulled the knife out of her shoulder only to see the ghost stepping through the gaping hole. As the creature poised to strike, Maxine used both her clawed feet and kicked the woman in her ribs like a kangaroo before extending her wings to lift her to her feet. She stabbed the woman in her leg, leaving a second knife in her body. Maxine didn't waste a second longer. She leaped upon her bed and pulled down the art of metal-crafted horses above her headboard. She tossed the art aside to reveal a bolt-action rifle mounted in an inlet. Maxine retrieved it and cocked it, aiming for the monster. Only mist and two bloody knives remained.

An ethereal mist trailed out into the common area of Maxine's apartment. Maxine followed. She looked about the room, staring down the sights of her rifle with tactical intent, her finger on the trigger. She moved into the center of the room, aiming her weapon about, scanning for any life. What frightened her most: she couldn't see the mist anymore. She stood there, for a minute or so, nothing but the sound of moths fluttering under lampshades. Silence seemed to have returned to her humble abode. Maxine lowered her weapon but kept her finger on the trigger. *Did she retreat?* Maxine thought foolishly.

From behind, she heard the somber sound of a woman sobbing. She spun with her weapon aimed again, seeing nothing. Out of her peripheral vision was a blur of white. Using her rifle to block the attack, Maxine turned on her heel and was knocked back by the blows. The first severed the weapon in half. The second, a vicious strike to the belly, the woman's fingertips stabbed into the soft tissue of Maxine's abs. The mothwoman opened her mouth, incapable of screaming through the pain. Maxine was forced to kneel, the talons digging into her muscles. She reached up to push off the woman, to no avail. The vile woman smiled widely with gnarled teeth and stringy hair about her face. Maxine began to lose strength, allowing the creature to stab her deeper, the horrible squishing sound louder than her thoughts.

A group of moths fluttered about the woman's face. Soon, several dozen were attempting to fly into her mouth and eyes. She wailed again, pulling her fingers out to slash at the flying insects, hitting Maxine in the face and arms in the process. Maxine fell to the floor, slashed and bloodied. Desperately, she crawled to escape, pulling the bleeding, crumpled mess that she was back to the center of the room. She looked about under the desks, reaching out for survival.

Upon freeing her face of the moth infestation, the woman noticed Maxine still lived. "No te pares." The woman said, stomping over to Maxine. As she flipped her over, the click of Maxine's sawed-off being cocked caused the creature to look, for a moment, feeble. The first blast was a skim, taking some flesh off her shoulder. The other was a more direct hit, shearing off the left side of the woman's face and jaw.

Maxine lay there, silent and still, her breath ceasing for a moment. The two rather alien beings lie on the ground, lifeless. As blood pooled beneath Maxine, and her heartbeat slowed, she closed her eyes, entirely still.

A pounding from the subfloors startled Maxine awake.

"Keep it down up there!" Her neighbor complained.

"Hated… all of that," Maxine groaned, slowly picking herself up and cursing.

A few failed attempts later, and she was standing and capable of finally observing the carnage. She managed to lower herself into a wooden chair, reloading the shotgun, just in case. She looked at the dead woman— and the holes in her ceiling, quietly thankful that she lived on the top floor— and hung her head in shame.

"Gods damnit," she lamented. As Maxine began to stress about having a corpse in her apartment, it, along with 50% of the blood and gore, evaporated into mist. The mist coagulated into a cloud that flowed out of the room from under the front door. Once the cloud was gone, not a single trace of the wailing woman's blood was left.

Beneath where the corpse lay, a collection of papers from the current case was rustled about, now covered in moth blood. On top, a Jack of Hearts with an eloquently penned phone number. She swooped up the card and began dialing the number into her phone. After a few rings, a groggy-voiced young man answered the phone.

"Hello?"

"It's Maxine," she said, still short of breath. "Maxine Mothman."

"I know who you are," he replied.

"You bug my phone?" Maxine blustered.

"No, I have caller ID," the man said, confused. "They came after you like I said they would… didn't they?"

"Yes… sent an undead or a Cryptid or some shit," Maxine puffed, lighting a do-over cigarette then wiping blood from her eye.

"… So? What do you say?"

"I'm in."

Cross the threshold into the next installment…

LOS ANGELES OCCULT

For updates, author bio, and more go to www.thecryptidchronicles.xyz

www.ingramcontent.com/pod-product-compliance
Lightning Source LLC
LaVergne TN
LVHW100505110826
845146LV00002B/516

* 9 7 9 8 2 1 8 7 3 8 6 2 4 *